Forever Indeed

Forever Indeed

John J. Jedlicka

Alpharetta, GA 30005

ISBN: 978-1-61005-489-8

10 9 8 7 6 5 4 3 2 0 6 0 4 1 4

Printed in the United States of America

∞This paper meets the requirements of ANSI/NISO Z39.48-1992 (Permanence of Paper)

To my girlfriend, my lover, my wife, Eileen,
who never, ever, never gives up, for what we have is
forever, indeed.

Preface

Forever Indeed is a work of fiction. Except for the known historical figures, all others exist only in the author's imagination to tell a timeless story. The author uses the historically acceptable *CE* for the Common Era rather than the more widely published *AD* designation for the years depicted in this novel.

The story of Masada itself is wrapped in tales, uncertainty, and, some say, myth. But it is an enduring tale of a proud people who will never again give up ground in their homeland. Masada (pronounced *metz-ada*) comes from the Hebrew word *metzuda*, which means "fortress." For that, indeed, is what it was.

The Romans occupied Masada for much of the first century CE, only to lose it to a determined sect of Jews, the Sicarii (from the Latin word for "dagger") in 66 CE. The Sicarii ruled Masada until another Jewish sect, the Essenes, began to migrate to Masada. The Essenes were peaceful Jews who strictly observed the Law and repudiated the practices of first-century Jerusalem.

In time, the Essenes outnumbered the warlike Sicarii and controlled Masada. This is where *Forever Indeed* begins. The Roman historian, Flavius Josephus, upon whom the author relied for much of the historical information in this novel, provided the only eyewitness account of the siege of Masada. Archaeological evidence contradicts his story.

The plateau of Masada is a treasure trove of Jewish history, dating back to the days before King Herod in the time of Jesus, Antony, and Cleopatra. Masada does exist. It is now a historical park run by the Israel National Parks Authority. Ruins of Herod's palaces exist on the plateau. The Roman ramp may still be seen. The Snake Path is used still by tourists from all over the world who have forsaken the easy way to the top—via cable car.

But what of the mass suicide, the one firmly entrenched in Jewish lore? There is no evidence of a mass suicide. Archaeologists have excavated fewer than thirty bodies from the time of the Roman siege on Masada in 74 CE. But there is evidence of a large conflagration on Masada.

The controversy doesn't end there. Shards of pottery with eleven names inscribed in Hebrew including that of Eleazar ben Ya'ir have been found. This directly contradicts the account of Josephus who has written that ten men took their lives as the last survivors on Masada.

Much of this period in Jewish history and Roman history remains conjecture. To be sure, there are the recordings of Roman officials—even Josephus himself—but they tell little about daily life. Archaeologists, historians, and true believers may debate the "facts" endlessly. We shall never know the full truth of what happened on that spring afternoon in 74 CE. Nor will the debate be ever settled.

What we do know is that the image of Masada, the spirit of the Jewish people, and the resolve to shout into the heavens "Never Again" lives this day on top of that dry, high plateau.

Acknowledgments

Many of the characters in *Forever Indeed* are based on real people I have met and who have fashioned my life. Teachers, professors, friends, antagonists, and lovers contributed the rich portraits of the characters in this novel. I shall not name them. Not because they would be embarrassed or reticent to see their names in print, but in this time of Internet exposure of all of our secrets and life happenings, some things should remain locked away in the vaults of our private memories.

Introduction

The truth of what happened on Masada shall never be proven. The mists of a time long forgotten provide a fertile ground for an author to create a tale of what could have happened. *Forever Indeed* plants the seeds of "what could have happened" and provides the reader a realistic tale of four young people separated by two thousand years, drawn together by the plausible forces of love and devotion, reaching across the millennia to be joined, once again.

There are no secret codes, no mystical objects, no sinister societies populating the pages of this novel. Just people, who in all their frailties and with all their emotions, prove that the human spirit and, yes, love, is forever indeed.

The Cast of Characters

In Classical Times

Nero Claudius Caesar Augustus Germanicus – known as Nero, ruled Rome as Emperor (54 CE–68 CE), the last in the Julio-Claudian line of Roman emperors

Titus Vespasianus Flavius Caesar – known as Vespasian, ruled Rome as Emperor (69 CE–79 CE), generally accepted as the Roman emperor who quelled the Jewish revolt

Titus Flavius Caesar Vespasianus Augustus – known as Titus, the son of Vespasian, ruled Rome as Emperor (79 CE–81 CE), led the destruction of the temple in 70 CE and was in overall charge of the assault on Masada as commander of the Roman army in Judea

Valerius Sixtus – a general of the Tenth Legion who led the legion up the ramp to conquer Masada

Procranius Livator Sixtus – the father of Valerius

Flavius Silva – leader of the Tenth Legion

Gaius Longinus – senior centurion of the Tenth Legion

Joseph of Jerusalem – young Jewish rebel

Levi bar Adon – Joseph's closest friend on Masada

Eleazar – leader of the sect on the plateau of Masada responsible for the historical event of the Jewish suicide

Joab – wool merchant living on Masada
Aleya – Arabian princess
Ahmal al-Fasheal – ruler of all Arabia and Aleya's father
Narif al-Sharah – Aleya's uncle and the king's vizier
Ezekiel – hermit living in the oasis of Ein Gedi
Orshu'u – slave
Obabe'e – countryman of Orshu'u
Gamaliel – Jerusalem trader
Boaz – Chaldean caravan master
Juventius – Roman tax collector and port official
Baalcath – Chaldean herdsman and chief camel driver
Iraeea – Chaldean giantess
Rhenus – captain of the *Bonus Nauta*
Ruwalah – Bedouin leader and Aleya's principal protector
Mattias – Joseph's servant and Christian convert

The Modern Era

Khalif – Bedouin treasure hunter
Edmund F. X. O'Brien, S. J. – a Jesuit priest
George – Palestinian guard at the Shrine of the Book
Father Osinsky – Vatican librarian
Henri Denouard – professional assassin
Andrew Wagner – New York librarian
Jordan Barash – Israeli archaeologist and IDF captain
Julian Hirschberg – Mossad official and "uncle" of Jordan Barash
Daniel Bensouk – Arab terrorist
Hassan Bensouk – brother of Daniel Bensouk
Giacomo di Sistio – Vatican cardinal
Jim McCoy – New York FBI agent
Jill Benson – retired classics professor
Ettore Scala – Italian government representative
Reb Whitlow – contract killer

Prologue

The bright desert moonlight washed the cliffs with a silver glow, the soft light reflecting on the calm waters of the Dead Sea. Small openings in the cliff, no bigger than a man's body, stood in dark contrast against the glimmering white rock. The openings led to caves carved out by the rushing waters flowing through the Judean and Arabian deserts millennia before civilization sprung from the lands of the Fertile Crescent. Midway up the cliffs, a merchant scrambled up the rocky slope, skinning his shins against the stones' sharp edges. He stopped, looked sideways across the face of the cliff, and cursed his failing memory.

He was no simple desert dweller. Gold rings encircled his fingers. His finely tooled sandals were no match for the sharp rocks and loose pebbles under his feet. The straps broke, and he kicked them off. The soles of his feet were soft, the sure sign of a city merchant. The tender flesh scraped and bled against the stones of the Judean hillside. He inhaled deeply, wiped his brow, and resumed his ascent, remembering his youth when he regularly navigated the treacherous slope of Masada. So far away and so long ago.

A few feet from the top of the cliff, he saw twin openings in the hillside staring back at him like the hollow eyes of a dead man's face. One of them held the scrolls of the holy men of Qumran.

This is what he was looking for. But, which one? On a whim, he entered the cave on the left. He struck a flint from his fire kit and caught the spark on a rag soaked in the thick, black liquid he brought back in stone jars from his travels in the south. The torch burst into flames.

Shadows danced on the walls, the smoky torch illuminating a row of stone jars lying against the back wall. He scrambled to the back and looked into the jars. Each held several scrolls. One jar lay on its side. Joseph directed the light from the torch into the mouth of the jar. There were two scrolls in the jar. One was sheepskin; the other, curiously, was made of copper.

He touched his fingers to his lips, praying thanks to the God whom he believed did not exist. If He did, Aleya would be his.

He removed the square of copper from his robe. It was his fortune. He must protect it. Today he would travel into the territory of the enemy. Qumran was but a day's journey from the holy city of Jerusalem on the Roman Road. Jerusalem had become a dangerous place for Jews. The Romans controlled the city and ruled with an iron fist.

He didn't know what to expect once he entered the city's gates, but he did know he must protect the copper square from falling into unfriendly hands. Joseph of Jerusalem secreted the square between the leaves of the copper scroll. He removed the half-medallion from around his neck, looked at it, kissed it, and remembered the last words they spoke to each other.

Until the last star gives up its hold on the night sky, until the moon races her course through the heavens, until there are no stars, no moon, no heaven, just the two of us, alone in God's universe.

He slipped the medallion into the jar, and then fished it out. *No. I should keep it. Her children will have their half. And my son and his children will need this half.*

Chapter One

1947

Khalif licked the sweat off his upper lip. He could feel the soft, downy hair that appeared just a few months ago. Soon he would be a man and take his rightful place alongside his father and friends. Today was important for him. It was his first hunt for the treasures that the English would buy. For as long as he could remember, the men told stories around the cooking fire about how the English would buy the old tools and jars his family found in the hills surrounding the salt-encrusted hills of the Dead Sea.

How foolish, he thought. *This land is covered with those useless items.* What Khalif wanted was a new Ford truck, the kind that started with a key. It was 1947, and the war was over. The Americans were building those trucks again. He would be the first in the village to own one. He would find the treasure that would make his family rich and famous. He would lift his family out of poverty and one day assume his place as tribal chief.

"Khalif, what in the name of Allah are you doing up there?"

The young Bedouin looked down. His father stood at the base of the cliff, shouting and waving his arms wildly. "You stupid boy.

There's nothing up there. Come down here now or I'll come up and beat you instantly."

Khalif shrugged his shoulders and raised his slight five-foot frame to his full height. "Father, I'll be down soon."

He ignored his father's warnings and climbed up the side of the cliff. He paused to drink from his water skin. His ears caught the soft bleating of a kid. He looked around, saw nothing, and assumed it came from the valley below. He climbed the cliff. Again, he heard the animal's cries.

I must find this animal. The imam in the village told us it is better to find one lost goat than rejoice in the health of the entire flock.

Khalif cupped his ear against the wind and listened intently. He followed the sound—now softer and more plaintive—to a small cave about three meters above his head. It was almost inaccessible and probably empty, except for a sure-footed goat.

He scrambled to the cave's entrance and shone his flashlight. In the dim light, Khalif made out the shivering figure of the small animal. "Be good, my little one. I will rescue you."

Khalif moved gingerly toward the frightened animal. As he grabbed the goat's forelegs, the flashlight fell from his hands, the beam piercing the darkness at the back of the cave. The kid wriggled free and ran toward the light.

Khalif didn't mind going into the cave and looking for the little animal. He just wanted no part of exploring the darkness. He was afraid. He knew that *djinn* lived in these desert caves waiting to swallow the village's children. He knew this for a fact. His brothers told him so.

The foolish English teacher gave him books showing *djinn* waiting under bridges to capture little children. They were fools, those English. Everyone in the desert knew that *djinn* avoided the daylight. It would kill them.

Khalif gulped, the taste of supernatural fear rising in his throat. He reached for the flashlight and crawled back. He tussled with the goat, trying to avoid the animal's sharp hooves. He bumped his head against the cave wall. A loud knock resonated through the darkness.

Khalif stopped for a minute. *Cave walls don't make a hollow sound. What is here?* He squinted and looked into the darkness. There were clay jars. Dozens of them! That's what he'd hit his head against.

He forgot about the *djinn.* He forgot about the goat. These jars would fetch a nice price from the English. *I'll tell them they are thousands of years old. They'll never know. The English think everything from the desert is old.*

Khalif crawled and pushed the flashlight in front of him, saying a prayer against the *djinn,* just in case. He tipped over one of the jars and shone the flashlight into it. Inside, he saw rolled up pieces of paper, like the maps the English used to spread out on the tables in the *souk* during the war. He pulled one out and looked at the writing. It was undecipherable, not that Khalif, an illiterate village boy, would know what it said. But the blood of treasure hunters ran in his veins. He knew he had found a treasure. Better yet, he'd found the keys to his new truck.

Khalif edged out of the cave and into the sunlight, far away from the *djinn.* "Father, come here quickly. Look what I have found!"

Amal looked up at his son scrambling in the rocks of Khirbet Qumran and prayed that the boy had not gotten into trouble.

The times were bad. It was three years to the half-century mark. The war was over. Displaced Jews from war-torn Europe arrived at the ancient ports on the Mediterranean. He had no quarrel with the Jews of Palestine. The Jews and his people had lived side by side for generations.

It was these new ones—the ones from Europe struck by a fervor to build their own country—who caused the trouble. They wanted their own country now. Already, a blue-and-white flag flew over land that had been his, the land of his father, and his father's father, and many generations stretching back before men counted time.

He had heard the news on his cousin's wireless. Somebody voted in New York. They called it the United Nations. He had seen New York in the newsreels at the picture shows—even a picture of the building where the vote took place. New York was a sinful place—rich beyond imagination. Soon, he had heard, the Jews were going to form an individual state, separate from the rest of Palestine.

Much worse than the question of statehood was the possible end of his business. The new state of "Israel"—he spit as he said the word—wanted to stop the looting of their birthright. *What about* my *birthright?*

Oil lamps, trinkets, and occasionally gold jewelry unearthed from these brown hills provided a livelihood for those who knew where to sell them. And the tribe of Khirbet Mazin was among the best. Collectors and museums from all over the world avidly sought artifacts uncovered by Amal and his family of Bedouin goat herders.

Tribal leaders assured the provenance of the artifacts. They swore nothing was stolen from archaeological sites. Only items found while wandering the parched desert lands foraging their goats would be sold by the tribesmen of Khirbet Mazin. This assurance satisfied the consciences of the collectors who bargained with them in the *souk*.

Amal looked up and saw his son, Khalif, standing at the mouth of one of the many caves that pockmarked the hills overlooking the Dead Sea. "Khalif, come down from there. There is nothing in there but bones left by the desert predators. If you're not careful, your bones will join them."

"No, Father. I have found something. There are jars. Dozens of them."

"Khalif, we have sold so many jars in the marketplace that there is no longer interest in them. Come down. It's time to go home."

"Father, come up here. Look. The jars have rolls of paper in them."

"Khalif, they are nothing. They're probably maps brought by the English. Let's be away."

"Father, no. These rolls of paper are old. Come see."

"Khalif, I will come. If this is a trick, I will beat you. Your brothers will beat you. I will even have your sisters beat you!"

Amal lifted his robe and climbed up to Khalif. His son stood outside, respectfully, and stepped aside to let his father into the cave. Amal entered, flashlight in hand. He saw several dozen jars arranged upright against the back of the cave.

"See? I told you, Father. I have found something that we can sell. I am now a treasure hunter," Khalif said proudly.

"Stay here." He pushed his son aside. He crept into the cave, steadying himself on the upright jars. He pulled a roll of paper out of one of the jars. It crumbled in his hands. "This is no army map. These are old. You have done well, my son."

Amal's eyes bulged at the treasure in front of him. Collectors from around the world would travel to his village for a simple look at these scrolls. Who knows what they would pay for them? There was enough here to buy a Ford motorcar, and he would be the first in his village to own a new one.

"Father, look in here." Khalif's voice shook Amal out of his dreams. The boy reached into the narrow neck of the clay jar and came out with a greenish-gray cylinder. "Father, what is this?"

Amal shook his head. He didn't know. But he knew copper when he saw it.

Chapter Two

Present Day

"It's late, Monsignor. The sun has long set over those hills you love so much. Go home."

Reverend Monsignor Edmund F. X. O'Brien, S. J. looked up at the slight, Palestinian watchman and nodded. Not a word passed between them. The noise from the air conditioner barely broke the silence in the empty museum. The guard could no longer stand it. He shifted on his feet and spoke.

"Monsignor, what keeps you here? Those dusty scrolls have been in the desert for almost two thousand years and in this museum for over half a century. That ragged boy who found these is now a great-grandfather and sits blinded by his days of stealing artifacts in the desert sun! Another hour won't make a difference. Go home. Come back tomorrow when the sunlight streams through the dome and makes it easier to see."

"George, old men like me have no one to go home to. I am home among these dusty scrolls with you as my only company at the Shrine of the Book. Go. Go look around like you're supposed to and come back for me in an hour. Then, I promise, I will leave."

"Yes, Monsignor. But before you leave, say the blessing over my meal. My beautiful Fatima has prepared for me a lamb dish like you have never tasted. Perhaps you'll stay and share it with me? It has pine nuts, cumin, and a hint of orange. A meal truly fit for one of the Twelve!"

"Come back later, my young friend, and we shall eat together." The Palestinian guard beamed at the priest and made his way out through the central hall of the Jerusalem museum. The clanking of the guard's watch key was a familiar sound to the silver-haired Jesuit. He knew all of the night sounds in the museum from the regular cycles of the special air conditioning system to the steady drip of the bathroom faucet down the hall.

He riveted his eyes to the work on his desk. He turned over the last words of the watchman in his mind before tackling the translation problem that had been giving him fits ever since he accidentally discovered the copper square two years ago.

A meal fit for one of the Twelve, indeed. The watchman belonged to an ancient sect of Christianity, and he was proud of it. George, a Maronite Catholic, claimed Thomas the Apostle the founder of his church. Like the "Doubting" Thomas of infamy, the priest doubted George's claim to the historical founding of his church.

No matter, I have one hour to work before sitting down and eating with him. Maybe George thinks having a priest bless his meal makes it more like the Last Supper.

The Atmos clock moved silently. It had been a gift to O'Brien after he "retired" as headmaster of a preparatory academy in the Bronx. The clock followed him to whatever job the New York province of the Society of Jesus assigned him.

O'Brien liked the clock. It worked on atmospheric changes, and someone told him it was worth quite a bit of money. It didn't tick. It just moved. The clean lines of the clock case were only broken by the gold nameplate, *Edmund F. X. O'Brien, S. J., Headmaster*. The clock moved silently, its thin gold hands a mute testimony to the twelve hard years of his life that it took to revive a moribund boys' high school in the Bronx. When he left, the school reached the standing a Jesuit preparatory academy deserved.

And what did he get for it? A posting to a politically charged, no-win position as the Jesuit representative to the always rancorous committee of Dead Sea Scroll scholars. This was the same committee that spent the last sixty-five years protecting the most widely reported archaeological discovery of the twentieth century and dribbling information to the public bit by bit, year after year—the last in the 1990s.

From the bright lights of Lincoln Center, fundraisers, and corporate boardrooms to a quiet Jerusalem museum, the once-promising career of Edmund F. X. O'Brien stalled in the antiseptic laboratory of the Dead Sea Scrolls in a country far from New York and a land quite different from the Catholic Bronx of his boyhood.

O'Brien looked at the Atmos again. It was half-past ten. George hadn't come back. *Probably poring over those magazines his cousins brought back from Amsterdam. So what? Let him look. I'm going home.*

He shut off his desk light, shoved the small copper square under his desk blotter, and locked his office door. He walked down the central hall and left the museum.

Entering the cool Jerusalem night, he said a quick prayer intended for George's lamb sandwich, turned down the alley, and made his way back to his apartment.

Chapter Three

He wore his working clothes—black Versace jeans, the black turtleneck his mother gave him for his birthday, black Reeboks, and the black backpack from Bottega Veneta on Fifth Avenue. His idiot friends back in France infuriated him when they asked, "Fifth Avenue, where?" as if there were another Fifth Avenue.

But they were from desert Arab stock destined for little more than a life of petty street crime in the back alleys of Marseilles. He, Henri Denouard, was different. He had a particular skill involving his favorite weapon, a black-handled stiletto, custom-made for him in a goldsmith's shop in Florence. And his skills were much in demand.

The stiletto's handle was burnished iron, made black by countless rubbings of unrefined oil. The thick liquid worked its color into the metal until he could see the depths of the ore reflected in his eyes. The goldsmith had worked a braid of soft and hard steel into a blade so thin and sharp that it would pierce skin, muscle, and sinew as easily as a finger dipping into a bowl of rose water.

He favored the murderous history of the Italian weapon. Let others use guns or piano wire garrotes like the clumsy Mafia. For him, nothing else would do. His employers in Geneva trusted and admired his skill.

"You must be quiet, Monsieur Denouard. And you must be right. Kill the guard. Leave the priest alone, even though leaving someone alive pains you. Photograph the piece of scroll on the Jesuit's desk. Photograph his notes. And get out. Leave the rest up to us and you'll be whoring and drinking in Marseilles in no time."

The man in the gray suit had given him his instructions, cash, and false traveling papers and walked out of the café in Geneva.

Henri remembered that afternoon. The natural water jet bursting through the surface of the lake. The stone bridge supposedly used by Hannibal to cross into Italian Gaul still standing. He had a job. *Now go and do it.*

The Palestinian watchman made his rounds through the darkened corridors. His eyes swept over the display cases of the scrolls. He was surrounded by thousands of years of Jewish history. He reached his broken-down desk the priest had given him. George opened the desk drawer and reached for his dinner. He never saw the shadow behind him. The thin blade pierced the soft spot at the base of his skull.

The intruder propped the dead watchman upright in his chair, carefully unwrapping the sandwich and popping the lid on his yogurt drink. "Now, that's a good Palestinian dinner. Too bad you can't enjoy it."

He grabbed the alarm key from the watchman's belt and walked over to the wall where the master alarm box hung. He inserted the key and punched in the code the men in Switzerland had given him. The red light blinked once, twice, three times and turned green. He was clear.

He walked to the back of the museum's main room, looking about enviously. He could make a fortune if he could find a collector foolish enough to buy these.

"Don't touch anything. You may not take anything; leave nothing, not even a cigarette butt from your filthy habit. You have a job to do. Do it," his Arab contact had told him when they met in the shabby café in the old quarter of Jerusalem. He had left the meeting with more money, a new set of immigration papers, and a miniature camera.

He felt for the camera in his backpack. The bag was awkward for this job, but necessary. When the job was over, he would assume the role of a lost but wealthy tourist. The Jews were contentious people, but they respected wealth, especially when wealth was spent on useless fashion designers and premium Fifth Avenue names. No policeman would question him. No soldier would stop him. Yes, he was an Arab, but a rich one, and he wasn't looking to live off the Jewish welfare state.

His job done, Henri would wander around Temple Mount like any other wide-eyed tourist and then leave the backpack by the Wailing Wall, keeping only his money and the small camera. His treasured stiletto would be in the Bottega Veneta backpack. Some street urchin would make a lucky find, and the stiletto would disappear forever in the Arab underground.

Henri would take the bus to the Palestinian border. The Israeli guards would be happy to be rid of him, and friendly Palestinian guards would let him pass.

From there he would travel to Jordan, board a plane to Paris, and be on his way out of this miserable part of the world. He savored the pleasures the money would bring him in the forgotten back streets of his native Marseilles.

Henri snapped out of his thoughts and got back to work. The alarm was off, but still he carefully crept through the darkened rooms. He found the priest's office, opened the door, and approached the desk. He pulled out the camera and cocked the silent shutter. It was a Minox Digital Spy Cam. He took pictures of everything on the priest's desk.

He looked but couldn't find the copper square the Swiss wanted. Cursing, he swiveled his head around the room, trying to think where it would be. He saw the slight bulge beneath the blotter. He lifted it. There was the prize—his passport to a life of ease and maybe retirement from this work.

He was careful not to move the metal square or the priest's notebooks next to it. They wanted the picture of the square, but they especially wanted pictures of the notebooks. He lifted each page, one by one, with the point of his stiletto, now cleaned of the guard's blood. He shuddered at the thought of losing his treasured knife to a street beggar. But it had to be. No fingerprints. Nothing left behind. That was his way.

The Minox snapped repeatedly, no flash to reveal his intrusion to anyone looking into the museum. He would hate to have to kill a casual stroller. He was only paid to kill the guard.

He replaced the blotter and backed out of the room. Henri walked to the rear entrance and left. He never looked back at the dead Palestinian.

"Damn him. What's taking so long?" The aristocratic figure elegantly clad in a Loro Piana wool suit stormed about the boardroom.

"Mein Herr, these things take a while. Maybe we sent our man in too soon, yes?"

Jurgen van der Velde spun around and confronted his subordinate. In his hand were the pictures Denouard had taken in the Shrine of the Book, the Jerusalem museum containing the Dead Sea Scrolls.

"Look at these! How long does it take to decipher this? Why did we send in our man so soon? What good are you people?"

The men, assembled around the large table in the boardroom of the Société des Bains de Basel, stared at the tabletop saying nothing. No one dared speak when the chairman raged. "That fool priest has been with this thing for, how long, two years?" Again, the men in the boardroom were silent.

On the table were the developed pictures from the Minox. The assassin had done a good job. The pictures of the copper square were clear, and they could read the priest's notes under lamplight. But, still they knew little more today than they did two years ago.

Van der Velde calmed down just enough to issue another order. He turned to a young man standing stiffly against the boardroom wall. "Stay close to this. Have our men in New York and Jerusalem on twenty-four-hour alert. And find out what miserable whorehouse in Marseilles that idiot Denouard is staying in. Make sure our friends in the police dredge his body out of the harbor by tomorrow."

Chapter Four

O'Brien leaned over his desk, the copper square reflecting the halogen lamp he positioned over it. The concentration gave him a headache. He stretched back in his chair, saw a small piece of the police crime tape still stuck to the wall, and said a silent prayer for George. The Jerusalem police came and took statements from everyone. The Antiquities inspectors came and took statements from everyone. Unknown government police came and took statements from everyone. Nothing was touched. The alarm was turned off, but nothing—not even a simple oil lamp—was missing. That was a week ago.

The police said George's death was a blood feud, perhaps a warning to Palestinians not to work for the Jewish government. Not to worry, just another Palestinian worker. No need to expand the case any further. The murder would go unsolved. George's death was just another in this tumultuous part of the world.

O'Brien mistrusted the official explanations. In his gut, which was turning over with excitement and disgust, he knew that it was all connected to the small copper square that lay untouched on the middle of his desk.

On his right lay a stack of papers. Each page had a single line on it, painstakingly transcribed from the obscure paleo-Hebraic script etched on the copper square before him. O'Brien had broken the code to the language after researching long-forgotten texts in Jerusalem and the Vatican. Decades ago, before entering the Society of Jesus, he had received a degree in biblical languages at Fordham University in New York. While his classmates protested against the injustices of society and the Vietnam War, O'Brien further honed his ancient language skills at the Oriental Institute in Chicago. Never did he think he would use his student expertise in so august an institution as the Shrine of the Book.

Tonight, he was close to deciphering the entire message. He knew who owned it. He knew who had written it. He didn't know what it meant.

He got up from the desk, rubbed his eyes, stood on his tiptoes, and looked into the deepening gloom of the Jerusalem evening. The thin ribbon of windows at the top of the room protected the artifacts surrounding him from the harsh glare of the Middle Eastern sun. They also kept him in darkness as he studied the small metal square he had discovered hidden between the leaves of the Copper Scroll.

O'Brien sat back in his desk chair and thought about how he was able to examine the Copper Scroll in the Jerusalem museum. What was truly amazing was that the Jesuit was given permission to examine it outside the museum in Jordan. The scroll was reportedly "discovered" in 1952, but O'Brien had reservations about that date. The more he got involved in Dead Sea Scrolls research, the less likely he was to believe anything of their discovery. He declined to get involved in the constant political debate concerning the scrolls. Research was his only concern.

O'Brien knew the official history of the Dead Sea Scrolls and never challenged it openly. Bedouin goat herders found the first cache of scrolls, supposedly all parchment and papyrus. The Bedouins sold most of their find to antiquities dealers. In 1952, archaeologists uncovered the Copper Scroll in Cave III at Khirbet Qumran near the shores of the Dead Sea.

Ancient scribes had incised the text on thin sheets of copper and joined them together to make a scroll. The Copper Scroll consisted of two scrolls. When discovered, the copper was brittle and heavily oxidized. Scroll experts cut the scrolls into twenty-three individual sheets. Alone among all of the Dead Sea Scrolls, the Copper Scroll was the only one kept outside the Shrine of the Book in Jerusalem. The Copper Scroll resided with the Department of Antiquities in Jordan.

He reminisced about his persuasive arguments that had resulted in the scroll coming to Jerusalem. It was just two years ago that he sweet-talked the Jordanian authorities into granting him access to the scroll. If O'Brien had known that his request would lead to the murder of poor George, he would have reconsidered. *Who could predict what happened?* At the time, the priest's only interest was his academic pursuit of translating the Dead Sea Scrolls. He neither expected the poor watchman would lose his life nor that his request would amount to an international incident. Nor could he conceive that he would focus upon the most difficult and most perplexing of all the scrolls—the Copper Scroll.

Jewish authorities, Arab authorities, Americans, French, and British all got involved over his request. He fashioned himself as a simple Catholic scholar. O'Brien was certain that a phone call from Rome by an interesting and well-connected cardinal took care of the problem. He didn't know who the cardinal was, but in the Bronx, they would say he had a lot of "juice" in this part of the world. He recalled his fateful visit to the Jordanian museum that held the Copper Scroll.

◆ ◆ ◆

"Monsignor, we prefer that you work with the scroll here. There is no reason for you to take it across the river."

"Your Excellency, may I speak? If you permit, I have the facilities in Jerusalem, far better than here. Plus, I have no political aspirations. I am a simple Catholic priest working on an archaeological discovery."

Mansour al-Jamedi looked at the "simple Catholic priest," instantly liking him. The director of the Jordanian Department of Antiquities considered the Jesuit's request.

"Tell me, Monsignor O'Brien, what are you looking for? You're not planning to do a movie on the lost treasures of the Jerusalem Temple, are you? Let me know if you do. I always wanted a small part in a Hollywood movie."

The heavyset Jordanian grinned at his own joke and eyed the priest through a thick stream of smoke from his Arab tobacco. O'Brien had quit years ago, but the scent of a well-made cigarette brought back fond memories.

"Monsieur Jamedi," he said, inhaling the fragrant smoke, "I am sure the soldiers of the Tenth Legion looted the temple long before this scroll was written. Whatever treasures remain are probably in the basement of the British Museum." The Jordanian smiled slyly and motioned with his cigarette for O'Brien to continue.

"I have a background in paleo-Semitic languages," he said, careful not to say *paleo-Hebraic*. "Let me examine the scroll back in Jerusalem. Maybe I can help the Kingdom of Jordan reveal all the secrets of the Copper Scroll."

O'Brien was convinced there was more in the Copper Scroll than what was known. True, the scroll contained a list of sites scholars alleged to be the secret burial grounds of the fabled treasures of the Jewish temple. The ancients wrote the scrolls in an obscure form of Hebrew, but O'Brien suspected that rearranging the letters would reveal other messages, written in a form of paleo-Hebraic. He really wanted to examine the Copper Scroll in his offices at the Shrine of the Book.

"Monsignor O'Brien, you are not a Jew as your clerical garb plainly proves. In fact, my people tell me you come from a part of New York—the northern Bronx, no?—that has its own problems with terrorists. So you understand why I must question your motives. What is so special about the Shrine of the Book that we cannot provide here?"

"Monsieur Jamedi, I have worked with the committee for these past two years." At the mention of the committee, the Jordanian rolled his eyes. O'Brien took note and moved on. "There's a belief that by keeping the Copper Scroll in Jordan, you are cutting out a serious part of scholarship. Now, let's be reasonable. The Shrine of the Book is a multinational effort. It is not political. Nor do any of the scholars have an agenda.

"Look at me. It must be forty degrees Centigrade today, and still I wear the black of the Society of Jesus. Do you think black clothes in the desert are political?"

"Monsignor O'Brien, you are a persuasive man. The Irish, I have been told, are persuasive, no? Let me think about your request. My driver will take you back to the checkpoints. And, Monsignor, I do not know who is right. But say a prayer to your God for me as I will do to mine."

Monsignor O'Brien left Monsieur Jamedi with a prayer on his lips and little hope he would ever study the Copper Scroll in the Jerusalem office. A few weeks later, a knock on his door shook him from his scholarly concentration on a dictionary of ancient languages. He looked up from his desk, trying to imagine who was behind the door. "Come in."

It was George, the Palestinian Catholic who worked as a night watchman. He also took freelance jobs from the museum during the day.

"George, what are you doing here in daytime? I thought you just worked nights."

"Monsignor, you have a special package from Jordan. The museum officials called me at home and asked me to come here to help you. And I am here to do my duty.

"There is a contingent of Jordanian soldiers in the outer room of the museum asking for you, Monsignor. What have you done? I can protect you!"

"I have done nothing." *Or, maybe,* he thought to himself, *I have done too much.*

George closed the door and walked down the corridor to the waiting Jordanian contingent, never knowing he would pay with his life for helping the only man in the museum who befriended him.

Monsignor O'Brien got up from his desk, straightened his suit jacket, and waited for the next act in this play he had unwittingly written.

George opened the door without knocking. He stood stiffly in his security guard uniform, looking like a child in a Halloween costume next to the sharply attired soldier to his right. "Monsignor O'Brien, I present to you, Colonel Madif."

"Thank you, George. Colonel, welcome to the Shrine of the Book. How may I help you?"

"Monsignor, it is I who may help you, not the other way around." The Jordanian colonel spoke in a clipped Sandhurst accent. "I have here with me in this box what you have requested. Guard it carefully. We have entrusted it to you." The Jordanian officer saluted and left.

Chapter Five

O'Brien was spending his last few years as an active Jesuit priest representing the Vatican's interests in the study of the Dead Sea Scrolls. Deciphering just one line a week was a major accomplishment. His Jesuit superiors in America thought that a man used to the limelight would be driven into the quiet arms of retirement working on a project as slow-moving as the Dead Sea Scrolls. Little could they know or dream.

In Israel, O'Brien found peace. Handiwork from millennia long-gone evoked a sense of serenity and affected him deeply. He scanned the artifacts on the shelves. *Who fashioned that clay bowl? Did a pretty woman carry the water jug? Was there a man waiting at home to take her to his bed? Could that scrap of wool have come from sheep tended by Abraham or his son, Isaac?*

His eyes drifted over the shelves, his gaze returning to the glass cases on the floor of the room. His eyes focused on the crown jewel of the museum's collection, the Dead Sea Scrolls, named after their hiding place high in a cave overlooking the Dead Sea near Qumran.

Bedouin shepherds discovered them in 1947. Two years later, an international scholarly committee made the discovery public. The shepherds who discovered the scrolls were from a well-known family of thieves who scoured the countryside for antiquities to sell to ill-informed tourists. "Shepherds" sounded better than "thieves," and the romantic notion of the scrolls' discovery lived on. The scrolls changed hands several times before their arrival as a state treasure at the Palestine Archaeological Museum, now called the Rockefeller Museum and finally, more colloquially, the Shrine of the Book. Scholars have been examining the scrolls for over sixty-five years, always in secret. Public pressure forced them to reveal their findings in the 1990s. The revelation settled none of the religious debates. Not one scroll detailed a contemporary account of the life of Jesus, though they were written during his lifetime. Neither did any of the scrolls prove, nor disprove, the origins of Christianity.

The scrolls were simply a library of religious texts. Only one scroll captivated the unending interest of scholars, the enigmatic Copper Scroll, so named because it was inscribed on two continuous sheets of copper. The ancient scribes always used parchment or papyrus and ink for their writings. The Copper Scroll was special.

Some believed the Copper Scroll to be a treasure map pinpointing where in the Judean wilderness the high priest buried the treasures of the Jerusalem Temple before the Roman Tenth Legion sacked and destroyed it in 70 CE. Others linked the Copper Scroll to the mysteries of the Kabbalah, the medieval Jewish book of mysticism written in middle Europe almost 1,500 years after the Dead Sea Scrolls were placed in their jars.

O'Brien walked back to the windows and stared at Temple Mount, envisioning what it was like when the soldiers of the Tenth Legion ran through the great building. He closed his eyes, imagining the wailing and weeping of the temple officials and the cries of the soldiers' curses as they looked for treasure.

The Roman legion ran down this very street I'm staring at. Their hob-nailed sandals pounded the pavement as they rushed through the outer doors into the temple's courtyard, hacking away at the fine wooden temple furniture and piling the rubble in the middle of the courtyard ready for the torch.

O'Brien envisioned the frustration on the soldiers' faces as they charged through the temple, coming up empty-handed except for a few offering coins.

No one knew where the fabled treasure of the temple was. Popular theory had the priests burying the most select pieces days before the actual sacking. These same priests were said to have recorded the location of these treasures on a long-forgotten scroll that changed hands from generation to generation. That particular scroll was rumored to be the now-famous Copper Scroll, part of the Dead Sea Scrolls collection.

The unfamiliar topics in the Copper Scroll had puzzled scholars for decades. It was the only Dead Sea Scroll not devoted to a religious treatise.

That's what drew O'Brien's attention. The Copper Scroll was mysterious and fairly inaccessible. It was the only one of the Dead Sea Scrolls to reside outside Israel. It was held in Jordan at the Citadel Museum in Amman. Its inaccessibility and mysterious history piqued the interest of the American Jesuit.

His attraction to this most unusual of the Dead Sea Scrolls was natural. His entire career as a member of the Society of Jesus was unusual. In a priestly order that prides itself on scholarship, individualism, and iconoclasm, Edmund O'Brien stood out. He was too witty, too outspoken, and too unmindful of his ranking superiors. He quickly made enemies in the American church, relying on his provincial superiors to bail him out of impossible situations. He was irreligiously charismatic, movie-star handsome, and wildly popular among the Catholic moneyed set in New York.

As he grew older, O'Brien lost none of the good looks women found attractive in his college days. His dark brown hair turned silver but remained thick. His right shoulder became arthritic after a lifetime of playing tennis with the rich and famous, but that was a small sacrifice. A regular schedule of exercise and good genes kept his weight down, and his wit never left him.

When O'Brien was in his mid-thirties, he accepted the leadership of a slowly sinking Jesuit high school in the Bronx. That was in 1970. His success at reviving Rose Hill Preparatory Academy and his unblushing pride about his accomplishments led to a clash with his superiors and his removal as headmaster. But he couldn't be shunted aside, no matter how hard his detractors tried. He belonged to that exclusive group of Jesuits who took the Fourth Vow, the promise of obedience to the pope. That still counted for something among his brother Jesuits. So his provincial superior revolved him through a series of prestigious and unrewarding jobs in America before sending him to an exclusive Jesuit office in the Vatican.

The Society for Missionary Affairs was one of dozens of offices in Rome staffed and paid for by the American Catholic church. O'Brien headed the society and immersed himself in the politics of diplomacy and charity as practiced by the *eminenza* of the Vatican.

His job took about two hours each day. As the clerical director of the office, he was a figurehead. Vatican rules demanded that clergy head each office. Professional staff carried out the real work of the missionary society. With time on his hands, O'Brien luxuriated in the beauty of the Vatican. Surrounded by the magnificence of the papal buildings, the ancient ruins of Rome, and the glory of St. Peter's, he fell in love, once again, with the academic regimes of his college days. He dove into a reacquaintance with obscure biblical languages, the same ones he had studied in college and at the Oriental Institute. Finishing up what little work he had to do each morning left him afternoons to study his beloved Near Eastern ancient languages.

The languages spoken in the time of Jesus seemed more real than ever as O'Brien studied under the shadow of the great dome of St. Peter's. He pestered the genial but slow-moving librarian of the papal library as he went about his studies. The old man wasn't used to students asking him for long-forgotten manuscripts, but O'Brien wasn't a usual student. He wanted to study and to know. The librarian would sigh and give the American everything he wanted. But nothing escaped the librarian's memory. He kept his eye out for O'Brien and reported in his diary meticulous details of what the New York priest studied. The librarian was a priest, a Slav like a previous pope, and he curried favor with the Vatican bureaucracy by reporting on everything he saw and heard in the library's halls.

Father Osinsky, too, shared a passion with O'Brien for ancient Near East languages, but he never revealed his interests to the American priest. As the chief librarian of one of the most important repositories of ancient documents in the world, Father Osinsky cultivated a circle of influential and important librarians and researchers around the world. Growing up in communist Poland taught him the importance of keeping contacts with everyone, including government authorities and shadowy organizations. A word here, a note sent there—all resulted in a steady stream of "donations" that ended up in his pocket.

Something about the American priest's interest in ancient documents troubled him. Father Osinsky knew he had to keep a close watch on this man. O'Brien could turn up something that would be interesting. The information might be worth a good deal of money to the right people.

Osinsky would watch this O'Brien and pass on what he learned. Academia was vicious, and—in the high-stakes world occupied by top-level professors and researchers—inside information was precious.

Careers might get hurt, even derailed. But thankfully, no one ever got hurt.

Despite O'Brien's removal from the power centers of the church hierarchy in America, the irrepressible former headmaster had found a way to endear himself to the Vatican power structure. He hadn't severed his ties to New York money, and he coaxed some of that to flow into the coffers of the pope's favorite charities. For his work, Pope Benedict XVI had bestowed upon O'Brien the title of protonotary apostolic, the highest ranking monsignor in the Catholic church. His irreverent friends referred to his title as "almost bishop."

To his Jesuit brothers toiling in the world's parishes, O'Brien's elevation rekindled the campaign that "something" must be done about him. And it was. A few months after donning the crimson-trimmed cassock of a monsignor, O'Brien, an El Al ticket clutched in his hand, walked through the terminals of Rome's Fiumicino Airport and boarded a flight to Tel Aviv. He had been sent to a museum in Israel where, once and for all, he would be permanently off the backs of the American hierarchy.

He arrived in Israel on a typically hot summer morning and by evening was at the Shrine of the Book in Jerusalem, the final resting place of the Dead Sea Scrolls. This should have been his last assignment for the Jesuits. For five years he toiled as an outsider in that tight-knit community of scroll scholars. Some of those men had guarded the scrolls and what they contained for well over sixty years. The multinational community could never agree on anything except to keep their research private. On this, even the warring French Benedictines and the irreligious Jewish scholars from the Israel Antiquities Authority could agree.

O'Brien couldn't agree less. But he was powerless. The Society had finally found a way to neuter him. Or so it thought. He dove into his work, translating minute portions of the scrolls with a religious fervor. Picking up pieces ignored by the rest of the scholarly community, O'Brien wrestled with the Hebraic and Aramaic script, trying to discover what those ancient writers meant. It may be his last official "job" as a Jesuit priest, but he would approach it with no less zeal than he had any of his jobs during his career.

Chapter Six

Two years had passed since Colonel Madif stood in his doorway delivering the Copper Scroll. A week ago, he concelebrated the funeral mass for poor George. After paying respects to the widow and comforting his four daughters and three sons, he returned to his office and began pulling strings for George's family. The hundred American dollars he left with the family also helped lessen his guilt.

It just took a few calls here and there. Each of George's children would be assured a full scholarship to any Jesuit university in the States. Work-study jobs awaited them when the time came, and there was no doubt "his" graduates in the State Department would secure student visas for them. It was all worked out. What else could he do for the proud man who guarded the treasures of a proud and ancient people?

After the funeral, Monsignor O'Brien returned to his work with a vengeance. He stared at the small copper square and savored his academic triumph. All the more amazing was that he found the discovery of his lifetime by accident!

For two years he had studied art-quality photographs of the Copper Scroll, trying to unlock its secrets. He constantly shifted his concentration between the photographs and the scroll itself, hoping that he would find inspiration by gazing at the handicraft of the scroll's actual authors. He knew he hadn't much time to complete his work. The past two years were just seconds in the lifetime of research the scroll committee had dedicated to the study of the Dead Sea Scrolls. O'Brien was certain he would succeed where others failed. He had to succeed. He knew this assignment would not last much longer before the Jesuits forced him into retirement.

Late one night, exhausted by his examination of the scroll, he made a fateful decision. He jumped to the last fragment of the scroll for no particular reason, except maybe guidance from unseen hands, ones that reached across two thousand years and would never entwine themselves in a lover's embrace.

He opened the protective case holding the fragments. Against all museum rules, against the traditional conventions of scholarly research, O'Brien held the pieces in his hands. He prayed fervently that his touch would unite with the touch of long-dead fingers and reveal the mystery of what he held.

Each night, he would return the pieces to their protective case. The next night, he would remove them, holding the pieces, looking for a clue, praying for a divine spark of knowledge, and trusting in the warmth and grace of a human touch.

Most people think the Dead Sea Scrolls are neatly rolled and stored upright in clay jars. Not the case! There are over 15,000 pieces being examined by the committee. O'Brien had just a few pieces of the Copper Scroll. The rest remained in Jordan, awaiting his call for more material.

Scholars spent more time on the papyrus and sheepskin scrolls than they did on the Copper Scroll. True, it was not easily accessible. Yes, it was hard to understand. But the difficulty of understanding this two-thousand-year-old record of something is precisely what drew O'Brien.

No one had held the scroll in over sixty-five years. Of course, all of the scrolls were harshly treated before finding refuge in the Shrine of the Book. But the hands of those people cared little for what they held. It was treasure to be bartered, to be sold to the highest bidder, and scholarly cautions be damned.

Inside the museum, curators used surgical tweezers in hands encased in soft cotton gloves to examine the scrolls. Never did they actually bond with the scrolls themselves. The Dead Sea Scrolls were precious, historical, and sacrosanct, not trivial items to be held by modern-day humans. O'Brien cared not for research protocol. He needed to touch, to feel, and maybe connect.

One evening, alone in his office and free from the prying eyes of his fellow researchers, O'Brien picked up one section of the Copper Scroll, held it, and stared intently. In his heart of hearts, he was willing it to tell what secrets hid in the script.

His fingers numbed. He placed the piece of the Copper Scroll on his desk and shook his hands to get rid of the pins-and-needles feeling. Picking up the section of the scroll, the pins-and-needles effect came back.

This is strange, he thought. *My circulation is fine. I don't have high blood pressure. What the hell is wrong with my hands?* He dismissed it as a chemical reaction between the salty sweat of his hands and the oxidized copper of the scroll, creating an ancient version of a battery.

But there was more. He shook his hands again and again and began tracing the faint wording on the scroll. The more he held it, the more his hands prickled.

Why has no one reported this before? Am I the first to get this feeling? I guess the cotton gloves they wore prevented any chemical interaction with the scroll.

O'Brien held the piece, gently running his still-tingling fingers over its surface. His index finger lingered on the incised lettering, outlining line after line of the crooked and chaotic letters. As he continued handling the scroll, his fingers telegraphed a very distinct message that something was wrong. The Copper Scroll was in pieces, worn and torn by its two thousand years in a clay jar overlooking the Dead Sea. It was bumpy, corroded, and missing sections. It was anything but linear and precise, which was exactly what O'Brien's fingers felt.

What could this be? he wondered, as he rubbed a fingertip along an almost-imperceptible crease in the scroll. It was too straight to be a natural crease, yet wearing a curator's thick gloves would cause one to miss it. Dismissing it as a chemical reaction to thousands of years spent in the Judean desert, he continued his research. But the crease kept bothering him.

What is this? I've been staring at this for two years, examining it line-by-line. Now I notice a difference? It doesn't make sense.

Again, setting aside all museum rules and all rules of scholarly research, he began to examine the piece of ancient copper in his hands. *There is something here. Something extra. Something that no one has found.* He placed the section of the Copper Scroll on his desk and shined the bright halogen lamp directly on it.

Father O'Brien looked at the copper fragment. He looked harder. This was definitely a section of the Copper Scroll that seemed to have a line drawn directly down it. Still unsure of what he was looking for, the priest reached into his pocket, feeling for the nail clipper on his keychain.

O'Brien was fastidious. Generous friends allowed him to wear custom-cut suits and bespoke shoes. He would get haircuts that cost a minor fortune when most men spent three dollars for a weekly trim at the neighborhood barber shop. His pet peeve was unkempt fingernails. He always carried a nail clipper so that a sloppy finger wouldn't betray his Bronx Irish past.

He slipped the small file from the clippers underneath the backside of the scroll. He worked the file along the crease, becoming more convinced that there were two pieces of copper stuck together. Gently, ever so cautiously, he worked the crease and eventually separated the two pieces he was so certain were there.

A small copper square fell away from the scroll. O'Brien stared at it, wondering what it could be. It looked the same as the Copper

Scroll. The faint lettering he could see seemed to be in the same language of the Copper Scroll. But it wasn't a part of the scroll.

He stared intently, finally matching just a few faint Hebraic glyphs in the last passage on the square to his Copper Scroll dictionary. He tried a translation on the fly. Nothing clicked. His brain stopped working. All he saw were a couple of letters in the middle of the page. Nothing else. The letters just stopped in mid-sentence. It was like staring at a blank TV screen waiting for the picture to come on.

But that couldn't be. Messages from antiquity just didn't stop mid-page. This wasn't a novel trying to keep readers hooked so they would turn the page to the next chapter.

His fingers ran over the square, feeling for tell-tale indentations that meant there was more writing or, to be archaeologically exact, incised lettering. He reached for his nail clipper.

With the clipper's file extended, he scraped away, carefully and gingerly, the deposits of two millennia of copper oxidation. He knew he wasn't supposed to do that. The Shrine of the Book had experts who cared for the museum's artifacts. But he couldn't wait. Besides, the scroll and now this find had lasted for almost two thousand years, could a little bit of scraping harm it?

He removed the jeweler's loupe he wore to examine this copper piece. The hard plastic of the magnifying glass had pressed into his eye socket, and O'Brien rubbed it vigorously. He wanted so desperately to be the sole scholar who, after over sixty-five years, would be the one to discover the earliest references to the words of Jesus.

O'Brien blew away the greenish copper dust. He peered intently at the square piece of corroded metal, fitting the loupe back into his eye socket. He lowered the desk lamp just inches above the copper square. Something was on the square, but he couldn't tell what. Again, he scraped the file across the corroded metal. Again, he blew away the dust. Again, he examined the copper square with his jeweler's loupe.

The hidden message from two thousand years ago emerged. The oxidized copper dust had filled in the neatly incised letters of a long-forgotten paleo-Hebraic language. Now that the metal was scraped away, the letters stood out as clearly as the front page headline in the *New York Post*.

O'Brien matched the new text to his private dictionary. He read the last few lines. And read them again.

He had hoped to find a contemporary account of the carpenter from Nazareth. That discovery would have shaken the tenets of Christianity to their very foundation. Instead, he found something that would resonate throughout the known world—Muslim, Christian, and Jew.

The small copper square was a deed. He trembled as he read the words. He dared not write them down. Instead, he burned them into his memory.

The square was a record—a record from the court of a South Arabian king. O'Brien wondered about the court scribe who pressed his stylus into the softly yielding surface of the metal. *Was he nervous? Was he worried that one wrong stroke would cost him his life?* Copper was expensive and used only for permanent records.

The man must have had a special post in the king's court. Not every scribe was trained to etch copper. Besides knowing how to prepare the copper, the scribe had to fashion his own etching tools. The king's vizier had probably given him a small lump of hard metal, a metal so precious that it was only held in the king's treasury. The vizier probably taught him how to work it into a needle-pointed stylus that would inscribe the copper with ease. The strange traders from the north with their dark curly beards and flashing black eyes called the metal "iron."

O'Brien held the piece of copper in his hands, trying to think like the scribe. *He was writing the words of his king. What was going through his mind?* "In perpetuity," the king commanded the scribe to write. The diminutive palace scribe, no doubt worried and nervous in the king's presence, etched those words into the copper. Across his knees was a lap desk, acknowledging his position in the palace hierarchy. The small, wooden desk probably jiggled, keeping in time with his knocking knees.

The scribe finished etching the king's command, burnished the copper plate, and gave it to another official for his approval. The scribe would never again approach the august throne of the king. It was for others in the palace to do that. He just wanted to return to the counting rooms where he could go about tallying the collection of the king's taxes and recording the official words of the king's ministers.

He would go home and tell his children and his children's children that he, a lowly palace scribe, one day wrote the words of the king on copper. He would remember those words for all his life. After all, they came directly from the mouth of his king and his lord. Never in all of his twenty-seven years on this earth would he believe that what he had written would someday threaten the fate of the world.

Joseph of Jerusalem, favored of the king, I, Ahmal al-Fasheal, ruler of the desert, of all the lands from north to south and from east to west, from the lands of the black water to the blue waters of the pearl sea, give you and your family, your sons and their sons, their sons and their sons' sons, in perpetuity and forever, all the land as far as a camel can ride from east to west along the journey you took to return my daughter. You and yours shall rule forever over the land of black water from the dunes of the Empty Quarter to the pearl beds of the sea. This I have said. This I have written.

Edmund O'Brien, a late vocation into the Roman Catholic priesthood and a member of the prestigious Society of Jesus, reached for his mobile. He punched in a speed-dial number.

On the western side of the Mediterranean, over a thousand miles away, a hushed voice answered, "*Pronto!*"

O'Brien held his breath for a moment, and then spoke carefully into the phone. "I must speak with the Holy Father."

◆ ◆ ◆

The magnificence of the Renaissance chamber was set off by the simplicity of its furnishings. The Pope sat, bent over some papers on his desk. There was a knock on the door. He was not surprised at this late intrusion. He himself had summoned the man. "Enter."

The priest entered. Dressed in a cassock embroidered with the markings of a high Vatican official, he waited respectfully for the Pontiff to speak. One never knew what language he would use, though his innate courtesy invariably meant he spoke Italian to his Vatican counterparts.

"Please, sit with me and pray. Or, if you prefer, use my priedieu. I am afraid that this body God has given me no longer allows me to kneel when I speak to Him. Do you think that will get me a rejection notice when I arrive at the gates of heaven?"

The priest looked at him, pleased by the man's genuine modesty and pleased even more for his use of Italian, even though it was haunted by his Bavarian accent. "Holiness, I may come at another time if it is more convenient. Your secretary said that you wanted to see me right away. How may I serve you?"

The leader of his church and pope to the whole world looked across the room at the standing cleric and addressed him by his first name. "Giacomo, we have seen more horrors in our lifetime than is fitting for any one man. We know of many more that are never reported by the American media. But we have never, never known of such a thing that could be totally ruinous to our lives."

"Yes, Holiness."

"One of our sons has unearthed a secret, a terrible secret that should have remained buried in the desert. He is in Jerusalem, but we are sending him to America, to New York, for his safety. We must ask you to go there and help us."

"Holiness, may I ask the nature of the assignment?"

"Giacomo, do you know the bible?"

"I am a prince of the Church, a cardinal archbishop. My current duties may make me seem, ah, more worldly than some of my brothers in the College of Cardinals, but—"

"Giacomo, please, don't explain yourself to me. I know better than anyone in this city who you are and what you do. My son, you are going to New York to keep the world from crossing into Megiddo. You will know everything once you get there. Now, let an old man pray in peace. God bless you."

"And you as well, Holiness."

Cardinal Archbishop Giacomo di Sistio closed the door silently behind him, nodding to the Swiss Guard outside the pope's chambers. The guard's presence was merely comforting. Much more sophisticated measures protected the man who wore the Shoes of the Fisherman.

Megiddo, he thought, rolling the biblical place name over his tongue. *Megiddo, the place of Armageddon!*

Chapter Seven

73 CE

Valerius Sixtus could smell the boredom of the 15,000 legionaries camped at the base of the mount the Jews called Masada. *With so little water in this blasted Judean wilderness to carry away the mounds of shit and garbage, it's a wonder more men don't sicken.* Valerius needed to talk to the camp's sanitation officer.

Have a few men dig latrines farther away from the camp. Maybe I'll put them right under the noses of the rebels. That should get them down from the mountain.

"General, your centurions are waiting for you at the legion's campfire." Valerius looked at his orderly, a young man from some well-connected family in Rome, and ignored him. The battle-tested general officer would rather deal with real soldiers than some sycophant delivered on his doorstep by one of the emperor's *cunni.*

He walked into the firelight. His camp commanders, centurions like he once was, stood respectfully when they recognized who was among them and saluted. Valerius barely returned the salute and charged directly into his questions. "How are the men doing? Are they eating well? What of their health? What are all of you doing here? Why aren't you with your men?"

"General." Valerius glanced in the direction of the speaker, the senior centurion, Gaius Longinus. "The men are tired and bored. Camping in the Judean desert and waiting for orders from Rome wears on our nerves. We are the Tenth Legion of Rome. Why are we sitting here and waiting? Since when does the Tenth conduct a siege? Let's take the fight to the rebels and be done with this."

Valerius looked at his senior centurion, a grizzled veteran of many campaigns fighting in Germania, Boetia, and the furthest reaches of the empire. The old soldier, reaching into his fourth decade in service to the emperors in Rome, spoke the truth.

Valerius hurled his cup of cheap Judean wine into the fire and looked at his camp commanders with disgust. "Gaius, I know what you're thinking. When will this end? I must confess, my friends, I have no idea. The latest I have heard from Rome is that a new commander is coming, one who supposedly will take back Masada and bring order to this unruly province."

"General, with respect, sir." Generius Tullus took a step into the light of the fire. "I fear for the health of all of us here in this accursed desert. This legion is not an encampment legion. The men are used to action, battles—not sitting around campfires waiting to starve the enemy into submission."

"Generius, you are right. What do you suggest I do?"

The others gasped in mock surprise at Valerius's question. They knew he was setting up his youngest officer for a lesson as Valerius had done with all of them.

"Well, sir, I would organize nightly patrols around the base of the mountain to make sure none of the rebels escape. Then I would have daily patrols harassing the rebels with pretend assaults. And I would vary this routine among the centuries so that all of the men would get a taste of the action."

"And exactly what would we accomplish other than committing our men, most of whom are seasoned battle veterans, to nothing more than a daily run around the Masada fortress?"

"General, if you please, sir. I think..."

"I will take your observations under my consideration. Until then, I suggest you talk less and listen more whenever we have these campfire meetings. You'll learn more."

He walked away, motioning for his senior centurion to join him. "Gaius, don't tell that pup this, but I like his idea of night patrols around Masada. Take care of it. And oh, put Generius on permanent night watch duty. It's his idea. Let him stay up and supervise."

Gaius grinned. Once again, the general would teach a young pup a lesson about Roman army life, one that Valerius had taught him so many campaigns ago. When a senior officer asks for suggestions, put your head down and keep your mouth shut.

Valerius continued his patrol. It was important for his men to see him. He thought deeply about his centurions. In truth, they, and not his Roman-born officers, ran the Tenth. More than a non-commissioned soldier, but less than a privileged Roman officer, the Roman centurion was the heart and soul of the army.

"You there. Come here."

A stocky man, arms and legs bulging out of his uniform, walked briskly toward the commanding voice. He didn't know who it was, but he recognized a voice of authority. "Yes, sir," he said loudly, his clenched fist banging against his breastplate in salute.

Valerius recognized his accent, a country twang whose rough edges wore on his ears. *Our language was meant to be spoken by Romans, not by country peasants from the hills outside the city's walls!* Unfortunately, few Romans hailing from the blessed seven hills served in the army. Foreigners, mercenaries, and men from the empire's client states filled the ranks of his legions.

"Soldier, who is responsible for that garbage pile in front of the tents? Never mind—fetch your centurion...now." The soldier ran off and returned within minutes, young Generius Tullus behind him.

Valerius was almost pleased to see Generius. Now he had the opportunity to teach him a double lesson. "Centurion, what did I tell you about keeping the camp clean? Why is this place filthier than a whorehouse in Pompeii?"

"Sorry, sir. I'll have the men get on it in the morning."

"For you, the morning is now. Grab some torches and clean this place up."

"Yes, General."

"And, Centurion, I did like your recommendations about what needed to be done. Be sure to see the senior centurion. He has some plans for you."

Valerius stepped briskly through the camp and stopped at the tent where the standard of the *Aquila* century was planted firmly into the ground. This was his century—the one under his command when the emperor awarded him the first of his three *civica corona*.

Soldiers called the *civica corona* the "grass crown" because temple priestesses wove it from grass growing in the courtyard of the Temple of Jupiter in Rome. It was the highest decoration in the army and bestowed only for saving a companion's life in battle.

Valerius had won three of them. But there was no chance for glory in Judea. He regretted that this was his career-ending command. Soon he would be on a ship back to Rome, slipping away into retirement.

"General, welcome to my camp. I see you always seem drawn to the *Aquila*. Could it be because you have had some experience with this command?"

Valerius laughed at the senior centurion's gentle jibe. Like him, Gaius Longinus was a committed and capable veteran of the army and his companion through many battles. As Valerius advanced in the ranks, so did Gaius, though it was unlikely that Gaius would ever wear the crimson robe of an officer. "How goes my high-flying command?"

The centurion grinned, knowing the general's question played on the century's name, the eagle. "It goes well, General, though I wish that, like our namesake, we could fly to the top of that damned mountain and get rid of the rebels. This waiting is torture."

"Patience, my friend. There is a plan. We'll know soon enough."

Valerius walked away, ashamed that he lied to his trusted centurion. The truth was that neither he nor Rome herself knew what to do with Masada.

The Jewish people were a pain in the ass. The country yielded little treasure and caused nothing but trouble for such a small return. But how could the great Roman army, represented by its strongest legion, get stymied by a small band of rebels? *How did we get stuck here? I know how* I *got stuck here, but what about the 15,000 men camped beneath Masada?*

Whenever troubled, Valerius muttered to himself and clasped the *Aquila* pendant he still wore, long after he had given up command of the century. The first century in every legion was the *Aquila* or eagle century. The army reserved command of the *Aquila* for the most experienced and most decorated centurion and filled its ranks from the legion's most capable and fiercest soldiers. It was always the first in battle and the last to leave the field. Few centurions advanced to officer. Those who did enjoyed a special relationship with their legionaries and had made the best officers in the Roman army. Valerius was one of those officers.

The emperor made him a general for two reasons: his unprecedented three "grass crowns" and a father well connected in the bizarre world of Roman-Judean politics. Had he been born in Rome of two Roman parents, he would clearly have had command of his own legion as a *legatus,* capped off by a lucrative political posting somewhere in the empire. Instead, Valerius, a half-breed born of a Jewish mother and a Roman father, would serve out his army years as a general officer, answering to the politician-soldiers who trekked to Judea from Rome.

"I shall never achieve a rank higher than what I have," he would say to his companions. "The emperor does not promote half-breeds."

His men would yell and swear allegiance to him and throw their cups of wine into the campfire, calling upon the gods to bless the name of their commander. Yet, they knew the truth of what he had spoken. They knew his background. And they knew the suspicion he had come under during the Judean campaign.

Chapter Eight

33 CE

"Valerius, my son, have the house slaves adjust your toga. Today is the Ides, and we must present ourselves at the temple."

Young Valerius looked up at his father and reached out his hand. Together, they would walk to the Temple of Jupiter. Valerius adored his father and knew he was some kind of Roman official. He also knew that his father was a fabled Roman legionary. *One day,* young Valerius thought, *I, too, will be a fabled Roman soldier.*

His father, Procranius Livator Sixtus, served as a legionary in Judea. When he separated from the army, Governor Pontius Pilate appointed him a minor official responsible for orderly trade between Roman and Jewish merchants. He stayed in Judea, had a son, and never returned to Rome.

One trading holiday, a merchant whom he knew well brought his daughter to a dinner sponsored by a group of Jewish and Roman merchants. "Benjamin, this is highly unusual. What's a woman going to do at a merchant's dinner?"

"My dear young Procranius, I intend to have my daughter recline with us and discuss business. She knows more about wool rugs than any man at this table."

He started to protest again but closed his mouth when Benjamin's daughter entered the room. Instantly, Livator Sixtus fell in love with her and made every excuse thereafter to visit the rug merchant's shops.

Against the advice of his friends, he married the copper-haired beauty and settled into a life as a Roman official in Judea. Together, they had Valerius. The boy learned all he could about the capital city of the Jews. His father's duties took him all over Jerusalem, the epicenter of the country's trading activities. Wherever they went, men greeted his father, treating him with the respect that a Roman official commanded.

Procranius Livator Sixtus raised his son as a righteous Roman citizen. Valerius honored the gods and made the usual sacrifices in the name of this god or that emperor. He never missed a Roman holiday and enjoyed walking with his father to the temple erected by Tiberius before he became emperor.

During those quiet walks, father shared with son his hopes and dreams, encouraging the young boy to look to the might of Rome for a career. "We live in a region where mighty empires rose and fell. But Rome, my son, will always be. Look under your feet. What do you see?"

Young Valerius looked down and had no idea what his father was talking about.

"There, right there under your feet, is the success of the Roman Empire."

He was hoping his father would be more specific. He kept his head bowed.

"We are master engineers. Under your feet is the proof of this. You are walking a Roman-built road, the arteries that connect all points of the empire to Rome. Someday, when you are a Roman officer, you'll thank your ancestors for insisting that all soldiers be engineers. Mark my words, Valerius; you will thank your ancestors."

Valerius listened, knowing that once his father got started on the "glory of Rome," there was no stopping him. For the life of him, he couldn't figure out how being an engineer was going to help his army career. His answer was far ahead in his future, unknown to him or the gods.

If daytime was reserved for worship of the Roman gods, the evenings involved other activities. Valerius knew where his father went. The elder Sixtus met with his clients before visiting the temple whores. It didn't matter to him. He knew his father loved his mother. That's just what Roman nobles did.

When his father was away with clients, Valerius and his mother would sit in the courtyard by the reflecting pool with its cascading fountain. He would sit and listen to her stories about her people and their history. Late into the evenings young Valerius would read with his mother, even when nightfall forced them to retreat into her sitting room and light extra lamps so they could see. He sat by her side, the oil lamps highlighting the copper tints in their hair. Valerius had inherited the look of his Sabine ancestors. He was solidly built with thick arms and legs.

But he shared his hair color with his mother's Jewish ancestors, a rich copper-gold that was unusual for a Roman soldier.

He listened, transfixed by the stories of great Jewish generals, the innumerable battles in the Judean wilderness, and the successful wars waged by the great Jewish kings. In later years, Valerius came to understand why the Jewish people were so difficult to subdue. With a fierce history like they had and a devout belief that their God would come and fight on their side, how could any conquering army successfully subdue them?

When the Jewish feasts came—there were so many of them—he shared secret meals with his mother right under the nose of Governor Pontius Pilate. His father knew about the meals but never let on that he did. Nor did it bother him that his wife and son were participating in practices that the empire frowned upon. *Let them enjoy themselves. It's only a meal.*

Valerius's mother taught her son more than the Jewish rituals. She taught him not only Jewish scriptures but also the language of the common people. He would walk into the marketplaces, clad in his *toga virilis,* and bargain for himself. Jerusalem was truly a wonder for a young boy. Wandering through the city's streets and markets, Valerius would stay close to his father, excited by the din raised by traders and visitors from all over the Roman Empire.

One day, close to a major Jewish holiday, Jerusalem was packed with visitors from all over. The entire city came out to honor a young rabbi. The crowds surged to touch the man's robe, shouting hosannas and laying palm branches beneath his feet as he entered through the gate. Just five days later, those same crowds turned him over to the Roman garrison to be crucified outside the city walls on a hill called Golgotha.

He recalled the day when the rabbi died. He remembered running frightened into his father's office at the governor's palace when the midday sky darkened and the earth shook under his feet. His father, racing down the palace halls, grabbed him and held him tightly until the earth settled. "Be still, son, it's just another earthquake. I don't know why, but the land is cursed with them."

"What about that rabbi that died today? I heard some people say that he caused this."

"Nonsense. No man commands the earth. Besides, he was a common criminal executed for preaching rebellion against Rome. He got what he deserved. Good riddance to him."

Valerius snuggled into the safety of his father's arms, and both of them waited for the earth to stop shaking.

Chapter Nine

63 CE

Thirty years ago, that rabbi died. And we are still occupying a land that does not want us here. Valerius paced the outskirts of the camp, keeping his thoughts to himself. *My father was a good man. May the gods grant him peace.* Too many years ago, years before Valerius had a chance to share his military success with him, his father joined his mother in the Judean sand hills reserved for Roman burials.

He walked to the stables and told the guards to get his horse. *It's time to take a ride around the outside of the camp. Besides, I think better on a horse.*

This Judean assignment was his last. Throughout his career he had served in most places where Rome had planted its eagle. The place names ran through his mind—Germania, Hispania, Persia, Magna Arabia, Gaul, Britannia, even a short stay in Helvetia. Now, he had come home to finish his career.

For the next five years—when he was due to retire—he would live near the house his father built. That is, if he ever had time to retire to a rich trading position in Rome under the patronage of the emperor himself.

All he had to do, the emperor said, was bring the pugnacious Jews under the yoke of Rome.

Valerius had an intimate knowledge of Judea that he gained years after leaving his parents' house. The legionary had managed to return home often enough to know the Jews held tightly to their myth of freedom and an all-powerful Messiah would proclaim a Jewish kingdom on earth. Always the talk of freedom and a savior to deliver the Jews from the Roman yoke!

He yearned for the normalcy of Rome. Once there, he would establish himself as a trader to the Near East. Maybe, if he worked hard enough, he could even raise himself to the equestrian class. Anything more than that was out of the question for a citizen born far away from the seven hills that made up the mightiest city of all time.

A commotion some fifty paces from where he sat astride his horse jolted Valerius back into the real world. "Centurion! What's wrong here? Why aren't the men tending to their weapons? This is a camp of the Tenth Legion! Not a bawdy house!"

"Honored General, we caught this Jewish thief sneaking around our weapons pile."

It was Generius who replied. The young centurion had already started his nightly patrol around the perimeter of the camp.

"What have you there, Centurion? It's barely nightfall, and already you have captured a rebel prisoner?"

Valerius looked down at the centurion who had his hands full of a young boy, barely thirteen. Rather than be afraid, the boy stared defiantly at the general on his horse. He cursed him loudly and vigorously. The soldiers looked at him cluelessly. None of them spoke Hebrew.

Valerius peered at the young captive and flung back the boy's insults in his own tongue. That, more than the commanding presence of the Roman general, startled the boy.

"What is your name?" Valerius asked him in Hebrew. The boy just stared at Valerius, twisting helplessly, trying to break the centurion's hold on him. "Tell me your name, boy, and why you're sneaking around the camps of the Tenth Legion. You don't look like a messenger or a favorite of one of my men. So tell me, what were you doing skulking around our camps? In our weapons armory? What does a mere boy like you intend to do with a Roman weapon?"

Valerius hoped it was mere curiosity that brought the boy into the camp. Otherwise, if he were a thief, the penalty could be severe. Boys of all ages and all countries were naturally attracted to the instruments of war. Valerius was especially aware of the attraction boys felt to the fearsome gear of the Roman legionary. *How long have boys played soldier? And how come no one told us what this life was really like?*

"I come to arm myself against the day when we do battle," the boy screamed.

"Well, my little warrior, with whom are you going to do battle and with what? And tell me your name or you'll be carrying buckets of legionary shit until your hair turns gray."

"My name is Joseph, and I arm myself for the day when we throw the legions out of our homeland."

Valerius looked down at Joseph. *Is this our legacy to Judea, that we, the mightiest army of all time, turn the hearts of thirteen-year-old boys against us? And what is Joseph fighting for? A land that sits in the way of every invading army from the east. A land so arid and divided that this couldn't possibly be the promised land their God spoke about.*

Even the Jews fight one another. The Jews in the south revile their Samaritan cousins in the north. Nobody likes the Canaanites, and we are constantly settling disputes among the small tribes that ring Galilee. Have these people forgotten that the Jewish legends say they were all part of the tribes that trekked across the desert to this "Promised Land"?

"Well, little man, if you must fight us, then you must be properly equipped. Centurion! Go to the armorer's gate and retrieve one of the old swords he's working on. Make sure it isn't sharp and the tip is blunt. We don't want our little man harming himself."

The general's words brought peals of laughter from his men. *Little man, indeed.* Every Roman soldier had his little man safely tucked under his tunic, waiting for the opportunity to meet some of the saucy Jewish prostitutes who came to the legion's camp looking for a few silver *denarii.*

Joseph knew army slang, and their laughter enraged him further. That's when Valerius stepped in and took him away from the grasp of the legionary. "Wait with me, Joseph, and you'll soon have what you want." The Roman general looked fondly at the boy, imagining the day when he would grasp the arm of his thirteen-year-old son.

The centurion returned with a battle-weary *gladius,* the short sword every legionary carried. But this sword saw more use as a pickaxe than as a weapon in battle. The blade was dented, the metal pitted, and the grip broken. Joseph would do more damage to himself with this sword if he dropped it on his foot.

"Here's your sword. And remember who gave it to you—spare my life in battle when we meet." Joseph grabbed the sword without thanks and ran off. Valerius wondered if he would ever see him again.

Chapter Ten

69 CE

The desert wears on men. The heat of the day, the cold of the night, the unrelenting sun in the summer, and the fierce winds in the winter draw life from even the strongest of bodies. The weary Roman general surveyed the activity around the camp. After ten years, the camp was a full-grown city, so long had the Tenth Legion been in Judea.

The soldiers had replaced the embanked dirt walls with a sturdy wooden palisade. The general officers lived in stone houses. The men stayed in their barracks or found living accommodations with the women in the camp. There was a regular marketplace. The younger officers had erected a temple to Mithras and practiced the eastern religious rites so favored by legions all over the empire.

Valerius Sixtus felt his years wearing the insignia of the legion every day. Thirty years of toiling under the Roman standard had worn him down. He had reached an age when most high-ranking Roman officers were comfortably settling down to positions in public life and not worrying about the rigors of another campaign. Yet, there he was in Judea, still. *Three emperors have come and gone, and I'm still in Judea. When do I leave?*

The occupation was especially hard for the army. The troublesome province was known throughout the army as "tough duty." It wasn't like this in other provinces. After a while, they all adopted Roman ways and lived peacefully under Roman rule. Even the pugnacious Gauls stopped fighting and sought Roman citizenship. But not the Jews. Every day saw a new incident between his soldiers and a local. Valerius spent more time mediating these battles than he did in fighting the enemy, whoever that was.

Years of dealing with the people's growing resentment against the legions of Rome had worn him down. Valerius was the legion's unofficial ambassador to the Jews. He spoke their language, had a Jewish mother, and knew their history.

The governing procurator, recently appointed by the new emperor, Vespasian, desperately sought from Valerius an answer on how to subjugate the Jews. Making matters worse for him was that Vespasian had placed his son, Titus, as the officer-in-command of the Judean campaign. Titus regarded the ongoing revolt as a personal affront against the majesty of Rome. And he believed Valerius was too sympathetic to the Jewish cause.

"General, you know that Titus will solve this problem in the most brutal way possible. He is not a gentle man, nor does he have any feeling for the people in this part of the world. I have to ask you this: Can you follow him?"

Valerius looked into the sad eyes of Linus Talmeus, the new procurator, and held his tongue before he spoke. "Lord Procurator, I am not privy to the thinking of General Titus. I am a Roman officer. I do what I am commanded to do." With that, he pleaded duty in the camp and left the procurator's palace, riding back to the base of Masada.

The Romans considered all Jews to be a stiff-necked people. Their stubborn leaders refused all the accommodations Valerius had extended. The rebels on Masada, that accursed mount that occupied most of Valerius's time, were particularly suspect. Jewish elders mistrusted the inhabitants of Masada. They were too pure, too clinging to the old ways of religion. They refused to get along. It was ironic that neither the Jewish leaders nor the Roman generals knew what to do with Masada. But, Titus had a plan.

Flavius Silva and Valerius Sixtus shared the midday meal at Silva's villa. Flavius had excellent cooks and the best supply of Falernian wine this side of the world. Flavius Silva was the *legatus,* the Roman officer-in-charge, a post given to him by Emperor Vespasian as a favor to the Silva family. Valerius was truly the officer-in-charge, a general in his own right, but he deferred to the emperor's appointees. Flavius was one of them. They both awaited the arrival of Titus, Vespasian's son, who had been given command of the entire Judean campaign by his father, the emperor.

"Flavius, the Jews on Masada are more trouble to their own people than they are to us. I am convinced they are a peaceful people, more given to farming their fields in Ein Gedi than leading a revolt against Rome."

"What you say may be true, but then again, you may be too close to the question."

There it is again, Valerius thought. The suspicion that he was a Jewish sympathizer. "Sir, I have camped here ten years. Let's wait them out. After all, how long could they live? They took a vow not to live with women. And unless their God is all-powerful as they claim, I know of no relationship between men that could produce offspring."

"Those 'peaceful' Jews on Masada overtook a Roman camp and massacred our men. Are we not rulers in Judea? Do we not punish rebels? Think about what you say!"

"Listen to me. Don't confuse the Zealots with the Sicarii. It was the Sicarii who overran the Roman garrison on Masada and massacred the Roman garrison. The Sicarii, led by that devil, Menahem, are the enemies of Rome, not the Zealots."

"Valerius, don't bore me with Jewish history and politics. Find a way to retake Masada. You may leave."

Valerius turned on his heels and left without saluting. *What can he do to me? Exile me to Judea?*

On the way back home, Valerius pondered the Masada conundrum. He was right about the Sicarii. They were the true revolutionaries, once led by the man the Jews selected for Roman mercy on that long-ago feast day. *To think the mob picked a revolutionary and handed us a gentle carpenter.*

Valerius had spies on Masada and knew the group of Jews couldn't last much longer. The Sicarii no longer cared about the mount, and he was certain the Zealots wanted to depart to a more peaceful place. And there was the ever-present political wrangling among the Jews.

Menahem had taken over leadership from Barabbas. The old leader still lived with the Sicarii on Masada but ceded control to Menahem who had struck up a friendship with Eleazar, the Messianic leader of the Zealots of Masada. Some called the Zealots "Essenes," but Valerius never concerned himself with all the labels Jews gave their rival sects. The Zealots let Menahem and his followers live with them. Eleazar's disciples criticized him severely for his decision, but he pleaded with them: "Menahem and his men conquered Masada for us. We live here free from Rome."

In Rome, Vespasian cared little about the trivial differences among the Jewish sects. Though he spent time in Judea, now that he was emperor, he had more to consider. He would take care of the Jewish revolt the same way Rome took care of all upstart peoples. The Roman legions, his mighty Tenth, would crush them.

66 CE

Years ago, before Vespasian became emperor, Nero, who was the emperor then, dispatched him to Judea as his favored general. There was talk that the sexually ambivalent emperor also favored Titus,

Vespasian's young son, but in a different way. Whispered rumors in the imperial court were never spoken aloud.

Nero had sent Vespasian to survey the Judean scene. Valerius Sixtus and Flavius Silva had labored long and intensely in this godforsaken country. Now, they awaited a visit from Rome and the imperial court of Nero.

Just after dawn, the blaring horns of an honor escort shattered the early morning calm of the villa. Slaves scuttled about, preparing to ready the house before the Roman dignitary appeared outside its gates. Flavius and Valerius, caught unaware by the escort's horns, rushed to present themselves. "Where did he get the escort?" Flavius whispered to Valerius.

"I wouldn't put too much faith in them as an escort. They're harbor police. I figure they'd run at the first sight of a Roman sword. Believe me, the escort is a Roman thing. So is a litter. If Vespasian wants to conquer the Jews, he'll have to relearn his horsemanship."

Flavius Silva looked at Valerius, hoping his companion would be on his best behavior. Vespasian was, after all, the direct representative of Nero.

The litter pulled up to the gate. A slave hurried to place a portable step by the litter and waited for its occupants to emerge. First came Titus, rumored to be Vespasian's favorite son and likely heir. Then came the general. He accepted the salutes and walked directly to Valerius. "Read this. It will answer all of your questions."

Vespasian turned to his son and said, "Let's go in, Titus. It feels good to be on solid land. Flavius, do you still have that storehouse full of Falernian? I could use a good cup of wine to wash the taste of the sea from my mouth."

Without waiting for an answer, Vespasian, Titus, and their party walked into the villa. Flavius followed, but Valerius stayed outside reading the scroll.

The Tenth Legion was to quell the Jewish revolt. The emperor, Nero, had had enough of the bad reports coming out of Judea, and he wanted the rebellion to end. Nero ordered that the subduing of the revolt come first. Too much was left unsaid. It seemed the emperor gave Vespasian discretion on how to finish the Judean campaign. Valerius knew the legate was a fair man, but who knew what would follow once he went home.

Valerius left the villa and met Flavius outside. They both turned and went into the garden. There, Vespasian sat as if he were waiting for Valerius. "Tell me, my friend, what do you think of our emperor and his plans for your Jews? You've read his orders but let me tell you my plans."

Vespasian gathered his cloak around him and laid out the Judean strategy. The plans were clear, almost brilliant. Use the legions like a hammer, he often said. And that's what he meant to do in Judea.

"Flavius, Valerius, I need you to split your legion into smaller forces. I plan to move into the cities of Judea and put down all armed resistance. With extreme force, if necessary, I will put down this constant insurrection."

The legate turned to Flavius Silva. "I will have done my part, Flavius. Masada shall be your problem. I'm sure the emperor, Nero, will want you to plant the Roman eagle atop the mount as soon as possible. When I get back to Rome, I'll explain the situation to his divineship. You shall be hearing from us soon."

Chapter Eleven

73 CE

The stars pierced the violet sky as night darkened the view from the top of Masada. Joseph looked up. The desert sky deepened into a rich blackness, and the bright stars with their twinkling points of light shone in contrast against the black.

Joseph sat alone in the magnificent baths of King Herod's palace on Masada's northern slope. The palace was deserted. The gaily painted women and loudly playing orchestras were but memories, ghosts of another time. The Zealots never used the old king's buildings. They built simple huts and avoided the lavish structures built by Herod.

Beneath him, 1,500 feet away, more lights pierced the blackness of the night. Hundreds of campfires sparkled on the plain below. Gathered around the fires, telling stories and passing wineskins, were the soldiers of the fearsome Tenth Legion.

Joseph was a wanderer. His family had died in the Jewish revolt, and he lived on the streets of Jerusalem. He picked up enough camp Latin to survive off the Roman garrison billeted at the base of Masada. Joseph was a familiar figure in the city of the Tenth Legion. He thought back to his years as a camp follower. His conversations with the Roman quartermaster were nothing but the unabashed salesmanship of a street urchin looking to survive.

"Decimus, where else could you get such fresh fruit for the tables of your commanders? No one, I tell you, no one will deal with you Romans anymore. You're lucky to have me."

"I don't care if you steal from the orchards of your people. Just don't steal from me. I can give you no more than twenty *sesterces* for this load."

"Twenty *sesterces*! What am I offering you? Swine fodder?"

"You best be careful, or you will become swine fodder."

The grizzled quartermaster leaned in and drew the young Jew close. Joseph smelled the sour wine on his breath and saw the hairs growing from moles on the man's face. "Tell me, boy, that you have a whore on the top of that mount. Tell me that you go up there to get your little man exercised. Only don't let me find out you're a spy. You're too good of a fruit peddler."

He threw a leather bag at Joseph and told him to get lost before he changed his mind. Joseph ran away quickly, darting into the camp stables to catch his breath. He sank to the ground and drew his knees close to his face.

What have I gotten myself into? I thought I was careful. If that drunken quartermaster knows about my trips up and down Masada, who else knows? He should have thanked the Roman legionary. The soldier had given him a plausible explanation for his journeys up the mountain, one that any of the horny soldiers would believe. Any young man would willingly travel up a mountainside to lay with a pretty young girl. And on the top of Masada, the quartermaster reasoned, there were plenty of young women who would gladly welcome such a handsome young man into their beds.

If Joseph had a polished metal hand mirror, he would know what the quartermaster meant. Despite a life on the streets, he had grown up to be a good-looking man with close-cropped hair and a hard-muscled body conditioned by years of working in the Roman camps.

His life on the streets of Jerusalem had made him unwelcome in many quarters of the city. He was a thief, a petty criminal, and a temple robber. He left the city for his own good and decided to make a living working and stealing from the Romans camped at the base of Masada.

In the Roman camp, Joseph could look up and see Masada. The mount didn't fascinate him like it did some of his countrymen. He could care less about the Zealots, Pharisees, or any of the sects that bubbled to the surface of daily life in Jerusalem like scum on a pot of boiling meat.

True, he was a thief. At least he was an honest thief. He never overcharged his customers. And those on Masada could use his fresh fruit as much as the Romans. And, he could charge them more for hauling the food. One day, he told his Roman quartermaster friend he'd be gone for a few days to look for new sources of food.

"Where are you going to look? This is a goddamn desert. You think orchards spring up every ten paces?" The other quartermasters broke out in derisive laughter, following the lead of the older soldier who taunted Joseph.

Before he left, Decimus grabbed him again. "Boy, you better not be a spy. For your sake, I hope it's your little man that's leading you up there. Be good and take care. Better yet, be careful and come back...with fruit."

That was seven months ago. He became a regular visitor to Masada and continued to fill the produce orders for the Roman quartermasters. Slowly, the Zealots on Masada had accepted his presence. They bought food from him. Above all, the leadership valued Joseph's working knowledge of the Roman camp. Over the months, Joseph knew that he had to work with the Zealots. Below were Romans, his people's sworn enemy. On Masada were his own.

"Eleazar, I think I can help you." The self-proclaimed leader of the Jews on Masada looked at Joseph. They stood nearby the ovens where the women cooked the daily bread.

"You are a trader. You bring us fruit you steal from our orchards, and you eye our women. You probably sleep with them. I know nothing of this since I follow the rule of celibacy. Why should I trust you? More importantly, how can you help me?"

"Eleazar." Joseph trembled as he spoke his name, for he knew it would put his life in danger. "Listen to me. Go back to your men around the campfire. Tell them you have someone who can slip in and out of the Roman camp like a shadow in the night. I can help you."

The gruff leader of the grubby pack of Jews on Masada snorted and walked away. Joseph could not have predicted that the Masada leadership would eventually appreciate his value as a spy and send him on regular missions to the Roman camp.

The Roman soldiers and leaders of the Tenth Legion were tiring of the Judean campaign. Some of them had been in the region for over ten years. Nero had posted these veterans to Judea after a particularly hard-fought campaign in Britannia. They thought they had deserved better than to be sent to another impossible posting. There were many other places to choose since the Roman army spread throughout the world. There was Hispania, Helvetia, even Germania—all these would have been preferable. But, no, the emperor wanted them in Judea to continue the empire's unwinnable campaign.

After leaving Britannia on a fleet of the empire's triremes, they marched through Gaul, down the coast of Italy, and camped at Brundisium. Eventually, they boarded ships for the port of Caesarea in Judea.

Joseph knew the mood of the soldiers. He still worked the camp like a simple merchant, selling the sweet oranges the Zealots grew in

Ein Gedi. Sometimes, he cleaned the slops the legionaries left over, a filthy job but one that paid well in a country where jobs were scarce.

The Roman occupation hadn't brought any riches to Judea. On the contrary, it sucked the lifeblood out of the people. The economy of the once-rich province had come to a standstill. Except for the Sadducees who cooperated with their Roman masters and profited from the war trade, most of Judea's citizens lived in poverty, scraping a living from day to day.

The Roman quartermasters took from the people at below-market prices, sometimes paying, sometimes not. The occupation was harsh. The Romans were strict, taking their frustrations out on the common people. Daily, the floggings of Jews and the burning of peasants' hovels by Roman soldiers stoked the people's resentment. It was a disaster in the making, and it would come to no good for either the Jews or the Romans.

Over the years, working the Roman garrison, Joseph had absorbed enough Latin to make simple conversations as he went about his daily trade. He would often overhear the soldiers grumble to one another about the misery of the Judean assignment. Lately, he started to pick up snatches of conversations indicating that something was afoot. The rhythm of the garrison had changed. So had the mood of the rank-and-file soldier.

The soldiers seemed more alert. Routine camp life quickened overnight. The armorer's forge glowed through the night, sharpening and repairing their killing tools.

It had been a long time since Joseph had seen all of the forges burning brightly. Wagons loaded with timber from the farthest reaches of the province rolled into the garrison. The camp's palisades were sturdy and the houses were made of stone, so Joseph reasoned that the timber was not to be used for living accommodations. Only one use for the timber made sense—engines of war.

A few years back, he thought he saw that Roman general who grabbed him when he was a young boy and saved him from a round of teasing or worse at the hands of his legionaries. The general eyed Joseph in the marketplace, searching his mind for a bit of recognition. The years hadn't been kind to him. His hair—what was left of it—was an iron gray. Years of care and worry lined his face, and his shoulders hunched as if they carried the weight of the camp.

All these changes had taken place in a man that he first saw less than ten years ago! Joseph wondered about the general. *What does he care about? When is he going home? Why has he undergone such dramatic physical change? It isn't just age. There are far older men on Masada who look better than he does.*

Joseph wondered what the general was doing now. *No doubt,* he thought, *planning to kill as many Jews as possible.* Something was amiss in the Roman camps, but Joseph had yet to identify exactly what was happening.

Chapter Twelve

Cries from the nightly sentinels on top of Masada broke through Joseph's isolation. Just above where Joseph sat, the camp on Masada settled for the night. Herod had built his palaces on several levels so it was easy to escape from the milling humanity occupying the top of the mount. Almost one thousand men, women, and children sought refuge on Masada. They trusted the leadership to keep them safe.

He looked up from his perch on the side of Masada and saw a faint glow hovering over the southern slope of the mountain. He knew what caused the glow, and he knew that it meant the end to life on Masada for all who camped there.

On the far slope of Masada, hundreds of torches shone on Jewish slaves and Roman soldiers toiling on a massive engineering project. Joseph couldn't see the work that was going on—it was on the other side from where he was sitting—but he knew what it was and what the consequences would be.

After Jerusalem fell during Vespasian's campaign and the temple that Herod built lay in ruins under the feet of the Roman legionaries, the Jews that did not escape to the countryside became slaves. Flavius

Silva had good reason to enslave the Jewish populace. His engineers would use them to wipe out the last holdouts of resistance on top of Masada.

Joseph knew what the Romans were doing. He saw his people carry buckets of dirt by the thousands. The Tenth Legion would march to the mount of Masada on a massive ramp they were building up the mountainside. Each day, the ramp drew closer to the top, and soon the legionaries would be coming over the walls.

Eleazar ben Ya'ir, the leader of the Masada encampment, had discussed his defensive strategy with the men of the camp. In Joseph's mind, there was no defense. How could a pitiful group of unarmed men stand against the might of the Roman army? Once the ramp was completed, the battle-hardened soldiers would storm over the walls and slay every last man, woman, and child in revenge for what the Sicarii had done to their comrades years ago.

Eleazar was the titular leader of Masada. The Zealots had forsaken worship at the temple in Jerusalem, practicing instead their religion through study groups led by the Zealot teachers. Eleazar was the principal rabbi, the self-described Teacher of Righteousness, who led his people with a strong and willful presence.

Joseph could never understand Eleazar's physical attraction to the people. He was an ordinary man, same as the hundreds of men Joseph saw on the temple grounds. Eleazar was shorter than Joseph, standing no higher than a mule wagon. He was thickset with the large hands of a manual laborer. His voice, gentle and commanding, did not fit his body.

For all his physical ugliness, the people on Masada revered him. Some even called him the Messiah and looked to him to deliver them from the hands of Rome. Little did the people know what deliverance Eleazar would bring.

The Roman threat occupied talk around the campfires, by the cisterns that captured and stored the spring rains, and near the ovens where the women baked the bread. Though the ramp wasn't even half-finished, Masada's inhabitants knew what its completion meant. The few married couples clung to each other like every day was their last. The unmarried people, for all the prohibition against sexual relations between men and women, found time to be alone, to be with one another.

For the little ones, the children who knew nothing except endless games among the ruins of King Herod's palace, life remained the same. Scrambling around the palace, chasing the few goats the families kept, and picking the wildflowers that sprouted after the sparse winter rains, nothing but living occupied the minds of the children on Masada.

How many of these boys will grow to manhood? Already, the pairings between girls and boys had begun. The Zealots practiced celibacy, but no one had told the young ones yet. Girls plaited crowns of yellow wildflowers for their boyfriends, and the boys pledged their lives for their girlfriends' honor.

Eleazar had also made a pledge: the Romans would never take him to be crucified on the criminals' hill outside Jerusalem. Better to die a free man than live and die under the yoke of Rome.

"They shall not take us alive. They shall not take our families alive. Promise me that," he exhorted his followers at campfire after campfire. The charismatic Jewish leader had worked his followers into a frenzy, believing that the Romans would subject them to the cruelest of cruelties and that only death would spare them.

Eleazar had it all worked out. When the Tenth Legion finally breached the wooden wall the Zealots had erected in front of the ramp, the Romans would come into a camp occupied by the dead. First, the men would kill their families. Then, with just ten men left alive, they would draw numbers, dictating who would be the last to live. Only one of Eleazar's followers would live. After killing the other nine of his brethren, the last Jewish survivor on Masada would fall on his sword. The Romans would be greeted by the specter of death and the fallen bodies of the Masada inhabitants.

Joseph was part of this campfire of men listening to Eleazar nightly. The young man had earned his place at the campfire because of his daring forays into the Roman camp. But the suicide pledge Eleazar required was too much for him. *I am in the prime of my life, ready to take a woman and make a family. If anyone is to taste the edge of my sword, it will be a Roman and not one of my own people.*

That night Joseph sat transfixed by Eleazar's words. He didn't want to surrender and commit suicide. He thought about the Roman general. *He had hair when he gave me the sword and laughingly kicked me out of his camp. I think I saw him just a little while ago. Could I kill him if he led his soldiers up the ramp? He did ask me to spare his life if we ever met again in battle. What would I do? What would Aleya want me to do?*

Joseph's mind drifted to Aleya, the freed slave who fled to Masada with the wool merchant. She was not of his people, rumored to come from one of the tribes in the far southern desert. She was exotic and mysterious. She captivated him.

Her skin was dusky as if burnished by the golden warmth of the sun. Her upward slanted eyes were large, black pools of light. Her voice was musical, and she spoke Hebrew with the most attractive accent Joseph had ever heard.

Joseph judged her to be about fifteen years old, old enough to take a husband. She was slender, but more a girl than a woman. Joab, the merchant, hadn't worked her hard. She had no calluses on her hands or feet, and her face was smooth and unlined.

Aleya's hair was dark but not black. It was dark brown with streaks of reddish gold. Joseph had assumed that her exposure to the clear sun of Judea had lightened her hair. He was certain she did not color it. Where would a slave get the money to pay for such frivolities?

Joab had bought her from a sea captain making passage from Alexandria to Judea. The captain had bought her from the strange dark peoples who lived south of the cataracts on the Nile. The Romans called them Nubians, and Joseph used to see them in the governor's palace. The only Nubians he ever saw were slaves. So how could a people of slaves sell slaves? And how did Aleya fall into their hands? Where was she from?

"Joab, tell me, please, where your slave girl comes from. I am interested in her."

"Join the crowd of young men on Masada who are 'interested' in Aleya. That's her name. Don't call her a slave girl. Sit down, young man, and I'll tell you what I know. But let me tell you first. Aleya says she's a princess."

Joseph sat in the merchant's tent on a pile of the softest wool rugs he had ever felt. In the dim glow of the oil lamp, he let the old man's words weave a magical tale of the slave girl from the south.

"She comes from a land beyond the Red Sea. She told me she was on a caravan with her brother, the prince. A slave trader in a port city grabbed her and sold her to a captain on a slave ship. She has never seen her family again. She thinks it was two, maybe three, years ago."

Joseph had never seen the Red Sea. He knew all the stories of how Moses parted the waters to save his people from the Pharaoh's army. And he knew some merchants who sailed across the sea to Egypt. He would sit silently around their campfires, listening to tales of fierce warriors who lived in the sandy wastelands along the coast.

The nearest port was several weeks' travel from Masada, according to Joab. If Aleya came from a country beyond the Red Sea that meant she probably lived in what the Romans called *Arabia Petraea,* a dry land of desert dunes and strange black streams.

"I freed her a year ago, but she stays with me and treats me like her grandfather. What is strange about her is that she remains aloof from our God and the practice of our religion. And yet, she has more in common with us than she knows.

"Years of keeping trading accounts have dimmed my eyesight. My hands are useless. That young girl you want to know about keeps me alive. If you value her, if you grow to love her, treat her well. And keep her alive."

Joseph just looked at the merchant and nodded his head, saying nothing, waiting for the man to continue his story. For all his physical frailties, Joab's spirit soared with God. A simple word from him would calm a crowd. Sometimes, at the nightly council campfires, he would speak so softly that the entire group of men would lean in to catch every word he said.

"Joseph, my son, heaven has granted my wish for someone to care for me in my old age. I have only sons. Each followed in my footsteps but none married. And none cared for me. After my wife died, if it weren't for Aleya, well, I might have quickly followed my beloved wife."

Joseph leaned into Joab and spoke softly in his ear. "Listen, old man, you bring her to the men's campfire, but she never says anything. But she entices me. I find myself staring into her dark eyes and paying less attention to the words of the men around the fire. You know that romance between us is impossible. She is a heathen. I am a Jew."

Joab listened intently and glanced at the belt around Joseph's waist. "I see you carrying that sword, polishing it and keeping it sharp. For what? Are you going to kill me first, then Aleya? Better you had never lived than to think of such a thing. Forget Eleazar's plan. Leave here. With her. Take her home to her own people and come back to Jerusalem. Forget you ever met her. I tell you no good will ever come from anything between you.

"We Jews do not believe in casting signs to tell the future. But this I feel. This I know. If you continue to pursue that young girl, you and your family will regret it."

Chapter Thirteen

The morning sun burned brightly on Masada, the crest of the mount thrusting up sharply to meet the first rays of the dawn. Aleya was already at the water trough, washing clothes and preparing for the week. None of the women spoke to her. Even the other slaves kept their distance. She was different, even a little haughty. Not that she was too foreign. There were many foreign slaves on Masada. It was clear the young woman who claimed to come from across the Red Sea cared little for the Jewish way of life. She cared even less for the eligible young men who always managed to be around to assist Joab.

Aleya went through life on Masada in a trance, as if her time with Joab were a dream. She only smiled when she was taking care of him. Joseph pitied her. Aleya didn't need his pity. In her own lands she was a princess whose father was far wealthier than most men could dream.

Her father commanded armies of men. He lived in a palace with a roof so translucent that she could see birds flying in the sky. The riches of the mountain slopes brought all kinds of fruits and vegetables to her feet. Caravans came daily to beg her father's blessings to trade their goods for the kingly gifts of frankincense and myrrh that her people produced.

She was the daughter of the man who ruled the Arabian Peninsula as far as a camel could ride from coast to coast and from north to south. Even the nomads who left the cities of the south for a life back in the desert paid homage to her father.

Anywhere she rode, any dhow she boarded, any army she met, all were under her command because she was the first daughter of her father. She was the princess royal of the desert.

How had Aleya ended up a slave? How could fate be so cruel to turn her into a washerwoman, serving people who would be beneath her notice back in her father's palace? Her only hope, her only salvation was the young man the other women called Joseph. He was different from the other Jewish pigs who lived in the miserable hovel they called a camp.

She knew from watching him that Joseph had a way out of here. He would leave for weeks and mysteriously return as silently as he left. When Joseph arrived from these trips, the sentinels took him immediately to Eleazar. He was young, but he sat around Eleazar's campfire. Surely he could help her.

The other men considered her a temple whore, hoping that Joab would allow them to take her for a small fee. The Zealots' law demanded cleanliness. But the men went unwashed, smelling of the fire and the disgusting food they ate. She always avoided their stares and comments, but her beauty attracted the men like wild animals to a desert watering hole.

Joseph was different. During the day, when she went about doing the small tasks that Joab had asked, she saw Joseph looking at her. At the well, at the ovens, he always seemed to be near the place where she was. When other men cast eyes at her, Joseph was always the quickest to divert their attention. Yet, for all the attention he paid to her, he never even came within ten paces of her, except at the council meetings when she helped Joab.

When Aleya attended Joab at the council of campfires, Joseph was always the soldier who stood nearest her. She dared not think of

Joseph in any way. He was a simple soldier, not even a decent Jewish merchant. And he followed a religion with strict rules, one God, and commandments by which he followed his life. How could she even consider a man like that?

She was a princess. Her father ruled all the lands from the sea to the oases to the caravan routes. What could this uncouth Jewish adventurer offer her—except freedom? Joseph could save her. She wept silently, her tears mixing with the pure water she took from the cistern.

In the privacy of his tent, Joab addressed Aleya as "Granddaughter," for that was how he thought of her. His family was gone. His sons chose not to follow him to Masada and sought their fortunes elsewhere outside of Judea. But this one—with the dark eyes, the slender figure, and the promise of youth blooming all over her body—could be his granddaughter.

One night, before they both went to bed, Joab began asking her questions. "Tell me, my little one. What are you thinking? That you are tired of hugging an old man good-night and wish you had the strong arms of a younger man around you instead?"

Aleya was horrified by Joab's words! Of course, she wished for a younger man to take care of her. But she would never desert him. "Oh, don't say that, Master. Of all the men on this mount, I care for you alone."

"Is that true, Aleya? What about the young warrior I see following you about the camp like a wounded puppy? The one who pretends not to look at you but drinks in your every move with his eyes?"

"I do not know of whom you speak, Grandfather," Aleya said, catching herself at the use of the familiar title. She had never called him anything but "master."

Joab's heart swelled when the word slipped past the rosy lips of his little one. To be called "Grandfather" by such a gift of God swelled his heart with pride and filled his soul with love. "You called me 'Grandfather,' Aleya. Do you miss your real one so much that you give that title to a merchant who bought you in the marketplace like a cow?"

Upon hearing this, Aleya burst into tears and fell into Joab's arms.

"There, there, my little one. No doubt you miss your family. But you have a new one here. Do I not treat you like one of my own? At the next council of campfires, I'll make it official. I will declare you my family, adopt you, and no one will ever think that you are a slave again."

Aleya looked up at Joab, and some of the pain in her eyes went away. She loved the man, but no one, not even the kindly merchant, would ever replace her real family. It wasn't the palaces. It wasn't the servants she called her own or the riches her father bestowed upon her. She would gladly give them all up today if she could see her family tomorrow.

Better to be a servant in the kitchen of my father's house than the adopted daughter of this rich merchant. She looked across the brazier and saw the old man's chin resting against his chest. Deep snores issued from his mouth, and his craggy features had sunken into a relaxed pose. "Come, Grandfather, it is time to sleep. Let me help you to bed."

Outside Joab's tent, Joseph sat and watched the shadows thrown against the canvas walls by the dim light of the brazier. He watched Aleya escort Joab to his sleeping quarters and then watched as she prepared herself for bed.

He felt guilty, like a spy peering over a garden wall while the women of the house bathe themselves in the courtyard fountain. But he couldn't take his eyes away from the shadow. The shapely outline of Aleya's body, backlighted by the oil lamp inside the tent, only served to arouse him further.

I could take her if I wished. She's only a slave, and I am a member of Eleazar's ruling council. No one, not even Joab, would dare prevent me from taking Aleya. No! That wouldn't be right. I am not like that. I am not like those Roman rapists who come in and take the women of the village at their will. I shall make her mine. No one, not Eleazar, not Joab, will stand between us.

Chapter Fourteen

"Hello, Joseph! Why so moody? Can't you see that flowers have sprung up in this godforsaken wilderness? And there's work to do. There's always work to do. We need to get back to work. I mean, you need to get back to work," shouted Levi bar Adon, Joseph's closest friend in the camp.

Joseph rested from his job of building the fortifications that Eleazar had planned as the first line of resistance against the Roman invaders. Eleazar had gathered the young men and put them to work constructing a wooden wall at the point of the Masada fortress where the Roman ramp would end.

Joseph laid down his shovel and crept over to the end of the camp to spy on the Roman engineers. He needed the time alone. He half looked at the Romans and half looked into his heart, pondering his future with Aleya. Sadly, he knew, there would be no future when the Romans overran Masada.

The Romans had finished building the wooden supports that would bring the earthen ramp up to the walls of Masada. When the ramp reached the lip of the mountain, the advance guard of the mighty Tenth Legion would leap over the walls and overrun the camp of the Zealots.

Joseph spied on the work of the Romans, oblivious to the work going on behind him. *We are but a handful of people compared to the might of the Roman legions. Can wood hold up against the iron of the Roman sword and shield? Why doesn't Eleazar just lead us down Masada and sue for peace with the Roman commander?* Joseph asked these questions in his mind, hoping that, somehow, he would find the answers.

He drifted away from the work site toward the northern boundary of Masada. Looking down the side of the mount, Joseph examined his escape route. This was the one he took on his excursions into the Roman garrison. And this was the only route to safety once the Roman soldiers charged over the wall.

Sitting on the dusty, dried-out soil, Joseph let his mind drift back to his first trip up to Masada. When Joseph joined the Jewish defenders there, he climbed up that very same path to the camp. It was treacherous, allowing only one person at a time to scale the heights. It wound around the mount, rising the full 1,500 feet to the top. It was said that Herod would not allow any other path up the side of the mountain. The better to defend himself against his enemies. A handful of soldiers could hold off a whole army.

The leader of the Sicarii, Barabbas, assured him that his men would fight against the Romans "until the stars withered in a wrinkling sky and this earth faded in a whirl of smoke."

Joseph did not believe the old warhorse any more than he believed in the fighting capabilities of the Sicarii. Joseph considered the Sicarii to be worthless troublemakers. He would just as soon send them tumbling down the side of Masada to their certain deaths as defend them in a fight against the Romans.

When Joseph first arrived on Masada, its residents were divided evenly between the Sicarii and the Zealots. They avoided each other but respected each other's goals. After all, weren't they both groups of Jews who found fault with the current Jewish leaders? For a while, the balance between the Sicarii and the Zealots held evenly. Slowly, more people joined the Zealots' camp. The Zealots began to outnumber the

Sicarii, and Masada became more of a religious haven and community than a hiding place for outnumbered Jewish rebels. No longer was Masada an encampment of revolutionaries who would pull the tail feathers of the fierce Roman eagle. The way of the Zealots overcame the combative atmosphere created by the Sicarii. A battle against the Romans was becoming less likely each day.

Joseph could see how every day the arrival of more Jews into the Zealot community changed the nature of the camp. The Sicarii were exclusively male with a few camp followers. Families began joining the Zealots, turning Masada into a real community, not just a collection of ruffians living in the desert.

Unlike the Roman garrison that preceded them, neither the Sicarii nor the Zealots took advantage of Herod's sumptuous buildings. Though long abandoned by the king's family, the magnificent buildings the Tetrarch had built remained. The dry desert air and minimal rainfall preserved buildings for centuries.

The inhabitants on Masada did use Herod's water collection system. Joseph recalled when he first arrived at Masada how dry the environment was and questioned how anyone could live there. He examined the giant cisterns that were empty when he arrived. They were huge. If four men stood on one another's shoulders, the man on top still wouldn't be able to touch the ceiling. Joseph had no idea how anything this big would fill with water, that is, until he experienced the first spring rains on Masada.

The giant cisterns collected the sudden desert downpours, assuring a year-round water supply. The water was for drinking, not farming. It was difficult to grow anything on Masada. Thankfully, the oasis of Ein Gedi was not far off. It supplied Masada's residents with all the fruits and vegetables they needed, with some left over to sell to the Roman camp. Joseph knew the oasis because Ein Gedi was his resting place when he travelled back and forth between Masada and Jerusalem. For the limited amount of meat they ate, the Zealots kept a small flock of sheep and goats.

As Joseph looked around the camp, he realized Masada provided the perfect environment for a group of people who wished to live apart from the world below them. It would have been the ideal place for the Zealots to live, if it hadn't been tainted by the massacre of Roman soldiers by the Sicarii. And they would pay for it…with their lives.

"Come get back to work," bar Adon cried. Joseph looked over to his friend covered with desert dust and grinning foolishly. Levi bar Adon was Joseph's childhood friend. It seemed their lives were always entwined. Soon after Joseph joined the camp on Masada, he returned to the Jerusalem marketplace and recruited his childhood friend to join him in his crusade against the Romans.

When they were little, they played Jewish soldier against Roman soldier. Of course, Levi was always the Roman, even though Joseph had his Roman sword. Levi used to complain that the game wasn't fair. He never got to win. Joseph and his army of Jewish warriors always overcame the Roman army led by Levi.

Their childhood games gave way to more serious things—games may live forever, but not so little boys—and the two of them found themselves united against a real Roman enemy who would soon come storming up the side of Masada. This game was deadly serious, and it wasn't likely that the Jewish warriors would overcome the Romans this time.

Though lifelong friends, the two young men were completely different. Joseph was passionate about himself, his people, and his history. He was a strict observer of the Law. Levi would flit from belief to belief and from sect to sect. There were dozens that circulated in Jerusalem in the years after the death of the young rabbi. Levi had joined and left most of them.

Levi is a fool, Joseph thought. Eager to grasp any new belief that simmered to the surface in the fringes of the Jewish community, Levi had first joined the Sicarii. Then he transferred his loyalties to the gentler touch of the Zealots. He had given himself completely to the Zealots' way of life, even going so far as forsaking the comfort of women. Levi's celibacy lasted a few weeks, interrupted by a chance meeting with a woman wandering on the grounds of the Herodian temple. The others may resist a woman, but not Levi. He reveled in the lack of male competition. Joseph always suspected that Levi followed the Zealots because they abandoned the touch of a woman. This left the field totally open to him.

He stopped his daydreaming and rejoined Levi at the wooden wall. *Levi may be a fool, but at least he's a happy one. He has his pick of the women on the mount, and no night goes by without Levi coupling with yet another woman in her tent.*

Eleazar, on the other hand, is a hopeless fool. Reasoning that not even the Romans would drag siege engines up the ramp, the Zealot leader figured that a high palisade would provide a good defense against the Tenth Legion. *Hasn't Eleazar ever heard of fire? Doesn't he know what a few well-placed torches will do to a wall of wood? Why are we working for months on a wall that could be destroyed in hours?* He kept his thoughts to himself rather than raise doubts of his loyalty to Eleazar and his cause. He knew he had to leave. And take Aleya with him.

Chapter Fifteen

74 CE

The Romans pushed the slaves to work faster on the ramp. Joseph and his camp-mates worked like slaves themselves to erect the barricade Eleazar ordered.

Down below, a centurion in the work party made his way from the ramp into the Roman camp. He was to report to his commander and give him an estimate for the completion of the ramp. The centurion strode through the camp and entered the command tent of Flavius Silva.

"Honored Commander," the centurion said, striking his breast in respect for his officer, "the engineers have finished building the wooden supports for the uppermost reaches of the ramp. We should have it completed by the Ides."

Flavius Silva looked at the veteran. Covered with the dust of the wilderness, dripping with sweat, and undoubtedly chafed where his leather breastplate rubbed against his chest and shoulders, the centurion stood silently waiting for his commander to say something.

He turned to the Jewish slave girls attending him. "Bring this man some refreshment. No, not that. Get the amphora of Falernian wine and some Rhodian grapes. This man has been working to set you free," Flavius chortled.

Some of the Jews can be accommodating, even if they are temple whores, he thought. Flavius had promised the slaves a letter of manumission once Masada was cleared of the Zealots. No doubt, those temple harlots would never make it past the camp's gates once his legionaries decided to celebrate their revenge on Masada. Flavius had seen what was left of women who were passed from drunken legionary to drunken legionary. He shuddered at the thought of what would happen to these beautiful girls.

The centurion stood and waited for Flavius to speak. Instead of addressing him, the Roman commander turned to his side and addressed Valerius. The centurion, knowing when to stay quiet, remained at stiff attention in the tent and kept his mouth shut. "A mouse does not squeak when elephants gather," was a Roman proverb. In this company, the centurion certainly felt like a mouse.

"So, General, what think you of this news? Are you eager to lead your men up the ramp and over the walls? You of all people should welcome the completion of the ramp. Once we take Masada, your exile in this godforsaken land will soon be over. Then it's back to your comrade-in-arms, Vespasian, and to the life of luxury you deserve in Rome. Who knows, Titus may even let you ride behind him in the triumph."

Valerius rose to answer but stopped as the flaps to Flavius's tent were thrust open. In strode young Titus, acting like the emperor himself. In recent months, the son of Vespasian styled himself in the dress of a noble senator of the republic. He dressed in a *toga virilis* made of the whitest Egyptian cotton pounded with chalk and soaked in urine to make it even whiter and fringed with the imperial band of purple. Titus strode into the commander's tent with the look of a man who was demanding action. The *legatus legionis* looked impatient.

"So, where are we with your infernal road to nowhere?" Titus demanded. Both Flavius and Valerius looked at the centurion who stood caught in the crossfire of the three most powerful men in the Tenth Legion.

The centurion sweated nervously. The elephants were playing with the mouse. *Let me face the arrows of the Parthians, the blue-painted devils of Gallaecia. Even send me back to Britannia, but please, mighty Mithras, watch over me now and put the right words in my mouth,* the centurion prayed silently.

"Centurion, tell the mighty Titus what you have just said to me," demanded Flavius.

Seeing the centurion's discomfort, Valerius stepped in, rescuing the tongue-tied soldier from further embarrassment. "Go, Centurion, back to your men and the dirt-haulers. I shall give your report to my Lord Titus. Here, take this wine with you, but mix it with water. I doubt if your men have ever tasted the likes of this Falernian. It could get to your head too quickly and take you away from the ramp."

The grateful centurion exited quickly after a sharp Roman salute to the three commanders and a quick prayer of thanks to the soldier's god, Mithras.

"Always the centurion, eh, Valerius, though you wear the crimson of an officer and soon may be invested with the purple of a noble," Titus said.

The Zealots occupied the top of Masada for ten years. For a decade, Masada had been a thorn in the side of the Roman governor. The Roman army had occupied Masada for forty years before losing it to the Sicarii.

Naturally, Flavius was not on Masada when the Jewish rebels massacred the Roman garrison. But he pledged he would teach the Jews not to trifle with the might of the Roman Empire.

Flavius would still stay in the camp, but the results on top of Masada would be vastly different. To be sure, though, Flavius needed more information. He had Valerius search the garrison for any soldier who had served on Masada before its recapture by the rebels. He wished to know more about the fortifications on top before committing the men of the Tenth in an all-out assault.

Valerius knew the best way to find the soldier would be to tap into the centurion grapevine. It took Valerius two weeks, but he had found the man.

"General, I am reporting as requested." Valerius looked up from the papers laid out on his campaign table. In front of him stood a gray-haired veteran of the Tenth, not a centurion, not even a non-commissioned officer. The man had scars on his arms, Valerius noticed, indicating he had seen his share of battles.

"Silva wishes to know more about Masada. What can you tell him?"

"Sir, I left Masada just weeks before rebel troops stormed the mountain and killed our garrison. My knowledge isn't current, but I doubt if the rebels have made many changes."

So you left Masada while your comrades perished to the last man. Is that why you have achieved no rank? The Tenth is punishing you for your good fortune, Valerius said silently to himself. "Soldier, tell me your name and duties."

"General, I am Publius Quintulus, and I am assigned to the quartermaster's staff. I have always served as a quartermaster. I left Masada to replenish our supplies. I have never returned."

"You will have the opportunity to return. If you wish, I shall have you serve in the front ranks that will lead the assault on the mount."

"General Sixtus, you will have done me a great honor. How may I help you now?"

"You will accompany me to the commander's quarters. Be prepared to tell him what you know about Masada. I presume your memory is still good, or have you rotted your brain with the Judean wine you pilfer from the officers' wagons?"

Valerius added the good-natured ribbing to ease the old soldier's fears. A summons to Flavius's quarters, especially for an old, failed soldier like Quintulus, was nerve-wracking, and Valerius knew it.

They waded through a crowd of soldiers hanging around Flavius Silva's tent. *The men in the legion know that we are going to attack soon,* Valerius thought, *and are hoping to pick up tidbits of information from their officers coming in and out.* He nudged Quintulus.

"Don't say a word to any of these men after the governor dismisses you," Valerius warned. Quintulus clasped his fist to his chest and nodded. Valerius returned the salute, fully knowing that the old soldier would keep his mouth shut for maybe twenty paces away from Flavius's quarters.

As they approached, the outside guards saluted. Valerius and Quintulus entered and stood before the seated governor. "Well, Valerius, what have you found? Tell me this is a Masada expert? I thought you were going to bring me one of your Jewish friends."

It was apparent that Flavius knew nothing of the old soldier's past. Valerius decided not to inform him. "Publius Quintulus served in the century that previously occupied Masada. The Jewish fort stands out clearly in his mind like a mural in a Capitoline temple."

"So you say. Well, draw up a bench and begin. But don't take too long. We haven't much time."

His offer of a seat shocked Quintulus. Ordinary legionaries never sat during a formal audience, even with their centurions. And the man in front of him was the legion's head of the entire province of Judea.

"General Sixtus has said you wish to know more about Masada. What can I tell you that your engineers haven't discovered already?"

"Soldier, tell me what it is like on top. What will my men encounter when they get there? How fortified is the camp of the Jews?"

Quintulus drew a breath, sighed heavily, and leaned his forearms on Flavius's campaign desk. "This is what I know." And the unintentional survivor of the Masada massacre began to speak.

Chapter Sixteen

King Herod, some hundred years before Flavius arrived in Judea, created his fortress on Masada. Herod was an unpopular ruler. His people hated him, believing he sold his birthright to the Romans in exchange for the crown. Always a nervous ruler, Herod feared for his life and his kingdom when the Roman Republic fell into disarray after the death of Julius Caesar. Marc Antony and Tiberius, the adopted son of Julius Caesar, battled for the right to lead Rome, forgetting about the Judean province. Cleopatra, Queen of Egypt and Antony's lover, always coveted the land across the Red Sea. She convinced Antony to give the province to her when he beat Tiberius. This terrified Herod, so he built his fortress on Masada.

"Quintulus," Flavius Silva interrupted the survivor's summary, "where did you hear this story about Cleopatra, Marc Antony, and all these Roman nobles?"

"I became friends with a woman whose great-grandfather was a stonemason. He was part of the crew that constructed Herod's buildings on Masada. Over the years, she has told me the history of the fort. Shall I continue?"

Flavius wordlessly flicked his fly whip in the direction of the soldier, motioning for him to continue. "Some of Herod's soldiers came to the towns of Judea recruiting workers. The Jews thought Herod was crazy. Who would build a palace on top of a dry mountain, miles outside of Jerusalem? But Herod had his own reasons. His Masada palace would keep him safe from Cleopatra's armies and his rebellious subjects.

"Herod created a desert masterpiece. He imported engineers from Persia whose Babylonian ancestors built the beautiful gardens for their king, Nebuchadnezzar. The Babylonians designed an aqueduct on Masada to catch the spring rains and channel them into a series of cisterns that would hold a year's supply of water."

"So unless we overrun the rebels, they have enough water to hold out forever?"

"My Lord, water, yes. But they have to eat. There is almost no food supply on Masada. That's why I took the wagons..."

Valerius jumped in. "That's enough, Quintulus. The governor has no time for your reminiscences. Continue with your description of Masada."

Quintulus looked at Valerius, grateful that his general had prevented him from talking about how he survived the massacre. "Let me get back to the water supply. When Herod and his family lived on Masada, he had plenty of water for his two palaces, his magnificent Roman baths, and the servants' quarters.

"Since his death, Romans and Jews alternately occupied his palace free from attacking armies. Only stealth or an all-out assault would overcome the occupying troops encamped on Masada."

"Thank you, Quintulus. You may go." The soldier left. Valerius remained behind. Flavius sat at his desk, staring blankly ahead. He knew that Masada was unassailable. King Herod made sure of that. The only path to the top made it impossible for a force of any size to mount an attack. So Flavius had decided to build a ramp large enough that would allow his men and his siege machines to rid the empire of the Jewish revolutionaries once and for all. Masada could only be taken by brute force. Flavius was determined to supply that force.

70 CE

Flavius received word that a ship flying the imperial banner had landed in Caesarea. Titus, the emperor's son and now an adult, was on board.

It didn't take long for Flavius to receive more news. Ports offered men as much pleasure as they could pay for, and Titus had the backing of the imperial treasury. The emperor's son spent several weeks in Caesarea, bragging to whores and drunkards that his father sent him to direct the Judean campaign. Word reached Flavius. The Roman commander of Judea thought Vespasian had removed him from command. The prize that he sought, the destruction of the Judean revolutionaries, appeared to be out of his grasp.

Titus arrived in Jerusalem two months after he landed in Caesarea. The imperial escort accompanied him to the Roman garrison at the base of Masada. The haughty son of the ruler of the world looked around the camp and sneered. "My dear commander," he said to Flavius, "can't you find better accommodations for me? It is hardly fitting for the commander of all the Roman army to bed down in a tent that isn't even fit for your lowliest centurion."

Flavius and Valerius stood at attention, listening to the complaints of the emperor's son. Flavius had no desire to be a manservant to this young whelp. The emperor's son needed a general officer as an aide, but it wouldn't be him. Flavius assigned Valerius to look after every need of the man who would probably be the next emperor.

"My lord," said Valerius, "let me go to Jerusalem and find you proper accommodations."

"No, that's not necessary. Just make this pigsty more comfortable for me," Titus commanded Valerius. When the emperor's son spoke, legionaries jumped. Valerius excused himself from the imperial presence and sought help to make the tent Titus was to occupy that night "more comfortable."

The young emperor-to-be can sleep like a legionary tonight, Valerius thought, as he made his way back to his humble tent. *I'll take care of his needs tomorrow.*

As Valerius prepared himself for bed, Titus and Flavius locked themselves in a discussion of strategy. *Now, I will learn what the emperor wants,* Flavius thought, *but not until we have drained another amphora of Falernian wine.*

Flavius made sure that his servants had stocked Titus's temporary quarters with a good supply of the best wine they could find. He thought of securing some jugs of Egyptian beer, but the sweetish taste of that drink didn't sit well with all men. Flavius preferred the beer to wine, but, of course, he had to drink what Titus drank.

A mule-drawn wagon pulled up outside Flavius's tent. A centurion guard entered the tent, clasping his fist to his chest. "My Lord Flavius, the quartermaster has arrived. Where shall I tell him to put the provisions?"

Just then, Titus jumped up and ran outside the tent, brushing past the centurion as if he were a marble statue. Inside the tent, Flavius and the centurion could hear the commotion caused by the appearance of the emperor's son. Titus was speaking loudly. They had no idea what was going on. They waited, tensed, wondering what the son of the emperor was doing.

A centurion threw the flaps of the tent open, and Titus walked in, hugging an amphora of wine. "Flavius," he shouted, "never tell my father that his son is not prepared to do the work of an ordinary soldier." He placed the jug of wine on the carpeted floor of the tent and cut off its neck with his sword. Precious drops of the best wine in the empire spilled onto the carpet. The centurion looked enviously at the wine that was being wasted.

"Flavius, dismiss your men and let's get to the strategy of this campaign." The centurion departed quickly but not before grabbing the broken neck of the jug, which still held a half-cup of wine.

Titus and Flavius huddled around his table and began emptying the jug. Well into their cups, Flavius learned the nature of his assignment. The emperor, Titus said, was determined to put down the Jews forever.

"My father successfully tamed the wild Britons. We have Gauls who are citizens of the empire. The Visigoth hordes remain on their side of the Rhenus. All that is left is Judea. We mean to strike at the heart of the Jewish revolution. We, meaning you and your legion, will take down their temple stone-by-stone and salt the earth so that nothing grows there. Then, we will deal with the rabble on top of your mount," Titus told Flavius.

Titus's words stunned Flavius. *My greatest desire is to stop the Judean revolution. But tear down the Jews' temple! No Roman ever defiled the sacred place of any god. Weren't there temples in Rome to Egyptian gods, Babylonian gods, and Greek gods? We respect the gods of all people. We do not destroy temples. We take them as our own. And the God of the Jews was powerful. Do we dare to go against so powerful a god?*

"My lord, Titus, do you think that is necessary? I have been here for many years, and the Jews have impressed me with their devotion to their God. If we destroy their temple, are we not bringing down the people's wrath upon us?"

"Flavius, Flavius, do you really think gods exist except to serve our purposes? The Jews believe their God is powerful and brought them out of slavery. Ha! What a great God he is! Aren't they enslaved now? And what about our gods? Do you really think that boy-lover, Tiberius—dead though he is—is a god as we are supposed to believe? Do you really want to worship a catamite?

"Flavius, we destroy their temple, and we destroy them. Then we move onto Masada and rid our garrison of those vermin. I am aware of your letters to Rome. So is my divine father. You can have your wish. You can lead your men and take back Masada for us. But, first, you must destroy the temple and give your men an opportunity to get the treasures that they say are hidden there. Didn't that young rabbi so many of the Jews are following these days prophesize that the temple would be torn down? Well, think of it this way—we're just helping the prophecy come true. And, Flavius, I will lead. Make sure your legion is ready."

Titus left Flavius brooding about his commander's orders. Never did he think Rome would seek to rip the heart out of the Jewish people. *Destroy their temple! Raze the building! Steal their sacred objects! Anyone who takes part in that undertaking is doomed. I fear their God, but I fear the emperor more. It will be done as he wishes.*

The next day Flavius ordered Valerius to gather the centurions. In Flavius's tent, the centurions learned the emperor's command. The men disliked it as much as Flavius. Stealing the temple's gold and silver didn't disturb them but tearing down the building? That was a plan hatched by a madman.

Flavius ordered the centurions to get their soldiers ready for the task. "Valerius, this should be easy. Probably no more than two cohorts will be needed for the task. Just keep the other centuries in reserve. And, Valerius, I'm suspending construction of the ramp for now. Masada can wait until we finish tearing down every stone of their precious temple."

Valerius left his commanding general's tent with a sour stomach and a bad taste in his mouth. He turned to his centurions but kept quiet. The emperor had spoken.

In the ensuing weeks, the soldiers prepared for the task. They trained as if they were to fight an enemy, not a collection of old priests and weak temple whores. Thirty-seven years after the death of that rabbi, the Romans would march into Jerusalem to destroy the temple, and with it, the spirit of the Jewish people.

The Roman plan leaked to the Sanhedrin, who alerted the temple priests. In that darkest part of the night, after the moon had set but stars had not risen, the priests spirited away most of the treasures for safekeeping in hidden desert locations. Buried in obscure caves, some high up the face of rock outcroppings, the fabulous temple treasures were hidden until it was safe to retrieve them. Only the high priest knew the exact location of all the treasures. He recorded the locations on sheets of copper to be passed down to future generations of high priests. He rolled the thin sheets of copper into a scroll and secreted them in a cave overlooking the Dead Sea. Only he, and future high priests, would know the location of the scroll and possess the key to unlock its secrets.

The high priest recorded the locations of the buried temple gold using an ancient form of Hebrew which was only taught and practiced by the temple priests. The language was no longer spoken by the people, and none, except a few temple priests, could read the ancient script.

The high priest, knowing that the Roman army would be marching at any time, entered into a period of mourning in anticipation of what was to come. He cut off communication with the other priests in the temple and rarely made public appearances. His actions covered his real mission—to hide the temple treasure. Some temple treasures he could not save. The fabled golden grapes adorning the temple doors and the seven-foot silver menorah had to remain. These, the priests knew, would fall into the hands of the Roman soldiers.

"Valerius, prepare your men for the march!" Titus shouted down to his soldiers from astride his war horse. He watched as the men formed into marching order and prepared to strike at the very heart of the Jewish people. Under Titus's orders of a forced march, the legionaries soon approached the gates of Jerusalem. The city's inhabitants knew what the Romans would do and scattered into hiding places. The streets of Jerusalem were no place for a Jewish citizen when the Roman army appeared in force.

Titus halted his horse at the foot of Temple Mount. Looking up at the magnificent temple, he ordered the men to regroup and prepare to enter the temple's courtyard.

Valerius had no stomach for this fight. For the first time in his career, he held back, unsure whether it was in respect for his mother's memory or a soldier's fear of angering a powerful god. It wasn't war. It was a treasure raid with the only defenders a handful of old men and cheap whores.

Titus directed his men to storm the temple doors. Using a leaden battering ram, the soldiers easily broke through the massive cedar doors and ran into the inner courtyard. There in front of them, or so they thought, was the temple proper with all its hidden gold and silver. The soldiers streamed throughout the temple grounds, seeking the treasure and killing anyone who got in their way. They charged about in a frenzy, and none of the officers could control them. The killing and looting went on all day.

At night, the flames from the burning furniture illuminated Valerius's face. He walked about the ruined temple, gingerly stepping over rubble that once was a holy place. *What have we done here? What have we accomplished? I know these people. Their building may be destroyed but not their spirit.*

"Sir, what did you command me?"

Valerius looked to his side and saw a legionary standing there, holding a bag of produce from the many vendor stalls that lined the outer courtyard.

"Nothing, soldier. Nothing. Enjoy your bag of fruit." And he walked away in disgust.

The soldiers and officers who took part in the raid were disappointed. Perhaps the rumors of the great temple treasure were untrue. Except for some very large objects affixed to the walls and a handful of coins left as donations, the soldiers found none of the fabled silver plates and golden utensils.

Titus tortured several priests to discover the truth about the treasure. The old men died before revealing anything. Valerius was positive they knew little about the treasure. He suspected the high priest was the key to the location of the treasure, but the high priest was sacrosanct. Not even Titus would touch the revered old man.

Valerius sought Titus and asked him for his leave. Titus granted it, and Valerius made his way back to the Roman camp in the desert, leaving the destruction of the temple behind.

The soldiers stayed in Jerusalem for well over two months, dismantling the temple of the Jews. Like the young rabbi prophesied, not one stone was left standing upon another. The soldiers only left one wall standing near the western part of the temple. Valerius could only guess they left it standing because they were tired of demolishing the building.

Valerius could understand the soldiers' fatigue. The temple was huge. Constructed at immense cost by the ill-fated King Herod, the Temple of Jerusalem was reputed to be one of the largest religious structures of its kind. It was larger than even the Temple of Jupiter in Rome where the Roman Senate met daily.

Less than half of the Tenth Legion participated in the temple raid. Valerius was glad that it was just half of his men. In the weeks after the temple's destruction, a mysterious malady befell many of the soldiers involved in the raid. Roman soldiers are superstitious, and word spread through the camp that the Hebrew God was punishing them. None of the men died, but all of them were miserable and afflicted with unknown ailments for well over half a year.

The destruction of the temple had the exact effect that Titus expected. It demoralized the Jewish people. Even Valerius noticed that their fabled feistiness deserted them. Titus, of course, considered his campaign a complete success and the only real accomplishment of the Roman army in Judea for the past forty years. Valerius reserved his words and never spoke his true feelings.

Chapter Seventeen

74 CE

The *Kalends* of March had passed, and the Judean spring, which had teased the Tenth Legion with a promise of pleasant weather, had stopped being coy. Cool breezes no longer wafted through the Roman camp. Gone, too, was the warm sunshine. Now, the desert showed its true face. The rainy season—as brief as it was—had come, dampening the spirits of the soldiers and the slaves working on the ramp.

The Jews on Masada welcomed the spring rains. It was the only time of the year they could replenish their cisterns. The rain washed down the side of Masada, and the dry stream beds gushed with sudden torrents. The clever placement of cisterns captured every drop of the precious liquid.

Down below, in the camp of the Romans, fifteen thousand men were readying for the spring festival of *Lupercalia*. The men paid no heed that the festival was a fertility rite. The centurions had rounded up plenty of wine, some women, and a few musicians to break the monotony of the legion's desert vigil. As long as there was wine to drink, meat to roast, and a few women to satisfy their cravings, legionaries in the Roman army would celebrate any festival.

Valerius looked about from the doorway of his quarters. The staff of the Tenth Legion marked his tent as the dwelling of a commander with his new rank of military tribune. Titus had bestowed this favor upon him after the destruction of the temple. Valerius did not consider it a reward but welcomed the title nonetheless.

In the days of the Republic, the people, the *plebes*, elected tribunes. The tribunes had the power to turn over any decision made by the Senate by simply saying, *Veto*, "I forbid." But those days were gone, and tribune was merely a higher rank in the emperor's army.

Valerius readily adopted the trappings of a tribune. After more than ten years in this godforsaken Judean desert, he deserved a promotion. His officer's crimson cloak, now edged in gold cloth, which he draped across his shoulders to ward off a morning chill, marked him as a tribune. The *augustclavus* banner that flew outside Valerius's tent proved that Titus, the *legatus legionis*, had elevated the grizzled warrior to the equestrian class. Now all Valerius had to do was lead his men up the ramp and kill a few hundred innocent people. Then his future in Rome would be assured.

Valerius grumbled that the emperor was turning his soldiers into murderers of women and children all because Vespasian let his courtiers talk him into a grudge fight. The rebel holdouts, they whispered into the imperial ear, had offended the *maiestas* of the Roman people. We must get rid of them!

Valerius questioned his emperor's wisdom. *How in the name of the bloody bull of Mithras did Vespasian allow his court* fellators *to convince him that a ragtag bunch of desert hermits had offended the sovereignty of the Roman people?* He worried that his last campaign in Judea would be a joke in Rome. He would lead the mighty Roman army—trained to fight and kill the toughest soldiers in the world—against a bunch of ill-equipped peasants.

There's nothing strategic about that mountain. We've crushed their temple and scattered salt on the earth, enslaved their people and compromised their leaders. Why can't we turn around and leave those fools on the mountain to love and die in peace? Does the greatest army in the world need to fight against a band of religious fanatics armed with cast-off swords?

At first light tomorrow he would lead his troops. Then it would be back to Rome, never to return to Judea. He took in his last sight of the desert. Yellow and blue wildflowers dotted the desert floor. The rocks of Masada gleamed like gold in the early morning sun. On top, the remains of Herod's temple glinted starkly in the clear desert air, touches of color indicating the murals decorating the walls of the kingly palace.

The sky was a pale blue, nearly all the spring moisture wrung from its clouds. The pennants in the camp flapped in the wind from a southerly direction. Valerius grunted in approval, thanking the gods for this small favor. A southerly wind was the usual and constant pattern in the Judean wilderness. *That will be good. The wind will be with us when we storm up the ramp.* He went to prepare the battle order for tomorrow's march.

On Masada the Sicarii and their allies, the Zealots, were also preparing. The Passover feast was near, and the Zealots prayed fervently that the pitiful flock of sheep that lived on the mountain would produce the lambs they needed. At the other side of the camp, the Sicarii went about preparing their own feast. Their God was not a God of deliverance but a God of war. The books the Sicarii worshipped told of an angry God who smote their enemies. They prayed fervently that their God would smite the Roman enemy when he came over the walls.

The desert night fell over the camp. This was Joseph's favorite time of the day. He rested his tired body against the wooden wall that his comrades foolishly thought would hold back the Romans. Only he knew how the Romans fought. Their engineers would bring their siege engines up the ramp and batter down the walls. Before tomorrow night's moon was full, Masada would be a Roman camp.

Eleazar had other plans for what would happen when the Tenth Legion came marching in. His plans, Joseph knew, were worse than falling upon the mercy of the legion.

Joseph looked over the side of the mountain and saw the army marching up the ramp. A night march was unusual. The Roman army never marched after dark. Seeing the thousands of Roman soldiers marching up the ramp below him convinced Joseph that Masada would not be standing the next evening. A fully armed Roman legion struck terror in the hearts of its enemies. Even Joseph, who knew the Tenth like the back of his hand, shivered at the sight of the marching soldiers. Joseph began identifying the units that would lead the attack.

First, the light infantry, made up of the legion's auxiliary, marched with their bows ready to rain destruction. Then came the first line of the legion, those veteran soldiers who would lock shields and hold them over their heads. This strategy was called a *testudo,* so named after the Roman word for *turtle.* No enemy spear or missile could ever penetrate the locked shields. After the first line broke through, the rest of the legion would follow.

Joseph doubted that the Roman commander, whoever he'd be, would need to bring more than a cohort up the ramp. A full legion would be choked by its own bulk.

Below on the ramp, Valerius sat astride his mount, his crimson cloak unfurling behind him, as he led his men to the brink of Masada. At the top of the ramp, engineers set massive blocks of stone to support the siege engines.

Legionaries dragged the woodworks behind them, preparing to erect the catapults and battering rams the night before the assault. Some legionaries carried siege ladders.

All Roman legions had siege engines artfully contrived for them, but the Tenth Legion's machines were especially designed for the Masada assault. Some threw darts; others hurled hundred-pound stones more than 1,200 paces through the air. No wall could resist that battering for long.

Archers readied their arrows, wrapping the heads and shafts in wool and dipping them in pitch. Titus had issued particularly vicious orders for Valerius to carry out. The governor wasn't satisfied with battering down Masada's defenses. He wanted to incinerate them. The preparations were done. The legion settled in for the night. Dawn would bring battle.

Morning arrived like any other spring morning in the desert. The wind blew at the backs of the Roman soldiers massed below Masada on the ramp the engineers had built. There was little for Joseph to do. Knowing that he was approaching his final hours, he sought comfort in Aleya. He had tried to prepare her for this day. Each night he attempted to tell her what the end would be like, but he could not. Eleazar forbade council members to reveal his plan.

"The people will find out when they need to. They will agree, for none of us here wish to fall into the hands of the dreaded Romans," Eleazar said.

When the nightly council meetings ended, Joseph ached to see Aleya, to hold her, to tell her what was coming. Over the past few months they had grown closer.

She was shy at first, and he was afraid she would reject him. Joab brought them together. The old merchant would often welcome the young man into his tent and inquire about activity in the Jerusalem marketplaces. Joseph still made his trips into Jerusalem, walking his way through the Roman camp. Once inside the city walls, he sought information of the Roman army's plans. He went to his usual sources but learned nothing. Judging by the activity within the camp, Joseph knew that the attack would be soon.

When Joseph returned he would report his findings to Eleazar, then seek Joab and tell him what was selling in the markets. Gradually, Aleya would join the conversations. Joab encouraged her participation.

The casual meetings between Joseph and Aleya had been going on for months. The slow pace of their relationship obviously tried the patience of Joab. The next time Joseph walked into the merchant's tent, Joab rose to his feet and called out, "Joseph, Aleya has been on this rock for almost two years and has never gone beyond the area of this tent or the women's well. The miserable women in this camp refuse to have anything to do with her because they say she is a pagan. I don't care. Do you?

"Please take her and show her the palaces of King Herod. Go to the end of the mount and show her the Dead Sea. She's been spending all of her time with me, and I am no company for a beautiful young woman like her."

Aleya blushed. Joseph's heart almost came up through his throat, it was pounding so hard. *God bless Joab and all his generations,* Joseph said silently to himself. Of course, he couldn't come out plainly and say he would be delighted to escort Aleya. He had to sound like it was an activity he could barely fit into his schedule.

"Joab, I have just come back from Jerusalem and was on my way to the bathhouses. Perhaps Aleya could accompany me there. But then I have to attend a meeting of the council, so I will have her back in your tent soon. Maybe at another time I could escort her around the camp."

Joab recognized the false bravado in his voice and chuckled to himself. "Well, go then, Joseph, and take Aleya. Maybe you can come back for dinner tomorrow, and we can plan a tour of Masada for Aleya."

That conversation had taken place several months ago. Since that first tour after they had dinner in Joab's tent, Joseph and Aleya had become inseparable. Several council members warned him about the relationship. "She is a pagan," they said. "Certainly there are other women here more suitable for you."

Aleya paid dearly for her relationship with Joseph. As a pagan, outsider, and clearly the favorite of Joseph, the women of Masada shunned her. When their relationship deepened, the women ostracized her. She became a non-person. When Aleya would walk to the well to fill her buckets, the other women would leave. When she would bring loaves to the communal ovens to bake them, the other women would remove their loaves—baked or not—and walk away.

She didn't mind. She had Joseph, and none of the other women ever would. *Let them ignore me. Joseph and I are leaving Masada someday and never coming back.*

One night, Joseph came to Joab's tent for Aleya. They embraced and walked to the far end of the mount overlooking the Dead Sea. "Over there," Aleya pointed into the distance, "you can almost see where my father lives and rules."

"Over there, my sweet, is the land of the Canaanites. And I hardly think you are a Canaanite. What do you mean over there?"

"Not over there in front of your eyes," Aleya smiled. "Over there, for many months of a camel ride. Near the great sea where my father's people bring him pearls and jewels and brightly colored fish for his pond. That is where I am from."

Joseph had heard of the peoples of the desert and the rumors of a civilization in the far south. Had not Father Abraham come from the desert and left some of his children there? Occasionally these desert dwellers appeared outside Jerusalem's gates during the great festivals.

Their appearance provoked wonderment among the sophisticated city dwellers who speculated where they came from. The priests said these people once believed like themselves but had fallen away into idolatry and worship of false gods. These desert-dwellers came to the outskirts of the city around the great feast days peddling their jewels, their precious frankincense and myrrh, and above all, their beautiful horses.

The Romans forbade any Jew from owning one of those horses. All were purchased for the imperial court in Rome. The Romans called the land where the horses came from *Arabia Petraea*. Farther down toward the water was *Arabia Deserta,* a forbidding land where the sand moved like waves on the Dead Sea. All who ventured there were captured by desert devils.

The Jews called the desert-dwellers "Arabs," from the Hebrew word for *nomad*. Arabs themselves were a mysterious people, swarthy in complexion with dark eyes. They wore layers of robes that covered all but their heads and made no obeisance at all to the Lord God of Hosts. They were outside the Law and were forbidden entry into Jerusalem.

Not all the Arabs who came to trade were from the same tribe. Some dwelled in the cities near the southern coast. Others lived in the desert, traveling from oasis to oasis, tending their sheep, and making war on each other. The city Arabs called the desert Arabs "Bedouin." However, to the Jews, they were all desert dwellers.

For weeks before and after the two principal holidays of the Jewish calendar, the Arabs camped outside the city, conducting twice-yearly horse auctions. They bred the most beautiful and fastest animals in the empire. Other horses worked harder. Still others were more sure-footed. But none could compare to the style and grace of *Arabia equus.*

"Tell me, Aleya, how you came to Jerusalem. You say you are a princess. What are you doing as a slave to the old merchant?"

"I will tell you, my love. But you must promise me that you will take me back. My father is a rich and powerful king, and he will reward you with treasures beyond your imagination."

"You are the only treasure I want. I will take you back after we repel the Romans from our sacred mount. There's nothing your father could give me to replace my longing for you. But this I swear: I will take you home."

Chapter Eighteen

Joseph never believed Aleya's tales. They were too improbable. Everyone knew there was nothing beyond the great desert. He knew Egypt was across the Red Sea. He had seen the dark-skinned people of Upper Egypt. But people living in the desert and creating a city that was finer than Jerusalem as Aleya claimed? No, that was impossible. But Joseph loved her too much to make fun of her fantasies.

"Listen to me, my love, and I will tell you how I came to be here," Aleya told him, breaking into his thoughts.

70 CE

Aleya lived the life of a pampered daughter of the greatest king on the Arabian Peninsula. She had everything and wanted nothing, except to be like her brothers. Her father, King al-Fasheal, doted on her and granted her every wish. But he did not want her to leave the safety of his palace.

However, she was headstrong. She listened to the stories of the traders who came to her father's palace, telling of wondrous places, fabulous jewels, and the streams of mysterious black water that bubbled to the earth and caught fire. Desperately, she wanted to go with her brother to one of the horse auctions he conducted outside the city of the Jews in order to see these wonders for herself. She wanted to meet the people he called Romans. It would be her first time away from her father's palace. She begged and pleaded with the king to let her go.

Aleya's father could not understand her wanderlust. In his time, women stayed home and made babies for their husbands. Did not his wives find pleasure with him? They never asked to go on a caravan. What was different about this little girl, the love of his heart and the center of his life?

"Why, my precious daughter, do you wish to bear the rigors of the sixty-five passages to the north? Don't you have enough here? What do you hope to gain by seeing more of the desert?"

But Aleya was determined and her father weak when it concerned her. She knew how to manipulate him, even though he was the ruler of the entire Arabian Peninsula. "Abdul will protect me. I am his favorite sister. Are you saying that twenty of your strongest and bravest warriors cannot safeguard a little girl? Father, maybe you need better soldiers."

The captain of the guard, who attended the king at all times, winced at Aleya's words. He had been in love with her since she was a little girl. "Your majesty, I will guard Her Highness with my very life. Only my best men will accompany me. I shall bring Her Highness back within two sixty-five passages. This I swear on my life."

Aleya's father knew that his captain, Abu Quraysh, was in love with Aleya. He also knew that Aleya thought nothing of the captain. But he was certain that the captain would be true to his words. He would bring down a desert lion with his bare hands before he let any harm come to Aleya. *Besides,* the king thought, *the caravan route was safe. Our people have been traveling the path for generations.* It took sixty-five passages from oasis to oasis to coast and sea. All told, a caravan could be back and forth in less than one year. The king knew he was going to grant Aleya her wish. But he enjoyed listening to her plead and pout like any father who totally loved his daughter.

"Please, Father, let me see what this big city looks like. I have been here all my life. Besides, the good captain here will be my constant companion. Oh, Captain, how many men have you killed in my father's honor?"

This was the first time Aleya had addressed Abu directly, and he was taken aback by her direct question. "M-m-many, Your Highness," the captain stammered, still struck by Aleya's forthright manner.

All her life, her father scoffed. *That's a grand total of twelve journeys of the sun. But her monthlies have begun, and Aleya is to be granted one request before she is bundled off to womanhood and married to the Prince of Idear.* The marriage would combine the strongest kingdoms in the desert and give him suzerainty over all the lands that he could see.

He granted his daughter's wish. He didn't know how fateful his decision would turn out to be.

The caravan left the royal palace as soon as the king's soothsayers said the time was right. Aleya's ancestors had lived on the Arabian Peninsula for several thousand years. The caravan route she and her brother followed had been carved out of the desert by generations past so many years ago that even the palace soothsayers were uncertain of the time that had passed.

Aleya knew she would be gone for months. She knew the hardships. She knew the dangers. Nonetheless, she bubbled over with excitement. This was her first real trip away from home. She'd be crossing the desert on a camel, riding on the sea in her father's royal dhow, meeting Bedouins outside her father's court for the first time, and who knows what other adventures. This trip with her brother was the thrill of her very short life, and she promised herself to remember everything about it and never forget.

The caravan departed Sana'a in the first month of the new year. Traveling conditions were ideal—not too cool and certainly not blisteringly hot. The first part of the trip was to take them from the middle of her father's country, down through the mountains, and over to the royal port city of Mocha, just across the straits from Africa.

"Abdul, can we go to Africa and see the animals? I've always wanted to go to Africa and see where our palace slaves come from."

"Little sister, you are my favorite of all our brothers and sisters. That is why I did not protest when Father said you could accompany me on this caravan. But this is a caravan to Judea for the sole purpose of conducting a horse auction for the Romans. This is neither a pleasure trip nor have we scheduled any excursions to Africa or wherever else you want to visit. Understand? I have agreed to take you with me, but I am not operating this caravan for your enjoyment. I swear there will be more than enough for you to see during our caravan. Save your trip to Africa for when you go back and get married."

Aleya knew her brother admonished her as gently as he could, but she still wouldn't give up. "But, Abdul, Captain Abu says you can see Africa from Mocha. Can't we just row across, please?"

Abdul looked at Aleya and smiled. *She is so precious. Just a little girl who's quickly becoming a woman. But I can't give in to her. This caravan is no pleasure trip.* He had to impress upon her the nature of this trip. "Before you ask any more questions, let me show you where we are going. Come with me and I shall show you a map of our route."

"A map! Abdul, you are going to show me a map?" Aleya shrieked with excitement.

Maps were extremely rare and heavily guarded. Even though Aleya was a royal princess, she had never seen one of the maps her father's geographers drew to help him rule his kingdom. All maps were kept under lock and key in the royal library. One needed special permission from the king to consult a map. Even then, it was done under the watchful eye of the royal librarian.

The king believed in educating his children. After all, they were to inherit a kingdom that spanned the entire peninsula and had trading arrangements in countries as far away as India and Africa. They needed to be educated. But, the king reasoned, neither they nor his subjects needed to know where they were or how to get to those far-off countries. That's why he kept his maps in locked vaults. The carefully drawn maps were more precious to him than the finest pearls his divers brought up from the bottom of the Arabian Gulf.

Abdul brought Aleya to the back of the caravan where a camel was packed with two enormous saddlebags, one on each side. Abdul called one of the captain's men to stand guard while he pulled a chest from one of the saddlebags. He opened it with a key that hung around his neck and lifted out an ordinary looking scroll. He spread a carpet on the desert floor and placed the scroll on the carpet and unrolled it. Abdul gave Aleya her first look at a map.

Aleya's eyes widened in wonderment. "Is this really all the land in our father's kingdom? Why is there water on both sides? What's this big space in the middle?

"Is that Egypt? I have never seen a map, but I know our father's boats make a trip of two suns to trade with Egypt. And Egypt is in that strange land the palace officials call Africa. Look, right here. That must be Africa. See, Abdul, I told you; we'll be close to it. Oh, is up there where we are going? How long will it take? How do we cross this land? Abdul, do you—"

"Shh, shh, little sister, I'll answer all your questions. But, please give me time to think about the answers. You have asked enough questions for a week's worth of thinking."

Abdul was not surprised at Aleya's excitement. He remembered the first time his father showed him a map of the kingdom. He could hardly sleep that night, thinking about all the places he was going to see and where he was going to travel. *Perhaps,* he thought, *it's a good idea that the king keeps his maps locked up. Otherwise, half the palace would leave for somewhere else, just for the excitement of the adventure.*

"Sit down here and look at the map, Aleya. Be quiet and I'll explain everything to you."

She sat down and stared at the map, captivated by the symbols and names. She was so excited that she remained utterly still and silent, hanging onto every word Abdul told her.

"Here is the land of our palace down at the point of the peninsula. As you can see, the land is bordered on three sides by water. That's why our geographers call it a peninsula. If there were no water, it wouldn't be a peninsula.

"We started here in the middle of the kingdom at our father's palace. See the place name, Sana'a. That's where we live. So far, we have traveled to about here, which is another two passages away from the coast and the port city of Mocha. So long ago that no one knows when, our ancestors determined that our caravan route to the north takes sixty-five passages.

"Each passage gets us from oasis to oasis, traveling the ancient dried-out riverbeds. These riverbeds or wadis are all that is left of a land once flowing with streams and rivers and abundant wildlife. Those ancient riverbeds still connect to oases."

Aleya looked at her brother. *What was he talking about? Dried riverbeds, indeed! I may be his little sister, but I'm not stupid. How could a desert have rivers?*

Abdul continued talking. "You know those drawings on the rocks that we see when we go into the mountains? Our soothsayers say an ancient people made them, our ancestors who lived at a time when this peninsula was lush with flowing water. I find it hard to believe, but I don't argue with the palace priests. Anyway, that's not important. Where we are going and how we are going to get there is important. Just listen.

"When we get to the city of Mocha we will board a royal ship, a dhow, and sail up the coastline of the Red Sea. Now, you see how close Africa looks on the map. Believe me, my little princess, it is more than two days in a boat. So your dream of rowing there is out of the question.

"We sail north, staying very close to the coast. We will land the ship each night and make our camp on the shore. The trip on the Red Sea is very safe. Our father controls all the land we see, and the people will respect us. But we still need to be careful.

"Once we have traveled up the entire coast of the peninsula, we will be very close to Egypt and Judea. But we will have to cross the Sinai before we can get back into the dhow.

"See here, Aleya, where the Sinai connects to lower Judea and almost to Egypt. In ancient times, a great king built a canal to allow his boats to go from the Red Sea into the large sea that people now call the Roman Sea. The canal is now overgrown with marsh grass and barely has any water, but we can have the dhow dragged across the marsh and launched into the Great Sea. Then we will continue by dhow up to Caesarea where we will meet the horse traders.

"The Great Sea is dangerous. Our father holds no power there, and the Roman navy hardly patrols those waters. We will stay close to the shore, but there is always the danger of pirates. When we get to the Great Sea, you'll have to stay out of sight.

"Well, Aleya, what do you think? I have shown you the map, and I have shown you the route we take to Judea. Satisfied, my princess?"

Aleya looked at her brother, her mind still trying to take in all he had said. He was ten years older than her, her father's first son and principal heir. And she loved him best of all her brothers.

"Abdul, I never knew the world was so large. Imagine, there are two big seas around us, and I never knew that. Wait until I tell our sisters back home what I have done. They will be so jealous! Thank you, my dearest brother. Thank you."

Abdul rolled up the precious map and placed it back in its locked chest. "Now the geography lesson is over. It's time to prepare for the night. Good night. Sleep well."

Abdul joined the men who were bedding down the camels. Although he was the first prince of the land, he was also the caravan master, and it was his responsibility to make sure that all the chores were completed. Taking care of the camels was an essential duty of the caravan master.

The king had given his son his fastest and most dependable camels. These animals had traveled the caravan route several times and could instinctively find an oasis even when the caravan was miles away.

Abdul went over to the string of camels. As the first prince of the kingdom, he had his pick of the beautiful horses raised in his father's stable. But camels were another story. Camels were work animals, and he had little to do with them.

Abdul petted the lead camels, trying to hide his distaste of the ungainly animals. Camels were disgusting creatures, but they were the life of the desert. Ill-tempered, hard to control, and more stubborn than mules, the camels meant nothing more than transportation to the king and his subjects in the royal city of Sana'a. Citizens of Sana'a lived in a city and were unaccustomed to the rigors of desert living. To those who made their livings on the caravan route, camels were more precious than gold.

There were other people in Arabia who knew no king, respected no laws except their own, and had a reputation as fierce fighters. They were the Bedouin. For caravan masters, knowing the Bedouin and their way of life was essential to surviving the long trek across the desert. Abdul knew the Bedouin and respected them. He always hitched an extra camel to his caravan as a gift for the first group of

Bedouin he met. He never understood how it happened, but once he gave the camel to the first group, all other Bedouin understood he was a man of respect and allowed him safe passage.

The Bedouin were not like the city people. They had no use for the exotic spices and carpets the caravans carried. Nor did they care for the frankincense and myrrh that were more valuable than gold. But a camel! That was another thing altogether.

For the Bedouin, camels were life. Those mysterious, independent people never recognized the authority of Abdul's father, yet they respected him as a far-away leader. The Bedouin lived from season to season, oasis to oasis, following the rushing waters of the nearest wadi and living on dates and camels.

They lived in the interior of Arabia, far from the cooling effects of the sea. They never enjoyed the annual rains that relieved the coastal regions of his father's kingdom from the dryness and saltiness of the interior desert. How they lived there was something Abdul could not understand.

The Bedouin were as mysterious to him as he was to them. This trip would be the first time that Aleya would come under the protection of the Bedouin as the caravan followed the trails traced by the ancients from wadi to wadi. Abdul wondered how Aleya would react to meeting them.

The Bedouin still followed the old ways, worshipping a number of gods according to the season. Their most important god was Zamzam, the bearer of all water. In the desert, water was more precious than the frankincense that the caravans struggled to bring to market. To the Bedouin, water was all. The Bedouin even had an ancient hero who saved his people from certain death in the desert by striking a rock and making water flow forth.

Aleya and her people had long forsaken the many gods of the desert and dedicated themselves to one god. Her father built a majestic temple, fourteen-stories high, dedicated to the one god, Almaqah.

Her father's ancestors knew him as "El," the one god. Over the generations, the holy men told stories that were revealed to them by El. There were even stories that told of one people who believed in El, but some of those people moved beyond the sea and no longer worshipped the same god.

Aleya wasn't so sure. How could the same people worship the same god but no longer believe in the same god? She would ask her father these questions, but he would quiet her, telling her that such questions should not be asked by women of the royal family.

"We believe in Almaqah. There is no god but him. We have a prayer. It says there is one god, and his name is Almaqah. His truths were revealed to us by our father, Abrim. Now, my little princess, stop asking questions and believe."

Chapter Nineteen

Aleya woke up to see her servants waiting to dress her. The hardest part of the journey had yet to begin. She finished her morning ablution. Turning around, she saw her old nursemaid holding cloths for her to dry herself.

"My lady, it's time to go. Meet your brother and his men outside these quarters. I have sacrificed a newborn lamb to Almaqah so that you will return safely to us."

"Oh, Nakrah, you have been worrying about me forever. I'm not a little girl anymore. My father doesn't think so. Otherwise, why would he allow me to travel to the Great Sea?"

"My lady, forgive me my worries. I forget how swiftly you've grown. If only your brother had your sense of adventure."

"Nakrah, that's enough! Help me with my chests. And pick a gentle camel for me!" *Nakrah has been with me all my life. She's closer to me than my mother. Why does she worry so? What does she know about the dangers of this trip that she's not telling me? Whispers around the court say that Nakrah isn't from our people but comes from the desert Bedouin. My grandfather found her after he raided the Sabean camp. She was a little child wandering around the campsite. Grandfather picked her up and brought her to his tent. She's been with us ever since. But there's something about the desert she knows and is keeping from me.*

"Aleya, let's go. If we wait any longer, the heat will rise, and our brains will be like dried camel skin. Come on," Abdul cried. She touched the sacred image of Almaqah that hung over the lintel of her tent and proceeded to meet her brother outside. Though the caravan had been traveling a week, it was still within the safety of her father's kingdom. Now, the caravan was preparing to go into the Great Desert, a no-man's-land where demons and *djinn* lived.

As she walked out of her tent, she ran headlong into the largest man she had ever seen. He was wrapped completely from head to toe in a long flowing garment and a headdress that covered all but his fierce eyes. He looked down at her and motioned for her to follow him. Was this the Bedouin? And what was he doing here so close to her father's city? A desert-dweller near Sana'a was as rare as a Roman official and a lot scarier.

"Come, my lady, it is time to continue the next portion of your journey," he said, guiding her to a sitting camel. Aleya stared at her brother, questioning him with her eyes. Her brother glanced back as if to say he would tell her everything later. The Bedouin helped Aleya mount the camel. Although the trained beast was in a sitting position, Aleya still needed to use the ladder to mount the beast. She mounted the camel, which stood up on the command of the Bedouin.

Aleya looked around her. She was so high off the ground! She could see all around her as if she were on the roof of her father's palace. *This will be so exciting,* she thought. With a shout from the lead driver, the rest of the camels rose, and Aleya began her journey.

The days and weeks passed. The excitement of the trip soon left Aleya. The first part was fun. The caravan had a royal send-off from the palace staff. Many of her friends and servants joined them for the first few days. But after a week atop the camel and sleeping in a tent each night, Aleya was growing tired. She knew they had to cross the desert to get to the port city of Mocha, but wasn't there a more comfortable way to do it?

For weeks, the caravan traveled. Aleya found herself sickened by the constant rocking motion of the camel. Throughout the trip, the Bedouin, who was called Ruwalah, never looked from side-to-side, never spoke, and never ate at her brother's table.

"He has his 'two black ones,'" Abu, the captain of the guard, told Aleya. "He doesn't need us. In truth, my lady, we need him more."

Aleya later learned that in Bedouin culture to possess the "two black ones"—water and dates—is the goal of every Bedouin trekking across the desert. With these two, it is said, the Bedouin can travel from the south near the coast all the way to the Red Sea. While water is preferred, the Bedouin saves that most precious commodity for his camel, and if he has them, his horses. Camel's milk is the drink of the desert, and dates are the only solid food a Bedouin might eat in weeks. He supplements his diet with camel meat but that, too, is rare. Bedouins do not kill camels for their meat. They wait until one dies.

When they return to their camps, which move from season to season, the Bedouin feast on sheep and goats that the women and old men raise. But on the sea of the desert, sitting astride his camel, goat and lamb are luxuries.

Each night the king's servants set up the royal camp. The tents were made of spun cotton grown in the fields across the Red Sea in the kingdom of the Ptolemies. Egyptian cotton was the finest in the land. Only that magical cloth from the east brought by ships from the men living past the Indus River was better.

It was said that the cloth—"silk" the traders called it—came from a land where the people were yellow-skinned. *How impossible was that! I don't believe those stories of yellow-skinned people. And I don't believe that silk comes from worms. Whoever heard of such nonsense? The traders must think I am a silly little girl who they could fool with their outlandish stories.*

How could anyone live under Almaqah's sun and not bear his mark? The sun darkens us, Aleya knew, *some more than others. It doesn't make us yellow, and no one can avoid the sun. To live under Almaqah's protection meant to live under his sun.*

Roman women, she had heard, took baths in calves' milk and carried cloths on sticks to keep the sun away from their faces. That was so their skin could stay fair and be white. *What kind of man would want a woman whose skin looked like the bellies of the dead fish that wash up on the shore of the sea?*

Aleya's caravan had made its way to the outskirts of Mocha. Ruwalah and his band of Bedouin disappeared during the night. When Aleya awoke, she found the mysterious-looking Bedouin gone.

"Abdul, where's that huge man who watched me like a hawk but never spoke to me?"

"Aleya," Abdul said, "the Bedouin try to avoid cities as much as they can. Ruwalah had pledged to accompany us while we were in the desert, but I knew he would be off as soon as we neared a big city. Do not worry. Ruwalah will show up to help when you least expect him."

The caravan broke camp and made its way to Mocha to begin the second part of the journey. There, in the city, Aleya's father still held sway, and the whole caravan would be treated like the royalty they were. Abdul had made the trip many times.

The city's prefect, a man who went by a single name, Rama'az, met them at the gates, bowing effusively and promising them whatever their hearts desired. Abdul addressed the man gruffly. "Just get some lodgings near the dock and have the port's best captains report to me tonight." He turned away and mounted his camel. Abdul grabbed the bridle of the camel that Aleya was riding.

"Stay very close to me, little sister, and do not wander about. Captain, assign your two best men to stay with the princess at all times."

Aleya looked at her brother and noticed the change in his character. No longer was he the gentle, loving brother satisfying every whim of his favorite sister. His face had hardened, and he barked out commands like the first prince of the kingdom that he was.

For the first time, Aleya realized that a caravan trip to the north was not the adventure that she had envisioned back in her father's palace. She suddenly felt like a twelve-year-old girl again and not a brave, adventurous princess. She was grateful that it was just the length of a camel bridle that separated her from her strong brother.

Abdul led the caravan into Mocha. He dispatched the captain and the remaining guards to secure lodgings for the caravan party. A litter came for Aleya. Satisfied with the two guards the captain assigned to watch Aleya, Abdul strode to the house of Rama'az where he would make the necessary arrangements for the rest of the trip.

Rama'az, meanwhile, had delayed returning to his house. After leaving Abdul at the city gates, he slipped away to the city's back quarter, a collection of alleys and dirty wine shops catering to the bottom-dwellers of the maritime trade.

Rama'az ducked through a low entryway and waddled to the back of a decrepit wine shop. There, at a table illuminated by a single oil lamp, sat one of the Arabian Peninsula's most notorious slave traders. Said to be the son of a slave himself, Izad, the slave trader, had indeterminate features that made it hard to place his birthplace or even his lineage. His fleet of pirate ships usually worked the coast of Africa, filling the need for slaves along the Arabian coastline. But, occasionally, he would take a chance when an unusual slave opportunity presented itself. That's why he listened to Rama'az.

Neither of the men liked each other. It was evident in the way they spoke. "Make it quick, Rama'az. I prefer not to be seen in your company. If my customers ever thought I was openly cooperating with port officials, my next voyage would be to the bottom of the sea."

Izad leaned forward into the light cast by the oil lamp. His sinister features looked demonic in the flickering light. Rama'az looked at him nervously. He had heard that Izad worshipped ancient eastern devils and that he could summon them from the depths of hell to strike his enemies. The city official no more wanted to be in this man's company than Izad wanted to be in his.

"Izad, I have a rare treat for you. A caravan has just come into my city from Sana'a and the palace of the king. There is a young woman with the caravan. My spies say she is truly a princess of the royal house. Not only is she a princess, she is untouched. Betrothed, but not yet wed, she comes to you in all her virginal purity. If you can manage to keep your filthy hands off her, she would fetch a ransom in any slave market in the world."

"A princess? A virgin? Since when have you become so bold that you would even dare to meddle with a member of the royal house?"

The slave trader knew the city prefect. He was no hero. He would turn the other way when Izad came to Mocha to do his dirty little business, then gratefully accept the bag of gold left for him on his doorstep. *Why would this little coward even suggest so bold a venture as to kidnap a princess of the kingdom?*

"Tell me, Rama'az, what do you want for your cooperation?"

"It is simple, Izad. I am sick of making my living as a minor official in this backwater port. I will arrange for you to do your business. You will pay me ten times the usual amount. And then I shall make my way to Alexandria, far away from the punishment of the Royal Court."

"Ten times! Have the desert gods addled your mind? No slave is worth that price!"

"Izad, no one at the port knows your face. Present yourself as just another coastal trading captain. The girl will probably be there with her brother and her guards. See for yourself. Then come and tell me that ten times is not enough. I'll meet you here in two days."

Rama'az gathered his robes and left.

♦ ♦ ♦

Izad seemed ready to make the deal and pay the price. But the only gold the despicable port official would see would be the handle of Izad's dagger sticking out of his chest. Izad grabbed the barmaid around the waist and teased another cup of wine from her jug.

While the two had been plotting, Abdul had spent all day at the docks. Making arrangements to cross the Red Sea into the Mediterranean would take at least one week. He had met up with another caravan master who was returning to Sana'a. Abdul had given the man a message for his father, telling him that all was well. The poor caravan master was shocked that the prince had spoken to him. Groveling his way out of the room where Abdul spent his days, the caravan master promised to bring his message back to the king.

Aleya's brother turned his attention to his ledgers. He knew that a successful caravan depended not only on the bravery of the caravan master but how much the master would be willing to spend. Abdul spent freely in the port. The price that his thoroughbred horses would fetch at the Roman auction would make him a wealthy man. There was no need to skimp on spending. Besides, how often did he have the opportunity to spoil his favorite sister? Abdul smiled, left his temporary office, and made his way back to the house that Captain Abu had secured for them.

At the foot of the dock, sitting on some sacks of grain, the watchful eyes of Izad followed Abdul. The arrangements were made. He would draw Abdul away from the house with a promise of more horses to trade at the auction while his men snatched the little princess. The loathsome slave trader would see that the guards were drugged and gave no fight. Meanwhile, Abdul and his men would be feasting at the home of a private citizen whose name they would never learn. Izad had taken the house for a week and would be with the prince for the entire evening while his sister was spirited away to the hold of his swift trading ship.

Aleya spent her time in the port city of Mocha shadowed by her two guards. Both men knew the dangers of a port city and would never let Aleya out of their sight. They even stood guard at the doorway to the bathhouse when she entered for her nightly toilet. They made sure that it was empty before Aleya entered.

Aleya had never seen so many different people. Mocha may have been a backwater trading port, but it was the first she had seen. She walked dockside, trailed by her guards, looking with wonderment at the piles of trade goods stacked on the dock. There were sacks of spices, grain and other foodstuffs, cloths of all kind, even animals in cages that were said to have come from Africa.

She peered in one of the cages and saw a huge monkey which looked back at her with knowing and inquisitive eyes. "Tell me, Sergeant, what kind of monkey is this?"

"Highness, I have seen these before. It is a great ape from Africa. They say that it is strong enough to crush a man's chest with a single blow from its hand. I beg you, please do not stand too close to the cage."

"It looks so sad caged like that. Where is it going?"

"Again, Princess, I cannot say for sure, but I have been told that the Roman officials favor animals like these as dangerous pets. Sadly, few of them live through the sea voyage."

"Sergeant, that is so sad. Come. Let's go back to the house. I have had my fill of sightseeing."

Her guards escorted her back to the house and left her in the company of her brother. Abdul was in the courtyard having a heated discussion with his men. "Prince Abdul, we do not need more horses. What we should—"

"I'll be the judge of that," Abdul shouted, cutting off his chief horse trader in mid-sentence. "We will go to this trader's house tonight and see what he has to offer. If the price is fair, we can arrange for another ship. I want you to be the judge of horseflesh. Let me be the judge of our business arrangements."

"Yes, Highness," the horse trader said and backed away.

Aleya walked into the house trailed by the sergeant of the guard. She ran to her brother and sat by his side. Abdul looked at her, and his face brightened. He knew he should not be taking on another consignment of horses, but the profits to be made at the Roman auction were too great to pass up.

"Aleya, tonight I am going to another trader's house. He has an interesting proposition for me. I want you to stay here with your guards. Do not leave the house for any reason. I'll be back late. We can explore the city tomorrow morning."

Later that afternoon, Abdul gathered his men to meet the horse trader. He made sure that his guards had secured every entrance to the house, kissed his sister good-bye, and left her safely in the hands of the king's own soldiers.

Abdul and his men arrived at the house of Izad. The slave trader stood at the entrance to greet his guests. In the stable were four magnificent horses, sleek and shiny as the mysterious bubbling black streams in the desert.

"Welcome, do you wish to see the horses or do you wish to eat? No, let me decide. We shall see the horses, then we shall feast," Izad said merrily.

As he led them back to the stable, a servant left the house carrying food and a jug of wine. Izad had sent a slave with baskets of food and jugs of wine to Abdul's house for the guards. It would be their last feast. The jug of wine contained a poison specially mixed in Africa. It was said to come from the mouth of a serpent. One sip would be a man's last.

Izad's slave approached the house. One of the guards came to the entrance and stopped her. "What do you wish?" he asked suspiciously.

"Captain," the girl said, fully knowing that the soldier was not a captain, "your prince has sent you a meal to enjoy. Here, you can look at it if you do not trust me."

The guard lifted the cloth covering the basket, opened the jug, and sniffed it. The girl was true to her word. The prince did send dinner.

"Put the food on the table." As she bent over with the basket, the soldier fondled her thigh. "Come back later."

"Oh, certainly, Captain." The slave girl smiled saucily. "I hope you enjoy the meal." She left the courtyard. The soldiers divided the food in the basket and poured cups of wine for themselves.

As the evening wore on, Aleya became curious. None of the guards had come to see her. There was no noise in the courtyard. And she hadn't heard their voices for a while. She left the room where she was staying and walked to the courtyard. Both of her guards were slumped facedown on the table. She thought it curious that they would let wine overtake them. She knew her brother would be furious and rushed back into the house to get a jug of water to splash in their faces.

As she entered the kitchen, a man clamped his hand over her mouth. She couldn't scream. She couldn't move. She was terrified, the terror showing in her eyes.

"Be still, my princess. No harm shall come to you. You are going on a sea voyage like you planned. You are going to Jerusalem."

Chapter Twenty

74 CE

"Pull, pull, you lazy *cunni,* or I'll have the flesh off your backs. Get those mules behind the wagon. We'll never make it up the ramp this way."

The centurion removed his helmet and watched his sweat drip off the nosepiece. His hardened leather breastplate and hammered brass greaves itched and chafed his body. Flavius ordered his centurions to have the Jewish slaves move the siege engines up the ramp. Each centurion was responsible for a section of the ramp. If there were any breakdowns, the legion's commanders would know exactly whom to blame.

Finally, after a year of moving half the earth from the desert to the mountain, the Tenth Legion was going to spring into action. The ramp was finished. The platform for the siege engines was built. Tomorrow, or so the rumor had it, would be the day of the final assault on Masada.

Anticipating the battle took the centurion's mind off his misery and concentrated it on the section of the ramp under his command. "Now pull, you worthless dogs. Any man who falls down will find himself in the *ballista* instead of a stone!"

The ramp reached just below the crest of Masada. The siege machines, some of which were nearly sixty feet tall, would batter the Zealots' wall to pieces. If the machines failed them, archers with fire-tipped arrows would complete the destruction. Once over the top, the battle should be swift.

Already, the centurion began to savor the victory. There was no thought of plunder, but there were women on the mountain. The women would be spared, and children sold into slavery. The men? Well, they would find out what it was like to descend the mountain without the aid of a ramp.

Once the ramp was complete, the centurions sent the slaves back to their camp. The Roman soldiers stayed at their outposts on the dirt road, waiting for the orders in the morning. The rumor among the men was that the general himself, Valerius, would lead the first cohort up the ramp. The soldiers banked their fires and bedded down for the night.

The next morning, the desert sun burned brightly. The Roman camp had been awake for two hours preparing for battle. Valerius was ready. He had his orders from Flavius and prepared to lead his men up the ramp, behind the siege engines, and into the Zealots' camp.

Valerius mounted his horse, gathered his centurions, and began the fateful march up the ramp. His heart was heavy. He did not look forward to the task that lay ahead. Halfway up the path, Valerius halted his big gray, Arinax. The horse was a gift from his father's clients, a mix of the desert pony and the swift racers bred by the southern tribes of the desert, the Bedouin. "Steady, steady, my proud one. This day shall be over soon, and you will feast on the sweetest hay and drink the coldest mountain spring water."

Valerius turned around and surveyed the scene behind him. In perfect four-by-four formation, the Tenth Legion marched up the ramp. How in the name of the gods they expected to fit on top of Masada was beyond him. But Flavius wanted a show of force to demonstrate to the crowd of Jews who gathered in the Roman camp to watch. The conquest of Masada wouldn't be the final act in his Judean campaign. There was still a whole country to subdue.

Thankfully, thought Valerius, *Masada will be the final act in* my *Judean campaign.* He sat astride Arinax and thought about his departure from Judea. Wagons loaded with his household goods and possessions were already on their way to the port of Caesarea. After the riots three years ago, most of his parents' household goods were burned or carried away. Twenty-two years as a soldier in the Judean wilderness left little time to accumulate treasures, so just two wagons in the caravan belonged to him. He wasn't bringing much back with him. His real treasure lay in Rome, safeguarded by the Vestal Virgins.

His father, may the gods bless his memory, dispatched his will to the Temple of Vesta, where the virginal priestesses held it in safekeeping. Their temple was inviolable, and a will deposited with the Vestal Virgins was honored throughout the Roman Empire. Because it was customary to also name the temple in a will, the Vestal Virgins had become the richest women in the empire. Unfortunately, they could only enjoy their treasure when they had gotten too old and were forced out of the temple.

Valerius knew that his father had set aside a comfortable sum for him, his only child. He also knew that his family owned land near the Sabine Hills. It wasn't Rome, but it was close. And the climate was mild enough to grow grapes. Perhaps, after all, Valerius would have his small business when he retired.

"Easy, Arinax, easy, boy. Why are you so skittish? Don't tell me all this inactivity has made you afraid of the battle line?"

His horse was uneasy and for no reason that Valerius could see. He was well away from the front line, and the assault had just begun. The *ballistae* threw large stones against the Zealots' wooden wall, but Arinax was used to the noise of hurling missiles.

The Zealots had done a good job of fortifying their camp. They had built two walls and fortified the space in between them with dirt. The battering ram, which followed the *ballistae* in the line of battle, knocked down the first wall, only to encounter mounds of dirt.

Centurions rushed legionaries to the front with shovels to clear a path for the siege engines so they could assault the inner wall. However, the machines could not stand evenly on the dirt, so the *primus pilus* ordered the archers with their firebrands up to the front.

Arinax bucked and nearly stomped a Jewish slave underfoot. "What's the matter, Arinax? What's troubling you?" Valerius had never seen his horse act so nervously on the field. Even when crossing the inland sea to Britannia, Arinax held his calm. But something was happening or about to happen. The horse could sense it.

Valerius prayed to the gods that it wasn't going to be the earth-shaking that he knew plagued this region of the world. Sitting astride a horse halfway up a mountain was not a good place to be when the gods decided to open the earth.

The horse whinnied nervously. While Valerius was attending to his horse, the archers let go with the fire arrows. They penetrated the wooden walls, and the burning pitch dripped off the arrowheads, igniting the dry wood of the Zealots' defense. There was plenty of water in the cisterns but no way for the Zealots to get it to the burning wall.

Legionaries bunched together, waiting for an opening to pour into the camp of the Zealots. They had dipped their scarves and cloaks into water buckets and wrapped the wet cloth around themselves. Nearly five hundred men stood ready to charge the final paces into the Zealots' camp.

As Valerius looked up the ramp, he immediately sensed why his horse had been acting skittishly. A different desert smell assaulted his nostrils, and he knew why. The dependable southerly winds, which were blowing into the Zealots' camp, had just turned course and blew northerly.

The winds never blow in the northerly direction. Something must be amiss! More importantly, Valerius had to warn his men. The change in wind direction meant the flames and smoke from the burning wall would blow away from the camp and into the onrushing Tenth Legion. The flames would engulf the siege engines, the archers, and the first two centuries of legionaries turning the charge into a disaster. *Maybe the God of these Jews is a powerful God,* Valerius thought.

The Roman commander spurred Arinax and galloped up the ramp, knocking aside slave and soldier alike to warn his men of the impending disaster. Higher on the ramp it was difficult to tell which way the wind was blowing. But in the desert, wind directions changed quickly and fiercely.

"Back, back. Leave the engines and get back before you are roasted alive," he shouted above the din of battle. But it was too late. Already, the flames—invigorated by the strong northerly wind—blew down on the legionaries and burned the foundations of the siege engines.

It was complete chaos at the top. Legionaries, roasting in their own armor, ran screaming down the ramp. The siege engines tottered and threatened to crush the men beneath them.

The vaunted discipline of the Roman legion fell apart under the flames. Valerius had never seen anything like it in all his years of battle. Men would stand and fight hand-to-hand with the fiercest of enemies, the blue-painted devils of Germania, but against flames, no, there was no fighting them.

He called for his standard-bearer and jammed the *Aquila* into the ground, serving as a rallying point for the men who remained on the ramp. The whole legion was behind him, waiting for the flames to die out.

Then, as quickly as the wind charged down the ramp, it reversed direction again and began its usual southerly course. *Mithras has favored us once more,* Valerius thought, as he moved to take command. Valerius surveyed the dying embers on the Zealots' wall. He was prepared to lead his men into the camp on Masada but decided to hold back until what was left of the wooden walls cooled. If he only knew how fateful his decision was and how it would reverberate through the centuries!

All Valerius knew as he was waiting to storm the mount was that the meager opposition from the Zealots had stopped. Valerius led Arinax down the ramp, wondering what could have happened in the camp to still the Zealots' resistance. As he walked his horse down, he saw his soldiers milling about in the confusion caused by the unexpected shift in winds that drove the fire into their faces. They bunched together just below the top of the mount. Seeing his men still prepared for battle, Valerius considered what he should do next. Continue the battle or wait until the next morning? The absence of any response from the defenders of Masada gave Valerius his answer.

"Centurion, follow me." The first centurion of the legion drew his horse up behind Valerius and trotted up to the brink of the ramp. The general and the centurion waited and listened. All they heard was the hissing of the burnt wooden wall and the crackling of the timbers as they broke and fell.

"Centurion, return to your men and tell them to make a battle camp. We will take the mount tomorrow morning. I want all the men in full battle armor and the engineers up here with me to lay the planks upon the siege ladders the first thing in the morning. Until then, tell the men to rest."

With this order given, Valerius rode past the centurion and returned to his men, ready to make battle camp as he had ordered the centurion. The weary general removed his armor and rested on the ground like a common soldier.

Valerius leaned back on his saddle and dozed. *We can wait until tomorrow morning to attack a handful of pitiful men, their women, and children.* If Valerius had decided not to wait to send his men over the walls, it was possible that the course of history might have been changed. But gods, not men, write history.

Chapter Twenty-One

Eleazar gathered his lieutenants and council members around the campfire that fateful night before the final Roman attack. The wall had initially repulsed the Tenth Legion, and God had granted them favored winds. But each man knew that the next day would bring death.

The night was clear, and a mild breeze blew in from the south. The men were solemn, knowing that tomorrow they would have to face the soldiers of the Tenth Legion. The fire burned down to a few wispy flames on top of a pile of glowing coals.

Eleazar looked around at his council. He was to give a speech that would be handed down through generations of Jews and make the name of Masada live forever. Joseph was one of those men around the campfire, waiting for their leader to share his war plan. No one except the council members was prepared for what Eleazar was going to say.

The short, thickset leader stood up. His men looked at him with anticipation, waiting for their final instructions. Eleazar circled the fire, touching each man on the right shoulder as if to quiet him. The men looked at him in complete silence.

He started off by recounting the atrocities his people experienced at the hands of their captors. "Have you forgotten the Egyptians? Do you not recall when the Syrians slew eighteen thousand of us in Damascus? And in Egypt that year—our messengers tell us that more than sixty thousand of us were slain. Do you think the Romans will be any different?" Eleazar challenged his subordinates.

"We shall fight them for our liberty and freedom, but we shall cheat them of our death. Tell no one of this. We were the very first to revolt against the Romans and the very last to fight against them. Do you think they will spare us?

"No, they will not. But first, they will abuse our wives and toy with our children. We shall not let that happen. By our own hands we shall cheat the Romans so that we may not live in slavery, and they shall not profit at our defeat."

Eleazar then called his lieutenants to summon the people around him. "Tell them to bring torches, for they must be able to see each other," Eleazar shouted. They went through the camp, rousing men and their families, telling them Eleazar wanted to address them.

When the people had gathered, Eleazar stood on a millstone so he could look out on the thousand or so souls who followed him to the mount of Masada. He looked out at them, and doubts began to race through his mind. *What do I tell them? How do I convince them to take their lives rather than submit to the Roman sword?* Then he thought of the old man, Barabbas, who lived his entire life under the threat of Roman reprisal. Yes, the Jewish people may have saved his life so many years ago, but the Romans watched him closely, always hoping to catch him in another insurrection.

Is this what I want for my people and me? To be living under the Roman yoke like slaves and handmaidens? No! My way is better.

Eleazar gathered his thoughts. He walked slowly to the end of the women's well where the people of Masada stood. It was a fitting place for an address by their leader. The women always gathered there and talked about the future.

Now, they imagined, they would hear how they would deal with the Roman soldiers. The women had tired of living on Masada, away from their families down in the city. They longed for a normal life and an end to the futile resistance to the Romans. Like women throughout history, they knew that war was not a way of life. They had children to nurture, families to cherish, and futures to build. Eleazar was coming, they thought, to lead them to a normal existence.

Eleazar concentrated on what he was going to tell his people. He had no care, no concern for what the women of Masada were thinking. All he knew, all he felt, all he believed would come pouring forth in his speech like a spring freshet coursing through an ancient wadi. Eleazar walked toward the well to address his people.

He looked about and saw the entire camp gathered. Men, women, children, babies in arms, expected him to end this madness. Only that handful of men who made up the ruling council had an inkling of what their leader was going to say. And they dreaded it. Eleazar pushed through the crowd and leapt to the low wall surrounding the well. He drew a deep breath and began a speech that would captivate Jews for as long as they existed on this earth.

"My people, we have waged a long and unsuccessful war against the Romans. For those who have been killed in the war, they are blessed. But those who have been captured and remain alive suffer the cruelties of the Roman people, which is suffering beyond imagination. Would you yourselves go through that? Some of them have been put on the rack and tortured with fire and whippings. Some of them have been half-devoured by wild beasts but kept alive so that they can die again and provide sport for the Roman people.

"And where is that great city now? Jerusalem, which the Romans took so easily from us. Where is this city that was believed to have God Himself inhabiting therein? It is now demolished to the very foundations and has nothing but that monument of it preserved—I mean the camp of those that destroyed it, which still dwells upon its ruins. Some unfortunate old men still lie upon the ashes of the temple and a few women are there preserved alive by the enemy, for our bitter shame and reproach.

"I cannot but wish that we had all died before we had seen that holy city demolished by the hands of our enemies. Or the foundations of our holy temple dug up in so profane a manner.

"We revolted from the Romans with great pretensions to courage and when, at the very last, they invited us to preserve ourselves, we would not comply with them. Who will not, therefore, believe that they will be in a rage at us if they take us alive? Miserable then will be the young men, who will be strong enough in their bodies to sustain many torments!

"Miserable also will be those of elder years who will not be able to bear the calamities, which young men might sustain! Will we be obliged to hear the voices of our sons imploring help of us when their hands are bound by our captors, the Romans? I say, No!

"We have another choice. Certainly, now, our hands are at liberty and have a sword in them. Let them then be subservient to us in our glorious design. Let us die before we become slaves under our enemies, and let us go out of this world with our children and our wives in a state of freedom. That is what our laws command us to do; that is what our wives and children deserve. God himself brought this necessity upon us. The Romans hope that we live, and they shall capture us. Let us deny them of their pleasure.

"Let us make haste and instead of affording the Romans their pleasure, as they hope for, let us leave them an example and the world an example which shall cause their astonishment at our deaths and their admiration at our hardiness and faithfulness to each other."

Now, Eleazar was going to continue his exhortation of the people, but they cut him off with their activity. Men, who had been prompted by the leaders on the ruling council, started to collect their families together and say good-bye. In tearful kisses and hugs, husbands and fathers, grandfathers and uncles, looked after their families, kissing them and praying over them.

The women remained in shock. They could neither believe their ears nor fathom the actions of their men. Listening to Eleazar speak, the members of the ruling council circulated among the men of Masada and encouraged them to do as their leader had said. And the men began to kill.

Fathers embraced their children one last time before plunging a dagger in their breasts. Husbands held their wives for the last time—but in truth, for all eternity—while they raked knives across their throats. Then the men turned on each other, until there were ten. And one of the ten, according to the number he drew at the campfire, slayed the others, until there was one. And he fell on his sword. And there was silence.

Joseph and Aleya disappeared in the darkness, slipping away from the religious fanatics who were implementing their leader's plan. "Joseph, where are we going? I want to hear what Eleazar is saying. Let's help Joab. Come. Let's go back."

"Aleya, you have no idea what you're talking about. There's no going back. There's only going forward. That's what we'll do tomorrow. We'll get off this accursed mountain and make our way to the land of your people. I have experience in the desert. I can lead you home."

"Joseph, you've been carrying that sword since I first met you. Isn't it about time you finally used it against our enemies? Surely, Eleazar has a plan to deal with the Roman legion."

"My love, we cannot stay here. Eleazar has no plans to make a treaty with the Romans. Listen, can you hear that?"

The Arab girl cocked her ear in the night and listened to the faint sounds coming from across the top of Masada. They sounded like screams, but she wasn't sure. The wind on Masada often played tricks with her ears.

Joseph ran over to her and grabbed her by the shoulders. "Listen! That's not the wind. They are killing each other. I know that. Eleazar's plan is for all of us to die before the first legionary crosses the wall. You have asked me why we did not join the group. I knew what his plan was. And I knew we weren't going to be part of it. I'd rather kill myself ten times over than lay a single finger on you.

"I know a way off this mountain and into Jerusalem without anyone knowing. I will surely not die here by my own hand. Nor will I raise my hand to take your life." Aleya looked at Joseph, shocked by what he said and too scared except to follow.

Joseph planned to climb down the mountain path when the Romans attacked and the confusion of battle occupied the soldiers. No one would see him and Aleya escape. When they got to the plain, he and Aleya would melt into the Roman camp like he always did and make their way to Jerusalem. Once in the city, he had no idea what he was going to do next. For now, just getting away from this place of death was a great accomplishment.

They weren't the only ones who wanted no part of Eleazar's suicide pact. An old woman, her friend, and five grandchildren scrambled off the rock into an outcropping formed by the floor of Herod's palace. Like Joseph and Aleya, they waited through the night in the underground cave. While the young lovers were making plans to leave, the women and children hid farther back in the outcropping so that the Roman soldiers would not find them and kill them.

On that night of death, nine survivors huddled on Masada, waiting for the onslaught of the Tenth Legion. They knew it was coming with the rising of the sun. By then, no Jew on Masada would be left alive. Just the nine who chose not to follow Eleazar.

The women hugged the children. Joseph hugged Aleya tightly, listening for the noise of the camp. It was silent. So many people were dying, and it was silent! Joseph held his love and let the desert night wrap around them.

Chapter Twenty-Two

In the darkest hour just before dawn, the Roman army prepared its assault. Centurions marched through the camp below the mount, waking soldiers, preparing them for the final assault on Masada.

"Get up, you dogs! Do you want the Jews to come down here and slay you in your sleep? Get up! Get up! The battle calls us."

Valerius was awake and fully dressed for war. Sitting astride Arinax, he looked down at the centurions who were busily waking up the stragglers.

It is strange; I am not at all challenged by the battle ahead of us. My usual mix of fear and elation that I feel before I go into battle is missing. Is it because it's not a battle I'm headed for but a slaughter? Let's get finished with this. He wheeled his horse around and shouted to ready battle formations.

The rising sun bounced off the polished armor of the Roman army. The first century of the Tenth Legion was in its place at the head of the legion. Formed in the Roman-style four-by-four battle array, the men waited for the order to storm the mount.

The first line of men had already laid the planks of wood across the top of the smoldering embers of the wooden fortification wall the

Zealots built. The archers had nocked their arrows to repel the first line of defenders. They waited for the final order from General Valerius.

Valerius nudged Arinax to the head of the formation. The horse couldn't walk across the narrow planks, but the men expected their general to be mounted to lead the charge. When the engineers designed the ramp, they never expected a Roman general on his horse to lead the men across the top so the planks were just wide enough for two men abreast, which was still too narrow for a horse.

Valerius held his men back while he dismounted, tethering Arinax to a piece of construction timber. He was the first over the wall, his soldiers right behind him. They walked silently into the camp of Masada, ready to spring an attack on the unsuspecting Jews.

Valerius surveyed the landscape. Nothing prepared him for this. His men reacted the same way. Eager to charge and beat back the Jews, the soldiers simply stood still. They were battle-tested legionaries, hardened veterans of the proud Tenth Legion, but they were also husbands, fathers, and grandfathers. Nothing prepared them for this.

Bodies choked the area around the Masada wells. Men, women, children, and babies, all lay in the stillness of death. A few soldiers walked to the edge of the mountain, spewing last night's wine down the side of the rock. Breakfasts of olive oil and plain bread splattered the earth beneath their feet.

The Tenth Legion had stormed Masada to take it back for the Roman Empire. What they had taken back for the emperor was a cemetery.

Valerius walked among the dead Jews, wondering to himself why they did this. A centurion ran up to him and broke his concentration. "General, we have found survivors. We found two old women and five children hiding in the cave beneath the old king's palace." The centurion pushed the women forward. They held the five little ones close to their bodies, fearful of what the Roman demons would do.

"Come here," Valerius said gingerly, for the old women were frightened. *They probably believe the nonsense that the leaders of Masada spread about us terrible Romans, so I must be careful with them.* "Tell me what happened here."

Fear paralyzed them. They believed what Eleazar had said about the Romans, but they were unwilling to take their own lives and the lives of the children. Now, they had no hope except to trust the goodness of the man in front of them.

"Lord General, Lord General, spare us. We are but old women with no use for anyone. Please, Lord General, spare us and the children."

"Easy. You should have no fear of us. Besides, all our work is done. Tell me. What has gone on in this camp?"

"Lord General, Eleazar ordered the men to kill everyone. Look at these little ones. How could I let them drag a knife across their throats? They are babies. Are the Romans so terrible that they slay babies as they sleep? I thought not. I hid in a cave below the old king's palace. That's where your men found us."

"You can do us a great service. Guide me through this camp and identify Eleazar. I never knew him. I wish to see my adversary before we throw his body on the funeral pyre."

Valerius took the women's hands and walked through the camp. The children they had saved trailed behind them. It was an unusual scene for an end of a battle. It was silent, and soldiers milled around. Their weapons were drawn but not used. There were no dying enemies lying on the ground calling for mercy.

The men obeyed Valerius's command that no desecration of the bodies take place. But he had no need to give that order. The legionaries walked around the camp as if in a trance, unable to comprehend the slaughter in which they had no hand. Some of the legionaries wept as they turned over the bodies of the children. Fathers themselves, they could not begin to understand what powerful force gripped the minds of the Zealots, compelling them to kill their wives and children. No, this was not a usual battle scene. It was a funeral.

"Centurion! What is that noise? What's going on?"

"My Lord General, some of the men have broken into the Jews' wine stores. They need relief from the horror they have seen. Please, General, let them be."

Valerius kept silent. This was a scene like he had never seen, but he must maintain discipline. He had given a strict order that there be no looting. Yet, some of his men ignored his command and decided to go their own way.

"Centurion, round up the drunken sots and take them to the camp below. And put them on latrine duty. Maybe cleaning out the shit of a couple of thousand men will restore their senses."

"Yes, General."

Valerius turned to the old women. Together they walked through the camp, eventually coming to a large campfire site. The ashes were black and cold, the squat stone benches unoccupied. The bodies of ten men were scattered around the campfire.

One woman broke the silence, still fearing for her life. "This is the ruling council, my Lord. These men were the last to go. Here is Eleazar."

Valerius walked over to a body that lay supine before the cold ashes of the campfire. Valerius knelt over the body but did not touch it. *So that is Eleazar. He's the man who had his hold over so many people, a hold so powerful that his men would kill their women and children for him rather than seek Roman justice.*

Valerius turned over the body, the blood ringing his neck like a jeweled diadem. In Eleazar's lifeless hand was a clay square inscribed with the number four.

So, thought Valerius as he looked at the terrible enemy and leader of Masada, *you couldn't even be the last to die. You left it up to chance.*

You drew number four. Why didn't you leave your people up to the chance of Roman justice? What did you think of us? That we're murderers, idolaters, rapists, and child buggerers?

He stared at the lifeless form of the Masada leader. He looked around the campfire at the other dead Jews. *These are the people of my mother. I may wear the eagle of the empire, but these are my people.*

His polished greaves reflected the dying embers of the Zealot campfire. His crimson cloak swirled the smoke about, and his eyes misted as he surveyed the carnage at his feet.

"General, what are we to do here? No one can tell us what happened." Valerius turned to Gaius Longinus, the first centurion of the Tenth, rubbing his eyes as if the smoke drew the very moisture out of them. Neither the centurion nor any soldier would realize that it wasn't the smoke that dampened their general's eyes.

"What can they tell you, Gaius Longinus? What more do you need to know than that these people so feared you and your comrades that they'd rather die than face you?

"There's no need to search. I have found all that I need. This woman is my guide. She can tell me all I need to know. Let the men rest and we will make our way down from this accursed place at daybreak."

The centurion clasped his chest in a sign of obedience to his general and went away to tell his men to stand down. The battle was over. The general was satisfied. And there would be wine, food, and the fine Jewish wenches in camp tomorrow night.

"Centurion!" The soldier stood as still as a hare who knew the falcon had seen it.

"What, General? Have I forgotten something?" The centurion was nervous. He had less than one year left before he retired to his tavern, woman, and two children who waited for him back in Germania. Maybe he would even marry her and make the pups she whelped into Roman citizens. Then again, maybe not. Maybe he'd stay here and become a spice merchant.

As these thoughts ran through his mind, all he could think was that his future would come crashing down if he fell into the general's disfavor. It was Valerius, after all, who would discharge him from the army and see that he would receive the emperor's patrimony.

"Centurion, remind your men that no one touches anything on top of this mountain or your woman in Germany and the spice merchant's daughter in Jerusalem will have to wait for another Roman soldier to make them happy. You have already let some of your men break into the wine stores. Don't push your luck." It troubled Valerius to talk this way to his old friend, but he had to.

He scurried off with as much dignity as he could to relay the general's command to his men. By the bloodied balls of the Mithraic bull, if he caught any man with anything but his sword or his little man in his hand, there would be one less soldier marching down the ramp to the camp.

With his final command of the Masada campaign issued, Valerius surveyed the camp of the Zealots for the last time. He brooded in silence until the revelry of a small number of his troops shook him back to action. He dismissed the woman, ordering a legionary to bring her down the mountain into the Roman camp before letting her and the others return to Jerusalem.

"Legionary, make sure the woman, her friend, and the children are fed back at the camp. And, legionary, if they have no way to make it back to the city, I'll hold you personally responsible to find a wagon to take them back. If anyone gives you a hard time, tell them they will have to deal with Valerius Sixtus if they have a problem. Understood?"

"Yes, General."

He turned to another of his officers. "Centurion, how many of these Zealots are dead here? Have you taken their number?"

"Lord General, we have counted 960 of them."

"Mark it down in the scroll, then. We have taken the Zealots' camp on the fifteenth day of the month of Nisan."

"Nisan, my Lord General? Is it not the Ides of Xanthicus?"

For a moment, the proud leader of the Roman army forgot himself. He had dated the slaughter according to the calendar of the Hebrews. *How is it that I have reverted to the time of my mother? What is it about this place that brings my mother's blood to boil in my veins?*

"Of course, you are right. I have been looking at this tablet left by the Zealots. That's why I identified the month as Nisan. I'm sorry. Have the scribe mark it down in the scroll and deliver it swiftly to my Lord Flavius."

Best I be rid of this place. It has been profaned by all these deaths. It is accursed. Oh, these damnable Jews will remember for all time the name of Masada! I pray they leave my name out of it.

Chapter Twenty-Three

Behind him, Valerius heard a scrabbling as if someone were trying to get near him, but was afraid to approach. Valerius whirled about and confronted the intruder who dared to enter into his private thoughts. "Who are you? What do you wish of me now?"

"My Lord Valerius, I am but a simple friend of Caesar who wishes to write a dispatch to his most august majesty telling him what went on here."

"And what does my Lord Caesar need of a 'simple friend' when he has several generals here who will tell him the truth?"

"I am a historian and a Roman citizen. Do you question my ability to send a truthful dispatch to the imperial court?"

Valerius looked at the man in front of him. *A Roman citizen? Maybe, but not born on the seven hills. I know enough about Judea to know that this man was born within smelling distance of Galilee. Let me flush him out like the game birds my father and I hunted in the hills outside of that sea.*

"You say you are a Roman citizen, yet the look of Judea abounds about you. Who are you, I ask again, and what are you doing here?"

"My Lord General is most observant. Yes, it is true, I am a Roman citizen, but I was born in this humble part of the empire. I served as a general in the Jewish army, but I came to see the error of my ways and now serve the Roman Empire. I was known as Joseph, son of Matthais. When the emperor granted me citizenship, he gave me a new name, Titus Flavius Josephus. I am a Jew, but no more loyal subject of the emperor exists in this land.

"His august majesty has commissioned me to write an account of the Judean wars. That is why I am here. I followed your men up the ramp and waited until I could speak with you. May I speak to the old women you have found? They will give me information that is of incalculable value."

"Josephus, or whatever your real name is, you have my leave to do your job. But do not get in the way. This is still a battleground. And, my little historian, when you write your dispatch to the emperor, do not forget the part that I have played in this campaign. I seek the favors of the emperor when I return to Rome. I could use the notice of his eyes."

"It will be done, my Lord General. You shall be hailed as the 'Hero of Masada.' Mark my words."

The proud general walked away from him; he didn't see the smirk on the historian's face. "Not a letter, General Sixtus," he muttered under his breath, "nor an inscription, nor even a drop of ink shall I waste on you, a Sabine country bumpkin. Generations from now, no one will know who or what Valerius Sixtus was. But they will remember the account of this battle written by Josephus."

Valerius left the historian with a bad taste in his mouth. To clear his head, he walked over to the western slope of Masada directly above the ramp his men had erected. The routes up and down the mountain were impassable. That's why his engineers had chosen the easier western face of the mount to construct their ramp.

Valerius stared over the edge of the mountain. The bright, white landscape of Masada was a stark contrast to the brown desert lands.

The ramp, built from the soil excavated from the western promontory of the mount, was white, while all around it was brown, dried, and dead.

The Roman legions will leave. The bones of the Zealots will turn white and crumble. But the ramp up the mountain, that great slash of white will remain. And with it will remain the story of how a great Roman army marched up the side of Masada to conquer, only to find that they had been conquered.

Valerius turned and walked alone along the eastern edge. Behind him, the sun was setting, casting an orange glow through the smoke of the ruined camp. Below him, just a few paces from his feet, was the cave where the two women and five children had hidden from his legionaries. They, alone, of the almost one thousand people who lived on Masada, survived.

We conquered this godforsaken place, and we killed no one. Thanks be to Mithras, no one can say I turned my sword against my own people.

In the silence of the setting sun, Valerius rested alone against the edge of the palace walls. Behind him, the colored tiles of Herod's palace glistened.

Valerius stared at his surroundings, assessing Masada as a military fortification. The tyrant knew where he had built. The palace was unassailable. The spring rains filled the cisterns for the coming year and caused small desert flowers to bloom. If not for the stink of death, this would be a wonderful place in the memory of the Jews. *How will they think of this now? Will it be a place of wonder or will it always be a place of death?*

A scrabbling of rock and a small puff of dust shook Valerius out of his melancholy. To his right, just over the edge of the mount, he saw shadows.

That's impossible, he thought. *Save for the women and the children, there are no Jews left. And my men are quickly forming to descend the ramp to the comforts of their camp. So the noise cannot come from a Roman soldier. What else could be making the noise except the accursed scavengers and animals that lurk among the rocks here?*

Valerius moved to the edge of the palace wall overlooking the precipice of the mount. Still seeing nothing, he drew his sword, ever ready on the defensive. "Show yourself; I extend the cloak of Roman justice if you are survivors of this camp. There has been too much death. Come out and I grant you safe passage."

The movement below him stopped. It was as if the animals of the desert and the night-blooming flowers stilled, awaiting the end of this confrontation between the might of Rome and whoever was hidden below.

"Come out. You have nothing to fear. It is over."

At the edge of the rock, Valerius saw a linen garment flutter in the desert wind. *Ah, a woman,* he thought. *She chose not to follow the Zealots to their death.* Valerius climbed down the edge of the palace wall, sword drawn. Suddenly, an armed man jumped out, the short sword of the Roman legionary in his hand.

Valerius peered at the man and thought he recognized the face. Clearly not a Roman soldier, he had to be a Zealot. He thought back to all the Jews he had dealt with over the years. *Who could this be? Why do I know him?* Then, in an instant, the memories flooded his brain. The laughing legionaries. The feisty little boy on the verge of angry tears. The would-be Jewish resistance fighter with a dull and broken sword in his small hand. And the thought that he, Valerius, might one day see that boy with his sword drawn.

"Joseph! So you have decided to use the sword after all." Valerius laughed. So many years had passed since he gave a useless stub of a sword to a snot-nosed camp follower. That little Jewish boy, now a fully grown man, was challenging him with a sword made by his own armories!

"Roman, leave us be. We intend to leave here."

"Boy, remember who gave you that sword in your hand? I always wondered if you would draw it in anger against me. Put it down. I mean you no harm."

Panicked, Joseph's mind couldn't focus on the man in front of him. *Who is this? He is a Roman general to be sure and a battle-scarred, decorated veteran as well. This is no man to be trifled with. Why is his face so familiar? I have known many soldiers. My sisters many more than me. Why do I linger in my memory over this one?*

"My little warrior, you are now a full-grown man, and you challenge me. Do you really want to go against a general of the Roman army, especially with his own sword? How many times do I have to give you my leave?"

All of a sudden, Joseph was thirteen years old again, scurrying around the camp of the Romans, looking for weapons to arm his fellow Jews. He looked at the face of the man. *Yes, that's him. That is Valerius Sixtus. But what has happened to him over these so many years? Has Judea caused that?*

The full-bodied Roman soldier who had tossed him a rusted *gladius* stood before him, wearing the cloak and regalia of a decorated Roman general and the color of a noble. But the man, the man inside the regalia, was nothing like Joseph remembered. He seemed smaller, sadder, and more careworn than Joseph remembered. *Is this what seeing so much death does to men?*

"What's the matter, Joseph? It is I, Valerius, and once again, I spare your life. Don't be a fool. You can't win against a full general in the Roman army. Go. Leave me be. Take your wench with you. And may the bloodied balls of the bull of Mithras watch over you."

Joseph looked at the man, smaller, less powerful than years ago and so tired. There was nothing else to say. "With your leave, General."

Valerius stood on Masada, looking at the carnage created by the mad dreams of the Zealot leader, Eleazar. The Roman general was no stranger to dead men. This was different. The bodies on the ground were not the bloodied corpses of soldiers who fell in battle. These were not warriors fighting for their country. These were ordinary, gentle people—families, mothers, fathers, little children. Like soldiers fallen in battle, though, they were dead all the same.

Valerius shivered with horror at the sight of the Masada mass suicide. The deaths of all those innocents affected his men, too. They walked about the camp, looking lost, with nothing to do. Valerius felt dirty and unclean as if he had just finished a *taberna* brawl, not a properly organized Roman campaign.

There was nothing left for him to do on Masada. He had taken the fortress. He could report to Flavius and Titus that he secured their objective. *But what has Rome won? The Tenth Legion has Masada as a Roman outpost, once again, and we defeated the Jewish rebels. Masada was the last pocket of resistance left in this accursed Judea. The destruction of their temple and the installation of a Roman government scattered the Jews across the Judean wilderness and out into the stretches of the Roman Empire. We have won,* thought Valerius. *But what have we won and at what cost? Will what we have done echo through the centuries? Will we somehow pay for destroying these people and their way of life?*

These Jews are tough. I know. My mother was one. Already I have received reports of rabbis conducting classes in desert caves. Can those rabbis maintain their religion? I think not. We have destroyed their temple. They are finished.

Better I think of my own life than dwell on what happened on this mount. I have completed the task set before me. I have conquered the Jews and made Judea a Roman state. Now, I shall go back to Rome to collect my reward and set myself up as a member of the equestrian class. Who knows? Maybe my family, if the gods give me one, will become honored Romans, and no one will look down upon them as peasants from the Sabine Hills.

Valerius ambled to the northeast side of the fortress. If he had looked hard enough down the side, he would have seen the two figures scrabbling their way down the rocky slope. But the embittered Roman general lost himself in his own thoughts and paid little attention to the activity below him.

Chapter Twenty-four

"Joseph, where are we going? If I remember correctly, the land of my father is the other way. We are going in the opposite direction from where I want to travel. Why don't you tell me where we are going?"

Joseph held Aleya's hand even more tightly as they scrambled down the hard rock face of Masada. Joseph kept quiet. He couldn't tell Aleya just yet that they were going back to the very same place where she was sold on the slave blocks.

He wasn't sure if he should be going back there either. Surely, someone would recognize him. *It doesn't matter that the general gave me his leave. I'm a Jew. He's Roman. And he could turn on me at any time. What if he sees me in Jerusalem? What would I do? I could become a Roman prisoner and spend the rest of my life in the galleys of Roman ships. God knows what would happen to Aleya.*

Just then, Aleya cried out and let go of Joseph's hand. She was slipping down the treacherous mountain path, tumbling to her death. The loose white rock gave way beneath his feet as he chased after her. She tried to grab hold of the rock outcroppings, but her grip was too weak, and she continued to barrel down the path. With steps honed by experience, Joseph chased after Aleya, trying to grab some part of her body to break her slide to a sure and painful death. "Reach out to me. Give me your hand. I have to grab your hand, Aleya. Reach out now!"

With the last bit of strength in his body, Joseph scurried down the side of the mountain and dove for Aleya's body. *Somehow, some way, I'll reach her. She means more than life to me. I must reach her!*

Aleya slid faster down the path. The sharp stones cut into her flesh and tore her meager slave girl's cloak to ribbons. Dirt flew into her hair and eyes. She knew that she was going to die.

She careened closely to the edge of the path, tottering slightly over the edge and a fall to certain death. Joseph stretched out his arm and grabbed her by her leg. He held onto her thigh and brought her back from the precipice.

She was filthy, dusty, bleeding from scratches and cuts, and he held onto her as if she were the only thing in the world. He looked at her frightened face. And Joseph knew that he loved her for now and all eternity. He would love her forever, indeed.

Evening was coming quickly, and Joseph had no desire to traverse the rocky path at night. He guided the wounded Aleya to a small overhang that marked the halfway point down the side of the mount. "Rest, please. We'll stay here tonight and finish our way down tomorrow. We'll meet a caravan and follow them to Jerusalem. People in the desert always welcome strangers. And when one of the strangers is a pretty, young girl, the welcome will be even warmer."

"You talk about merchants and caravans and traveling. Where are we going? You know I must get back to my father's kingdom. That was our plan. The two of us would travel south and eventually get back to my father."

"Enough talk for one day, my sweet. I shall tell you where we are going. To Jerusalem."

Aleya was exhausted and hurt, but her mind was still focused on going home. "Joseph, why are we going to Jerusalem? That's too far north. My father's kingdom is to the south. Why are you taking me back to Jerusalem?"

"It is simple. Think. How would we ever get back to your father by ourselves? We must meet up with a caravan. We would never survive in the desert by ourselves. How else would we get to your father's kingdom except as part of a caravan?"

Joseph said these words, not believing a single sentence. His Aleya was no more a rich Arabian princess than he was king of Jerusalem. But he loved her all the same and wrestled with how he would make her his wife.

He was telling the truth about meeting up with a caravan. Jerusalem was the best place to find a merchant group headed south. He had no other reason to go back to that city. There was nothing there for him. Joseph had no family in Jerusalem. There was no one to protest that he wanted to marry a pagan.

Somehow, though, he would take his Aleya south to meet up with her father, the king. *Some king,* Joseph thought. *We'll probably find him squatting in his filthy camel-skin tent surrounded by the dung and smell of his sheep. But it would be home for Aleya, and I promised to bring her back.*

Joseph looked over to where Aleya had lain down for the night. She looked so small, so promising, so tender. Joseph lay next to her and gently reached his arms across her small body. Before Joseph closed his eyes, he saw a shooting star traveling across the black desert sky.

Make a wish on a shooting star, his mother would tell him; make a wish, and it will come true. All Joseph wished for was lying next to him in his arms.

"We have to get down the side of the mount before we eat or drink anything. There is no water on the mountainside, but the path I have marked passes through an oasis where there are dates and a small stream. We shall wait there for a caravan to take us to Jerusalem. We'll never make it alone through the wilderness."

Aleya, still sleepy, rubbed her eyes and rose to follow him. The two of them walked down the path to the foot of the mountain. Joseph knew why it was called the Snake Path. It wound down around the mount, and it was impossible to see who was on the path. Joseph had heard that King Herod's brother—his name was Joseph, too—cut the path out of the side of Masada. That was the last time Judea was free of foreign oppression. It was a Roman client-state, but the Herodian Dynasty declared Judea a free kingdom. And, by all accounts, it would be the last time Judea was free. *The might of the Roman Empire has re-occupied the fortress of Masada, and my country will never be ours.*

He and Aleya continued down the Snake Path. It was on the eastern side of the cliff, directly opposite the ramp Valerius's engineers had built on the western side. There was no chance of Joseph and Aleya running into patrols of Roman soldiers. They just didn't come this way.

Aleya looked around. As far as she could see, the land was brown. In the far distance, there was a haze created by the evaporation of the waters of the Dead Sea. The sea was actually an inland lake with no streams or rivers feeding out of it. The River Jordan fed into the northern end of the lake. The only other source of fresh water was the meager two inches of annual rain that fell in the hills above it.

The Dead Sea had six to seven times the salinity of the world's oceans, making it an unlivable environment and unable to sustain any form of life. The rainfall was enough to keep the Dead Sea at a reasonable level, but it would be nothing more than a salty inland lake forever.

Joseph had followed the shoreline of the lake many times in his travels to Jerusalem. He knew its curves and dips intimately. He only wished that he knew Aleya as well as he did the Dead Sea shoreline. As usual, Aleya broke into his thoughts with another of her one thousand questions.

"When do we get to this oasis? I'm tired, hungry, and thirsty. Why didn't you let me bring anything from Joab's tent like I asked? Joseph, are you going to answer me?"

Joseph said nothing and continued to walk, expecting Aleya to follow him. *Maybe the women at the well were right. Aleya just might be some sort of princess. Certainly no Jewish woman would complain of walking after only a few hours. She's certainly pretty enough not to be of simple desert stock, and she's definitely not fit to walk through the desert.*

But where in Magna Arabia is there a kingdom like what she's hinted at? There's nothing but sand, heat, and more sand. The place is so forbidding that I hear it has black rivers of undrinkable water. Desert devils send something oozing out of the earth into the rivers to make them undrinkable to all but the demons. Sometimes, the rivers catch on fire!

Joseph hesitated to tell Aleya where the oasis was, for it was still a good day's walk through the wadi from the Roman camp. He wasn't sure she could bear the news of the distance. Of course, they went nowhere near the Roman camp. The army had attacked Masada. All Jews, even the slaves who served the Romans, were suspect.

Joseph unrolled a map of his route from Masada to Jerusalem, from when he was the unofficial courier between Eleazar and friendly Jews in the city. That seemed like a lifetime ago.

One day, he had asked the old merchant, Joab, for a piece of sheepskin and a writing instrument so that he could record the distances between Masada and Jerusalem. *Eleazar had hinted of his plan to the council. Joab was an unofficial member of that council. The old merchant must know why I am asking this.*

"Joseph, who needs maps? Merchants like me have been traveling with the caravans so long that the map of where we are going is part of our mind. Why is a young man like you in need of a drawing?"

"Please," said Joseph, "there are things I do for Eleazar that you don't need to know about. Should I disappear one day, the map will help Aleya get back to Jerusalem where she can meet a caravan to take her back to her father."

There was no need to tell the old man that he, the merchant, would not be accompanying Aleya wherever she went. Joseph knew what Joab's fate would be and so did Joab.

"Of course, my son. Come into my tent and I shall provide you with the writing materials. In fact, why don't you stay here and draw your map. I'll light an oil lamp. No one comes into my tent. You and your secrets shall be safe."

Now, on the desert floor under the looming presence of the mount of Masada, Joseph fingered the map that he had secreted under his robe. "Aleya, let's stop here under this rock and take a rest from the sun." They had been barely walking for an hour, but already Aleya was showing signs of exhaustion. She gratefully stopped and joined Joseph in the shadow of the rock, away from the heat and glare of the early afternoon sun.

Joseph looked at her. She looked nothing like a princess. The slide down the mountain had left her dress in tatters. Her shapely body exposed itself through the rips in her robe, shaming Joseph as he stared, trying to place the rest of her body in his mind. Not that he had ever seen it. The closest he had come to possessing the body of his beloved was the shadowy outline of Aleya undressing for the night inside Joab's tent. Now that he was alone with Aleya in the desert, he had, by right of the ancient practices that ruled life in the desert, full possession of her body and her rights. But Joseph had no wish to force himself upon this beautiful young woman though his loins ached at night, and too often he would awake in the morning with wetness on the front of his loincloth.

"Aleya, let me show you where we are and where we are going and how far it is to Jerusalem. I have a map here." They rested under the rock outcropping that created a sunshade over their heads. On the flat desert floor, Joseph laid out his crude drawing. He had seen the almost perfect drawings of the Roman engineers, so he knew what he did was little better than the scribbling of a schoolchild. Yet, it did chart the way between Masada and Jerusalem.

As he unrolled the map, Aleya could hardly contain her excitement. Joseph leaned down and withdrew the parchment from his side pouch. He spread the map out on the sand and looked up at Aleya. He knew she was excited, but over a map?

Aleya looked down at the parchment and frowned. It wasn't exactly a frown. Her mouth didn't move, but her cheeks drooped slightly. Joseph looked over at the girl-woman by his side and knew immediately that something was wrong.

This map is nothing like my father's. My nieces and nephews drew better pictures to impress their grandfather. This is supposed to get us to Jerusalem? This adventure of Joseph's will take us a lifetime.

Chapter Twenty-five

1987

The unpaved desert road bounced the occupants of the Land Rover around like the amusement rides at Tivoli. Jordan shifted every time they hit a pothole, and her body rose from the seat of the open vehicle.

The two men in front made no noise at all. The trip to the Qumran caves was not an adventure for them. It was work. But for Jordan, it was an adventure of a lifetime. Imagine! Her father—everybody called him the renowned archaeologist—was taking her to his latest dig.

She never thought it would happen. Certainly, her mother didn't want her daughter anywhere outside of Jerusalem. The lightning success the army achieved in the Six Days' War was twenty years old and never brought the peace it was supposed to. The country was still, as always for all of Jordan's short life, "on alert." Her mother didn't want her only child crawling around in the desert with her crazy husband.

"Yigael, what are you doing taking Jordan into the desert with you? Haven't you had enough excitement for a lifetime? You need to go out there and prove no one can harm you?"

Jordan's father looked at his wife, the beautiful woman who gave life to his treasured daughter. "Ariel, we are going out to a heavily monitored government site. Julian and I represent the Israel Antiquities Authority. We have to be there. I've promised Jordan for years that I would take her to Qumran. She has thoughts, you know, of becoming an archaeologist."

Ariel said nothing. There was no arguing with her husband over his dusty pots. "Just be careful. You know how I worry."

He gave his wife a full-mouthed kiss, called for his daughter, and left the apartment building. They found Julian Hirschberg waiting for them in the open Land Rover.

"Hello, Jordan. How's my little girl this morning?"

"Uncle Julian, you can hardly call me a little girl anymore. I'm entering high school."

Julian chortled and shoved his unlit cigar between his teeth. "Let's go, Yigael, before those shepherd thieves steal even more than we let them."

Yigael jumped into the driver's seat and adjusted the rearview mirror. As he twisted it, his daughter's face came into full view. *She's looking more like her mother every day. It's for her generation that we old guys continually fight these wars,* Yigael thought.

Ariel and Yigael had met on the boat that took them from war-torn Europe to a new life in a new land that was old before their parents' parents' parents were born. They arrived in Palestine like the hundreds of thousands of other refugees looking to make a life in a country that didn't exist. But they had faith that it would.

Yigael was a survivor of the camps, one of the lucky children never subjected to the experiments that the Nazi monsters routinely performed on Jewish children. Ariel was fortunate. Her parents saw the coming of the end of their world. They were both university professors in Munich and had a worldwide circle of friends. Long before the Nazi brown shirts arrived, Ariel's parents contacted their Sephardic friends in Spain, begging them to shelter their daughter.

On the day she boarded her train to Spain, Ariel's mother pressed a wooden box into her daughter's hands. She looked at her mother, wondering what could be so precious.

"Keep this, *mein liebchen,* close to your heart. It is our legacy. Save it and give it to my grandchild." Ariel's mother kissed her and stood on the train platform, waving good-bye to her future as the train left the station. Ariel would never see her mother again.

At the end of the war, Ariel was a little girl looking to start her life all over again. The horrors revealed by the American troops' discovery of the Nazi death camps destroyed her memories of the good times in Germany. She just wanted to get away. She decided to emigrate to Palestine, supposedly the place where a new country—just for Jews—was being built.

As she walked down the dock toward her future, she carried all of her worldly possessions in a simple cloth bag. Tucked in the corner of her bag was the box her mother had given her. Her family was gone—erased from the face of the earth as if they never existed. All she had left was the box and what it contained.

Yigael and armies of other young men fought to create their country. They fought and won despite worldwide disdain of their cause and nearly impossible odds. He remembered how he and his new bride held hands listening to the radio broadcast announcing the United Nations' vote that gave life to their new country.

Nearly forty years later, they were still fighting. But it had to end. It must end. Yigael shook his head to clear his thoughts and pay more attention to the atrocious Jerusalem traffic. He drove the Land Rover east toward the northern end of the Dead Sea and the Qumran caves.

The country between Jerusalem and the Dead Sea was harsh. Water was scarce, life sparse, and roads non-existent. Yigael and his wife, Ariel, weren't meant to live in a desert country. Their Eastern

European ancestry never prepared them for a life in a land where the sun beat unmercifully upon their fair skin and bleached their blonde hair. Yigael's skin tanned, thanks to his Bavarian genes. But his darling Ariel could not so much as take a walk down the street without turning pink.

Yigael looked at his daughter behind him, sitting on the hard bench seat of a government Land Rover. She was like him—blonde and green-eyed with skin that turned dark as an Arab in the summer months. The only difference between father and daughter was that the sun never erased the tattooed numbers on his arm.

"Father, how much longer do we have to go? You said it wouldn't be long, and I don't want to miss what's going on."

"I wouldn't bring you this far if it meant that you would miss the excavation's high points. This has been going on for forty years, and it will go on for a few more lifetimes. Every day we find something new. I promise you, you won't miss anything."

The man in the seat next to her father just laughed.

"Uncle Julian, stop laughing at me. I'm not a little girl anymore."

"I know, Jordan. One day you will make a commanding soldier and a great archaeologist. Make sure you come and see me before you enlist. I might have a spot for you in my old unit."

Chapter Twenty-Six

74 CE

The desert sun rose early and with a vengeance. The temperature went from the freezing of nightfall to the baking of the morning sun in an instant. By the time the sun was fully up, Aleya and Joseph were already halfway to Ein Gedi.

Joseph and Aleya walked along the caravan paths that merchants had been traveling for thousands of years. The ancient wadis held a secret that, if they could, would tell of a land that flowed with water and bloomed with greenery. But there was no water, no greenery to comfort the travelers. It was just a route that followed the path of long-dead rivers that flowed from the once-living Dead Sea.

Joseph followed the shallow bed of the wadi. It was a safe path, just a little bit away from the shore of the Dead Sea, pointing north to Jerusalem.

Their first destination on the journey back to Jerusalem was the oasis of Ein Gedi, a haunted place occupied by the memories of the inhabitants of Masada. For it was in Ein Gedi that the Zealots had planted their crops to feed the thousand souls on top of Masada. Not that the enterprising people on Masada didn't grow some crops. Masada, for all its isolation in the middle of the desert, was a miracle unto itself.

When Joseph first arrived on Masada, he was struck by the desolation of the place. Masada was stuck in the Judean wilderness, days from any civilization. *Why did Eleazar choose to situate his people here? How can anyone live without water? Surely, this is not the place to encamp over one thousand of your followers.*

Joseph had joined Eleazar in the dead of winter. It was cold, isolated, and miserable. Food was scarce. Water was scarcer. Joseph thought over and over again about his decision to join Eleazar. He was close to losing his faith in the man and the life he was preaching.

Then, the spring rains came. Masada overflowed with clean spring water. The immense cisterns that Herod had built filled to the brim. Two weeks of rain provided enough water for the inhabitants of Masada for an entire year. And there was enough water to nurture the meager crops the women had planted on the mount.

But the residents of Masada still depended on the riches of the Ein Gedi oasis. Joseph knew the place well enough. It was his first stop between Masada and Jerusalem. And it was the place of rest that he sought as he led his love back to her father.

Ein Gedi was due north of Masada, just near the Dead Sea coastline. He could smell the sea, he could hear the sea, but he couldn't see it. The path to Ein Gedi led away from the sea. It was just as well that the Dead Sea did not encroach upon the land of the oasis. Seepage from that great inland sea, poisoned by millennia of minerals and salts concentrated in the water, would have ruined the freshwater source the oasis afforded to travelers.

Ein Gedi was always an improbable site to Joseph. To come upon springs of fresh water, date palms, irrigated fields, and relief from the sun in the middle of the desert seemed impossible. But Ein Gedi and others like it spread throughout the Arabian Peninsula and made travel and commerce possible and encouraged the rise of great Arabian empires.

Joseph knew the oasis like he had a map of it in his mind. Near nightfall, after walking all day, he and Aleya approached the outer fringes of Ein Gedi. He could smell the water and the scent of fresh greenery wafting across the cooling desert sands. In truth, he was as anxious as Aleya to get to the oasis, but unlike Aleya, he knew the troubles that awaited a single armed man accompanied by an attractive young woman.

A group of large boulders marked the approach to Ein Gedi. Joseph guided Aleya to the backside of the boulders and knelt down. "Wait here until I return and tell you it's safe to come. No, wait until I come back to get you. Listen to no voice that calls to you in the night. Understand? I will come for you."

"How long will you be gone, Joseph? I want a bath in these waters you talk about. Imagine, a spring of fresh water in the middle of the desert! I wonder if my father knows of the place. He must. He's King. He knows about everything."

"I am quite sure your father knows all about Ein Gedi. He probably had those wonderful royal mapmakers plot this oasis and draw it out for him in exquisite detail. I'm sure they didn't miss a single palm tree."

Joseph snuck away from her. The desert night swiftly descended upon them, wrapping Joseph in the safety of darkness. He had approached the oasis many times in the past, never fearing for himself. But this time it was different. He had with him a young and beautiful woman who would be captured and sold into slavery immediately. He trusted no one. Joseph could take care of himself, but he feared for Aleya.

The oasis was deserted. Not one traveling caravan had called it a night at the banks of its cool streams. No one lived permanently at Ein Gedi, so if there were no travelers, the oasis would be empty. He walked through the field so lovingly cared for by the Zealots. He wondered who would take care of them now. Man had cultivated Ein Gedi for generations. Now, there was no one left to care. It was too close to Jerusalem to merit a small town of itself. Ancient Jericho was only half a day's walk. So, a permanent settlement never grew around Ein Gedi. It was to remain forever a wayfarer's stop. *When these fields ripen and mature would that be the last harvest at Ein Gedi?*

He didn't have the time to be philosophical about the demise of Ein Gedi. He needed a safe place to sleep for the night. He needed to bring Aleya into the permanent camp that hundreds of travelers had used through the centuries.

The Ein Gedi camp was a simple place to rest. It consisted of a few baked mud huts around an open fire pit. Its singular attraction in the camp was an artificial waterfall some would-be architect constructed to create a pool in the center of the camp. The ancient unknown builder had cleverly tapped a stream flowing through the oasis and directed it through the middle of the camp.

The camp was set in a hollow, and the water flowed down the sloping hills surrounding it. Ordinarily, a camp in a hollow was an indefensible position, a site just waiting for the enemy to come rolling down the slope. The Ein Gedi camp was a different story. Its location protected it from the stinging sand storms that blew across the desert. And it was considered a safe-haven. Nonetheless, when a caravan was in place, hired guards ringed the top of the slopes leading to the camp.

Joseph crept to the slopes around the camp and peered down into the hollow. Like the entire oasis, the camp was deserted. He scrambled down the slope and scouted the buildings.

The ashes in the fire pit were cold and no longer had an acrid, smoky odor. There were no signs of cooking or any kind of habitation for a long time. Joseph took his time going from hut to hut. On the walls, centuries of travelers had inscribed their names in every language spoken by the merchants who crisscrossed the Arabian Peninsula. There were Greek, Hebrew, Phoenician, archaic Latin, and a few languages he didn't recognize carved into the soft, clay brick walls.

Joseph never spent too much time in this camp when he traveled on Eleazar's missions. He would spend just a few hours at the oasis, arriving after dark and leaving before dawn, always staying on the fringes. He stood in the middle of the deserted camp, wondering why it was empty. *Everything else looks normal. What stopped the wheels of commerce?*

The night air was cooling. Joseph wrapped his cloak around him and grabbed his Roman sword. He looked once more around the camp and made his way back to Aleya.

Chapter Twenty-Seven

1991

The Mediterranean sparkled in the afternoon sun. Jordan Barash sat with her two friends at a seaside café, drinking mango juice mixed with champagne. Jordan thought it was an awful concoction cooked up by the Indian owner of the café. The only reason they were there was that the owner wasn't too careful about checking their ages. Besides, this was Israel where eighteen-year-olds regularly gave up parts of their lives to serve in the army.

Jordan and her friends had taken off for the coast once high school ended. All of them attended schools in Israel, but for different reasons. Once they returned to Jerusalem after their interlude on the Mediterranean coast, each of them would be off to a summer internship before entering university, except for Jordan.

She would spend the summer preparing for entry into the Israel Defense Forces while fitting in a mini internship. Her father, Yigael Barash, got her a job on the Masada excavation, joining him as part of the excavation team that had been working on the historical site for over four decades.

After her internship, she would join the army for a couple of years and then go to university. Her life would be much different from her friends who sat across the table from her.

"Jor, what are you thinking about? School's over. Enjoy yourself!" Penny cried out.

Jordan looked at her friend and smiled. Penny was an American who decided to study in Israel. She was all fired up over Israel's prospects now that peace seemed to have settled over the region. Penny was a hopeful American. Jordan was a pessimistic Israeli. Jordan knew that peace had not come to her country, though you'd never know it by the look of all the tourists enjoying the summer months at the seaside.

"Jor, what's the deal with all these languages on the walls? You know Aaron, the guy who wants to go to the University of Chicago to study classical languages? Well, he took me to a part of the Old City and showed me a wall that had all these languages on it. He started translating, but I lost interest in the wall. He has the cutest blue eyes and black curly hair! Who thought an Israeli would have black hair and blue eyes!"

"Penny, do you realize how long young couples have been reading walls in Israel written in many languages? This country has been a crossroads for travelers from all parts of the world for millennia.

"By the way, Penny, you should study Greek. Your name, Penelope, comes from the *Odyssey*. Penelope was a Queen of Greece who waited decades until her husband, Odysseus, came home."

"Jor, you take this history stuff too seriously. Order me another mango-and-champagne, will ya?"

Penny was going back to work on a kibbutz. Sharon, Jordan's friend since they were both toddlers in Jerusalem, was going to work at a hospital. She was anxious to get to her internship before she went to the army.

"Maybe I'll get to take care of some cute soldiers, Jordan. A hospital doesn't seem like a good place to meet a husband, but you never know.

When are you getting serious with a boy? All the guys in class just stare at you when you walk in. It's that blonde hair. Maybe I should dye my hair. What do you think?"

"Sharon," Jordan said absentmindedly, "I think you should leave your hair alone. The guys look at me and think I'm an American. I guess they have never seen an Israeli woman with blonde hair."

Jordan gazed past her friends out into the water. Her friends knew she was going to work with her father on some archaeological dig. They didn't know that her Uncle Julian had pulled strings to get her into an elite unit once the dig was finished. Jordan wasn't going to be teaching or going to a kibbutz or looking for husbands in a hospital. She was taking a step that was going to take her life in a whole other direction.

Jordan had known from early girlhood that she was marked by the government elite for a job that only a few of her high school friends even knew about. Her uncle had made sure of that. She never really knew what he did nor would he say.

"Jordan, my sweet little girl," Uncle Julian used to say, "you are special. I knew it from the first day Yigael brought you home. I held this precious baby in my arms and saw the face of my future. You are our hope. You are our dream.

"Later you study your archaeology, like your father, but first, your country. Keep your eyes open. Learn from the past. Study the Torah. Those of us who are religious look to the Torah for the word of God. I study the Torah and see the war plans of God. Nothing has changed in three thousand years.

"We are a small tribe of people surrounded by much larger tribes who want nothing more than to kill us. And what hurts me more than anything is that these tribes were once us. But who can argue with history? Enlist. Then go to school. When we call, you'll know it's time."

Jordan snapped back to the present with her two friends sitting at the seaside table. She looked at the peaceful-looking Mediterranean just a couple of hundred yards away from the café. She wasn't going to tell her friends that she already signed-up for the IDF.

Chapter Twenty-Eight

74 CE

A pair of eyes watched the young Joseph stride through the camp in the darkening hours of the desert evening. The eyes peered between the lush trees that surrounded the meandering streams in the oasis. The eyes watched him leave and waited for him to come back.

Aleya reclined against the boulders right where Joseph left her. *He's never coming back,* she thought. *He made his way to the oasis to meet up with a caravan.* She was deep in her thoughts about the rest of her life when she heard a scuffle away in the bushes. She peered into the darkness but couldn't make out any shapes. Though she was the first princess of Arabia, she knew nothing about the desert or what lived in its burrows or under its rocks. She gave no thought to the noise and laid her head on her arms and tried to sleep. But she couldn't help thinking about Joseph.

She was halfway asleep when, all of a sudden, a callused hand grabbed her across her mouth. She was too terrified to move, and the small dagger Joseph gave her lay in the desert sand too far from her hand to reach it.

"Be quiet, my little one. Don't scream. And don't get mad," Joseph whispered to her. He removed his hand. Aleya immediately stood up, ready to scream her lungs out at him. "No, Aleya. Please don't make a sound. I'm sorry I snuck up on you, but I had to. I had a very uneasy feeling that I was being watched when I left the oasis. I didn't want you to greet me when I returned. At night, any noise here in the desert travels for many paces."

"Well, you didn't have to come up on me like a thief." Aleya slumped against the boulder and looked up at Joseph. "Where are we going now?"

"We will make our way slowly and quietly into the oasis. There's a clump of bushes where I have some supplies left from the last time I was here. Trust me. We'll stay the rest of the night in the bushes and make our way into the camp at first light. Let's go." The two travelers stood up and made their way into Ein Gedi.

Morning in the desert came quickly. The mountains were west of Ein Gedi, so there was nothing to block the early morning sun from shining on the sleeping faces of the young lovers. Joseph awoke first. Aleya mumbled something and just wrapped Joseph's cloak around her. Joseph welcomed the sun. He had given his cloak to Aleya and slept in the robe that he wore when they escaped from Masada. It hardly covered his legs. He had shortened it so the cloth wouldn't interfere with his escape. He was cold, and he anticipated building a fire.

Joseph couldn't shake the feeling that someone was watching them. He wasn't frightened, just aware. If it were a marauding group of desert bandits, they would have been taken already. But someone or something was out there.

He made his way down to the camp, leaving Aleya in the safety of the shelter he had built months ago. As he approached the camp, he saw movement in the bushes to his left. There was no wind in the desert this morning, and bushes didn't move by themselves. He unsheathed his Roman sword and crept into the vegetation lining the banks of the stream.

He walked slowly through the bush, trying to get a sense of what was there. He sniffed the air, trying to catch a scent of an animal. He looked from side to side, listened attentively, but couldn't detect another presence. He turned back to go to the camp and start his morning fire.

As he neared the bank of the stream he heard another soft noise. All of a sudden, something dropped out of the trees and covered him with slithering snakes. He rolled around on the ground, trying to make it into the stream to rid himself of the monsters. He heard a crazed cackling and looked up.

Standing above him was a desert devil, what the Bedouin called the *djinn*. The devil was dancing about clothed in filthy rags with a gaping maw that was cherry-red and toothless. He fought against the snakes encircling his chest and tried to stand. The *djinni* continued to laugh like a crazed monster and stood on Joseph's body. Then it addressed him in Hebrew in a dialect Joseph hadn't heard since he was a little boy.

This djinni *speaks Hebrew. The devil is trying to confuse me.* "Hear, O Israel, the Lord is God, the Lord is One," cried Joseph, reciting the most ancient of Hebrew prayers. Joseph had forgotten most of the prayers he learned in boyhood—religion and revolution did not mix—but he tried to recite whatever he remembered. Anything to chase this *djinni* and his spells away.

"I've got you. You're mine. Now you must do my bidding," the *djinni* said. "Come, sit up, and talk to me." The *djinni* grabbed the snakes still wrapped around Joseph's body and sat him upright. When Joseph had a chance to catch his breath, he looked at himself and at the *djinni* and realized that things were not what he thought.

The "snakes" around his body were actually ropes woven into a net. The ropes were so pitifully rotten that Joseph was able to break them with one hand. And the *djinni* wasn't a desert devil at all, just an incredibly old, incredibly crazed man. Joseph thought it best to humor him, for he knew not what else the man had in store for him.

"Hello, ancient and revered one of the desert. You have me in your power, and I am your servant. Tell me what you want, and I shall do as you command."

The old man cackled in his peculiar, high-pitched way and looked Joseph straight in the eye. "You speak Hebrew! Oh, God has punished me again. I had hoped you would be one of those desert pagans. I want my revenge, but I can't get it against a fellow Jew. Come. Let me help you to your feet."

Still humoring him, Joseph made as if he were under the power of the man and pretended the net held him securely and helplessly. Joseph struggled to his feet and looked down at the old man. "I thought you were a *djinni*. I have never seen one, but they would look like you if they existed."

The man emitted a high-pitched whine. "Oh, the *djinn*. Yes, the *djinn*. They do exist. I have seen them. But what do you know of the *djinn*, a young man like you? Have you ever traveled to the land of the black water where the desert pagans live in their great palaces and travel the seas in their one-sail boats? Well, have you?"

He began to sing in a tongue that Joseph didn't recognize. He had never heard such a guttural accent. The man began to dance slowly round and round. Joseph thought that the desert had robbed the man of his senses. In fact, he was sure of it, talking about black water, *djinn*, and desert palaces.

His "captor" paid him no attention and rocked back and forth in place, singing in a low voice in that strange language that Joseph found beguiling. His crazed motion had Joseph so captivated that he never heard Aleya approach. "Joseph, what is it? Who is this man?"

"I don't know. He's just some crazy old hermit who lives on what travelers have left behind. From the look of him, he has been here in Ein Gedi a long time. He must have also stolen food from the field cultivated by the Zealots of Masada. Come, let's go to the camp and leave him be. He's harmless. We'll leave him some food before we make our way to Jerusalem."

Aleya stopped for a minute, listening to the man humming his song. She tilted her head, straining to pick up the tune coming from the man's toothless mouth. Joseph looked at her. There was a spark in her eyes. Something about the man's babbling kindled that spark.

"The song he's singing. I recognize it, I think, but I don't know why. It sounds familiar as if I have heard it in another life."

"Aleya, the camp is over that hill. Forget about him and walk with me to the camp. I'll make a fire and cook breakfast. There is always a supply of grain in one of the huts, and the fields of the Zealots will yield some vegetables and the trees some fruits. We can stay here for a few days and get our strength back. We have come a long way from Masada."

Joseph and Aleya left the old man in his reverie and headed toward the camp. They followed the path to the camp. It meandered down the slope, past the stream, and around the bubbling waterfall. Aleya's eyes widened as she took in the improbable scene of a waterfall cascading down a rocky slope in the middle of the Judean desert. All around the camp, the desert bloomed. There were leafy palms, heavy with dates and golden-green fronds.

Farther from the camp lay the fields of vegetables the Zealots had planted to feed themselves. Beyond the vegetable patches were orchards, the trees heavy with fruit. An intricate system of irrigation canals watered the earth.

Aleya walked next to Joseph. Her eyes took in everything. She still couldn't believe she was in the middle of the desert. She was dazzled by the beauty that could spring up in the middle of desert nothingness.

Together they walked, until they got to the group of mud huts that made up the camp.

"Here, Aleya, this is where we will stay. We can rest here before pushing ahead to Jerusalem. There's enough to eat and plenty of water to drink. We owe it to ourselves to rest. The trip to Jerusalem is a full day's walk. It is not easy. We need to rest."

Aleya did her best to make the mud hut inhabitable. She swept the floor of the animal droppings, rid the eaves under the straw roof of old birds' nests, and picked up old food discarded by other travelers.

Joseph walked to the fields and orchards, promising to bring back enough for a veritable feast. "Just you wait. This will be the best dinner you have ever had!"

If the truth be known, she thought to herself, *any dinner right now would be the best I've ever had.* After leaving Masada, she and Joseph existed on a handful of dried grain and meat. What water they drank came from tepid pools captured in the hollows of rock formations. The water was sandy and stale, but it was wet and kept them alive.

But that was behind them. Here in Ein Gedi, the water flowed freely—clear, sparkling, and cool. The most inviting part about this oasis was its water supply, and Aleya took advantage of it.

She walked out of the hut and looked around the oasis. Except for Joseph in the distance, she was alone. Ein Gedi was deserted. Aleya stepped down to the pool underneath the waterfall. Someone had carved the pool out of the rock. *This is definitely for bathing,* she thought. With one last glance around to make sure she was alone, Aleya slipped off her robe and sank into the pool up to her neck.

The cool water wrapped around her body while the warm desert sun, filtered by the trees surrounding the pool, gently heated her face. She lay in the pool, her head resting on a rock, and swished her hands through the clear water. Aleya couldn't remember the last time she felt so clean and free.

She was no longer a slave. That she knew for sure. But what was she? Of course, she was an Arabian noblewoman, the princess royal of the peninsula. But, if she and Joseph never made their way back to her father's kingdom, what kind of princess could she be? Who would know? And, most of all, who would believe her?

She thought she loved Joseph, but she wasn't sure about him. He was always so gruff, so soldier-like, that he was hard to read. And he treated her like a little girl. She became a woman years ago—how many, she wasn't sure. But Joab had celebrated two feasts of the angel passing over his ancestors' houses in Egypt. So, it must be at least two years since she was captured and sold into slavery. The next feast day was not too far off. That meant she must be at least fifteen years old! She would have been married by now, the mistress of her own palace. Maybe, if Almaqah favored her, she would have given her husband a fine son or two or maybe a son for him and a daughter for her.

This is not to be, she thought sadly. *Joseph is a brave man, and I think he loves me, but how can he get me back to my father? All he knows is the Judean wilderness and the path between that miserable Masada and Jerusalem.*

Tears welled in her eyes, and she pushed her face into the pool of water to cover them. She stayed under the water and listened to the rushing water bubble in her ears. When she could no longer hold her breath, she raised her head and looked straight into the face of the *djinni.*

Aleya held her breath and cowered under his gaze. She looked again at the *djinni* and realized he wasn't a desert devil, just a hermit driven mad by living alone in this godforsaken part of the world.

Chapter Twenty-Nine

1991

Jordan was pigheaded. She struggled up the Snake Path to the top of Masada, determined not to fall back on the military transport her Uncle Julian had arranged. Jordan had the same determination of another young woman who had once walked down Masada. Two millennia separated them, but soon their lives would be intertwined. Neither of them would ever imagine what the Fates had woven for them, but Jordan would soon find out.

Ever since her father took her to the excavations on top of the mount when she was a little girl, Jordan had a strange, almost mystical connection to Masada and its history. Now, she was completing a summer internship helping out with the Masada excavations.

Jordan started up the path. If she were to participate in the ongoing excavation of the ruins on Masada then, by God, she was going to walk up the mountain. Those brave Jews who took their lives to avoid capture by the Romans didn't have four-wheel-drive Land Rovers to take them to the top. And neither would she.

Most of the real work had already been completed by famed archaeologist Yigael Yadin and his multinational band of volunteers, but there was still more work to do. Her father, whose first name, coincidentally, was also Yigael, wanted to send her to America to spend the summer with his sister on Long Island. But Jordan would have none of that.

"I have plenty of time, Daddy, to travel the world. But I only have one summer to volunteer at Masada. You know well enough that my next two summers will be spent in the Defense Forces' training camps. How can I be an archaeologist and ignore the opportunity at Masada?"

Of course, her father gave in. All Jordan had to do was turn around and look at him, and his heart would melt. She was the only person in his life. Cancer had taken his beautiful wife despite the best care that modern medicine could provide. The trip to the hospital in New York, underwritten by his wealthy American brother-in-law, had given him some hope.

"Yigael, believe me, Sloan-Kettering is the best cancer hospital in the country. If there's any hope for Ariel, it will be there," Arthur Lieb told him over a bad connection between New York and Jerusalem.

Arthur had sent them two first-class tickets on El Al. Yigael accompanied his weakened wife on the trip. Ariel went to the hospital. Yigael lived with his sister and brother-in-law on Long Island. Arthur ran a wholesale furniture store on Thirty-Fourth Street in New York and was floating in cash. Yigael suspected his brother-in-law did a lot of business off the books. How else did he have enough money to plant an entire forest in Israel in memory of his parents and in-laws?

While he and his wife were in America, Jordan stayed in Israel with Julian Hirschberg, Yigael's old friend from the independence wars. Julian was connected to the Israel Antiquities Authority, like Yigael, but he also had shadowy connections in the Mossad. Jordan's father worried over the influence his old friend had with his young daughter.

Ariel completed her treatment at Sloan-Kettering and returned to Jerusalem a little bit better. She soon turned for the worse. Two months after the trip to New York, Yigael and Jordan buried Ariel. Since then, his beautiful blonde-haired, green-eyed daughter was the only woman in his life. Yigael was determined to protect his little girl like he couldn't protect his wife. No one could guard anyone against the insidious devil of cancer. Yigael knew that. But, against the evils of the world, he would try his best.

When Jordan was little, he would take her out on the balcony of their Jerusalem apartment and tell her about the desert that lay far beyond her vision. And he would tell her stories of the old people, the ones who believed in the *djinn* who lived in the desert.

And, when the Jerusalem sky would darken into night and all he and his daughter could see were the lights of the city below them, he would hold her close, protecting her against the make-believe *djinn*. Only Yigael knew that the *djinn* were real. They weren't mythological monsters preying on little boys and girls in the desert. The real *djinn* were the hateful monsters who wanted to see Israel wiped off the map.

Yigael would sit there on his balcony, holding his little girl and praying silently to himself that someday the real *djinn* would disappear and never affect her life. He never could have anticipated how well his little girl would fight those *djinn*.

Chapter Thirty

74 CE

The *djinni* was silent, not moving, and not scary like the *djinn* of her childhood tales. And the quizzical look on his face calmed Aleya in a strange way. *Maybe he is bewitching me. I must be careful. These* djinn *take human women to their beds and create foul monsters that haunt the travelers of the desert.*

Aleya was so enchanted with this strange man, she forgot she was lying naked in a pool of clear water. She let out a scream that rang across the oasis.

Joseph was making his way back to the camp, arms loaded with vegetables and fruits, when he heard the scream. He dropped everything and ran toward the camp, not knowing where Aleya was or who else was with her. He looked about for horses, camels, anything that would tell him who had invaded the oasis. But he saw nothing.

He ran down to the pool and saw the hermit crouched over Aleya's body. Joseph withdrew his Roman sword and smacked him across the back with the flat of the blade.

"What have you done, old man? By God in heaven, I swear I will kill you if you harmed a single hair on her head."

He rolled on the dirt away from Joseph, cackling and looking at him through crazed eyes. "So, my gallant soldier, you will show your sweet one how brave you are by killing a defenseless old man? Come, run me through with your sword and wipe out my miserable existence on this earth. I have done nothing to the girl. These loins are useless. But, I must admit, I couldn't help but look at such a tasty morsel. So, now, General, what will you do?"

Joseph looked at him, ashamed of what he did and amazed at how much he said. *Perhaps this one isn't as crazy as he looks.*

Aleya draped herself with her robe and arose from the pool of water. She looked at Joseph disapprovingly. "Joseph! Leave him be. He did nothing but look at me. How many times have I caught you doing the same thing, sneaking around when I was refreshing myself by the spring?"

Joseph looked away, embarrassed that he had been caught.

"Let's share some of our food with him and find out who he is. He may be able to help us find a caravan to get back to Jerusalem. It's obvious that he lives here depending on the generosity of the caravan masters who pass through this oasis."

The old man rocked back on his haunches, listening to the two young people, examining them through rheumy eyes dulled by age and living alone. "Well spoken, my princess. I am Ezekiel. I do live here. I am hungry. Will you feed me?"

The embers of the fire glowed red, the same color as the sun's rays reflecting off the Judean hills in the distance. Aleya got up and cleared the bowls that held the evening's supper. They had no meat, just boiled barley, fruits, and vegetables that Joseph scavenged from the fields and salt scraped from the rocks in the oasis. They drank the cool water that was a blessing from God for the poor travelers in the Judean wilderness.

While Aleya put away the bowls they found in the hut, the two men sat around the fire not speaking, but thinking deeply of what they were going to say. The hardest part of the evening was how to begin the conversation, the real conversation, that is, the one that would reveal who Ezekiel was, and in return, the one that would reveal the true mission of Joseph and Aleya.

Aleya returned to the campfire and eyed the old man. He was strange looking, like the desert hermits Joab spoke of. His hair was white and scraggly. His back was stooped like a cave dweller. When he spoke, his voice was raspy and set her teeth on edge. But his eyes! His eyes reflected the light of the fire and sparkled with knowledge so deep that she doubted few men even knew what he was thinking. She kept on looking at him but dared not break their silence to ask questions.

No one spoke. The fire crackled, and the evening sky deepened from crimson to purple to black. Still no one spoke. All three sat around the fire, looking into the coals as if the answers to the questions in their lives danced in the small flames that hovered above the dying embers.

Ezekiel began crooning a strange song in a different tongue that sounded like Hebrew but barely. Its tones and melodies reminded Joseph of the prayer-songs the temple priests chanted.

He said nothing. He just kept rocking back and forth, singing the mindless song in a low monotone.

Aleya stared at him with just the barest hint of recognition in her eyes. And then, from nowhere or from somewhere in her past, she sang the melody that Ezekiel hummed to himself. In the dark of the night, around the dim, reddish glow of the dying fire, words began to flood her memory. She mumbled them and rhymed them with the melody. Ezekiel glanced at her, smiled, and began to fit his own words to the tune. Joseph sat and wondered what was going on.

Together, he and Aleya began singing a childish rhyme in simple sing-song melody. Aleya's face glowed in recognition until it looked like her cheeks were about to burst.

"So, my little princess, you know the lullaby?"

A lullaby, Aleya thought. This crazy hermit chanted words and a song from her childhood when she nestled in her nurse's arms in her father's palace. That's what was so familiar about the tune Ezekiel sang. *But how did this desert dweller come to know a lullaby sung in the palace of the great Arabian king?*

"Oh, Ezekiel, you crazed old fool. Yes, I know that song. It is a lullaby my nurse would sing to me. How is it that you know the song as well? Did you pick it up from some caravan from the south? And why is it you keep on calling me 'princess'?"

"Joseph," Ezekiel said, "put more wood on the fire. I have a story to tell you two, a story that I haven't told in a long time."

Joseph jumped up and gathered wood. He threw the wood in the fire pit, and the flames blazed. The burning tongues of fire illuminated the faces of Aleya and Ezekiel. And, strangely, the old man neither looked crazed nor half-mad. It were as if the presence of Aleya breathed life into him and gave new meaning to his solitary existence in Ein Gedi.

"Sit down and listen. If you want to help this young woman, pay heed to what I say," Ezekiel said in a voice stronger than he used since Joseph and Aleya met him.

"My name is Ezekiel ben Mizrah, and I was a trader to the kings. Every two years, I would make the sixty-five passages between Judea and the land to the south, which the Romans call *Arabia Felix*. I would bring the treasures of Judea on the backs of great strings of camels in a caravan that stretched for many paces.

"Our first stop out of Jerusalem was always Ein Gedi. And when the caravan of Ezekiel made its stop here at Ein Gedi, it was a feast day for all who rested here. Indeed, it had become a fair, the first place where I traded some of my goods for the luscious dates, news, and comely women who always flitted about this place.

"Most important to me was the news of the desert. I was trading in the rarest of jewels, commodities more precious than gold, goods desired by kings and queens all over the empire. I was a dealer in frankincense and myrrh, the largest and most prosperous merchant in all of Judea.

"My life was the desert, the caravan, the stink and cries of the camels, and mysterious meetings with those outcast Arabs, the Bedouin. Year after year, I would go south with my treasures from Judea and from all over the Mediterranean and return north with saddlebags bursting with the precious spices, oils, and incenses from the mysterious south. I never had time for a family. There was no one back for me in Jerusalem. My only family were those I would meet each year in the caravans, hopping from one oasis to the other, and the petty nobles from the southern kingdoms who were authorized to trade in the king's commodities—the sweet-smelling resin from the myrrh tree and the frankincense they created.

"The peoples of the south do not trust us in the north, though it is said we come from the same ancestors, dividing into two peoples at the time when the wadis flowed with clear water and lakes irrigated the thirsty land—long before this peninsula became a desert. No one knows what happened or when this land died and the waters went away. But ever since, we have become as two different peoples with different customs, languages, and gods.

"I traded with them for over ten years before I received an invitation to the king's palace. It seems His Majesty had a few thoughts in mind for greater trade between the north and the south. His navy had opened new trade routes down the coast of Africa, way past Egypt and to the east where the people look like us but have dark-colored skin. They had little use for the spices and oils of the southern desert but greatly desired the goods from the Roman Empire. The king thought that I could help in securing a favorable trading agreement between him and the Mediterranean merchants.

"I asked for time to think about it and would come back next year with an answer. It is not easy to set up another trading agreement. There are schedules, shipping, delivery points between the sea coast and the inland ports, assembling caravans, hiring reliable caravan masters, and the list goes on. I knew that if I opened this route, I would become the richest merchant in the entire desert.

"But I also knew that the peoples of the southern kingdoms were treacherous. I needed time to talk this over with my merchant friends in Jerusalem, especially my good friend Joab."

Aleya cried out when she heard Joab's name. "Ezekiel, you knew a merchant by the name of Joab? Was this Joab your age?"

"Are you asking me if this Joab is a beaten-down old man like me? The answer is yes. But I don't think you'll ever find him in any bazaar or marketplace. Some years back, he joined the Zealots on top of Masada, and you know what happened there."

Aleya looked at Ezekiel quizzically since Joseph had bundled her away from Masada before she learned the entire truth about the massacre. Neither she nor Joseph ever told the old man that they had come from Masada. For all they knew, Ezekiel probably thought they were just desert travelers from the nearby town of Jericho. But Ezekiel knew a lot more than either suspected.

"Surely, Joseph, you learned about the Roman massacre on top of the mount. You used to travel back and forth between Masada and Jerusalem. Tell me, did you two leave before or escape after the Romans had their way with our people on Masada?"

Joseph looked at Ezekiel in amazement. *How could he know what happened on Masada just days ago? And how did he know I would stop at Ein Gedi on my missions for Eleazar?*

"For a desert dweller, Ezekiel, you seem to know a lot more than you should. Tell me, how did you get the story about Masada?"

Ezekiel repeated what he had heard about the massacre on the mount of Masada. He declined to reveal his sources, saying that the oasis was a fount of knowledge for those who look. Ezekiel's account of the Masada massacre reflected what the Jewish community believed for years. After no Jew came down from Masada following the Roman assault, the Jews believed the worst. There were no Jewish survivors, it was believed, so the Jews naturally assumed it was a Roman army massacre.

Joseph chose not to correct Ezekiel's version of the Masada story. Nor would he confirm the starting point of their journey. *The less that is known about my connection to Masada, the better it is for me.*

Ezekiel didn't press Joseph for more information and returned to his story. Before he would start, however, he asked Aleya about Joab. "Tell me, little one, you know Joab. How did you come by his acquaintance?"

Aleya regarded him with a guarded expression. "Yes, I knew him quite well. He bought me in slavery and treated me like his own granddaughter. He was a famous merchant, and he said he moved to Masada to atone for his sins. I could never understand what sins he was talking about. To me, he was a kindly old gentleman. I loved him," Aleya sniffed.

"You were a slave? How did that happen?"

"I will tell you everything. The retelling of my capture and slavery pains Joseph. So, please, Ezekiel, let me reserve my story for the morrow. For now, we both want you to continue yours."

"Very well, I shall continue. It is difficult for me to recall everything. This happened many, many years ago, when that sexual deviant, Caligula, assumed the imperial purple. But I remember very clearly how it started. I returned to Jerusalem and conferred with Joab. We agreed to go ahead with the plan proposed by a petty noble of the southern kingdom. Joab would serve as the merchant master in Jerusalem, and I would be the caravan master and chief trader. Even as a young man, Joab had no taste for adventure.

"We already had established a brisk and prosperous trade between Jerusalem and Caesarea and imported the treasures of the western empire to the east. Roman glass had established a reputation as the best in the world. The Romans also controlled the world's grain production.

"Joab and I would act as middle men in the trade, arranging for the purchase and transportation of the Roman goods to the southern kingdoms. In return, we could bring frankincense and myrrh to the west more cheaply and more reliably than the seafaring merchants. They typically lost half their cargo between the Red Sea and the Mediterranean to pirates, weather, and other unforeseen circumstances.

"To cover their losses, these merchants would double the price of the frankincense and myrrh. And people gladly paid the price. Joab and I were beside ourselves, thinking about the money we would make and how we would grow into the empire's most important merchants.

"In late winter, I prepared for my first trip. I knew it would take me a year because the trip through the desert was described as being one of 'sixty-five passages.' I inquired what this meant and was told that it signified the number of stops a caravan would make along the entire trading route.

"Joab and I worked feverishly to put together a caravan. No one could know the purpose of the trip. That's because no trader in Judea ever imported frankincense and myrrh in the quantities we were considering. It was an exciting and heady time. Both of us were young, and all we could count were our riches. The hardship meant nothing to us.

"I was the caravan master. We neither bought camels nor hired men in Jerusalem. That's how great our secrecy was. I was to meet with the Bedouin a month outside Jerusalem and set up the caravan. Those savages cared nothing for trade. But they knew camels, and they knew how to sell protection. We were making a deal with the devil but for a devil's ransom!

"The day of my departure finally came. I was excited as we set off that morning. Little did I know that it would be my last trip as a free man.

"The first part of the trip was normal. I followed the usual route I had taken many times in the past. However, after two months' passage, I found myself in completely unfamiliar territory. The great desert, what the southern peoples call the 'Empty Quarter,' loomed ahead of us. I questioned how we were ever to cross that wasteland. But cross we did. Then, little by little, the country began to change.

"We came to the places of the black waters. The superstitious peoples say the black waters were a creation of the desert devils. I think—like sulfur and other minerals beneath the earth—the black waters, too, are a kind of mineral that seeps to the surface. There is nothing supernatural about them. But what their use is, I could never figure out.

"We continued to travel south. I was told that to the east and south of me were the great waters that offered a route around the world. Not knowing anything about the southern seas, I dismissed these tales as campfire gossip and a joke on me, the neophyte trader.

"After many months, we came to a great walled city that shone in the desert like a magic palace. It rose out of the desert as if placed there by the hand of God. If you think Jerusalem is a great and beautiful city, you should see this place!

"Its walls were blazingly white, and surrounding it were the lushest gardens I had ever seen. I wondered, if the gardens outside the walls were this magnificent, what possibly could the gardens inside be like?

"The caravan made its way to the city gates. A palace functionary, who told us to wait outside, greeted us. He refused us permission to enter the gates. He guided us to a city of tents outside the walls and treated us well.

"This tent city housed peoples from all over. There were the deep black princes from the lands below Egypt. Darker-skinned people, who looked like us in every form except skin color, sat in front of their tents festooned with precious and colorful silks. They wrapped cloths around their heads and decorated them with precious jewels. Never before had I ever seen such an abundance of wealth and treasure in a bazaar! Joab and I were truly going to become rich.

"Every day we had our pick of magnificent fruits, tasty vegetables, fresh lamb, and beautiful women. There was nothing for me to want, except to get inside the walls and begin trading."

The old *djinni* sat back and recalled that fateful day.

"Close to our tents was a bathing house, maintained outside the city expressly for use by the women of the royal family. The king's own soldiers guarded it, and a wall surrounded the interior courtyard. Each day, a long and beautifully attired procession would take place. The city's gates would open, and the procession would emerge. A bejeweled litter, carried by the largest men I had ever seen, would make its way inside the walls of the bathhouse.

"This took place for a few weeks. Finally, curiosity got the better of me. I know the time because I was keeping a calendar to determine how long it would take for an audience inside the palace. Despite the wonderful treatment we received, I was getting bored and restless, aiming to get about my business. I casually asked a guard the name of the woman in the litter. I knew it must be the wife of a high-ranking official. I thought if I got to know her, she would speak favorably for me at the king's court. So, I approached a guard who accompanied the litter.

"'Do not concern yourself with the royal palace, foreigner,' the guard warned me. He seemed to be annoyed at my questions."

"What happened, then?"

"I pressed him again for an answer. And he told me. Alas, I wish he didn't. 'Foreigner,' the guard said, 'the litter holds the high priestess of the women's temple. In three passages of the moon, she is to be wed to the young king. The family of the royal palace is of no concern to you. Now, go off and be away with you!'

"Nonetheless, I was determined to talk to the royal lady, still hoping she could advance my case with the king. I had purchased a slave from the Bedouin, one of those dark-skinned peoples from below Egypt. The slave knew I would free him when we returned to Jerusalem. This was his reward for his loyalty.

"The slave's name was Orshu'u. He resembled the men carrying the litter. I asked him if they were his countrymen. 'Yes, they are, Master. These desert devils raid my country and enslave the youngest and strongest people from our cities. What do you wish with me, Master?'

"I explained my plan, reminding him the quicker we returned to Jerusalem, the sooner he would be a free man. I even hinted I would make him a caravan master and share our wealth with him. Believe me, young people, I would have done so if I had succeeded. I do not believe in slavery.

"The next night, Orshu'u slipped out of our tent city and made his way to the palace walls. He pretended to be a bathhouse slave sent to the city for more supplies. The guards, who consider a slave to be no better than the king's dogs, let him in.

"Once inside, Orshu'u made his way to the slave quarters and found his countrymen gathered around a cook fire. He arranged for one of them to take ill the next day and asked to be his replacement. Now, this was going to cost me. I told Orshu'u to promise this fellow that I would buy him from the king and set him free once we got back to Jerusalem.

"Orshu'u stayed in the palace. The next day, when the procession emerged from the city gates, there was Orshu'u, shouldering the litter like we had planned. As the litter was passing our tent city, my faithful servant cried out in a loud voice and seemed to stumble. The other slaves, terrified for their lives, set the litter down gently, lest they disturb the royal woman inside.

"I rushed over to help. Before the guards could turn me aside, I saw the woman. She was the most beautiful woman I ever laid eyes on. Now I understand why David would turn aside his wife and kill his best commander, so that he could possess Bathsheba. Our queen, David's new wife, who bore us our good King Solomon, came from these lands. Our books tell us that Bathsheba was the most beautiful woman in David's kingdom. I believe it now after I saw the woman in that litter."

Ezekiel leaned back from the fire and exhaled a tired breath through his nose. He stretched his back and leaned over for the jug of wine near the fire. The wine was his present to Joseph and Aleya. He knew where the Zealots had stored the wine. Joseph knew it was in one of the caves by the field, but the exact location remained in Ezekiel's head. He took a sip, swirled the liquid around his mouth, and spoke to them.

"Young people, it is getting late, and there is so much more to tell. Let an old man rest. May I stay here tonight? This hut is certainly better than the goat-skin tent of mine," Ezekiel remarked.

"Yes. You have enchanted us with your stories of a fabulous kingdom in the south. Rest well and continue in the morning."

Chapter Thirty-One

1991

"Oh, shit!" Jordan screamed. Her shin hit a rock on the path up Masada, and she fell. The loose rock provided little footing, and she started to slide down the mountain. She braced her Eddie Bauer hiking boots into the dirt to stop her fall. *I wonder how many women fell down this damn path like me,* she thought, pulling herself back up the path.

Jordan was in the middle of the Judean wilderness, and there was no one to hear her profanity. She never used words like that in front of her father. He would not permit it.

She dusted off her hands and began her ascent, looking up the five hundred meters she still had to climb. Behind her, she heard a slight scuffle.

"May I help a damsel in distress?"

Jordan turned and saw a man about five meters behind her.

"I'll be glad to assist you up the mountain, though I must say, I enjoy the view from back here." The young man grinned foolishly and held out a canteen.

Jordan shot him a look that clearly said she had no time for stupid college boys telegraphing sexual innuendoes. "I'm quite fine, thank you. Why are you following me?"

"I'm not following you, miss. I'm on my way to volunteer at the Masada excavation and thought I should walk up the mountain instead of taking those air-conditioned tourist buses your army provides."

"My army? What about your army? You look like you're from here. Are you one of those horny soldiers looking to pick up women trekking around your country in search of adventure?"

Daniel's swarthy Middle Eastern looks, a gift from his Lebanese ancestors, resembled the young men serving in the army. It wasn't too much of a leap for Jordan to make that comment because she really didn't look closely at him…at first.

"Well, I'm sort of from here. And I assure you I am not a 'horny soldier.' Your words, not mine. I am an American. I'm a student in Atlanta. But I am from the Middle East—Lebanon. Rumor has it my family's descended from the Bedouin. Somehow, their camels led them into Lebanon where they put down roots and gave up their nomadic ways. I'm in Israel this summer to study languages and thought I should volunteer at Masada."

Jordan looked at him. He was gorgeous, like a young desert sheik. "Well, Mr. American, if you can stop staring at my butt, you can help me get up this mountain."

"Certainly, my beautiful lady. By the way, my name is Daniel."

Chapter Thirty-Two

74 CE

Ezekiel scuttled off to a corner of the hut and lay down. The desert cold worked its way into the hut. The dying fire warmed the air, giving the small hut a feeling of comfort. Joseph and Aleya arose and walked outside, each alone in their thoughts. Joseph was troubled. Could it be that his Aleya was speaking the truth when she described a magical palace in the south? Ezekiel kept calling her "princess." Why?

While Joseph walked by Aleya's side, she too had thoughts to herself, but she could not contain them. "Joseph, if Ezekiel is telling the truth, can you now believe who I am? My love, I know you doubted me since the day you came into Joab's tent. How could a slave girl be the princess of a powerful kingdom, you thought. But I loved you nonetheless. Please, bring me home!"

They walked back to their sleeping hut. Joseph spread his cloak on the rough bed left by past visitors. He held his love and rocked her in his arms until she fell asleep. Then he crawled to his own bed.

Joseph awoke to the smell of porridge cooking over a fire. He looked up from his crude rope bed and saw Ezekiel squatting over a pot, stirring something with a large stick. On the other side of the hut in her own rope bed lay the sleeping form of Aleya. Neither the smell of Ezekiel's cooking nor Joseph's restless stirring had awakened her. Ezekiel looked at Joseph and wordlessly motioned to him.

"So, you and the woman sleep together but separately? Come. Let's walk away and let the princess sleep."

"She is not what you think. We are traveling together, and I have pledged to return her to her father."

"Yes, quite so. But, still, you do not touch her. She is a slave, isn't she?" Ezekiel challenged him.

"She isn't what you think she is. She lived with Joab who treated her like his granddaughter. And I, well, I..." Joseph's voice trailed off.

"My young friend, I think I know very well what she is. It is you who does not know. Let us break the night's fast. I have prepared porridge sweetened with fruits from the orchards."

Ezekiel and Joseph walked back into the hut to be greeted by a strange sight. There was Aleya, busily stirring the porridge.

"There you are! You men. You think you can put a pot on the fire and walk away? What were you going to do, scrape the burnt porridge out with your knives? Come here and sit down. It's almost ready."

As hard as she tried to sound like a scold, there was a musical lilt to Aleya's voice. It was as if a burden had been lifted from her heart. Her disposition matched the beautiful day that had dawned.

The three of them sat down to a bowl of porridge, slaking their thirst with water that was mixed with wine. "Tell me, Ezekiel, if you know, why do we add wine to our water? It was not done so in my father's palace."

"Adding wine to water is a custom in the towns and great cities in the empire. If you drink the water directly pulled from the well, then you would get a terrible stomach sickness. Mixing wine in the water purifies it. Wherever I traveled and wherever there was a large amount of people living together, the water was always foul. So it was mixed with wine. It is a strange thing. Too much wine can make you sicker than water ever will, but just the right amount keeps you from getting sick.

"Now, I never experienced this problem in the desert. The water was always pure, sweet-tasting, and healthful. There were also very few people around to draw the water. That's why I think too many people make the water bad. How they do it, I do not know."

"Ezekiel, you promised last night to finish your tale. Aleya and I must make it to Jerusalem and find a caravan that will take us south. Please finish your story so we can be on our way."

"Very well. Where did I leave off?" Ezekiel said, glancing at the beautiful face of Aleya. "Ah, yes, the story of Bathsheba.

"So, I rushed to the falling litter to help and see the woman inside. One of the guards quickly fastened the curtain and drove me back with his whip. Believe me, those gilded whips they carried were not ceremonial. I retreated but not until I saw the beating Orshu'u was taking. I feared for his life," Ezekiel recounted.

"I was a few paces away when the curtains of the litter parted, and the woman commanded the guards to stop. I couldn't hear what she said, but I caught a glimpse of her face. I truly thought the king had captured an angel who fell to earth.

"Her skin was golden brown, and her hair was the deep rich color of last year's honey. Her eyes were the most beautiful I had ever seen. They were slightly upturned at the corner and colored a bewitching greenish-brown."

Ezekiel stopped to catch his breath. He looked over to Joseph who remained sitting around the fire, his eyes locked in Aleya's direction. Joseph was obviously studying Aleya's face while listening to the old man. Ezekiel said nothing and continued the tale of his life.

"The guards drove me away. I saw them taking a slave's still body back into the city. I returned to my tent.

"That night, something most unusual occurred. The city gates opened, and the guards threw out a sack. I and a few other merchants ran over to investigate. When I saw blood oozing through the cloth, I feared the worst. I pulled my dagger out and cut through the cloth.

"Inside was the beaten and almost-lifeless body of Orshu'u. He looked up at me and tried to smile. He said, 'Death will soon set me free. But you promised. You owe freedom to my kinsman who is still inside the king's slave quarters.' He died before telling me the man's name. I promised Orshu'u's memory that I would buy his countryman from the king's slave master and make him a free man.

"Now, more than ever, I was determined to get inside the city gates. But I still had to wait. We had been there for one full passage of the moon. I was getting restless. I wanted to forget about the woman and my promise. At that time, trading with the southern kingdoms didn't seem as good an idea as it did in Jerusalem.

"The king's vizier, Narif al-Sharah, learned through his spies that we were getting so impatient that many of us were preparing to leave. A few days later, another procession emerged from the city gates in the afternoon and made its way to our humble tent city. It was the vizier. He ordered us to prepare to meet with the king that very moment.

"I and a few others started to protest. The vizier made it plain that if we wished to see the king, it must be that afternoon. We prepared to join the vizier's procession, taking nothing with us except some small gifts for the royal family.

"I joined the procession when, all of a sudden, the vizier approached me. 'You are the merchant from the north? We welcome you, but take care of where your eyes rest.' I knew what he meant, but I refused to recognize it. I bowed slightly as he walked to his litter."

Ezekiel switched back to the present. "Excuse me, but porridge does not stay long in an old man's stomach," Ezekiel said as he rushed out of the hut into the bushes some distance away.

Joseph and Aleya looked at each other, wondering whether to believe what he was saying. Aleya was the first to break the silence.

"Do you think Ezekiel is telling the truth? I mean, well, you know, he doesn't look like a prosperous merchant. And, if he knew Joab, why didn't Joab say anything about him?"

Joseph sat in silence, waiting to reply. "I am not certain whether he knows what is truth and what is fiction. He has lived so long in this desert, alone, with no one to talk to. I think that these past two days have given him more companionship than he has enjoyed in years. Even if he is weaving a tale, he is a good storyteller. Shh, be quiet. Here he comes."

"Aaah, thank God my bowels still work. There's nothing better in the morn—"

"Ezekiel," Aleya chided, cutting him off in mid-sentence, "I'd prefer to hear more about your life than about your bowels. Please continue."

Ezekiel, mildly amused by the imperious tone of Aleya's voice, bowed to her and said, "As you wish, my lady.

"We entered the city through the massive gates. It was magnificent. Fountains and pools were everywhere. People lived in many-level buildings like the tenements in Rome. But much nicer. I swear they must have captured an entire river for the king's pleasure and changed its course so it ran through his city. Never have I seen a more beautiful and enjoyable place.

"We walked through the city and came upon the great square. At one end was this enormous building. I took it to be the palace of the king. In the middle of the square was this huge fountain which was illuminated at night by hundreds of oil-burning lamps. We strode past the fountain into a great hall of the palace. The light in the hall was very even, very soft, with none of the harshness of the desert sun but very bright. I did not know how the king's architects accomplished this until I looked overhead. The roof consisted of many panels..."

"...made up of a translucent mineral that let in the light," Aleya said, finishing the sentence for Ezekiel with her own words. She shrieked and jumped up and began hugging Ezekiel for all the old man was worth.

"Oh, Ezekiel, you are a gift from the gods. You are describing my home. You see, Joseph, I was telling the truth. Ezekiel has seen where I am from. It is no false story. Oh, thank you, Ezekiel. Thank you."

Joseph stood up abruptly and left the hut. Ezekiel followed him while Aleya just sat by the morning fire and stared into the glowing coals. She had a dreamy smile on her face.

"Joseph, listen to me," Ezekiel said.

"Leave me alone. You fill Aleya's head with fantastic stories, build up her hopes, and then leave. What am I left with but a disappointed girl? I'm telling Aleya to gather her things. We're leaving now," Joseph yelled.

"Patience, young man. I counsel you patience. Let me finish telling my story. I haven't told it for so many years to people who were willing to listen. Besides, you need my help in getting the right caravan to take Aleya back home."

Joseph still sulked near the edge of the pool, trying to shut out Ezekiel's words.

"What are you worried about? That she is a princess and that you will lose her? You have never told her that you want her. More likely, she was the bastard of a palace official. I remember there were hundreds of children running around the king's court in the old days. I don't think the king would let his royal children play with the offspring of the palace slaves. Come back inside with me. I'll finish soon, and you can be off," Ezekiel counseled Joseph.

"Now, I will finish my tale, and you will find out how I became the ghost of Ein Gedi.

"The king had agreed to see us. The vizier sent his slaves to greet us in the great hall and escort us into the presence of the king. All of us walked forward with visions of gold dancing in our heads. Trade with this rich kingdom would make us wealthy. I also had hoped to see the priestess again.

"We entered the royal chamber. The king sat on immense pillows woven of the finest silk. The floors had carpets as soft as a newborn lamb. The oil lamps burned brightly—with what, I did not know, for surely I have never seen our oil lamps burn as brightly. There, to his right, just below the pillowed platform on which he sat, stood the priestess.

"She was more beautiful in person than I could have imagined. The blood boiled in my young veins, and I could think of nothing—no trade, no incense, nothing—except her.

"The vizier's guard came behind me and prodded me to the front of the merchants. To the left stood the vizier, visibly annoyed. He knew what I was doing. He whispered into the king's ear. The king nodded and waved me away. My audience lasted all of a few breaths, but it could have been a lifetime to me, so dazzled was I by the beauty of the untouchable woman.

"'Merchant, we are interested in what you have to trade,' said the vizier. 'The pirates raid our ships, and we lose our cargo. Perhaps you will be luckier. But, merchant, not everything is to trade. Some things are forbidden, even to me,' the vizier cautioned.

"I returned to the tent city, determined to meet her face-to-face. Oh, I knew she wanted nothing of me—she was the king's betrothed. But I did catch her looking back at me. So I was emboldened and prepared a plan. But I needed someone inside the city to help. I thought about it and knew who I would pick: the countryman of Orshu'u.

"The following day the procession left the gates, making its way to the bathhouse. I approached the guards and said I wished to speak to one of the litter-bearers because his countryman, my slave, requested I give his meager possessions to the palace slave.

"The guard listened closely. Our languages were similar enough that he could understand me, barely. Just then, the curtains of the litter parted, and I saw the face of my angel. In a melodious, twinkling voice, the priestess let the slave meet me. 'Guard,' she said, 'let Obabe'e go to the merchant's tent tonight. He'll be back. There's nothing there for him.'

"I thanked her and walked away, my face never leaving the ground and my back never turning to her. Once the procession was inside the bathhouse, I practically ran back to my tent, leaping with joy. I now could follow through on my plan to see her.

"Later that evening, before the moon rose in the sky to spread her light, the city gates opened. Through them walked a single man with no weapons, no companions, just he alone. He walked to our tent city.

"'I have come to speak to the one who was with my brother, Orshu'u,' he told the first merchant he could find. The merchant brought the palace slave to me.

"As I recall, the slave entered my tent and announced his name. 'I am Obabe'e, prince-brother to Orshu'u. You have something for me,' he said. I motioned for him to come closer and unfolded my plot to get into the palace. I promised him his freedom for just a closer look at the priestess.

"'I have nothing to lose, merchant, in assisting you in your quest. I will take you to the palace tonight. I will say to the guards at the women's quarters that you are a slave offered to the vizier by the other merchants as a gift. The vizier will not be involved. He will not see you.'

"Obabe'e revealed his plan to me. 'We shall not be stopped. The guards let me come and go freely since the vizier's physician has made me a half-man—no threat to the women of the palace. We will make our way through the halls of the women's palace, looking for the physician. The guards will know why we are there. As you pass, they will hold their loincloths in sympathy, wondering why a man would trade his manhood for a life as a slave in the palace harem, no matter how easy his life would become. You and I are slaves. We mean nothing to them. And we trade our most precious gift for a life of ease.'

"I recall the looks the palace guards gave me as I walked down the halls with the half-man, Obabe'e, averting his eyes from the pity radiating from theirs. I had not intended to stay long enough for the physician to get near me. I looked at Obabe'e. I had heard of such half-men but never met one. He looked fine to me, though his loincloth was a bit loose.

"Everything went well. We went through the gates. The guard admitted us to the women-house. Obabe'e went to summon the physician, and I snuck through the rooms, looking for my angel. I turned the corner of one hall, and there she was, sitting on a mound of pillows, having her hair dressed.

"She took one look at me; I looked at her, and it was clear she was inviting me closer. I took two steps when I was forcefully grabbed from behind and thrown to the floor. I looked up; two palace guards and the vizier flanked Obabe'e, who was held in a tight grip by two more guards.

"The vizier ordered the guards to take us out of the women-house. 'Place them in the guard house. I'll deal with them in the morning.' Obabe'e and I were thrown into a dungeon to await our fate the next day."

"Ezekiel, will you finish this tale soon?" Joseph asked impatiently. "Aleya and I cannot waste any more time here."

"Joseph," Aleya implored, "let him finish. I want to hear what happened."

"There's not much more to tell. But, Joseph, I suspect you should listen closely. There is a lesson in my tale for you," Ezekiel warned.

"I remember vividly what happened the next day. The moon had yet to set, and the Dog Star shone brightly. Two guards came to the dungeon and dragged us into the vizier's court. To this day, I will never forget what he said or did," Ezekiel said, describing how he met his fate.

"'So, merchant, you were warned. You were told some goods were forbidden, but you did not listen. You wish to be close to the priestess. You shall. You wish to trade frankincense and myrrh. You shall. Guard, take these two to the dungeon. Tell the master there he has two new galley slaves for his trading vessels,' the vizier said and turned away.

"The king's soldiers marched dozens of criminals to the coast. Only Obabe'e and I survived the journey. For the next fifteen years, longer than anyone thought, Obabe'e and I worked as slaves on the king's vessels. We rowed his frankincense and myrrh up the Red Sea, pulled his ships through the canal, sailed around Africa to Egypt and across the Mediterranean. I grew stronger and morose. Obabe'e grew more silent and sullen. We were a perfect pair.

"You may be wondering how I got to my home in Judea and eventually to this oasis. On what was to be my last voyage on the king's galleys, a great sickness afflicted the entire fleet. There were four trading vessels. We anchored outside Caesarea, the new port Herod was building, and asked for help.

"The harbormaster refused to help. Obabe'e had collapsed, and I was near death. The captain of the galley had no need for dying slaves, so he threw us both overboard. By some miracle, we made it to shore, and I nursed both of us back to health.

"Obabe'e and I, our health restored, begged our way onto a caravan heading west and south. I knew there was nothing in Jerusalem, so I looked for a trading group headed past this oasis. When we got here, we ran away and hid in the hills. Since we were neither slaves nor hired help, the caravan master cared not that we were gone and left us behind. I have lived here ever since."

"That was a wonderful story," Joseph said sarcastically. "Aleya, let us prepare ourselves to leave. Ezekiel, I will come back shortly. Please tell me whom I should see in Jerusalem to find a caravan. That's the least you can do for making me sit through two days of tall tales."

"That I will, my son."

Aleya got up as well, but before she left, she asked Ezekiel where Obabe'e was. "He is still with me. And I fear we shall always be together. As you pass through Ein Gedi on your way out, you will see a crude tomb hewn out of the soft rock. That is where my friend of these past decades now sleeps and where I shall soon join him."

"How sweet and touching, Ezekiel. I shall never forget you," Aleya said, bending over to kiss the old man's forehead.

Before Aleya could straighten up, Ezekiel grabbed her hand and pulled her ear close to his mouth. "Aleya, my dear, that woman I loved—she was your grandmother."

Chapter Thirty-Three

The light from the desert sun shimmered on the calm surface of the Dead Sea as Joseph and Aleya readied their belongings for their trek to Jerusalem. "I shall miss you, Ezekiel. Thank you for everything, especially your stories."

Joseph was more circumspect. He still didn't know whether to believe the old man's stories. Images of a shimmering, white palace amidst the sands of the desert danced in Joseph's mind. *Was Ezekiel telling the truth or just humoring two weary desert travelers? I shall find out.*

Joseph leaned over and clasped Ezekiel in a hug. "Pray for us, old man. We shan't be seeing you again."

With Ezekiel's unspoken blessing, Joseph and Aleya began their walk to Jerusalem. "Remember, when you get to Jerusalem, seek out the house of Joab. You will find what you need there."

They pushed through the bushes surrounding the pool. Ezekiel, firmly planted in the place where he would spend the rest of his diminishing life, cried after them. "Stay well, my young people, and may God go with you." He murmured his blessing once more, losing sight of the couple as they crossed over a hill.

Joseph and Aleya walked silently out of the oasis. What they had learned from Ezekiel weighed heavily on both of their minds. Joseph—still unsure about Ezekiel's revelations about a desert kingdom—looked at Aleya, wondering what he was going to do. They began their journey to Jerusalem.

Neither Joseph nor Aleya had heard any news of Jerusalem or, for that matter, what was happening in Judea. Isolated on the mount of Masada, they had lived day-to-day. For his part, Joseph feared the worst. He knew the Romans occupied Jerusalem and had destroyed the temple. He suspected there was an exodus from the city by those Jews who wished no more of the incessant battles with the Roman Empire. But he hoped in his heart that some courageous Jews would make a stand against the mighty Tenth Legion. He swore that he would join the rebels as soon as he could.

The Romans had built two good roads from the shores of the Dead Sea to the hills of Jerusalem and Hebron to facilitate trade between the Dead Sea region and the northern cities of Judea. The Roman engineers had built their solid, paved roads on what had been ancient paths used by merchants and traders for several thousand years. Dusty paths were fine for merchants and caravans but not for the hobnailed sandals of the Roman legionary and his war machines.

Normally, Joseph avoided these roads. When Joseph was ferrying messages between Masada and Jerusalem, it would take him the better part of two nights to make the trip. He had to be careful, and he spent many hours waiting by the side of the road for other travelers to pass. Now that he and Aleya were making the trip as ordinary travelers, he had hoped to make it to Jerusalem by nightfall. He didn't worry about Roman patrols. The soldiers were too busy fortifying Titus's soldiers at Masada and keeping down the ongoing insurrection in the city. Any soldiers they would meet would surely be in a hurry to pass them.

Aleya and Joseph fell into a rhythm that would bring them to the gates of Jerusalem before the moon rose. The trip bored Joseph. There was none of the excitement or danger he experienced on his missions from Masada. There was no need to hide from anyone or worry about capture. The road was empty. No travelers, no soldiers, no merchants—no one was on the road. The road was built high in the hills above the Dead Sea. Joseph and Aleya had walked for half of a day when Aleya begged him to stop.

"Joseph, I have been a maidservant to an old man these past years. I do not have the stamina to keep on walking. Let's rest here for a bit." Joseph agreed and trundled off the road to a shady part of the hills. "Where are we? How much longer will it take to get to Jerusalem?"

Joseph knew exactly where they were. High above them, farther up the hills, was the encampment of a strange sect who called themselves the Qumran community. Joseph had once sought refuge with them. He had left after finding their rules too restrictive.

The members of the community walked around with white robes they would don after a ritual purification in a central bath. The inhabitants split themselves into two groups: workers and worshippers. The workers maintained the life of the community, doing the ordinary things that people need to live. The worshippers sat at the feet of their leader, whom they called the "Teacher of Righteousness." The community's scriptorium was always busy with copyists scratching the words of the teacher onto parchment scrolls. The chief librarian of the community stored the scrolls in the many caves that dotted the hillsides above the Dead Sea. They followed an extreme sort of Judaism that Joseph had no sympathy for. He often wondered how long it would take them to disappear from the map of history like all the other sects that arose in Judea following the Roman occupation.

As they rested in the shade, Aleya looked over her shoulder and noticed smoke rising from the top of the hills. "Joseph, there must be people up there. Let's find refuge with them. I am so tired."

"They are strange people. And you would not be welcome there. Few women, and no pagans, are allowed within their camps. I know them. They have left Jerusalem to practice, what they say, is a purer form of the Torah. They spend their days praying and working at the simple tasks of keeping the community alive. They do not welcome travelers. Rest here a little bit more, then we'll continue on our way to Jerusalem."

The two travelers rested their heads against the cool rock and sat silently. "Aleya, the sun is past midday, and we must make it into Jerusalem before nightfall." Aleya rose wearily and walked with Joseph back to the Roman road. Her feet dragged on the paved stones, and her sandals scrambled the pebbles.

The desert sun sank in the western sky, painting the Judean wilderness a brilliant red. Behind them was the Dead Sea, with its smooth surface reflecting the crimson sun. Ahead of them, Joseph knew, was the city of Jerusalem. They had long passed the fork in the Roman road that took travelers to the ancient city of Jericho. Once they passed this fork, Jerusalem lay less than two hours ahead.

The Roman road passed just to the south of the Mount of Olives, where trees—older than Joseph could know—still bore their fruit. He remembered that something had happened there with the young rabbi the Romans crucified, but he couldn't recall it.

They followed the road down from the Mount of Olives and there, just ahead of them, lay the city of Jerusalem. Joseph's heart swelled with pride as he looked at her white walls shining in the evening sun. The life of his people, the history of his race were all contained within that small area covered by the city. He could not contain his joy. He turned to Aleya and hugged her.

"We are here, my precious one. Now, we will get you home."

Joseph looked behind him at the Mount of Olives. The hillside was nearly bare. Most of the trees were gone, cut down for *ballistae*

and catapults the Romans used to seize Jerusalem. In front of him, his view of Jerusalem had changed forever. Missing was the magnificent temple. It lay in ruins. Yet, life within the city continued on.

There was no doubt in Joseph's mind that he would find what he and Aleya needed in Jerusalem. They had been through too much to fail. Joseph thought back to what he and Aleya had accomplished. They escaped from the horrors of Masada, walked the length of the Dead Sea through the Judean wilderness, crossed over the Judean hills, and dragged themselves through the dry valleys until they stood at the gates of Jerusalem.

In front of them was the key to their future. Ezekiel had promised Joseph that he would find a friendly merchant who would arrange a caravan to the south. The merchant's name was Gamaliel, and he had worked with Ezekiel and Joab when they were young men. Gamaliel used Joab's house as an office. "Trust Gamaliel," Ezekiel told Joseph. "He will find a way back for your young princess."

Joseph stood before the main gate of Jerusalem. Close to it was the Needle Gate, so called because it was purposely narrow, allowing only a man on foot to enter. No pack animals, horses, or camels could get through.

As he faced the gate he remembered what the rabbi said, the one the Romans crucified. One of his followers told him this. Joseph was too young to listen to the young rabbi.

"It is easier for a camel to get through the eye of a needle, than it is for a rich man to enter my Father's kingdom."

Joseph paid the rabbi's follower no mind. He didn't own a camel. And he certainly preferred being rich than poor. So, Joseph and Aleya confidently approached the Needle Gate.

Once inside, they would cross the Xystus Bridge and from there enter the Upper Market. From the marketplace they were to go to the Street of Potters and look for a cloth shop. The shop was once Joab's house. Joseph doubted that the house still existed. The Romans had sacked the city and leveled whole sections. But Ezekiel assured him that Gamaliel had a special arrangement with his Roman masters. The merchant supplied fine linens and silks to the Roman officers for their mistresses. No legionary would loot his shop, not as long as Gamaliel enjoyed the protection of the Roman commanders.

Joseph turned to Aleya, who, as always, stood by his side. "We are here, Aleya. Let's see what happens."

Joseph was perfectly at ease wandering the Judean wilderness, avoiding the predators that roamed alongside him. But, inside the gates, lived a different, far more dangerous animal—his fellow man. He had to be especially careful.

Joseph and Aleya walked through the Needle. The desert's dust clung to them. They came into the city like refugees, their necks craning, looking about and wondering where the city's great crowds were. Jerusalem was the greatest city in Judea. Its neighbor to the north, Jericho, was far older, but Jerusalem had eclipsed that ancient city in importance. Jerusalem was the main trading center for the Middle East and the seat of the Roman provincial government.

It was also the holiest city of the Jews and the gathering place for the world's Jewish community. But the magnificence and spectacle that was Jerusalem's glory no longer existed. The Roman army had broken the indomitable backbone of the Jews. The temple was destroyed. The Tenth Legion, still under the command of Valerius, occupied the city. After the mass suicide at Masada, Titus left a small garrison on top of the mount and ordered the rest of the Tenth Legion back to Jerusalem.

In Jerusalem, Titus maintained his relentless campaign against the Jewish rebels. Every Jew to him was a Zealot, intent on bringing down the Roman army. He forbade access to the city's markets and stationed Roman patrols throughout the city. Jews could move freely about the city if they had a special pass issued by Titus. The only other movement permitted to them was through the main gate and into exile. There was no in-between for the Jews—either be a favorite of the Romans and be despised by your own people or leave the city forever.

Joseph had neither the desire nor the intention to spend any time in the city. He was anxious to contact Gamaliel the merchant and make his way out of the city. Once in Jerusalem, all thoughts of joining the rebels left him. He wanted no part of the ongoing revolt against the Romans. Valerius spared his life twice. The old Roman commander would not be disposed toward sparing his life again.

The young couple cleared the Upper Market and made their way to the Street of Potters. The streets of Jerusalem were little more than goat paths winding this way and that. Jerusalem was already over one thousand years old. Some of the streets, named in the olden days for the merchants who gathered there, no longer catered to that type of merchant. That is why Joseph did not question Ezekiel's instruction to look for a linen merchant on the Street of Potters.

All around them, the rebellion against the Romans left its signs. Shops were gutted, some still smoking. A palpable fog descended over the city, certainly not from weather but from the fine dust thrown up by buildings whose stones were taken down one by one by the Roman legionaries.

By the time they had arrived at Joab's house, Joseph and Aleya looked like timeworn and weary itinerant travelers. The shop's door was long gone, probably used as a barricade by the Zealots. Joseph peered through the entrance, looking for the old merchant.

"I don't see how this man will get us on a caravan. It hardly looks like he has anything to trade," Joseph told Aleya. They both entered the shop and looked around. The shelves were empty, and the floor hadn't been swept in months. Toward the back of the shop was another doorway. Joseph walked ahead and looked through the second door. It was a pitiful room. A small rope bed lay in the corner. A rickety table held a bowl and jug. *Probably for ritual purification,* Joseph thought. A crude dining table stood in the center of the room. Two tiny windows on either side of the room let in weak shafts of light.

Joseph left the room and walked back to Aleya, doubt filling his mind that Gamaliel could help them. He even wondered if the linen merchant were still alive.

Outside, Joseph heard the unmistakable sounds of a Roman patrol arriving at the entrance to the shop. The *clump-clump* of the soldiers' hobnailed sandals stopped just outside the doorway, and a horse whinnied in protest as the bridle bit into the poor animal's mouth.

"Away with you, merchant. Figure your tally wisely. We will be back for you before supper." The harsh tang of Latin echoed in the alley.

Joseph and Aleya stepped back into the shadows of the shop's front room. Joseph thought it wise to avoid all Roman patrols. Besides, he felt comforted by the dark. He remembered the training he received when he joined the Zealots. The old Jewish soldiers would always tell the young recruits to hide in the shadows. It is better, they said, to peer into the light from the darkness than look into the darkness from the light.

The old merchant strode into his shop and looked about. Joseph paid attention to his training. He could see the merchant, but the merchant's eyes hadn't yet adjusted to the darkness. Joseph was surprised at what he saw. Gamaliel hardly looked like the downtrodden proprietor of an ill-equipped shop. He wore expensive clothes befitting a palace courtier. Finely tooled leather sandals fit his feet. His bejeweled fingers showed the favors he received from the Roman authorities. And the girth of his stomach told everyone that he was not one of the starving Jews eking out a subsistence living in the ruins of Jerusalem. When he spoke, Joseph's head nearly hit the low ceiling. He was so surprised to hear the man utter a word.

"You can come forward, my young people. The Roman is gone, and we can talk in quiet confidence." He lit a lamp, which threw a dim circle of light around the room. Joseph and Aleya, their forms illuminated by the lamp, approached the merchant. Gamaliel walked about the room, lighting the oil lamps spread along the wall. "So, you want to get on a caravan that is heading south, no?"

Joseph looked at him in amazement. How did he know what they came to him for? They hadn't even spoken one word!

Gamaliel noticed the surprise on Joseph's face. "News travels fast. You may think Ezekiel is some crazy old hermit living in the middle of the desert. But he's not. Consider us partners of a sort. Now, let's stop wondering what I know and how I know it and get on to the more important business of how I can help you."

"Sir, I was wondering," Joseph started to say, but Aleya stepped in front of him.

"Gamaliel, I don't know how you heard of us or how you continue to exist with the Romans. But I trust you. Ezekiel told us to come to you, and I trust Ezekiel. Please forgive my traveling companion. He has to know the insides and outsides of everything before he trusts anybody."

Gamaliel leaned forward, obviously enchanted by the twinkle of Aleya's voice.

"Joab has taught you well, my young princess. I have never heard Hebrew spoken so musically since my Adar died so many years ago."

Now, it was Aleya's turn to look at Gamaliel in amazement. She never mentioned Joab, and neither did Joseph.

"Both of you put aside your questions. If you are to survive in the desert, remember that information travels faster from caravan to caravan than it does by imperial post. How is it that the Romans' enemy in the desert always disappears before the Romans get there? I knew everything about you before you passed the caves of Qumran.

"What I know and how I know it is not important. That I can help you is of the utmost importance. Ezekiel said you were a friend, and especially you, my little one, were a friend of Joab. Why else do I exist these days except to help friends? You certainly don't think I enjoy helping the Romans, do you?

"Come. Let us discuss what we need but certainly not in this hovel." Gamaliel motioned for the two to join him outside. "We shall go for a short walk. You can wash, rest a little, and eat. Then, we will get down to the business of helping you."

Chapter Thirty-Four

They made an unusual party. Two young people, dressed like desert beggars, and a wealthy old merchant, attired in the finery of a Roman patrician, strolled through the streets of an occupied Jerusalem under the watchful eyes of Roman patrols.

They walked down the Street of Potters through the Upper Market and through the city until they got to the site of the destroyed temple. Joseph hadn't seen the destruction that the Romans had wrought. When he first came upon the rubble, Joseph fell to his knees in prayer, beating his breast and reciting the *Shema Yisrael*.

"Come, come, my boy. What have they done? Reduced a building to a mound of dust, rubble, and smoking ruins? This building was not our religion. It is in our hearts. We carry it in ourselves wherever we go. Let us go about our business. Besides, the Romans do not like Jews to gather about the ruins of the temple, even such favored Jews as I."

The three of them skirted the temple ruins and came to a street that was free of rubble, where the air was clean, and where, clearly, commerce ruled. "This is the new seat of commercial Jerusalem," Gamaliel said. "It is here we Jews practice our crafts under the watchful eye of the Romans. I keep my shop on the Street of Potters for legal reasons, but here, on this street, I do my business."

The merchant ushered them through a doorway to a large building. It was his warehouse. When they entered, Gamaliel lighted several lamps. Joseph and Aleya looked around them. Piled on the shelves were the treasures of an empire. There were silks from the east, woven mats from the Bedouin, the finest linens from Egypt, and in a back room, piles of seashells from which the imperial purple dye comes. The shelves were made of the finest Lebanon cedar.

Joseph had never seen so many riches in one place. He began to worry. If Gamaliel were able to trade in such expensive goods, then he must be in the employ of the Romans. And, if that were true, then Gamaliel could turn them over to the Romans as escapees from Masada. Joseph looked at him and wondered if his next stop was going to be the slave markets where he and Aleya would be put up for sale.

"Tell me, Gamaliel, how is it that you can trade in these goods when most other Jewish merchants are ruined?"

"You are right to ask. All about you, you see the ruins of a city, people scattered, houses and buildings destroyed. Yet, you come into this warehouse, and before you is more treasure than you have ever seen. You suspect I am in collusion with the Romans?

"Fear not. I am not an agent of the Romans, just a favored trader. And I pay heavily for that privilege. I pay triple the tax levied on all Jewish merchants and another exorbitant tax for the protection of my caravans. The Romans trust me and allow me to go about my business. Because I am so trusted, I am allowed to help my people without their interference as long as it doesn't become obvious. I have arranged the escape of countless numbers of my friends and acquaintances on caravans to Egypt, boats to Alexandria, and trading missions to the east. The Romans permit this as long as I fill their purses. That is why Ezekiel sent you to me."

"Gamaliel, please tell me, who is Ezekiel? At first, I thought he was a crazy man, but he doesn't seem so crazy now."

"He is called the 'ghost of the oasis' because no one knows his function or his role there. They think he's a crazed old man living out his final days in the middle of the Judean wilderness. Ezekiel, Joab, and I were friends and partners from the days of our youth. Joab would provide me with intelligence. Ezekiel made sure my caravans made it through the wilderness. And I stayed here in Jerusalem arranging all these things. Are you satisfied, now, Joseph?"

Joseph cast his eyes down to the marbled floor in shame. "I am sorry for suspecting you. I should have known that someone who was a friend of Ezekiel and Joab would not let us down. It's just that returning Aleya to her home is so important to me, and I…"

"Tut, tut, Joseph. There's no need for an apology or for an explanation of how you feel. I know what you have come through, and I know what Aleya is looking for. I shall help you, or my name isn't Gamaliel, the greatest trader in Judea! Let us go to the wine shop next door and get something to eat. With our bellies full, we can plan how to get you young people to the south."

They left the warehouse and emerged into the bright afternoon sun of Jerusalem. They walked a few paces down the street and sat at a table outside the wine shop. "It smells in there," Gamaliel said. "Sit here in the warm afternoon sun. It feels good on the bones of an old man."

The proprietor came over and greeted Gamaliel. "Shall I bring my best Falernian for you? We also have some fresh fish from Galilee. What say you just sit and let me bring what I have," the proprietor said. He didn't wait for an answer, just turned and went back into his wine shop.

As the shop's owner walked away, Gamaliel leaned over to Joseph and Aleya and said, "I helped his three sons leave Jerusalem and make their way to Alexandria. I just hope that if they open wine shops in that city that they will be more honest than their father! The Greeks deal much more harshly with dishonest merchants than the Romans."

Gamaliel quieted down as the proprietor approached with two jugs of wine, a plate of stewed fish, and some bread. "Here you go, my friend. Let the young ones eat up. Their last meal in Jerusalem should be filling," he laughed.

Joseph and Aleya looked at Gamaliel. "Does the whole city know why we are here?" Aleya asked. She pushed away from the table and ran into the street, tears welling up in her eyes.

Joseph ran after her and held her in his arms. "Aleya, come back with me. At least let's hear the old man out. If what he says doesn't satisfy you, then I'll get us out. I led us here from Masada, didn't I? Now, wipe your eyes and come back with me. I will never let harm come to you."

They returned to Gamaliel back at the tavern. The merchant looked at both of them, saying nothing. When they sat down, the proprietor joined them with another jug of Falernian wine. "This drunken fool of a tavern owner wants to apologize. His name is Ezra. Listen to him."

"I am sorry for upsetting you, pretty lady. I spoke out of turn. I know what you are going to do. For you see, I also am a partner of Gamaliel's. When he makes his final arrangements for you, you will come here, back to my tavern, to join the caravan."

"Now, be gone with you. I have much to say to these young people," Gamaliel yelled after Ezra got up from the table to go back inside his shop. "What Ezra says is true. He is a partner. The caravans do meet here. I just wish he could keep his mouth shut. Now, enough of him. Let's help you.

"You say you want to go south, back to Aleya's homeland. That is a tall order. There are no longer any direct trading routes to the south. Tell me, are you afraid of the water?"

The next morning, as Joseph arranged the textiles on their shelves, a group of men came in to see Gamaliel. "Slave, where is your master?" one of them called after Joseph.

Joseph turned, ready to spit out a word at the man who threw that insult. He was just about to jump down from the shelf and confront the man when Gamaliel stepped in. "Boaz, why is a worthless son of Baal like you darkening my doorway?" Gamaliel cried as he rushed forward to crush the man in a bear hug.

"Me, worthless? It is you, Jew, who is worthless. Taking my precious goods in trade for these rags," Boaz retorted.

The insults went on for a while between the two men. Joseph just stood to one side and listened. With their arms around each other, the two men walked toward the door into the courtyard. Gamaliel turned around and said, "Joseph, please join us and bring that bolt of Egyptian linen with you."

The two men sat on a bench in the sun. Joseph stood still, silently considering how he would repay this uncouth trader for the insult. The trader, who looked like a Chaldean from the east, rose from the bench and approached Joseph. "So, this is the slave you wish to accompany me. Why? Don't you trust me to get the best price for your cloths, Gamaliel?"

"We have been trading since both of us had brown in our beards, and the Lord knows when that was! You know I trust you. I am having my slave accompany you so he can learn the routes. He is quick with numbers, and he is bringing another slave with him, a girl. She can cook and take care of the caravan's cook fires."

"Well, he looks hard enough. Not like some of those city slaves you have sent with me. How far are he and the other one going? You know I have arranged a trading route to the lands of the south. Those Arabs are becoming Romanized. They, too, crave the purple dye for their robes. Bah! What happened to the rough days when we traveled with swords at our sides and daggers in our teeth?" Boaz yelled.

"You old pirate! You never held a dagger in your mouth in your entire life. Let's stop wasting time. This slave, Joseph, and the other one, a young girl named Aleya, are traveling to the south lands. It is time I reopened my routes to those peoples. Joab, Ezekiel, and I were the first Jewish merchants to trade there."

At the mention of Joab's name, Boaz became silent and bowed his head. *All of Judea now knows what happened on Masada,* Joseph thought. *Only, they do not know that Aleya and I escaped. I shall keep my mouth shut and listen.*

"Gamaliel, have them ready tomorrow before the sun rises. We leave from the wine shop. Make sure Ezra the cheat doesn't water down the wineskins he packs for us. It's a week's journey to Caesarea," Boaz shouted, leaving the old merchant and his new slave in the warehouse.

The departure of the large-figured Boaz created a vacuum. Both Gamaliel and Joseph filled it by speaking at the same time. Joseph respectfully deferred to the merchant.

"Don't mind Boaz. He bluffs more than he bites. I am sorry I didn't get a chance to tell you myself that you were leaving tomorrow. And I am doubly sorry that I didn't get a chance to tell you that you and Aleya were going as my slaves.

"It is the only way that Jews can leave the city. The Romans permit no free Jew to leave without paying an exorbitant tax. You have no money to pay the procurator, and I certainly can't pay him on your behalf. But the Romans could care less if a few more slaves left. That is the only way I can get you out."

Joseph's pride was still hurt, but his anger cooled. "I was told to trust you. And I do. Can I trust Boaz to keep up his part of the bargain?"

"Boaz and I have been trading since before you were born. I suspect he knows what I am doing since I have never owned a slave in my life. All of a sudden, I have a whole crowd of them. But don't think you are getting a free ride. Boaz will expect you to work. He'll be right along beside you. On the trading caravans, there are no slaves, no masters, only men trying to stay alive. Listen to him. He will get you and the princess home alive.

"Now, get back to Aleya and tell her what you know. Then come back this evening for supper. The two of you may as well stay with me. You leave before first light."

"Aleya, I have the news we have been waiting for. We leave tomorrow before dawn in the caravan of a Chaldean named Boaz. And, uh, you and I are going as Gamaliel's slaves." Joseph winced when he gave her the last part of the news.

Aleya looked at him, showing no disturbance whatsoever at her return to slave status.

Joseph was surprised. "It doesn't bother you to be a slave again?"

"How else were we to accompany a caravan…as lord and lady? Who would believe us, dressed the way we are? No, I knew Gamaliel had a tricky plan in the works. Besides, that's all I have been these past few years, a slave. I haven't forgotten how to act."

Joseph beamed at her, his heart filling with love. *What a sensible woman! And here am I, offended at being a slave, and my Aleya takes it as a matter of course. May God grant me her wisdom and His peace.*

The day was ending. The sun had dipped behind the Judean hills, and Jerusalem bathed in its golden light. Joseph and Aleya gathered their few belongings in a small purse for her and a shoulder bag for him and made their way to Gamaliel's warehouse.

The two of them turned into the street where Gamaliel had his warehouse and walked right into the middle of a traveling circus. Donkeys, camels, people, and wagons were everywhere. The courtyard was piled high with goods and trade merchandise. In the middle of all this commotion stood Gamaliel and Boaz, back-to-back, shouting out insults and spitting out commands.

The merchant looked up just long enough to notice Joseph and Aleya standing wide-eyed outside his courtyard. "Ah, there you are. Come inside. Boaz has promised to teach you all he knows about trading routes to the south. And you two, in return, will help him manage the caravan. You go as my representatives, even though you are slaves. Boaz knows how I treat my slaves and will not treat you unkindly."

Gamaliel took them by the hand and walked through the commotion outside, explaining what they must do. He introduced Aleya to the driver of the cook wagon and Joseph to the chief camel driver. In all, besides Joseph and Aleya, there were thirty men attending to the caravan. Not all of them, Joseph learned, would make the trip to the south lands. Some of them would accompany the caravan to the seacoast and find another caravan to serve. These were the ones who chose not to make the sea voyage south.

There would be nearly fifty camels and a dozen donkeys in the caravan. Not all the animals were in Gamaliel's courtyard. Only those beasts that would carry the rarest of his treasures were stabled in the courtyard. Tomorrow, the caravan would pick up the rest of the animals outside the walls of Jerusalem.

"Tomorrow, my young people, you begin your new life. For tonight, please enjoy my hospitality one last time." Boaz, his caravan master, and two others joined Gamaliel, Joseph, and Aleya for dinner. They ate Roman-style, reclining on a cloth-covered bench surrounding a low table. The merchant's kitchen staff had placed the table in the courtyard of the house. It was a beautiful evening, and stars were just beginning to appear in the darkening sky.

Boaz was having a hard time leaning on one hand while stuffing his face with the other. Gamaliel, meanwhile, had picked up the Roman custom readily and was enjoying himself. Boaz and his men were silent as to why he had two of his "slaves" accompany him to supper. Even though he and Joseph were the only Jews at the table, Gamaliel still recited the Jewish blessing over the food and asked

God's blessing for the trip ahead. Boaz, as boorish as he may have been, had enough sense to bow his head and stop picking at his food during prayers.

They ate silently, each privately lost in his thoughts. The smells and sounds of the caravan animals penetrated the air around them and assaulted their nostrils. *So, this is what my life for the next year will be like,* Joseph thought, *surrounded by animals and eating at night under the stars. It is all worth it, for my love is with me.*

Across the table, Aleya lay on her side, picking at a bowl of fruit. She was lost in her thoughts. *Tomorrow, I start for my home. Will they remember me? Will they accept Joseph? It is no matter. We will be together, and I am sure my father will honor him.*

Boaz broke the silence with a loud passage of wind. He got up and stretched his arms. "We better retire for the night. You, Joseph, get with the animals. Make sure they're bedded down properly. You, girl, make your bed in the cook wagon and make sure none of these thieves take any supplies. Gamaliel, we will see you in the morning."

Chapter Thirty-five

1991

Jordan brushed her sweaty hair underneath the Yankees cap Uncle Arthur gave her after her mother's funeral. She looked at the young American following her. "Look, if you want to see signs of the Roman excavation, you're wasting your time looking underneath your feet. You think you're the only one to walk up this path?"

"Beautiful lady, just tell me where to look, and I'll be happy."

"Listen, Daniel, stop playing with me. We're here to work and learn. So cut the crap and pay attention."

"Okay. What's your name?"

"My name is Jordan. And my friends call me Jordan. So don't shorten it like all you Americans do with first names."

"Like the river?"

"No, I was named after the almond. Now, shut up, come up here, and I'll show you what you're looking for."

Daniel scrambled up the path. About halfway up, he lost his footing and started to slide down. Jordan screamed after him. "Daniel, dig your feet into the dirt! This soil is loose, and you have to make like a goat to walk."

She sidestepped her way down the path and grabbed his hand. An electric feeling ran up her arm, but she avoided looking into his dark eyes.

Daniel did everything he could to make eye contact. "Your hands are hard, and your nails are cracked. Doesn't this country have manicure parlors? They're all over Atlanta. You should visit. I'll take you to a nail salon."

"I've been to America, and I'm not anxious to go back. So, thanks but no thanks. Tell me, Daniel, exactly what are you doing here? Your hands are soft, and there's no dirt encrusted under your fingernails. Yet, you tell me you're studying archaeology. What gives?"

"Jordan, despite the way I have been acting, my main purpose is not to track down beautiful Israeli women. There's a small but excellent antiquities museum in Atlanta. Some members of my family—they're in real estate—got caught up in a fund-raising campaign for an ancient Near East exhibit the museum was staging. They made significant contributions. In return, museum officials gave us VIP memberships.

"I started spending more time at the museum, later volunteering as a docent, and still later working as a volunteer on an archaeological dig of some American Indian burial mounds in northeastern Georgia. One thing led to another, and my father suggested I might turn my new-found hobby into a profession, so he funded this trip to the Middle East.

"We're originally from Lebanon, which truly is the crossroads of—"

Jordan saw a lecture coming, so she quickly interrupted. "Daniel, come on. Let's get to the top, and I'll introduce you to some of the working archaeologists up there. They'll take over and do a far better job with you than I can." But she kept her eyes on him. He really was cute and probably did have a legitimate interest in archaeology. But she neither had the time nor the temperament for a summer fling with a foreign student.

"Maybe we'll catch up in the city. There aren't too many places where people our age go, so there's a good chance we'll see each other again."

Daniel and Jordan did see each other again, in a small wine bar in the Old City; wine bars were just becoming fashionable in Israel after taking hold in America in the early seventies.

"Hey, Jor, do you see that table over there, the one with all the cute guys around it?"

Penny's male radar was on full alert ever since the evening began, and she never gave up her relentless pursuit of the opposite sex.

"Penny, for weeks we have been drinking those champagne-and-mango concoctions because you like them. I'm sick of them. We're here to have some honest Israeli wine pressed from grapes picked from thousand-year-old vines. We are definitely not here to pick up guys."

"Jor, don't be such an old maid. Would it kill you to be nice for one evening?"

Jordan hated when Penny, who Americanized everything, shortened her name. Every time Penny called her that, she felt like a cheerleader.

"Jordan, over here! Come join us." The group of girls turned to the corner of the wine bar where a table of young men sat. One of them was standing and was shouting in their direction. Penny just stared at her friend. *Jordan wasn't even looking, and now she's got this good-looking guy eating out of her hand.*

"Jor, wave back and get us over there. Quick. Where's the bathroom?" Without waiting for an answer, Penny ducked into the café's small unisex toilet to "freshen up." While Penny was in the toilet, Jordan casually walked over to the table and said hello to Daniel.

"Jordan, what happened to your friend? Three of you walked in, and now it's just the two of you."

"Daniel, what a surprise to see you here. Penny'll be back soon. This is Sharon, another school friend of mine."

Without waiting to meet his other friends, Jordan launched into her hard-to-get role. She looked at the four empty bottles on the table. "Sucking up some of the local culture?"

"No, I'm actually sucking up some of this awful Israeli wine that you bragged so much about. The Romans did a much better job of planting vines in France than they did here. Beirut is called the 'Paris of the East,' which is probably why I have such an affinity for all things French.

"Have you been there? We should go and visit my uncle. He has a seaside villa on the Corniche."

Does this guy never give up? Jordan thought. Just as Daniel was moving to a seat closer to Jordan, Penny came bouncing back in. The irrepressible American grabbed her and took her aside. "Jor, tell me. How do you know this guy? I thought you went out on digs with camels and old Arabs in cabooses. You told me you didn't have time for romance."

"Penny, they're called *burnooses,* and I don't 'know' him. He followed me up Masada, and we just got to talking. Now he's trying to get me to go to his uncle's house on the Corniche."

"Jor, what's his name?"

"Daniel."

"Hey, Daniel, you have a Corniche? Isn't that like a Rolls-Royce or something?"

Jordan looked at Penny and instinctively knew she'd be a Beverly Hills housewife with two lapdogs and a Mercedes convertible. Penny said she was staying in Israel, but Jordan doubted it.

"Penny, let me introduce you to Jerry. He's my cousin from Atlanta visiting family with me. Jerry, Penny's an American student who's fallen in love with the Middle East. She'd probably find your tales of the Bensouk family fascinating."

Daniel expertly cut Penny out of their small crowd and guided her to Jerry. Her bleached-blonde American looks contrasted sharply with Jerry's dark Lebanese coloring—like salt and pepper. But they would be good for one another—both seeking what they can't attain.

"Jordan, let's go to the courtyard. I feel the walls have something interesting to tell me. I hear this café was a merchant's warehouse, and I need you to help me read the walls."

Jordan had heard many lines in her life but "read the walls"? *This guy's trying too hard.* "Let's go and 'read the walls'? Daniel, can't you think of a better line than that?"

They left the wine bar and walked outside. Patrons looked up and knew there was something about them. What it was, no one knew. Neither did they.

Chapter Thirty-Six

74 CE

The donkeys began to bray. The camels shrugged and bellowed their displeasure. The two young bull camels began fighting again, exciting the donkeys even more. *This is not a pleasant way to start the day,* Joseph thought as he rose from his straw bed near the stable. Not only did the animals smell, they made the most annoying noises. The camels snorted, spitting large globs of phlegm wherever they looked.

The young bull camels got into a fight over a female. Both of the bulls asserted their rights to mate with her. The camel driver came over and separated them, pulling sharply on their bridles and hitting them with his whip.

Over at the cook wagon, Aleya was up, already having washed and prepared herself for the day. She was humming lightly and smiled at everyone who passed the wagon. The other men on the caravan—Joseph didn't know who was a slave and who was not—practically fell over themselves trying to assist Aleya to start the cook fire. Joseph rushed over like a young bull camel, pushing the other men out of the way and asserting his right to help.

"Why didn't you tell them you were with me?"

She looked at him and sighed. "We are slaves. No slave is 'with' another slave. I have spoken to Gamaliel. Boaz knows who we are. So do his principal men. The others you'll have to deal with. But don't you worry about me. I have spent the last three years as a slave girl."

Joseph walked away miffed by Aleya's offhand comments. He felt naked without his Roman sword, but slaves were not permitted to wear weapons inside the city walls. If the rich people needed protection, they could hire patrols of Roman legionaries at a very high price from the procurator. As soon as they were outside the walls, Joseph was going to the supply wagon to get his sword.

Gamaliel and Boaz were together in the middle of the courtyard. Boaz blew on a horn that looked something like the shofar, the horn the temple priest blew to signify the coming of the holiday. This was no holiday, and Boaz was no priest. He blew his horn to signal the men to ready the animals and prepare to depart.

All about him, men sprang into action, yelling at the donkeys and pulling on the camels' bridles. With cries of "Get up! Get up!" the animals slowly rose and formed a semblance of a straight line. Aleya, mounted atop the cook wagon, looked down on all the excitement. Joseph was caught in the middle of it all, right down on the ground.

"Let's go," Boaz cried. The caravan surged toward the main gate of Jerusalem. Gamaliel was busy with a Roman official looking over some documents and handing the official a large purse. For just a moment, Gamaliel looked up. Joseph caught his eye and waved. Gamaliel did not wave back, but he smiled, uttering a small prayer under his breath.

The hooves of the animals thudded on the wood of the Xystus Bridge that connected the city to the main gate of Jerusalem. The caravan passed through the gate, making its way west to its first stop where it would pick up the rest of the caravan's supplies.

Joseph looked back at the city's walls, knowing that he was leaving forever. *I will never forget this city, but I make my way to the south lands to be with my future wife.*

By the second day of the caravan, Joseph had prayed that he would never see another camel. The others warned him of the hardships. But he would not listen. His body was hardened by days and nights in the desert between Masada and Jerusalem. How much worse could a caravan be? For one, it traveled slowly. And, should he get tired, he imagined he could mount one of the animals. Joseph was only half right.

"So it took you and the girl a day to get from Ein Gedi to Jerusalem," remarked Baalcath, the chief camel driver. Baalcath was a mean-looking devil as befitted his name. Some peoples in the east worshipped Baal, but the Jews considered him a devil god. Baalcath was every bit his namesake. A camel had bitten off part of his right ear. One eye was completely opaque after a Bedouin stabbed it for cheating at a game of bones. He was permanently stooped from riding camels all his life. And his personality matched his ugliness.

"Just because you and the wench escaped and made it to Jerusalem in one day doesn't mean you're going to move fast with this caravan," he taunted Joseph. "You'll grow a long beard by the time we get to Caesarea."

Joseph was ready to jump up from his place around the campfire and throttle the stupid camel driver, but he stopped in his place. *So, Caesarea, that's where we are going. Gamaliel wanted to know what we thought about water. This is good. I have no desire to walk my way to Aleya's homeland.*

"Baalcath, you are as evil-smelling as the animals you drive and twice as ugly. Nothing you say can rile me."

"Nothing, eh! You were about to run me through with your sword. I saw you reach down for it. But it's not there. Slaves aren't allowed to have weapons, you know," Baalcath roared. His greasy locks swept back off his forehead as he threw his head backward in derisive laughter.

Joseph was about to charge Baalcath when Boaz stepped in between them. "Rest easy, young man. You are new to the caravan.

We have to see what you're made of. Baalcath has been my camel driver for years and has proven himself on many caravans. He likes to test the new ones. Don't lose your head. Someday he may save yours."

Joseph watched the caravan master walk away. He turned back to the fire, threw Baalcath a vengeful glance, and sat down. Baalcath kept chewing on the lamb's haunch in his fingers, greasy juices from the meat dripping down his chin into his beard. "Go easy, young bull. We have a long way to go," he said.

The third morning of the caravan dawned. Joseph slept with the donkeys, his job being to keep the extra donkeys in line. He had made his peace, of sorts, with Baalcath, taking to heart what Boaz had told him.

During a water break, when Joseph was required to bring the water skins to all the camel herders, Joseph tugged on Baalcath's sleeve. "Tell me, camel driver, why do we have so many donkeys?"

"Not so quick with the sword or your temper, eh? You asked. So I shall tell you. We never bring donkeys into the desert on the long trek of the caravan. But this is a short trip. We are bringing these goods to the port at Caesarea, where we will load them onto a trireme headed south down the Mediterranean. When the ship gets to the southernmost part of the sea, the goods will disembark for a short caravan trek to the Red Sea. Once at the northern end of the Red Sea, the ship will sail south to the end of the Arabian lands, to the country that the Romans call *Arabia Felix*.

"This is a combined caravan route with most of the travel done on the seas. This is a vast route covering thousands of miles, taking you to a far different world than you're used to.

"I sense that slave girl is depending on you to take her there. She looks like those people. Is that her home?" Baalcath asked.

At the mention of Aleya, Joseph tensed. *How much do these people know about us? Gamaliel said that we were to travel as slaves. It seems that even this lowly camel-driver knows my mission.*

"Baalcath, you have been honest with me. I shall return the same. Gamaliel is getting old. Aleya served his friend and partner, Joab, well into his old years. She has now come to serve Gamaliel, since Joab is dead.

"I have sworn to protect Aleya. Gamaliel bought me from the Romans and promised to teach me the trading routes to the south. If I do well on this caravan, I shall return to Jerusalem a free man and work for Gamaliel for the rest of his life."

Joseph was beginning to like Baalcath. It pained him to lie so blatantly to this simple, honest man. Joseph continued to weave his tale. "After Gamaliel dies, I shall inherit his business. Gamaliel has no sons, no family. As for Aleya, she has her own mind. I do not know what she will do. She has this fantasy that she comes from a large city in the south lands. From what you have said about the desert sands and the winds, such a city existing seems impossible."

Baalcath grunted. "Be careful what you say, Joseph. You have not seen enough to make such a judgment. I have never been that far south, but those who have made that trip come back with tales of wonder. Your Aleya may be telling you something that is very close to the truth."

"Baalcath, you are ugly, you smell, and I would not trust you with my money. But I will trust you with my life. Let us arise from this fire as friends. We must become friends. We have too many days ahead of us!" Joseph laughed.

Baalcath wrapped his greasy hand around Joseph's shoulder and gave him a friendly hug. The camel driver had the strength of two men and nearly knocked Joseph over. "Good enough."

The caravan moved slowly. Aleya and Joseph slipped into the mundane rhythm of caravan life. Joseph cared for his donkeys. Aleya was queen of the cook wagon. They rarely met, except at the evening meal, and even then, it was just a glance, a quick touch of the hands.

By custom, men and women slept in separate camps and ate separately. The women on the caravan, except for Aleya, were slaves brought along to serve the men's needs. They slept separately from Aleya, but all the women gathered each evening around their communal cook fire.

Most of the whores treated Aleya well. But one, an exceptionally large woman, resented Aleya's dignified and dainty bearing. "So, tell us, princess, why are you special? Do you have your own man, or is Boaz saving you for the market in Caesarea? You think you are above us, sitting on that cook wagon, never talking to us, never joining us when we meet with the men. I could take care of your pretty face right now," sneered Ireeae, a tough Chaldean woman who was Boaz's chief slave.

Aleya rose to walk away. The Chaldean woman would have none of that treatment. Ireeae jumped up and grabbed Aleya, turning her around to face the other women at the campfire.

"So you run away from us? We're not good enough for you? What are you? You're nothing but a slave like us. Boaz will take care of you. Just you wait. My pretty little princess will look so good under the caravan master's sweating body."

Aleya covered her ears with her hands and ran toward the safety of the cook wagon. She climbed inside and pulled the heavy linen flap over her body. Sobbing, she threw herself onto the bundle of rags that served as her bed. She cried for herself. She cried for Joseph. But most of all, she cried for her father, wishing his strong arms were around her, holding her, protecting her. She cried herself to sleep.

The caravan made its way down the Plain of Esdraelon, heading toward the coast. They were less than a half day's ride from Caesarea, and Joseph could detect a scent of the sea in the air. Joseph had never seen a real sea. The largest body of water he had ever seen was the Dead Sea. Baalcath teased him, saying that the Mediterranean, the "Roman Lake," would be the largest body of water he would ever see.

"You stand on the docks at Caesarea and look out forever over the blue body of water. And the port! What a wonder! You've never seen anything like it. King Herod tried to impress his Roman masters by building a port city that was greater than anything in Rome. Even the Romans agree that it rivals anything in Italia. Just wait until we get there."

Once the caravan reached the Plain of Sharon, Caesarea was just a few hours away. Boaz's caravan caught up with others making their way to the great city of Caesarea. The treasures of the east converged on a single path to the port city. Some camels carried amphorae filled with olive oil. Other camels had great bags of spices strapped to their sides. Silks from the east and woven rugs piled out of wagons. And sadly, there was the human trade—captives and convicted criminals making their way to the slave markets where they were sold to the highest bidder. Many would be chained in the bowels of merchant ships, destined to waste away while straining at the oars that propelled the ships containing the riches of the Roman Empire.

The caravan made its way to the city gates. Just outside, a Roman tax collector met it. Boaz called a halt. His camel knelt, and Boaz slid off. Boaz walked toward the Roman official and motioned Joseph to join him. "Keep your mouth shut and do as I do." The two men approached the official who motioned them to his tent. High above the crowds, towers manned by Roman soldiers guarded the entrance to Caesarea.

The tax collector was the true gatekeeper to Caesarea; the guards on the towers hadn't repelled an enemy for over one hundred years. Before any caravan could enter the city, the tax collector inspected the merchandise to ensure that the emperor got his due.

Boaz lifted the tent flap and followed the Roman inside. "Good greetings to you, Juventius," Boaz bellowed loudly. "We've come from Jerusalem with goods from all over the great and good empire for trade. Praise be to, er, the current emperor. And we wish good health to him."

"Boaz, you old pirate. You're back already! How do you stay in business? Your masters in Jerusalem must trust you. And thank you for your greetings. Tell me, Boaz, do you know who the emperor is?" Juventius said laughingly.

"I most certainly do, you Roman scoundrel. The emperor is the one who wants to collect taxes on my trade goods. Is that fair enough?"

"Never let politics get in the way of a good business deal, eh, Boaz? By the way, the emperor is Vespasian, may the gods watch over him. Tell me, who is that young man accompanying you? Yet another slave for the markets? I hope he's not damaged goods. A comely slave like him would fetch a very good price on the blocks."

Joseph felt uncomfortable. The Roman's bulging eyes roamed over his body as if he were inspecting a prize bull. "Might you allow me to entertain this slave for the evening? I shall return him none the worse for wear."

"Juventius, with what you have under that toga, you couldn't even wear out a chicken," Boaz roared, throwing back his head.

Joseph stood in silence, chafing at the discussion between the two men. *They treat me like a desert animal to be bought and sold and used by anyone for the right price.*

Just then, Juventius was called to the back of the tent. Boaz grabbed Joseph by the arm and spoke to him under his breath. "Be careful, boy. Juventius is a most powerful man here in Caesarea. If he wants to take you, then you go. But I doubt that he could handle you. Just follow my lead, and we'll get out of here intact, although a bit poorer for the tax that scoundrel will levy on us."

The tax collector strolled back to the table, trailing a cloud of perfume behind him. "I am sorry, Boaz, what were you saying?"

"Nothing. Just warning this boy here that he has to go back and tend to the donkeys. They are getting restless waiting for you to extort me. Come, Juventius, let us share a jug of your wine—no doubt stolen from one of my amphorae—and settle the tax."

Chapter Thirty-Seven

Joseph left the two men dickering over the emperor's levy. He was certain that less than half of what Juventius collected would be going to Rome. *There's no other way he could afford the fine clothes and jewelry he wears.* Joseph hoped Boaz would conclude his business with the Roman official quickly. He wanted to get inside the city's gates and see what Caesarea had to offer. Most of all, he wanted to get on with his journey back to Aleya's homeland.

Joseph trudged back to the camp where the caravan was waiting until it received clearance to enter the city. The men were gathered around a small fire cooking their lunch. Whenever a caravan got near the port city, dozens of merchants descended, offering food, wine, and trinkets and enticing them to visit some of the city's seedier establishments.

The Chaldeans gathered around a fire, cooking a strange-looking fish on the coals, a kind of fish that Joseph had never seen. "Baalcath, what in the name of God are you eating? It looks like a swarm of insects."

The men looked up at Joseph, shaking their heads at his lack of sophistication. "My boy, you apparently have never been near the sea. The merchants here call these prawns. Their flesh is white and as sweet as the summer's grass. Here, try some," Baalcath said, offering Joseph a skewer of prawns roasted in their shells.

Joseph looked at the prawns and turned his nose up at them. The Jewish dietary laws forbade the eating of any food from the sea that had no fin. Joseph had no knowledge of prawns. And, from the look of them, he had no desire to make their acquaintance.

"Baalcath, you are an animal. You smell like them. And you eat like them. I have no desire to sit down next to you and eat sea insects."

By now, the taunts and jibes between Baalcath and Joseph had become a friendly battle with no meaning. But Baalcath wasn't going to take Joseph's taunts without firing back. "You Jews would rather starve than partake of this fine food that Baal put in the sea for us to eat. Come back with me to Chaldea and I shall make a worshipper of Baal out of you, and then you can eat what you want. We'll even sew on another hood for your little man so you can look like us."

Joseph just waved him off as he made his way back to where the wagons were circled. He was looking for Aleya. Boaz wanted her to bring barley cakes to the Roman pig, and Joseph was the messenger.

As Joseph neared the wagons, he heard a commotion, like a fight was going on. He ran to the wagon encampment, fearing that robbers were looting the trade goods. But it was worse, much worse. When he got to the cook wagon, he saw Aleya and Iraeea down on the ground. The Chaldean giantess was on top of Aleya, pummeling her with her fists. Blood was pouring from Aleya's nose, her clothes were ripped, and she seemed to be getting the worse part of the fight. Joseph ran to the two women and pulled Iraeea off Aleya.

"What are you doing?" Joseph screamed as he pulled the huge woman by her hair. "Get off." Joseph wrestled with the much larger woman and smacked her soundly in the head. Iraeea lost her senses and fell back to the ground. Joseph immediately ran over to Aleya and took her in his arms.

"My sweet, my precious, what has happened?" Joseph glared at Iraeea. "If I ever see you touch her again, I will kill you. I do not care that you are Boaz's woman. I will run you through with my sword until your innards roll onto the ground. That I swear by the God of my fathers."

The ferocity of Joseph's gaze and the rage that quieted his voice to a whisper frightened the Chaldean woman. She slinked off but not before uttering one more warning. "We are not finished, princess."

Joseph jumped back to Aleya who was sitting up, wiping the blood off her face.

"What happened?" Joseph expected her to fold herself into his arms, seeking comfort.

Instead, Aleya stood up and raged with a commanding voice. "That slave woman is jealous. She is nothing to me."

She turned and stomped back to the cook wagon, holding her head up high. Joseph looked at her, wondering if she were truly a princess.

He returned to the tax collector's tent empty-handed. Boaz roared, "Where is the food?"

Joseph looked at him, eyes dulled by an inner rage, and said simply and softly, "The fire went out. There will be no barley cakes." And he stalked out of the tent.

Juventius watched Joseph walk away and sighed. "He does have beautiful leg muscles. Oh, never mind. Let us get back to the emperor's share." Boaz rocked back on his heels and dug in for another hour's worth of negotiations with the tax collector.

Joseph walked back to the campsite. *This Iraeea is going to be a problem. There's no way we can continue to Aleya's homeland with this witch in tow. But how do I solve it? How do I separate Iraeea from the protection of Boaz?*

As he continued to walk back to the campsite, he heard raucous laughter coming from the tent of the tax collector. *Juventius has a taste for young men,* Joseph thought to himself. *What about a woman with more muscles than most young men and a temperament to match? I bet that old sodomite would take a shining to Iraeea if I could only separate her from Boaz.* Joseph continued to walk back to the camp, scheming how he could take Juventius's mind off him and make Aleya's life easier.

Joseph walked around the donkeys, making sure they were fed and watered. He was about to walk away from the stables when Baalcath approached him. "Joseph, it's about time you learned about camels. After all, they are to accompany you on the sea voyage, and someone has to take care of them."

Joseph looked at Baalcath, wondering what the rough Chaldean knew that he didn't. "You son of the desert dog, if I had to know about camels, Boaz would tell me. Be off with you. I have much to think about before we enter the city."

Joseph started to walk away when Baalcath grabbed his arm. "Joseph, I think you need to know about the camels. I shan't be on the ship with you." Joseph just looked at the Chaldean camel driver and nodded his assent. The two of them began to walk toward the area where the camels were penned when Boaz, in a funk and spewing curses, walked toward them. Before Joseph had a chance to hail greetings, Boaz approached them, clearly in a foul mood.

"That bastard son of a renegade camel cow wants more money than I am supposed to give him. If I give him what he wants, then my portion of this caravan will be wiped out. But, Joseph," he said in a milder voice, "there is a solution."

Joseph leaned forward, listening to everything Boaz had to say.

"If you would spend a night—a week would be better—in the company of Juventius and his friends, all our problems would disappear. After a week, he would let us on our way. He has taken a liking to you, your smooth muscles and all, and he won't let this caravan budge until you become, let us say, friendlier to him."

Joseph stood on his feet, thinking how he could turn the sodomite's liking to his advantage. "Boaz, you are under a pledge and were given a considerable amount of money to deliver me and Aleya on our way to the south lands. Yet, you say I have to dally here with that tax collector. You have been paid to accompany me to Caesarea and see me on my way. You have also been paid to deliver the goods from this caravan to traders here in the port city. It seems to me you are caught in a most difficult position. You need to get me going. Yet, to sell your goods, you must make me stay here with Juventius. I have a solution that lets you deliver your merchandise and make good on your contract with Gamaliel."

Boaz leaned back and listened with interest as Joseph kept on talking. "It seems to me that Juventius is attracted to young, good-looking men with willing bodies. He cares not where he goes as long as it is into a well-muscled young body. Give him your slave, Iraeea. She is well-muscled and can easily pass for a young man. And from what I can tell of her, she cares not who enters her or where. Plus, she is a slave. There are many more like her in this city that you can buy with just a small portion of the earnings you will make from this caravan. You give Juventius what he wants, and you live up to your bargain with Gamaliel."

"You are a crafty young man," said Boaz. "Let me see."

The next morning Joseph saw Boaz leaving camp with Iraeea on another camel. Boaz called after him. "Juventius is looking forward to a younger and better-looking man than you. When we come back, I'll have our official pass. But you will have to accompany me to the villa of Juventius. We'll make believe he's choosing. But he won't turn down Iraeea."

Boaz strode through the camp, beating the animals and kicking the sleeping men. He walked over to the cook wagon and demanded that the morning's porridge be ready by the time he was finished walking though the camp. Joseph was already awake and did not need a kick from Boaz.

He sat up and thought through last night's events. He remembered separating Iraeea and Aleya and dealing with Boaz and Juventius. He also remembered escorting Iraeea to Juventius's villa inside the city gates. Everything else was a blank. It must have been when Boaz told him to bring another jug of wine that he lost his head.

Juventius invited Joseph to sit beside him and sip from the shared silver cup. He looked at Boaz, who nodded that he should sit down, and Joseph took his place next to the Roman tax collector. The wine in the cup went down smoothly, and soon Joseph felt himself drifting off into a dreamland where everything was warm and cozy. The walls of the villa closed in on him, and the cloying perfume that Juventius wore filled his nostrils. The last thing Joseph remembered was Juventius helping Iraeea out of her robe. Then it all went black.

Joseph paid heavily for last night's revelries. His head ached, his stomach was queasy, and his bowels were loose. He had never felt this way before. Maybe it was the quality of the wine—better than he had ever tasted—that affected him so. Joseph was no stranger to the wine jug. He had drunk his share of wine around many campfires. When his head cleared, he thought about the great victory he had scored in favor of his Aleya. Iraeea was gone, having joined the camp of Juventius. Joseph began to hum to himself as he prepared the camels for entry into Caesarea.

The city prefect strictly regulated the number of animals coming in and out of the city. The prefect claimed it was a sanitary measure.

Joseph suspected the Roman official wanted to keep down smuggling and make a tidy profit from renting wagons to the traders.

Without camels to carry the trade goods, incoming caravans had to rely on wagons. Since few caravans traveled with a large number of wagons, the extra wagons had to be rented from Juventius at a high price. This was Joseph's first exposure to trading between countries. He began to understand where the profits would be made and how.

Boaz came up behind Joseph and clapped him on the back. "When we enter Caesarea, we will go directly to the docks. There, I will find us a house. We will prepare the goods for the sea voyage. Joseph, you and Aleya are the only members of the caravan on the ship. I expect you to look out for our interests. Gamaliel will have traders waiting for you when the ship docks in Alexandria. Until then, it is up to you to protect our investment."

His brawny arms spread a map across the back of his camel's saddle. He traced the ship's route from Caesarea south to Alexandria on the Mediterranean Sea and from Alexandria to a port on the Arabian Peninsula. The goods would go overland through the shallow end of the Red Sea and head south to the Arabian port. From there, another caravan would pick them up and bring them into the kingdom of *Arabia Felix*, and hopefully, back to Aleya's father.

Once Joseph concluded his business with the king of the south lands, he was to return with a horse-trading caravan that the Arab king was sending north to Judea.

The trip would take Joseph nearly two years from start to finish. By the time he returned to Gamaliel in Jerusalem, he would be qualified to take over the old man's business as a full-fledged south lands trader. *Perhaps,* Joseph thought, *I will be able to fulfill the plans that Ezekiel, Gamaliel, and Joab started so many years ago.*

Joseph looked forward to his life as a trader. For too many years he had spent his time as a revolutionary hiding in the shadows, fearing the touch of the Roman soldier. As a trader, he would live out in the open, and at the end of every trip, come home to his Aleya. What better life could a man ask for?

Around him the caravan stirred. Men fitted the few camels with bridles and secured the goods on the animals' backs. Others busily loaded the wagons rented from Juventius. At Boaz's command, the entire group moved forward. Aleya, in the cook wagon, brought up the rear. Her wagon was heavily guarded. It now served as the caravan's treasury. Three of Boaz's strongest men rode next to the wagon on horses. The port city was safer than most because it also was the headquarters city for the Tenth Legion. The Roman commanders wisely billeted their men in Caesarea rather than in the outlying regions of Judea.

As the caravan rode through the gates, Joseph looked up in amazement. The largest building he had ever seen was the temple in Jerusalem. In Caesarea, there were several buildings larger than the temple and many more that were the same size. Herod had built the city to curry favor with the Roman emperors, naming it Caesarea in their honor. He had outdone himself.

In addition to the magnificent palaces and Roman temples, Herod had constructed a dock that covered the entire man-made harbor. In the middle of the dock was a monstrous tower that could be seen by ships out at sea from miles away.

Some traders said that Caesarea rivaled the great Roman port city of Ostia and was second only to Alexandria in its magnificence. Caesarea was clearly the western world's entry into the eastern kingdoms.

On the streets of the city, Joseph saw people from throughout the empire. Half of the city's permanent residents were Jews, and the other half were a mixture of Syrians, Romans, and Greeks. The presence of the Roman army created another class of semi-permanent residents. And then there were the traders. Goods of all kinds lay stacked on the docks awaiting a ship to take them to Rome, Africa, or Greece. Textiles, amphorae of oil and wine, fresh olives, finely carved cedar, and Arabian carpets piled out of massive warehouses lining the docks. And ships! There were ships everywhere and of every imaginable kind.

The most common were the Roman biremes and triremes, two-and-three-deck ships that were the fastest ships on the sea. Simple coastal ships with rounded bottoms and a single sail signaled the presence of Jewish traders who traveled up and down the Judean coast. These mariners never lost sight of land, pulling up to the shore each evening. There were also strange, single-sail ships with a rakish design. Joseph later learned that these were dhows, sailed by Arabian traders from the south lands.

Caesarea had one of the largest slave markets in the region, proof that the trade in human cargo was the fuel behind the expansion of the Roman Empire. Joseph and Baalcath walked among the markets examining the goods for sale. They turned down one alley and came upon a specialized slave market that traded in golden-skinned women with almond-shaped eyes.

Joseph stared at the women. He broke his concentration long enough to ask Baalcath, "Where do you suppose these slave girls have come from? I have never seen women who looked like this."

"There is a land down the African coast that I have heard of. It is from this land, I suppose, that these women come. Only Arabian traders traffic in these women, and only the Bedouin accompany them to the slave markets in Caesarea. They fetch a handsome price and are never sold on the open markets. Come. We better leave. We're not supposed to be here."

The two traders turned on their heels and made their way toward the opening of the alley. All of a sudden the light from the opening was blocked by one of the largest men Joseph had ever seen. He was swathed in white robes from head to toe and carried a strange-looking sword.

He looked down at the two men and said something in a dialect Joseph had never heard. Baalcath tried a language from the south of

Chaldea. It wasn't exactly like the language the man spoke, but he did understand some of the words. He answered Baalcath gruffly and made a menacing move with his sword.

Baalcath hurried Joseph past the large man into the light of the market square up ahead.

"Baalcath, who was that?" Joseph asked in amazement.

"First of all, my inexperienced trader, he was a Bedouin, actually a guard from the palace of the king in the south lands. And he made it very plain that if we were not interested in buying, our lives would be forfeited if we did not make haste to leave. Let's consider ourselves fortunate that we did not see one of the women unclothed. If that were so, we would have never left that alley alive."

Joseph just shook his head at their good luck. Nagging in his mind were Baalcath's words "a guard from the palace of the king."

Chapter Thirty-Eight

The two of them walked across the market square where they came upon a wine shop. "Come in with me, Joseph. I shall treat you to a drink like you've never had before."

"Baalcath, you old son of a whore. What miserable fortune of mine has brought you through my door?" the proprietor roared.

Baalcath ran to the back of the shop and embraced the man who stood there in the half-light cast by the shop's small windows. "Propertius, I have money to waste, that is, my friend's money to waste. I couldn't think of a better place to throw it away in than this smelly hovel of a tavern. Go in the back and draw us two cups of that miserable drink you learned to brew in the land of Britannia. And bring some of your worm-eaten bread, too."

Propertius withdrew behind a curtained doorway. Baalcath and Joseph were the only customers in the tavern. Nonetheless, Baalcath drew Joseph close to him and counseled him to listen closely. "He served in the Roman navy for over twenty years. He has been all over the empire, ferrying soldiers to-and-fro wherever the emperor wanted them. His knowledge of the shipping lanes and the threat of pirates are unequalled. When he comes back, listen to him. He may seem like a loud-mouthed bore, but he will start to make sense when he trusts you."

Propertius returned with a jug full of foaming liquid and three large cups. "Baalcath, you did say your friend has the money to pay for my drink, didn't you?"

"How you have lived this long without your throat getting slit is beyond me. Come, sit down and join us." The tavern's proprietor sat down and plunked the jug and three cups on the rough-hewn table. Joseph looked at the foaming liquid, wondering what it was.

"This is mead, boy. This is what the blue-painted devils in Britannia drink. I took a liking to it, having served in a campaign to take those blasted islands. We never really succeeded, but I did develop a taste for this sweet stuff."

Joseph looked at Propertius, thanked him, and took a drink. Immediately, the cloying sweetness of the honey-based beverage hit the back of his throat, and he began to cough. The liquid flowed out of his mouth and nose, and his eyes began to tear.

"What is this godforsaken stuff? How can you drink this camel's piss?"

"Now, now, Joseph," Baalcath said gently, "let's not insult Propertius here. After all, he brewed this mead."

Propertius just sat at the table and laughed. "You know, boy, this takes a while to like. I daresay one day at a tavern isn't enough time. But you're welcome to come here any time."

Joseph looked up, remembering what Baalcath said about the old tavern-keeper, and gamely swallowed the rest of the mead. "Fill it up again and fill me up with your wild tales of the sea. I will soon make passage to Alexandria."

"Propertius," Baalcath jumped in, "this is Joseph's first sea voyage. Gamaliel is training him to run the trading operations in Jerusalem. Joseph and his girl are on their way to Alexandria, then over to the Red Sea, and finally by caravan to the south lands of *Arabia Felix*."

"Aleya is not my girl, as you say. I am protecting her as she makes her way back to her father. She is also my partner in this trading venture," Joseph protested.

"Baalcath," Propertius joined in, "it seems to me that this young man is protesting too much about this girl for her not to share his bed. But who cares, eh? Let me share my stories."

Baalcath and Joseph settled into their chairs. The stories of this grizzled sailor could go on for hours, and both men wanted to be comfortable.

The light coming through the tavern's small windows had turned into the golden orange of the late Mediterranean sun. Joseph looked up from his cup of mead and realized that he and Baalcath had been at the tavern of Propertius all day. But it was a most profitable day. He had learned more about the shipping routes between Caesarea and Alexandria than he had thought possible. And he learned more about the danger of pirates than he had cared to learn.

The three men were draining the fourth jug of mead when one of Baalcath's camel drivers burst through the front door. "Baalcath, I have been looking for you all day. Boaz is on a rampage. A Roman trireme is to set sail tomorrow evening, and the trade goods must be loaded this night. You better get back to the docks now."

Joseph and Baalcath said good-bye to Propertius and stumbled drunkenly through the tavern's door. They locked arms and walked back to the dock to find their ship.

The massive Roman ship looked like a ghost vessel with the flames of its torches reflecting off the harbor's waters, illuminating the sides of the great ship. *If this is a Roman trading vessel, then what must a Roman ship of war look like?* Joseph thought as he walked up the plank to the floating ship.

He craned his neck to see the top deck. It definitely was a merchant ship. He walked around the ship, inspecting every line in her build. After all, she would be his home for the next three weeks as he and Aleya journeyed to Alexandria. When he got to the back of the ship, he looked at the lettering painted on the stern—*Bonus Nauta*. Joseph translated the name into Hebrew: "Good Sailor."

I only hope this vessel sails well. I don't care about the crew. The stories that Propertius told him about pirates on the Mediterranean made him shiver. *Thank God this ship is as big as she is.* He would hardly venture on the open waters in anything smaller, especially when the pirates, Propertius said, had commanded triremes themselves.

This leg of the trip south had come upon him unexpectedly. He had barely spoken to Aleya about the sea voyage, and yet here he was, standing on the dock in the middle of the night, preparing to cast off on the morrow. The trip to Alexandria was an important part of his promise to return Aleya to her homeland. All ships docked at Alexandria. All caravans used Alexandria as a staging area for trips south. When they arrived in that Egyptian city some three weeks hence, they would be ever closer to reaching their separate goals—Aleya to her home and Joseph to what he hoped was his marriage to Aleya.

Under the stern direction of Boaz, they succeeded in getting the trade goods loaded and stowed away safely. The sailors had conscripted Baalcath and Joseph to help with the loading of the trade goods. His muscles ached, but Joseph didn't mind. With each parcel safely stowed on board, he came that much closer to being with his Aleya. The ship's captain signaled to the men on the dock that the *Bonus Nauta* was fully loaded. They could go back to their bunks. With these thoughts in his head, Joseph left the dock and slowly walked back to his temporary lodgings.

Baalcath stumbled back to the house Boaz had rented. Joseph took some time for himself and walked around the docks. It had been days since he talked to Aleya. And he missed her. The press of the business getting the trade goods safely counted, paid for, and stowed away had stolen time away from her. Aleya was busy cooking for the constant stream of traders going in and out of the portside house. Boaz, it seemed, deliberately kept them apart so they could concentrate on the business at hand. *Soon,* Joseph thought, *we shall be together for a full three weeks. I will make my intentions known to her and tell her that I love her and that I want to make her my wife.*

The morning had come too swiftly. Joseph's body ached from working on the ship. His head ached from the mead he had consumed listening to Propertius. He walked out of the small house that Boaz had rented and saw Aleya making her way to the ship. He ran ahead and caught up with her. "Good morning, Aleya. Do you know where you are going?"

She looked at him as if she didn't know who he was and just kept walking ahead.

Joseph stood on the docks, trying to figure out what was wrong with Aleya. He ran after her again and grabbed her arm. "What's the matter? We're ready to begin the voyage that will bring us closer to your home. Why are you avoiding me?"

"Avoiding you!" She spat out the words. "We have been in this miserable port city for almost two weeks and what have I seen of you? Nothing but a head dipping into the bowl of porridge that I prepared! Did you ever come to me and say, 'Aleya, let's take a walk on the docks and talk about the future.' Did you even know I was here with you? No! You spent your time in the taverns listening to old sea tales and left me with the caravan whores. Is that what I am supposed to be? A caravan whore?"

She ran ahead to the *Bonus Nauta,* tears streaming down her face. Joseph stood on the dock, feet planted firmly as if they were made of stone. *What did I do? I had work. I couldn't take walks along the docks with Aleya. What does she expect of me? Why do I always seem to do the wrong thing in her mind?*

He shook himself out of his stupor and continued down the dock to the *Bonus Nauta*. Once at the ship, he looked up at the gangplank, the very same gangplank that Aleya had just walked up. At the top of the gangplank stood the captain. "You, boy, you there! What do you want?" the captain cried.

Joseph took some time to compose his thoughts. He had to give the man the right answer and with the right spirit. He may have joined the caravan as a slave, but he was still caravan master as long as he was afloat. Mustering as much bravado as he could, he shouted back to the captain. "I am Joseph, and I am in charge of all the trade goods on this boat."

"Very good, Joseph. I am Rhenus. I am captain of this ship. And, when the trade goods come aboard, I am in charge of them. You are a passenger and a slave to boot! Come up here and address me properly."

Joseph forgot his slave identity. If he dropped this masquerade for just a little bit, he could be returned as a fugitive from Judea and sold into slavery. "This is something I must not forget," he mumbled to himself as he walked up the gangplank to meet his lord and master.

"Worthy Captain. I am Joseph, a slave of Gamaliel who has been entrusted with this consignment of goods. I ask your pardon as I seek to find my lodgings on your ship."

"There are no slaves above deck on my ship. All the slaves are below. But mind you, take care and be alert. We have a troublesome trip head of us. The pirates from Wagonhage are out again, preying on Roman triremes. Are you handy with a sword?"

Joseph ran to his pack that he had left lying on the deck. He withdrew his Roman sword and brandished it in front of Rhenus. "I am accomplished with this, Captain."

"You carry the sword of the Tenth Legion. Either you stole it or you were a favorite of a legionary. What was it, my boy? Tell me. We'll be shipmates for the next three weeks, and I want to know how much I can use you. That girl that's aboard? She's too thin. I'm afraid I'll run her through with the first thrust. You might be more to my liking, especially if a legionary has trained you well," Rhenus laughed.

Joseph looked at him with rage and ran at the captain, charging headlong into his ample belly and knocking him to the deck. Hardened by the caravan trek, Joseph was a bundle of muscle. He held the flat of his sword against the captain's neck and goaded him to say more. "Now, Captain, exactly what were you planning to do with me or that girl? Tell me, you fat tub of lard, or I'll change the position of this blade 'til it cuts through your jowly neck."

The captain's back was flat on the deck, and he sputtered with surprise. Joseph's weight was too much to bear, and the look in his eyes spelled murder. "It was nothing, my young man. I was just testing you. I needed to know what kind of man you are. Let me up and we'll move to my cabin to discuss these things."

Joseph looked at the man, laying supine on the deck. He let the man up and pressed him against the ship's rail. "Tell me, Captain, what do you need to know?"

"Where do you want your goods stowed? That's all."

Joseph walked away. He didn't see the first mate of the ship hanging back in the shadows or hear the conversation between the captain and his mate.

"Captain, do you know who we will sacrifice to the sea gods the first time we run into trouble?"

"Lodus, there's no need to ask that question. That young man and his bitch will be the first people we send over to the pirates. And, we get to keep the trade goods. After all, abandoned trade goods are the property of the first ship that gets to them."

Chapter Thirty-Nine

Joseph said his good-byes to Boaz and Baalcath. Rhenus's men prepared the ship to set sail. Boaz's men had loaded the trade goods into the ship's hold. Joseph had already inspected them, passing through the lower decks where slaves manned oars to propel the ship when the wind died.

Joseph stood on the deck, looking over the harbor. He said a quick prayer for the unfortunate wretches chained below. *Slavery is as natural a part of life as breathing and eating, but there is no need to mistreat slaves. Our writings teach us they are to be treated well, and, sometimes, honored. I'll never be accustomed to the treatment of slaves under the pagans.* He shook his head once again, and walked down the gangplank where Aleya was awaiting him.

"All is well with the ship? You look a little troubled."

"Not to fear, my love. The ship is sturdy, and the captain is experienced. We'll be in Alexandria before you know it. Boaz gave that old pirate strict orders to leave us alone. The captain's name is Rhenus. He spent years in the Roman navy, and he knows his way around these waters. We shall always be in sight of land except for a day or two when we get close to Egypt and round the Sinai Peninsula on our way to Alexandria."

Rhenus saw the two talking on the dock. He whistled to them to get their attention. "You can't stay on land all day if you expect to get to Alexandria. Mark my words, it's a long walk," Rhenus shouted. Behind him, a few of his sailors joined in the laughter. Joseph and Aleya took note of the captain and made their way up the gangplank.

Rhenus turned his attention to getting the ship seaward. Lodus, the first mate, showed them to their quarters. He brought them to the stern where an overhang made of heavy linen was strung between rails. It provided relief from the sun and protection from the rain. It also served as a makeshift portico for the small room behind the wooden wall to which the canvas was attached.

Lodus motioned to Joseph to drop his belongings under the linen overhang. "You, my stalwart fighter, will sleep here. We'll tie up a piece of sturdy material between these two posts. You'll make your bed there falling asleep peacefully as my beautiful *Bonus Nauta* gently rocks you to sleep.

"And you, my lady, have the honor to sleep in the first mate's cabin. I have given up my unworthy accommodations for the duration of this trip. You will avoid the prying eyes of the crew and be able to entertain your man in privacy."

The last words dug into Joseph. He knew that Lodus was goading him. Joseph looked at him and decided not to take the bait. His sword was still in his baggage at his feet. Lodus had a wicked looking dagger stuck in the rope cinching his robe. There was little to gain in accepting the muted challenge from this seagoing vermin.

Joseph and Aleya stowed their belongings. They heard a great shout, and the deck began moving underneath their feet. Joseph heard a steady drumming from somewhere below his feet, and the *Bonus Nauta* slid gracefully into the open waters of the harbor.

Caesarea was a man-made port. There was no natural harbor to protect ships from the sea's storms. So King Herod had decided to create a harbor, a huge stone enclosure open to the sea from the front.

The ship slipped through this man-made harbor past the lighthouses on either side of the stone docks and into the open waters of the Mediterranean. Once it made the open sea, the wind picked up. Rhenus looked about, wet his finger to test the wind, and ordered his men to raise the two sails.

The *Bonus Nauta* was a trireme, a ship with three banks of oars. The lower decks held the slaves who manned the oars and the cargo loaded at the dock. The upper deck was open, providing a place for the captain and the crew. Like Joseph, the sailors slept on the top deck on fabric stretched between poles.

The ship was capable of navigating the open seas easily. But safety reasons and protocol required that all southbound ships in the Mediterranean hug the coastline. The Roman navy was weak in this part of the world. Piracy was always a problem. More cargo and human lives were lost to piracy than any natural disasters.

The hull consisted of one-foot-thick oak planks. It could withstand any battering ram. Fire missiles bounced harmlessly off the sturdy sides. A rounded railing enclosed the top deck. Its shape made it difficult for grappling hooks to grasp the railing. The ship was built to fend off any boarding attempts by pirates. Only a Roman warship could seize them, and that was unlikely. The Roman navy protected merchants. It did not attack them.

The brisk winter wind filled the sails and propelled the *Bonus Nauta* down the coast. Rhenus seemed satisfied with the ship's progress and made his way below. Joseph and Aleya settled into their little corner underneath the linen overhang. *The trip to Alexandria should be uneventful,* Joseph thought, *with only a coastal landing once or twice to break up the monotony.* Land was far off to his left. On his right was the open sea. In front of him was the way to the south lands.

The *Bonus Nauta* had been on the water for ten days—alone, it seemed, in a vast blue desert. Rhenus left them alone. Lodus only spoke to them when necessary. Only the ship's cook, a wizened old sailor good for nothing else but tending the cook fire, spoke to them.

At one evening meal—Joseph and Aleya ate alone—Joseph asked the cook, Adah was his name, why they hadn't seen any ships.

"Ships? You expect to see ships at this time of the year? No one in his right mind makes passage in these waters during the winter. If it weren't for the extra gold that Gamaliel sent along, I'd be home in Caesarea, sleeping in my house, safe and sound."

"Adah, no one told us about the winter storms. Could Gamaliel have given Rhenus enough money to make this passage worthwhile?" Aleya asked.

"Young lady, Rhenus is a pirate. He tells everyone that he is an honest merchant plying these seas with cargo. But the man is wanted in every province of the empire. Didn't you notice that he never set foot in Caesarea? Didn't you think that it was unusual that we loaded the ship at night and set sail before dawn? Rhenus had to get out of Caesarea before the Roman prefect knew who he had at the dock."

With that, Adah gathered up the dishes and left, cautioning the young people to keep their mouths shut. "The less you know about the *Bonus Nauta*, the better. Sleep well. We'll be rounding the Sinai tomorrow, and then it's to the open waters before making landfall at Alexandria. You are almost off this ship. It's best that you forget you were ever on it." They looked at each other and said nothing.

The next morning, the weather was rougher and so were the seas. Joseph mentioned this to Rhenus, asking him if there was a winter storm headed this way. "There is no storm. The Sinai Peninsula has a great effect on the waters around here. Whenever we take this route around the Sinai coast, we run into weather like this. Don't forget, just ahead of you is the great Africa. Her own currents and winds contribute to this roughness.

"I can handle these currents. I have sailed the cursed waters between Gallia and Britannia. Don't worry, this little bit of weather doesn't disturb me in the least."

Joseph wasn't worried about Rhenus's seamanship, just his reputation. African ports were known to be great slave markets. What was to prevent this pirate from selling him and Aleya once they made landfall?

At the midday meal, Adah was morosely silent. "What is it, Adah? Is there some reason you aren't talking to us?" Aleya asked.

"It is nothing, my lady. I just get nervous whenever we get close to the Sinai. It is the gateway to Egypt and Africa, and none of those places were ever to my liking. Come finish your meal. We have to stow away everything that's on deck. The passage will get rougher from now on."

The cook started to move away when Joseph grabbed his arm. "Adah, what is that land over there to my left?"

"That land? Oh, that is the Sinai," he replied.

The *Bonus Nauta* plowed through the choppy seas. No more smooth sailing. Joseph turned his attention from the land and turned around to look at Aleya. She was sleeping, curled up in a bundle of textiles that lay on the deck. How she could sleep when the waters were like this was beyond Joseph's understanding! He intended to stay awake as long as possible and keep his eyes open.

He went below to check the few animals he brought. There were three donkeys, his special charges, and four very disagreeable camels. All day long the camels bickered with each other. It was Joseph's responsibility to feed and water the animals and fill their stalls with clean straw.

Joseph bent to get some straw for the camels. One of the young males lowered its head and bit Joseph on his thigh. Joseph yelled and smacked the young male on the side of its head. The camel snorted, looked at Joseph, and loosed a glob of phlegm. Joseph avoided it just in time.

Joseph yanked down the camel's bridle and whispered in its ear. "I know your meat is tough. But I savor the day when I roast your flesh over an open fire." The camel just looked at him.

His animal chores finished, Joseph went up on the open deck and looked at the expanse of sea on his right. Far beyond the horizon lay Alexandria, Africa, and then Rome. *Shall I ever see Rome?* he wondered and let his gaze drift slowly to the left.

His eyes rested on the looming shape of the Sinai. Against the sand-colored backdrop of the Sinai Peninsula, Joseph thought he could make out a figure of something on the water. *Probably just one of those huge seafaring birds Adah taught Aleya and me about. Who else would be out on these waters during the winter?*

He turned aside and began tidying his belongings. Aleya drew up beside him. "Joseph, can you see out in the water, close to the Sinai? Is that another ship, or is the sun playing tricks on my eyes?"

Joseph rushed to the railing and, shielding his eyes from the sun, squinted in the distance. The haze from the sea made it difficult to get an accurate view from any distance, but the outline on the water was unmistakably a ship. Joseph ran to Rhenus.

"Captain, there is a ship off to our left! I thought you said no ship ventures into these waters during the winter," Joseph shouted up the deck where Rhenus was standing.

"Stand easy. That's probably a merchant ship that wandered off its route along the coast. There's nothing to worry about."

Joseph looked again out on the water. That ship wasn't wandering. It was getting closer to the *Bonus Nauta* every minute. Now, he could clearly see the ship. It was a sleek bireme of Roman design. On its deck were men with ropes. The ship was going considerably faster than the *Bonus Nauta* and would be alongside in a matter of minutes.

"Rhenus, what's happening? That ship is headed straight for us!"

"It is nothing." Rhenus laughed. "It's just going to be a little transfer of cargo for me and Lodus. I warned you about pirates and how dangerous these waters could be."

By then the ship was alongside them. Its sailors threw ropes to the *Bonus Nauta.* Rhenus ordered his men to tie them to the railing. The pirate captain hailed the *Bonus Nauta.* "Good sailing, Rhenus! You are just in time."

Rhenus waved back. "Epiphrates, you old pirate, we have wonderful cargo for us to sell in Alexandria. Come aboard."

Rhenus turned to his only passengers, Joseph and Aleya, and told them to sit still. "No harm will come to you. We will offload this cargo. Then Lodus and I will board the other ship. I'll leave you with enough men to make your way to the coast where you can report this piracy to the Roman officials. No doubt they will want to know about such acts on the 'Roman Lake.'"

Joseph was furious. He didn't trust Rhenus, but such an open act of piracy was more than he could handle. *Wait until Gamaliel hears of this.*

The pirates boarded the *Bonus Nauta.* They laid wide planks between the two ships and began taking the cargo that was stowed on the top deck. This cargo was the most precious. It consisted of Gamaliel's finest textiles, worth more than their weight in gold. Storing them below would subject them to mold and mildew and the teeth of the shipboard rodents. Epiphrates knew well what he was taking first.

With all the cargo gone from the top deck, Rhenus motioned Epiphrates and a few of his men to go below. "We have some fine material down there. Come, follow me," Rhenus said.

One of Epiphrates's sailors followed behind Rhenus and clubbed him hard on the head. He fell to the deck. They also subdued Lodus. Soon the two conspirators were trussed up in their own ship's ropes.

"What is going on here, Epiphrates? Take my share of the cargo. I don't want it. Just untie these ropes. There is no way I can steer the ship like this."

"You won't be steering the ship anywhere, Rhenus. It is only going in one direction and that's down," Epiphrates laughed.

Joseph looked around and noticed that the other sailors were also bound. Chains held the slaves fast to their oars below deck. Only he and Aleya were free. But what could one man do against a whole ship? They had escaped the pirates' attention so far by hiding under a pile of linen sails. Epiphrates was too occupied with looting the cargo to look for hidden passengers.

The cargo theft completed, the pirates boarded their ship and cast away. Before going too far, the pirates launched fire missiles into the *Bonus Nauta*. The dry timber of the ship's upper deck caught fire immediately. It spread quickly to the linen sails. Soon, the entire ship was in flames.

Rhenus screamed, "Epiphrates, stop, I can pay you well. Gamaliel has given me a bag of gold. It's all yours. Just untie me. The others can die. Please, Epiphrates."

The pirate captain called back to Rhenus. "Rhenus, didn't you know there was a bounty on your head? The Roman prefect has promised three bags of gold to anyone sinking your ship. I will give him this proof." Epiphrates held up the ship's nameplate that his men had torn off the stern. All that would be left of the *Bonus Nauta* was a carved plaque hanging in the prefect's dockside villa.

Epiphrates's ship quickly drew away. The fire on the *Bonus Nauta* raged. Joseph did not know what to do. He was too far from the shore to swim. Yet, if he and Aleya stayed on board to fight the fire, they would surely die.

He ran the length of the ship, looking for something to help them survive. He heard a loud cracking sound above him. One of the masts holding up the sail had given way. Before he could do anything, the heavy timber hit him in the head. The last thing he heard was the sound of the roaring water as it washed over the rails of the sinking ship.

◆ ◆ ◆

The camel snorted loudly, hacking up a mouthful of phlegm. The slimy glob sailed through the air and smacked into the back of Joseph's head. Joseph lay facedown on the shore, his body half in the surf and half on the sandy beach. Tiny waves lapped at his legs. The camel's spit hit him hard enough to awaken him. He looked up, groggily pressing his hands against his aching muscles. He tried to remember what happened. All he could recall was the sound of water. *Water! That's it! Where am I?* Ignoring his soreness, Joseph jumped up and looked around. *Where is Aleya? Oh, please, God!*

As if his prayers were answered, he heard the gurgling sound of someone throwing up. He scrambled down the beach, and there, half submerged in the surf, lay Aleya. Her head and face were on the wet sand, the small waves washing over the rest of her body. Joseph ran to her and held her in his arms. He caressed her face and prayed that she would live. Aleya opened her eyes, looked at Joseph, and smiled. She leaned over again, spewing seawater out of her mouth.

"Shh, my darling. It's all right. We are safe." Joseph held on to Aleya as if she were more precious than all the gold in Alexandria. "Somehow, we are safe," he murmured into her ear.

Aleya sat up, the bouts of vomiting over. "We are 'somehow' safe, Joseph, because I saved us," she said defiantly.

Joseph looked at her, wondering how this small girl could have saved them. "Aleya, we were both unconscious on this beach. How can you say that you saved us?"

Aleya pulled some seaweed from her hair and straightened her linen shift. She turned to Joseph, looked him directly in the eye, and answered his question. "When the ship started to sink, I went looking for you. You were under a burning timber that had hit you on the head. I dragged you to the back of the boat, looking for something to hold before we jumped off. But it was too late. The gods of the sea made our decision for us. As the boat started to go down, it broke in half. The front part must have been heavier. It sank immediately. The back half stayed afloat. I pulled you to the middle of the deck and fell on top of you, exhausted."

Joseph marveled at her story. He looked behind him into the surf and saw half of the ship foundering in the water. It was intact. Curiously, the wreck still floated, though the back end was stuck in the sand.

The ship was in shallow water. Joseph tested the waters with his feet and walked gingerly toward the wreck to investigate. The ship's hold had cargo, which he and Aleya would pick over later, and it had bales of hay. *Hay! Of course,* Joseph thought, *the hay kept the wreck afloat. That must mean that the half of the ship that stayed afloat held the stables.* He turned to the shore where several animals stood, including his friend, the nasty young male camel. With a crazed laugh, he thanked the God of his fathers for the company of the beasts.

The animals survived the trip standing in the hold of the ship. When the wreck had beached, they walked through the shallow water onto dry land. Joseph had never been so glad to see the camels. They were his salvation. With them, they could go anywhere. He returned to Aleya and lay next to her on the sand. She held him in her arms as the sun set into the Mediterranean Sea.

Joseph awoke before first light. The stars dimmed one by one. The moon had set, but the sun had yet to peep over the horizon. The animals had bedded down for the night. He got up and walked to the water. He waded to the wreck to investigate what he could salvage. The stove was intact and on its side. Adah's fire-making kit lay next to the stove in its watertight box. There were three full water skins. There was little to eat except some fodder for the animals. *Well,* Joseph thought, *if the animals can eat this, so can we.*

The sun rose over the surrounding hills. Joseph grabbed the fire-making kit and soon had a blaze going on the beach, feeding the fire with driftwood. He didn't know what to do except turn inland, try to find an old caravan route, and make their way south.

Joseph stood and gazed to his east. *This is the Sinai. My ancestors crossed the Sinai into the Promised Land. I can do the same, even if it means going in the opposite direction.*

Joseph was luckier than most shipwrecked sailors. He knew where he was. He knew where he was going. And his nighttime patrols from Masada to Jerusalem taught him to navigate by the stars. *We'll be all right,* he thought, as he walked toward Aleya to wake her and gather the animals.

Chapter Forty

1991

Jordan and Daniel walked down to the shore. Jordan refused to characterize their time together as "dating." She had no time for romantic involvement, especially with this American. She was headed to the army and then to university. He was headed back to the States to finish his schooling.

Since their chance meeting in the wine bar a few weeks ago, they had gone out a few more times. But to Jordan, it was nothing serious. She had convinced herself that Daniel really was interested in archaeology, so she served as his private guide.

"You know, Daniel, there are probably more relics of archaeological significance in the Mediterranean than in all of Israel."

She turned her gaze toward the blue waters of the sea. "Ships, boats, vessels of all sorts have ridden those waves for over three thousand years…maybe more. My father says that underwater archaeology will reveal more secrets about our past than any of the digs on land."

"That may be true, Jordan, but how do you get to them? The Mediterranean is over one thousand feet deep in some places. And I doubt that the US Navy will lend its deep-water submersible to help you find clay pots."

She gave him a playful slap and dragged him to the harbor's edge. "Right down there, who knows what's underneath all that sand and silt?"

"Who knows, Jordan? Maybe your friends out there can tell us."

Off to their left, about a quarter-mile offshore, just outside the entrance to the harbor, a patrol boat sped back and forth. It was just another grim reminder that her country was in a constant state of war with, frankly, people like Daniel. Or, maybe with his Lebanese family here.

In just a few weeks, she'd be training for that war. Uncle Julian had kept his promise and managed to get her into an elite unit. Her father was furious with his old friend. Not until Julian told him that Jordan was going to the unit just for specialized weapons training and would be more involved in "research" did her father calm down. She knew what "research" meant to Uncle Julian, and it had nothing to do with archaeology.

"Jordan, why are you fixated on that patrol boat? You haven't said a word to me since we spotted it."

"It's nothing, Daniel. I just wonder how much longer we can keep going like this."

"Like what?"

"Like, how can we always be at war?"

"That's why you should come with me to the States. A girl with your background could have her pick of any of the universities over there. And my family would welcome you with open arms. We Lebanese are famous for our hospitality."

"I can't go. You know that."

"I don't know anything. You never tell me anything."

"Let's not talk about the future. We've got now to worry about. Just think about the cargo on those ancient boats. They'd stop here in this harbor, offload their cargo, and send the goods by caravan to all points in the Middle East. Sometimes I wish I lived in those times. They must have been simpler than what we're dealing with."

"No, Jordan, you're wrong. Let's talk about the future. Our studies will unite us for the future. I'll switch to archaeology as a full-time student and come here for graduate work. The past can be our future. Somehow and for some reason I can't explain, I feel that the past is calling to us as strongly as our future. We can't ignore that. Listen to me…"

She turned away from him and stared at the boat.

Daniel spun her around and held her in his arms. "Jordan, I love you. Don't run away from me."

"Daniel, I can't. Let's go back."

Chapter Forty-One

74 CE

In a lifetime long ago, another couple led a most unusual caravan away from the shores of the Mediterranean Sea. It consisted of two people, four camels, three donkeys, and a handful of supplies. This caravan headed to the fabled kingdom of the south lands.

Joseph and Aleya sat astride two camels. He led the two other camels and the three donkeys on a tether. Joseph clucked his tongue, and the camels headed east.

They rode for days, Joseph navigating at night by the stars. He discovered a well-worn caravan route and followed it from oasis to oasis. None of the places they stopped had the lushness of Ein Gedi. A few mud holes provided barely drinkable water and spindly palm trees gave up their withered dates. The animals foraged where they could. Joseph tried to follow the coastline of the Mediterranean as far as he could, then turned further inland. He didn't know that when he headed inland, just behind him in the opposite direction was the Red Sea. On it sailed any number of ships that would have taken him south in return for the animals.

As they rode east, Joseph wondered if he had done the right thing. The land turned bleaker, far worse than anything he experienced in the Judean wilderness. He had no idea where he was. Immense dunes and shifting sands surrounded the small caravan. He relied solely on the camels now, for he had lost his way. Camels have the uncanny ability to sniff out water holes, no matter how small or how well hidden in the dunes.

Joseph suspected they were still following a caravan route. Something told him that this land, while it wasn't inhabited, did know the touch of man. Aleya was a marvel of patience and comfort.

Each night, they snuggled together. As extreme as the heat was during the day, even worse was the cold at night. At first, they kept their distance, trying to retain a measure of decorum. But the quest for survival soon took over. Not only were they sleeping closely wrapped about each other, they had the animals next to them, too. Their body heat and the animals' body heat kept them alive at night.

They pushed on day and night. The landscape never changed. Sand, dunes, and more shifting sand were all they could see. Joseph could tell by the sun's position that they were pushing farther south. He looked down at the leather saddle strapped to the camel's back. There were sixty marks on it, each one cut into the leather by Joseph's sword. Each mark signified the passage of another day.

He and Aleya had become seasoned desert travelers. Their skin was dried to a leathery brown. They had both become used to the sway of the camel's movement across the desert sands. Joseph had even made peace with the young male he rode. The camel, which he named Moses, because he hoped the animal would lead him out of the desert, had even stopped spitting at him. The donkeys had died weeks ago. Joseph and Aleya had feasted on their tough meat.

On the morning of the sixty-second mark on his saddle, Joseph was prepared to die. He weighed barely more than the empty water skin tied to Moses's side. Aleya drooped herself across her camel, never raising her head. Joseph held no hope. They had entered the land of the black water and the *djinn*. He prayed each night that the devils of the desert would come and take them out of their misery. The black water fouled whatever wells the camels found. Even those stupid animals refused to drink from such tainted sources.

In his heart, Joseph agreed to push ahead, if for nothing more than to fulfill the fantasy that Aleya still believed they would find the desert palace of her father. Night came and he prepared the evening camp. The landscape had changed slightly. The black waters still bubbled to the surface, but there seemed to be more rocks in this area. Joseph led his small caravan into the shadow of the rocks. Joseph could take no more. Aleya was dying. He had to stop.

In the stark moonlight of the Arabian Desert, Joseph steered the small group into the shelter afforded by the boulders that rose from the desert like an abandoned village. He looked around. *This is where we shall die.* Aleya dropped at the feet of her camel, too tired and despondent to prepare a camp. Joseph led Moses further into the rocks, fondly petting the animal that used to be his enemy. Moses dropped to his knees.

Joseph knelt by the exhausted camel. Moses looked at Joseph, the camel's long eyelashes resting on half-closed eyes. Joseph placed his arm around the camel's neck and spoke softly to him. "I know how you feel, old friend. You have brought me very far. But there is nowhere else to go. I promise you, you shall not wander these barren lands. Tomorrow, I will say my morning prayers and take you behind the rocks. You won't even feel my sword. It is that sharp." Moses blinked at him, clearly exhausted, and rested his head on the sand. All was quiet in the camp of Joseph and Aleya.

In the middle of the night, Moses began bleating. Joseph sat up, looking for a reason for the animal's discomfort. He raised his eyes to the sky and saw the Dog Star overhead. *It is the middle of the night. What is going on with Moses?* The animal pitifully rose to his knees and walked over to Aleya's mount. Moses nudged the other camel—Aleya never named her—and bit her on the rump. The camel coughed and tried to bring up some phlegm from her parched throat to spit at Moses, but she couldn't. Moses stood and butted the other camel until she stood.

Joseph didn't know what was going on, but he trusted Moses's instinct. He leaned over and shook Aleya. "Wake up! Wake up! I think Moses smells water."

Joseph would never know how close to death Aleya was. All he would remember was that he felt the flutter of wings pass over his body when Aleya came to and smiled at him. Later on, he would remember this night. Recalling the Passover services, he wondered if he, like his ancestors, had escaped from the Angel of Death.

"Aleya, please get up. Moses smells water. Something has revived him. Let's trust him one more time. He will bring us to water."

"I am almost out of hope. But where you go, so will I," Aleya said weakly. Joseph helped her onto her camel. He mounted Moses gently. The camel turned his head, and its ugly face looked squarely into Joseph's eyes as if to say, "Trust me." Moses took off in a weary lope. Joseph hung on, barely. Behind him Aleya held onto her mount with her last ounce of strength. Grasping the camel's neck, Joseph fell asleep.

Joseph startled awake. He had no idea how long they had been traveling. Moses had stopped. The abrupt cessation of the camel's swaying gait startled him out of his sleep. The loud slurping of the animal's rubbery lips gave Joseph a cause for joy. He opened his eyes. Moses had brought them to an oasis! Palm trees fringed pools of clear water. Joseph dismounted and looked for Aleya.

He found Aleya's camel busily drinking from the same pool as Moses. But there was no sign of his love. He searched the ground frantically. Several paces from the pool, he saw an inert form lying in the desert sand. He rushed over. There Aleya lay. Her skin was cool—not a good sign in the desert—and her breathing shallow.

Joseph said a quick prayer. *My God, have we come this far just to die here? Please, take anything, take my life, but give hers back.*

Joseph took Aleya's still form and gently placed her in the pool. His mind raced back to the time when he saw her lying in the Ein Gedi pool being spied upon by that devil, Ezekiel. He laughed and cried at the same time. *My God, my God, bring her back.*

Whether it was his tears of love, his prayers to his God, or the cool water, Joseph would never know. Aleya raised one arm weakly and caressed his face. "My love, here I am."

He pulled her out of the pool and held her until the last star gave up its hold on the night sky. He held her until the moon raced its course through the heavens. He held her until there was no moon, no stars, just the two of them, alone in God's universe. They fell asleep in each other's embrace.

The sun's warmth peeked through the palm fronds. A slight breeze bent the smallest palm trees, and their fronds gently slapped Joseph's cheek. He would have loved to awaken next to Aleya with nothing but the sun to remind him that he was alive.

But, his senses honed by the months in the desert told him something else was in the oasis, something that could spell danger. He opened his eyes slowly, fearing the blinding light of the morning desert sun, when a shadow fell across his face.

Standing over him was the largest man he had ever seen. From head to toe, the man was clothed in a brilliant white cloth. He looked down at Joseph and moved to the silent figure of Aleya wrapped in his arms. Joseph became alarmed, fearing for Aleya's life.

Aleya opened her eyes and looked at the white-robed man. Upon her awakening, the man fell to his knees. "Princess."

"Aleya, who is he?" Joseph rose to his feet, fevered from thirst and the heat of the desert sun. He wobbled on unsteady feet to where the desert giant was standing over them. He bent down to take her in his arms. More quickly than he could have imagined, two white-robed giants grabbed him and held him back.

Through eyes blinded by the incessant sun and with a voice cracked and parched by the dryness of the heat, Joseph asked again, in a small and weary voice, "Who is he?" The desert sun grew stronger and seemed to whirl in the sky. Joseph's eyes rolled back into his head. He collapsed.

When he awoke, the air was much cooler. The sun was setting. Joseph glanced down his body. He was wrapped in a voluminous white garment from head to toe. One of the desert giants was pressing a wet cloth into his mouth, feeding him drops of water, one by one. Aleya was off in the distance surrounded by a tribe of the giants. Joseph pushed away the hand of the man feeding him water and stood. He looked about, shook his head, and cleared his mind.

There, that's better, Joseph thought to himself. His lips were still cracked, but the constant thirst that almost drove him mad was gone. His belly ached, but he could stand the pain. He walked slowly toward the group of men around Aleya. Again, two giants grabbed him and held him by the arms. "You shall not defile the princess, foreigner. Stay here until she bids you to come."

Joseph's world had turned upside down. From the brink of death he found himself in a dream—a bad dream populated by giant desert *djinn* who kept him away from his only love. One of the giants approached him. "Come, foreigner, my lady shall see you now."

Joseph walked behind him until they got closer and he saw the figure of Aleya lying on the desert floor, wrapped like him in swaths of white cotton. He broke away from his escorts and ran to her side. Before he could kneel down and see how she was, a giant hand came out of nowhere and slapped him across the head. He immediately lost consciousness.

He lay on the desert floor. In his semi-conscious state he saw Aleya standing over him. She wore the most precious silks. Jewels covered her hands and neck. Servants stood beside her with bowls of apricots and the sweetest dates. Somewhere in the background, nightingales sang, trilling their sweet notes over the perfumed desert air. He was at peace. His Aleya was taking care of him. He lay back and fell asleep.

He awoke to another vision. There was his Aleya, pressing cool cloths to his forehead. Behind her stood the giants, almost deferentially, awaiting her next words. Joseph blinked his eyes and looked again. This was no vision. His love, his sweet, truly held him in her arms, wishing and loving him back to life. He felt the warmth of her touch against his body and drank in the love that flowed from her. The cloud lifted from his eyes. The outline of Aleya's sweet face became clearer. He began to speak. Aleya—the real one or the vision, he knew not what—pressed her hand over his mouth. "Hush, my love. We are saved."

Joseph cared not for this life, and he did not believe in the next. All he cared for, wished for, and hoped for was that his Aleya was still with him.

"Here I am, Joseph. Lay back. Rest." Her voice came to him through a dense fog. He fell back to the soft bed of desert greenery that lay under him. He had almost drifted off into unconscious sleep when he heard the unmistakable snort of a camel clearing its throat. Joseph opened his eyes and looked up. Moses stared down at him. And Moses was about to spit.

Joseph quickly rolled to his side and the phlegm from Moses's mouth landed on the dry desert soil. Laughing, but still weak, Joseph rose on one elbow and pulled the camel's bridle down to the ground. Moses followed the pull of the bridle until his head was nearly resting on Joseph's chest. The surly camel began to nuzzle Joseph.

Now, I know I am alive, Joseph thought to himself as the rank smell of Moses filled his nostrils. *No loving God would create an afterlife with camels!*

Joseph rose weakly to his feet, supported by two of the desert giants. Aleya rose quickly to meet him, the desert giant ever at her side.

"Joseph, Joseph," she said, holding him closely to her breast. He felt her heart beating, and her warm breath caressed his cheek. "We are saved. This is Ruwalah. He is Bedouin. He owes allegiance to no man. He is a prince of the desert. But he honors my father. We are less than a day away from my father's palace. Ruwalah will bring us there. Joseph, we are saved."

At sunrise, the noise of the animals fussing over their fodder awakened Joseph. The Bedouin were preparing breakfast. Two of them leaned over a cook fire, stirring porridge in a pot. Aleya was about to bring it to Joseph when her Bedouin guardian scolded her.

"My lady, it is not fitting that you serve a foreigner. Here, let me."

Aleya grabbed the dish out of his hands. "He is my man. I will look after him." She fed Joseph like a mother would feed her baby. Her gaze rested solely on his face. All that existed in her world was right in front of her. She fed him gently and wiped his face.

"Ruwalah, we are almost ready to leave. Let Joseph wash his face and we shall be off."

Aleya got up and marched to her camel. Joseph looked after her, amazed at her transformation. No longer a slave, no longer a frightened passenger on a desert caravan, Aleya had taken on the airs of someone in charge. Aleya acted as if she were a princess. The Bedouin warriors heeded her wishes.

The head Bedouin ordered his men to ready the animals. Soon they had the camels arranged in a caravan. Ruwalah rode a magnificent horse, the beautiful Arabian breed Joseph had seen in the horse markets outside Jerusalem. *We must be near the Bedouin's home. No horse could live too far from home. The horse may be beautiful, but it wasn't a camel. Those ugly animals could march to the gates of hell and back without a problem.*

Joseph mounted Moses. The obstreperous camel turned his massive head and looked at Joseph haughtily. Joseph leaned forward and smacked the camel's face. "Moses, you have eaten. You have had your fill of water. You are, once again, the proud ship of the desert.

Don't you remember, just a few days ago, I was going to slit your throat?"

Moses hacked and the inevitable glob of phlegm flew to the desert floor as if to say he had heard nothing that Joseph said. Joseph laughed, threw back his head, and said a prayer of thanks that he was still alive.

Ruwalah called for the caravan to move ahead. Once again, Joseph and Aleya were on the move. They had traveled for less than two hours when the landscape changed dramatically. Gone were the shifting sands and the ever-changing dunes. Gone were the parched earth and the sun-bleached sky. Joseph peered into the distance and saw mountains, vegetation, and clouds—all things impossible in a desert.

The Bedouin giant said something to him. Aleya moved her camel closer to Joseph and translated. "Ruwalah says that is what the Romans call *Arabia Felix*. Joseph, we are almost home."

We, thought Joseph. *I think not. You are home, my love.* We *are not almost home.* He kept his thoughts to himself, sinking deeper into worry about how his Aleya was changing right before his eyes.

Chapter Forty-Two

They rode, getting closer to the mountains. The closer they got, the more signs of life Joseph could see. He began to make out terraced gardens on the hills of the smaller mountains. They were green with plants and full of life. Water coursed down the hillsides in a measured stream, irrigating the vegetables and orchards planted in the rich soil.

Joseph was amazed. He had never thought such life could be brought forth from the barren desert. But then again, he had left the desert behind him. After months of traveling in the harshest environment on earth, Joseph had stepped into paradise.

The caravan wound around the base of the hills. In the distance, Joseph thought he could see a shimmering building, the heat of the sun causing it to waver before his eyes. The Bedouin said something.

Aleya rode up next to Joseph. "Don't worry, my love, I am at your side always. Ruwalah says he will send men to my father to let him know we are here. The king will welcome us with a feast and treat you like a prince. Oh, Joseph, we are home!"

Two Bedouin rode ahead and entered the gates of what Joseph could see was a great city. Ruwalah stopped the caravan just outside the gates and brought them to a well. He bade them to get off the camels and make camp until further news arrived.

Joseph and Aleya dismounted. They walked to the well. He looked about at the buildings that surrounded the well. They were richer and grander than any buildings he had seen in Jerusalem. *Jerusalem! Masada! They seemed so far away and in another lifetime. Shall I ever see them again?*

Joseph walked to the well. He sat down in the courtyard and gazed at the buildings. Mosaics covered the walls depicting scenes from desert life. Several fountains graced the courtyard, spewing water. One building, more richly decorated than the others, stood in front of him. *Is this the well that Ezekiel spoke of? Was the old man telling the truth?*

Joseph walked by himself through the buildings and talked to no one about his fate. Stable hands fed his camel. Servant girls swirled around Aleya. Joseph walked alone and glanced over his shoulder at Moses who stood contentedly chewing on fodder. Aleya was unapproachable. He laughed. *Now I am missing the company of that irascible beast!*

He heard a commotion behind him. The gates to the city had opened. A large party was making its way to the well. A troop of well-disciplined soldiers led a string of impeccably groomed camels outfitted with rich leather bridles and saddles. Behind them trailed two wagons covered with gaily-colored silk led by snow-white horses wearing jeweled harnesses. Atop the wagons were some of the most beautiful women Joseph had ever seen. A troop of musicians followed the wagons, playing on instruments Joseph had never seen. After the musicians came another line of camels, more richly outfitted than the first. Finally, atop a snow-white camel, the first Joseph had ever seen, was a palace official, clad in silks and jewels that would cost a king's ransom.

The caravan stopped at the well. The soldiers halted the camels. The wagons came to a stop. The soldiers ran back to the white camel and grabbed its bridle, pulling it down so the camel came to a rest on all four knees. They placed a small stool next to the camel. The little man slid out of the saddle, stepped down the ladder, and walked slowly to where Joseph stood. He passed by him as if Joseph were a column of salt in the desert. The women dismounted from the wagons and ran into the building where the Bedouin had led Aleya. The women emerged from the doorway where Aleya was, spreading flower petals on the dirt. Joseph fixed his gaze on the building's doorway. He saw Aleya coming through and made a move to greet her. Burly arms checked his movement. The soldiers kept him in his place.

The official walked closer to Aleya. *She looks like a desert queen,* Joseph thought. Her hair was oiled, cosmetics adorned her pretty face, and the most luxurious silks caressed her body. Aleya shooed her handmaidens away with a few quick gestures of her hands. She wanted to be alone when the old man finally reached her. Aleya stood up and threw her arms around his neck. "Oh, Uncle, I missed you so much."

The man nodded and held her gently, but respectfully. "Come, my princess, your father—our king—awaits you."

Joseph watched the two of them. Aleya's transformation captivated him. No longer was she his little desert girl. Like a butterfly wiggling its way out of a cocoon, Aleya left behind her desert rags and had become a bewitching desert queen. If there were any doubts in Joseph's mind about her stories all these years, the past two days quickly dispelled them. *Imagine that,* he thought to himself, *I have fallen in love with a real princess! And the princess loves me!*

Off in the distance, Aleya's Bedouin protector, Ruwalah, stared at Joseph. He had become less wary of Joseph, but he still did not trust the young Jew. If the king's physicians determined that the Jew had known Aleya in any way, Ruwalah would take great pleasure in removing the rest of the Jew's manhood to join the piece that was taken from him at birth. He treated Joseph with respect, as the princess commanded, but he did not trust him. Not once did Joseph escape the piercing gaze of Ruwalah's coal-black eyes.

The old man, who Joseph later learned was her uncle and the king's vizier, stopped the caravan in front of Joseph's tent. Aleya remained hidden in the royal litter, curtains closed and guarded by four massive Nubians.

"Young man, the king wishes to thank you for safeguarding his precious one. Kindly present yourself at the palace on the morrow. I shall send a guard for you." With that, he clapped his hands and led the procession back inside the city gates.

For the first time in almost a year, Joseph was alone, sitting in the tent the Bedouin had erected for him. Joseph stared at the silk wall of the tent, brooding about his future. He was alone, well, almost. Moses had pulled his stake out of the ground and, trailing his bridle and chain behind him, trotted over to Joseph's tent. The camel slid his nose under the tent. Joseph walked outside his tent, looking for the ugly camel. He found him and petted his nose.

"Here we are, Moses. I go from companion of a princess to the only friend of a camel. I have done very well for myself," he sneered. Joseph turned away in disgust and snorted. So did Moses.

Joseph sat on a stool the king's slaves had set up for him outside his tent. The king sent his men to ensure that Joseph had the finest possible accommodations outside the city walls. The silk tent was nearly as big as his house back in Jerusalem. Soft carpets covered the rough earth. The slaves positioned regal furniture inside. They had even put in a bed! Outside, they left Joseph a stool so he could sit and watch the goings-on. Joseph rose from the stool and walked in the direction of the city.

Immediately, one of Ruwalah's giant kinsmen blocked his way and spoke to him in a tongue that sounded like Hebrew, but Joseph still could not understand him. Joseph stepped aside to walk around the Bedouin, but the Bedouin followed, raising his voice again. Joseph looked at the man and shook his head to signify he didn't understand what he was saying. A slave scrambled over to Joseph, head respectfully bent and eyes to the ground, and addressed Joseph in Hebrew. "Master Merchant, I beg you, allow me to help."

Joseph was so excited to hear his native tongue that he grabbed the slave by the hair and pulled him upright. His gaze caught the slave's eyes. Immediately, the slave, horrified at the personal contact, fell to the ground expecting the lash to strike his back. The Bedouin raised his horsewhip and started to bring it down on the slave's head. Joseph caught the Bedouin's wrist and checked his swing. For a moment, the two were locked in a silent battle of wills. The Bedouin, in the spirit of desert hospitality, withdrew. Joseph raised the slave to his feet. Ruwalah came over to inspect what was going on in his camp. The Bedouin chief stood over Joseph and the slave, listening intently to their conversation.

"Slave, look at me. We are kinsmen, Jews. There's no need to fear."

"Master Merchant, I am not allowed to speak to you. Besides, we are not kinsmen. I am a poor wretch from Samaria. Even the lowliest beggar in Jerusalem thinks himself greater than the richest Samaritan."

"Never mind and speak to me. What is your name?"

"I am called Mattias."

"Mattias? That's a strange name for a Samaritan. Surely you are joking with me?"

"No, Master Merchant. I follow the young rabbi, Yeshua bar Yosef, whom the Romans killed. I took the name of one of his followers out of respect."

"Tell me, Mattias, how did you find yourself among these heathens?"

"I will gladly tell you all. But I must seek permission to even stand next to you."

"I shall get it. Tell Ruwalah that I desire you as a personal body servant. I ask it as a favor in the name of the king."

Ruwalah glanced at Joseph at the mention of the king. This let Joseph know that Ruwalah understood more than he let on. Joseph looked at the giant Bedouin and smiled. Ruwalah looked back and nodded. He gave a command to one of his men. The Bedouin ran to where the other slaves gathered and brought back a smith. The smith took out his tools and removed the leg shackles from around Mattias's ankles. Ruwalah motioned to Joseph that Mattias was now his.

Joseph brought the wretched slave into his tent and rubbed salve the king's doctors had given him into the festering wounds around his ankles. He tore linen into strips and bound the wounds. "Now, rest, Mattias. You are mine now, and I command you to stay in this tent and attend me when I call." Joseph walked out of the tent toward the well, feeling good about what he had done. Moses snorted in assent.

The following day, in the late afternoon, Aleya's uncle, the vizier, came for Joseph. His entire retinue accompanied him. Behind them, a stable slave led a snow-white camel outfitted in a bridle of woven gold. "The king will see you now. He requests you join him for late supper. I will escort you to the palace. I have brought a camel for you," the vizier said.

Joseph made his way toward the beautiful camel when he heard a loud snort. By now, he recognized the source of that sound. Moses's baleful eyes followed him as Joseph reached the white camel. Joseph turned around and addressed the vizier. "Thank His Majesty for such a grand animal, but I prefer my desert camel who has seen me through this long trek to your magnificent city."

"As you wish, Master Joseph."

Joseph didn't know what to expect. He had heard Aleya's stories. He had listened to Ezekiel's tales. The sheer bulk and magnificence of the city walls and their fortifications told him something about the city. But there was nothing in all of his memory or the stories to prepare him for the sight that unfolded in front of his eyes when the guards opened the gates.

Every building was a shimmering, blinding white. Graceful arcades shaded the walkways between the buildings. There was water everywhere—in fountains, in man-made streams meandering through the city's squares, and in large reflecting pools. The entire effect was mesmerizing. Myrrh trees sprouted in miniature gardens, perfuming the air with their exotic scents.

Mattias, dressed now like a palace slave, met Joseph inside. With his hair cut and the filth washed off, Joseph realized that Mattias was younger than he. Yesterday, the Samaritan looked like an old man. "I shall stay next to you, Master, and be your guide and interpreter. I speak several of their languages as well as our blessed mother tongue. I can answer…"

"Be still," Joseph cut him off. "If I have any questions, I shall ask."

Joseph rode slowly into the city on Moses. The camel was on his best behavior as if the animal knew he was to be presented to the king. Mattias walked by his side, holding the camel's reins.

A royal party approached. The Nubians placed the vizier's litter on the ground, and he stepped out. To Joseph's surprise, he addressed him in Hebrew. "Come here, young man. We must purify ourselves before we enter His Majesty's chambers."

Joseph followed the lead of the vizier, washing his hands, arms, face, and feet. A beautiful slave girl rushed to him with a soft towel woven from the whitest linen Joseph had ever seen. The vizier told Joseph to remove his shoes and walk into the royal chamber with his eyes to the ground. He was to raise his head only when addressed by the king.

Two palace slaves opened a set of double doors. The vizier motioned for Joseph to follow, eyes downcast. Joseph sensed that the room was crowded, but he did not look up. More than anything, he wanted to see his Aleya.

"Brother," the king said, "you have brought me the Jewish merchant?"

"Yes, Your Majesty. It is he who guarded the life of the princess and brought her back to her father's bosom. He is called Joseph."

"Joseph," the king spoke out his name loudly, and Joseph raised his eyes. All of a sudden, the king rose and stepped down from the platform where his throne rested. There was a collective gasp in the royal chamber. Never had the king left his throne during an audience.

The king approached Joseph, accompanied by several palace slaves scurrying about spreading flower petals in his path. He was a large man, taller than Joseph, but with the fine features of Aleya. Joseph looked directly into the eyes of the king.

"You have brought me back my daughter. She who was dead is now alive. Joseph, you are favored of the king."

With these words, the entire chamber dropped to their knees. A slave, bearing a cedarwood chest, approached the king. The slave opened the chest. The king removed a ceremonial dagger on a golden chain and placed it in Joseph's hand.

"Brother, make it known throughout my city, throughout my kingdom, and throughout all of Arabia that Joseph of Jerusalem is favored of the king. I command you this day to do as I say.

"Joseph of Jerusalem, we shall feast later this day. Now, I presume, you wish to see the princess. Ruwalah, escort Joseph of Jerusalem to the women's quarter. Stay with him."

The king clapped his hands, and the audience was over. As Joseph walked out of the king's chambers, the palace courtiers bowed low to him, and the slaves fell to their knees. Only the vizier, begging indulgences for an old man, remained standing, but he bowed nevertheless.

Mattias scurried next to Joseph and walked with him to the women's quarters. The slave was beaming idiotically. "What is the matter with you, Mattias? You are smiling like a fool."

"Master, yesterday I was a dirt-eating slave, the lowest of the low in the vizier's household. Today I am the personal servant of the favored of the king. There is no higher noble in the kingdom. You even outrank the vizier."

That remark made him uncomfortable. He had no desire to outrank the king's brother and Aleya's uncle. He needed to see Aleya and plan their life together. Then he needed to leave this city before palace intrigue got the better of him.

Ruwalah stopped them in front of the women's quarters. Joseph motioned to go inside, but the giant Bedouin blocked his way. "You may not enter. No man may enter, not even the favored of the king," Ruwalah said slyly. "The princess's handmaidens will tell her you are here. Sit down by this screen. Her Royal Highness shall be on the other side."

Joseph waited by the screen, his eyes downcast. Suddenly, his heart suffused with hope and love, and his eyes brightened with joy. There was no need to tell him that Aleya was near. He could feel her spirit, sense her presence, and be soothed by her love.

Aleya sat down behind the screen, barely visible to Joseph. He raised his hand and stuck his fingers through the screen. Aleya raised hers and grasped his fingers. Joseph knew something was wrong. He knew his desert princess was sad. He knew her cheeks were drooping. They always did when she was sad. He heard her sniffle back tears.

"What is it, my love? Have you not heard? I am favored of the king. Should you not rejoice with me? What can stand in our way now that your father has honored me so?"

"Joseph, oh, Joseph," Aleya said and began sobbing. Joseph wanted to break through the screen, drying her tears with the flat of his hand. It was not to be. Ruwalah held him back. The king knew what he was doing when he commanded Ruwalah to accompany Joseph.

Aleya dabbed away the tears with a silk veil. "My father will not let us marry. I am betrothed to the Prince of Idear. It is an important alliance for my father, and I must do as he wishes. I cannot be with you, my love. I must obey the king."

Ruwalah grabbed Joseph's shoulder when he heard his anguished cry. The Bedouin stepped away to give the young couple some privacy. He knew the decision of the king. And he knew what it would mean to Joseph.

Joseph continued to cry out as Aleya got up and walked away. For the first time ever, the giant Bedouin gently put his arm around Joseph's back and escorted him to his suite of rooms in the palace.

That evening in the king's royal chamber, the feasting began. Palace slaves carried in tray after tray of sumptuous vegetables, roasted meats, fine wines, and sweetened dates. But Joseph had no appetite. Neither did the king. For both of them knew what was lost. The king knew he may have acquired more land and another kingdom, but he lost his daughter's love. Joseph, the favored of the king, lost his only love.

During the feast, the king rose from his throne. The music stopped. The courtiers silenced their chattering. The entire room awaited the words from the king's lips.

"Joseph of Jerusalem, favored of the king, hear me now. You have brought back my most precious possession. You have acted in honor. You wished to have more, but more I cannot give. But this I can."

And the ruler of all Arabia placed a gold medallion around Joseph's neck while he uttered the words that would last for many generations.

"Joseph of Jerusalem, favored of the king, I, Ahmal al-Fasheal, ruler of the desert, of all the lands from north to south and from east to west, from the lands of the black water to the blue waters of the pearl sea, give you and your family, your sons and their sons, their sons and their sons' sons, in perpetuity and forever, all the land as far as a camel can ride from east to west along the journey you took to return my daughter. You and yours shall

rule forever over the land of black water from the dunes of the Empty Quarter to the pearl beds of the sea. This I have said. This I have written."

The king got up and left. Joseph was to never see the king again. Near the back of the room a nervous scribe was busy etching the king's words on a piece of copper. Joseph saw the little man at the back of the room and felt sorry for him. All about him the courtiers feasted, but the scribe continued to work. Sweat dripped from his brow. His lap desk shook as he inscribed the king's words on the leaves of copper.

Joseph walked past the scribe as he left the dining chamber to go back to his suite. The low-born scribe was still there inscribing the king's words. Now he knew why the man's lap desk shook. The palace scribe's knees were knocking.

Joseph stayed in the palace for weeks enjoying the great sovereign's hospitality. Wherever he went, people bowed low, honoring him and envying him for his good fortune.

It was time for Joseph to leave. The king's word was final. He would never have Aleya, at least not in this lifetime. The vizier assembled a great caravan to accompany Joseph on his journey back to Judea. It was the greatest caravan the kingdom had ever assembled. There were over 2,500 camels and 300 merchants traveling north. The king had given Joseph trade goods to make him rich for several lifetimes. Joseph cared little.

The day came for the caravan to leave. Joseph mounted Moses. Mattias rode on a donkey at his side. As the caravan started up, the vizier's litter came to a stop next to Joseph. The old man got out holding a leather pouch. Joseph kicked Moses and the camel dropped to all fours. The vizier gave him the pouch.

"What is this?" Joseph asked.

"It is the king's words, his gift of land for you inscribed on copper. Guard it carefully, for it contains the words of a desert king, and those words last forever.

"By the way, Master Merchant, you may want to stop at the women's quarters on your way out. There may be somebody there for you." Joseph shouted his thanks, but the vizier had walked back to his litter. He never turned around.

The caravan threaded its way through the city. Joseph stopped Moses in front of the women's quarters and dismounted. He walked inside accompanied by Ruwalah and Mattias.

Behind the screen stood Aleya, as beautiful as he had ever seen her. He touched her fingers through the screen. Their lips met, and silent words were spoken between them. The two lovers were to part. Joseph reached into his robe and grasped the medallion her father had given him. He bent the soft gold back and forth until it broke into two.

Joseph slipped half of the medallion through the screen. "Take this, my love. And remember that I will always love you."

"Joseph, my Joseph, our love will never stop. I will see you someday, in some life. I will be with you again. This I swear. This I pledge."

Together, fingers grasping fingers, they pledged their love to each other, speaking softly, *"Until the last star gives up its hold on the night sky; until the moon races her course through the heavens; until there are no stars, no moon, just the two of us, alone in God's universe."*

Chapter Forty-Three

1996

The sun beat down on the dusty plateau of Masada. The troops stood at attention in front of the dignitaries on the reviewing stand. These were Israel's finest, the best of the best. Overhead, five jets from the Air Force screamed by in salute. The blue and white flag of the country fluttered in the breeze. The young men and women stood and sweated.

A gruff old man who looked like he could spit nails and eat glass addressed the troops. "You men and women will soon be part of the elite. There is none better in the world. The future of our country is in your hands. Colonel Hirschberg will now swear you in. Take your oath solemnly. We need you."

The old man stepped back from the podium and Julian Hirschberg stepped forward. His gaze settled on the soldiers stretched out before him on the top of Masada. In the front row, toward the left, her blonde hair gleaming in the sun, stood his "niece," Jordan Barash.

She wore the rank of lieutenant, a prerequisite afforded to her by his own wishes and her university degree. Today would be one of the few times she would ever wear the uniform of the elite soldier.

Julian Hirschberg had other plans for his niece. She would work with him and her father for the Israel Antiquities Authority. She was not only an outstanding military student—she would likely become one of the best archaeologists his country had ever produced.

Julian tapped the microphone on the podium. He knew that it was on, but the tapping helped him allay some of his nervousness. He could work very well in close quarters but giving speeches was not his talent.

"Soldiers, you stand here on hallowed ground. Almost two thousand years ago, one thousand Jews—men, women and children—chose to take their own lives rather than live in slavery under the yoke of foreign invaders."

Julian stumbled a bit, forgetting his train of thought. "Soldiers, we have brought you here to induct you into our country's finest unit. Never let the spirit of Masada leave you. Prepare to take the pledge."

A parade marshal called the troops to attention. They responded as a unit, their boots slapping loudly on the hallowed soil of Masada. Jordan looked at her Uncle Julian on the podium and swore a fierce oath. Under her breath, audible only to herself and the God of her fathers, she uttered the words, "Never again."

Chapter Forty-Four

78 CE

Joseph! Joseph! Where are you?" Miriam's screams echoed through the canyons above the Dead Sea. "Joseph, come here and kiss little Ezekiel."

Joseph finished his ritual washing and joined Miriam and his son in the small community at Qumran. It had been almost three years since he left the south lands. Aleya was but a memory, albeit a warm and cherished one, but a memory nonetheless. Here in Qumran, Joseph had the flesh-and-blood love of his wife, Miriam, and his son Ezekiel.

The trade goods he had brought back from the king's city made him wealthy beyond belief. Fasheal's grant as master merchant guaranteed Joseph's wealth for all time to come. He now supervised a profitable trading route from Judea down into the Arabian Peninsula. He had exclusive rights to import the resinous gum of the frankincense and myrrh trees that all of Rome coveted. The grim journey he and Aleya had taken from Masada back to her homeland was in the past. He had embraced his new life with a vengeance, establishing a business that so long ago, Ezekiel, Gamaliel, and Joab had tried.

Joseph settled in the Qumran community at the urging of his former slave, Mattias. The settlers at Qumran embraced a strict form of Judaism. The way of life appealed to Mattias who still followed the crucified rabbi. It held no attraction for Joseph. When they got to Judea, Joseph had freed Mattias.

His former slave left him, and Joseph traveled the countryside hoping to find the *djinni*, Ezekiel, at the oasis at Ein Gedi to tell him the news of the south lands. Joseph journeyed to Ein Gedi, arrayed in the trappings of a rich merchant. The humble huts of the oasis and the simple water pool brought back memories from another life.

Joseph found him, lying in the sandstone tomb next to his friend, Obabe'e. He said a prayer for the two friends and wandered back to the water pool. He sat down on the same rock where Aleya had sat, yelling at him for threatening the old man.

There are many memories for me here. Shall I be captive to them and stay here becoming the next "ghost of the oasis"? No. He was a rich merchant. He had a life in front of him.

Mattias came searching for Joseph and found him still camped at Ein Gedi. Joseph returned with his former slave, listening to him chattering about the new religion he had found. Mattias encouraged Joseph to join him at Qumran and embrace its teachings. Mattias had hoped that Joseph would follow the slain rabbi and his disciples. Joseph chose neither the rabbi's teachings nor the strict Qumran way of life, but he did meet Miriam in the little community above the Dead Sea. They married and soon the marriage produced his son, little Ezekiel.

The Qumran community was peaceful, far enough away from Jerusalem to be out of the hubbub of city life, but close enough to receive news of Jerusalem. He had never returned to the city, preferring not to experience firsthand the destruction the Romans had wreaked. He had agents in the city to do his trading.

Joseph was fond of Miriam, and he loved Ezekiel as any father would. His family was well cared for. Should his trading business ever falter, he had created enough credits to take care of his family for the rest of their lives. The gold chain and half-medallion given to him by Aleya's father were in safekeeping in the Qumran treasury. The value of the gold alone would take care of his family. Joseph wondered whether Aleya still held her half.

The deed Aleya's father had given him was well hidden in the caves near Qumran in a clay jar where the community stored its library. Joseph thought about the day in the magic city of S'ana when the king had given him forever, in deed, ownership of the land he traveled to return his only love to her father.

The vizier's scribe had engraved the king's bequest to Joseph on a square of copper. This was most unusual, since the favored material of the day was parchment—fine sheets of sheepskin thinly hammered out and dried to soft leather. It was an excellent medium for writing and held the scribe's ink very well. The scribes at Qumran used parchment or papyrus, storing the scrolls in the dry caves high about the Dead Sea. But copper would last forever like his gold medallion.

The crafty old vizier knew the importance of his brother's words. He chose copper to record the king's deed. Joseph was a younger man then, and the desert monarch's words signifying *forever* had little meaning. Now, he had a son. And his son would have a son. And his grandson would have a son. And his family would go on protected by the riches of the deed.

Over the years, Joseph learned much about the culture of the southern desert peoples. He knew the people held the words of their kings sacred. Even though the old king was dead, Abdul, Aleya's brother, still honored his father's gift, as would succeeding kings who ruled over the lands of the black water. And the deed, buried in the jar at Qumran, guaranteed their prosperity as a wealthy merchant family forever.

More than the deed, there was the half of the gold medallion. Joseph would pass the medallion to his son along with written instructions that it be given to the oldest child of each generation.

Gold was an excellent choice to mark the existence of the gift. Like his love for Aleya, it would last forever. *Until there are no stars, no moon, just the two of us, alone in God's universe.* Someday, Joseph was certain, those words would come true.

Life was good. His business prospered, and he enjoyed the love of his wife. Yet, the old revolutionary in him still craved action. He wanted to get back to Jerusalem to survey the city one more time before gray had colored his hair and his belly hung over his girdle.

Joseph had every sound business reason to return to Jerusalem. He might inquire about the ongoing revolution, but he had little desire to take an active part in it. He knew the Romans had taken over the entire city. They even changed its name.

He would enter as he was, a prosperous merchant coming to inspect his warehouses. The Romans would have nothing to do with him. Joseph would slip in and slip out and return to Qumran within a week. Maybe then his restlessness would disappear.

One evening, Joseph told Miriam about his decision. She, of course, fought his decision.

"Now, don't be worried, Miriam. I am just going to see what it looks like and to find a few old trading friends. I have been gone for almost three years. I must see Jerusalem again."

Joseph stared into the cooking fire. The thought of Jerusalem loomed larger in Joseph's mind in the past few weeks. Life at Qumran was good. The community's laws were too severe for him, but the leaders did not require all to follow them. Mattias submerged himself in community life, becoming an acolyte while still following the teachings of the slain rabbi.

By virtue of his marriage to Miriam, Joseph was shut out from all but the lowest levels of the community. That suited him fine. He had no desire for their strange code of celibacy. Had not God ordained man and woman to be together?

The years spent at Qumran went well. He had a wife who treated him respectfully. He had a beautiful boy who would carry on his name and his business empire. He would tell Ezekiel, one day, about the copper square and what it meant to the family. He had all a man could want. Yet, something kept nagging at him. Joseph knew what it was. He would go to Jerusalem and rid himself of the nagging feeling. He would strap his Roman sword about his waist, mount old Moses, and ride into the city. He might even be able to capture a bit of his past life.

His traders told him that the Romans had cracked down on all activity by the Jews. Valerius Sixtus, the Roman general who bid him farewell on Masada a lifetime ago, was leaving his command and finally returning to Rome. *Who knows*, Joseph mused, *I might even see the old man myself.*

The next day Joseph told Miriam he would be leaving for Jerusalem. "Don't worry, my dear, it's only a half-day's ride away. I can stay with friends there. I'll be back within a week. Look after Ezekiel. I'll bring something back for you and the boy."

Joseph kissed Miriam chastely on the cheek and hugged his little Ezekiel. "Don't worry, I'll be back soon." Joseph clucked his tongue. Moses raced down the hills toward Jerusalem.

"Centurion! Centurion! By all the gods who occupy space on the sweet seven hills of Rome, if my baggage and I are not on the wagon making our way to Caesarea in one hour, then you will wish you never had become a Roman soldier. And, should I miss the warship that is taking me back to Rome, then you will wish that whoever your father was never cornered whoever your mother was in the back room of some cheap *taberna*. Now get this baggage out of here."

"General Sixtus, my parents were—"

"I don't care who your parents were," yelled Valerius as he cut off the centurion in mid-sentence, "just get me on that wagon."

"Yes, General."

The centurion saluted and made his way quickly out of the presence of the great general of the Roman army, Valerius Sixtus. On his way, a comrade stopped him. "What's troubling the old man? I've never seen him so edgy before. Usually, he's good with us. You know, he once was a centurion and led the *Aquila* of the Tenth."

"Falcus," the general's aide said, "he has waited over two decades to leave Judea. Each year through a personal request of the emperor, he has stayed. Finally, Titus has agreed that it is time for the general to retire. You know, he's the last of the officers in Judea who was at Masada. That was almost four years ago. I never knew him before that, but others said it changed him."

"Marcus, you may be a general's aide and not a real centurion like me. But neither of us will have any rank if we don't get the good commander out of here and on that ship back to Rome. Let me give you a hand."

The two centurions resumed packing the wagon with a lifetime's accumulation of objects for Valerius Sixtus. Valerius was following with a personal escort on his horse, Arinax III.

"Imagine that! The commander has the temerity to name his horses like we name our emperors. Arinax the third, indeed! What is the old man thinking?"

"If I were you, Falcus, I would keep my thoughts about the general to myself. And I wouldn't even go near his horse. They say that the first Arinax saved his life when the general led the Tenth in the storming of Masada. Something about the horse sensing a wind shift. I don't know. All I know is that Valerius Sixtus came down that ramp a changed man."

"What is it about Masada that has cursed so many of our officers and men? I'll never figure out how battle-hardened veterans still refuse to talk about the Masada campaign, as if it were an embarrassment. Didn't we retake the mount and establish a garrison there? I would call that a victory. Wouldn't you?"

"I wouldn't talk about Masada in front of the general. I suspect he doesn't claim it as a victory although the emperor Titus did give him a salutation and a further donation of land. The only problem is that the land isn't in the city like most victorious generals get. It's not even a villa with slaves. It's off in the Sabine Hills somewhere. It's almost as if the emperor doesn't want to be reminded about Masada either.

"And there's another thing, Falcus. I don't know for sure, but I have heard that the general's mother was Jewish. Maybe that's why he was so upset. I heard our soldiers had slain over one thousand armed Jewish rebels on Masada. Why the general wouldn't be proud of a victory like that I don't know, even if his mother were Jewish. I mean, he's a Roman general, not a Jew."

The clatter of hooves ended the centurions' idle conversation. A troop of legionaries broached the gate of Valerius's villa and rode into the courtyard. The senior centurion dismounted and made his way toward his fellow centurions.

"Falcus! Good to see you. How did you pull such soft duty? Are you now a manservant wearing centurion's armor? I have a message for the general," the senior centurion said.

Though Linus Eclectus was the senior centurion, it was customary for all centurions to treat each other equally off the field of battle. Marcus and Falcus ignored the senior centurion until he made his request more plainly. They both needed a very good reason to disturb the general.

"Linus, the only message General Valerius wants to hear is that the wagon is ready to leave and his escort has arrived. Everything else can wait until the new commander arrives sometime next week. So if your message is neither about the wagon nor about the ship sailing from Caesarea, I suggest you repair yourself to the nearest *taberna* and thank the gods that we have kept you out of trouble."

"Marcus, Falcus, we are not on the battlefield, but I am still senior centurion. I order you to take me to the general," Linus said.

The aura of collegiality among the three centurions disappeared like the mist on the morning seas. "As you wish. I shall see the general now," Marcus said.

"Lord Commander, the senior centurion is outside with his men. He says he has an important message for you, sir. Shall I…"

"Marcus, what by the shadows of Hades did I tell you? Have you forgotten or do you wish to spend the rest of your career as the lowest ranking legionary in the army? Again, if I am not on that wagon in one hour, I'll personally melt down your centurion's armor and hammer out a slave bracelet for you," Valerius roared.

Marcus winced at the thought of slavery. Not that Valerius would do it, but it was in his power to have any of his men sold off to the slave market for disobeying a direct order from a superior officer. Marcus's only hope was that Valerius remembered the agreement among centurions when they gathered off the battlefield.

"Lord Valerius, Linus Eclectus is the senior centurion, and he ordered me to bring him to you. Sir, I had no choice. I will—"

"Enough, Marcus. I shall see him." Valerius waved off the centurion and sat on his stool. It would be the last piece of furniture he would load on the wagon. The stool's legs were scarred and marked. Valerius loved this stool. It was the one he carried with him throughout his entire Judean campaign. And it had survived that day in Masada.

Sitting, he reflected on the senior centurion's request. Rarely did one centurion pull rank on another off the battlefield. It just wasn't done, no matter how senior the ranking man was. The other centurions deferred to the senior centurion, but all centurions stuck together. They had to stick together. Didn't they have enough trouble dealing with general officers?

Valerius wasn't clear about the gravity of the situation, but Linus's invocation of rank told him that the senior centurion wasn't seeking an audience to wish him well. He called through the doorway to his aide. "Marcus, tell Linus Eclectus to come in now."

The senior centurion entered. "My Lord Commander," Linus said, striking his breast in the traditional legionary salute. "I have some news for you."

"What news do I need during this, my last hour in Judea? Can't it wait for the other commander?"

"General Valerius, I have a personal message for you from a dying man. You know, sir, that we always honor the request of the dying, especially when they have fought bravely. May I proceed, sir?"

"Yes, by all means," Valerius said, now that his interest was piqued by the centurion's words. *Who do I know who would want to speak to me before he died? There must be some mistake.*

"Sir, you know it is my duty to supervise the patrols of the city, looking for the last few Jewish rebels lurking about. One of the patrols came upon a rebel who claimed he had just come back to Jerusalem and was looking for the shop of the old merchant, Joab. You know the one who died on Masada."

At the mention of Masada, Valerius winced. He knew nothing of Joab or of any of his descendants. Well, if Joab did have heirs, they were entitled to what was left of his estate, after the emperor's share, of course.

"Go on. Finish. I have but less than an hour before I mount Arinax and leave this province forever."

"Yes, sir. We challenged the rebel and asked him to identify himself. He refused, saying he was just in the city for a short while and had only been in Judea after traveling for over three years. He declined to give us his name, so we approached him."

"Linus, who is 'we'?"

"Sir, I was not on the patrol, but it is customary to have two of our soldiers approach every suspected rebel. Too many of my men have been injured by underestimating the ferociousness of the Jewish rebels.

"As we approached him, the rebel fled. We cornered him in an alley near the old temple, you know, the one Titus and Flavius destroyed."

"There's no need to give me a history lesson on Judea. I wrote most of it. Now get on with your story."

"As I said, sir, we cornered him and were approaching him to further inspect his person when, all of a sudden, he pulled out a *gladius*! It was truly a Roman short sword, and it bore the insignia of the Tenth. Now, not only did we have a rebel on our hands, but a thief as well. We were all set to disarm him, but he put up a real fight. Believe me, General, he knew how to use that sword."

"Linus, did you disarm him?"

"No sir. Before we could surround him, he leapt up and slashed the chest of the patrol leader. The men rushed him and subdued him. During the fight, he received several wounds."

Valerius was now concerned. He had no use for Roman soldiers who abuse citizens on suspicion they were rebels. He was beginning to ponder whether he would take action against those men involved in this affair.

"Linus, tell me, is it customary to have a group of legionaries accost a single rebel and then have him 'receive' several wounds?"

"No, Lord General, it is not. But this rebel knew how to fight. And he was using one of our own swords! When the men finally wrestled him to the ground, they knew he was dying. He was bleeding from his cuts. There was blood all over the ground. I was on patrol less than a hundred paces away, and one of the men came for me. The legionary said the rebel wanted to speak with you. He knew we would never disturb you with a simple message from a Jew. So he held out his sword and asked us to return it to you."

"What exactly did this rebel say?"

"Well, General, he said to thank you for the use of the sword, but that he had no need of it anymore. I started to question him. But he died."

"Do you have this sword in your possession?"

"Yes, Commander, I do." Linus turned and shouted through the doorway. "Guard, bring that sword into the general's house. And do it quickly!" A junior legionary came running in, saluting both his centurion and his general. He gave the sword to Valerius and exited quickly.

Valerius looked at the sword. It was nothing special. Just another *gladius* like the dozens he had handled in his life. This one was rusted and pitted a little, but it had a sheen to it that could only come from the black water found in the Arabian Desert. *Who owned it? And why did he say it belonged to me?*

"What have you done with the rebel's body? I should like to take a look at it," Valerius said.

"I thought you would, sir, so I forbade my men to move it. You can view the body and be back in time to mount your horse for the trip to Caesarea. You, sir, of all people deserve that berth on the ship back to Rome," Linus said.

Here I am, thought Valerius, *all but retired, and still my subordinates flatter me. Will I miss that once I become a Roman merchant?*

"Senior Centurion, let us make our way quickly. I must be on that ship back to Rome."

"As you command, General."

Linus led Valerius through the streets of Jerusalem, their horses upsetting merchants' wagons and barely missing pedestrians. The relationship between the Jews and the Romans deteriorated to a point where both sides believed they lived in an enemy camp.

Jerusalem was slowly emptying itself of Jews. Once the temple was destroyed, many decided to leave, seeking their lives and fortunes elsewhere. As the Jews left, more Romans came to live in the city. Jerusalem looked nothing like his boyhood home.

Valerius saw a knot of soldiers standing around the dead man. They looked bored, yet worried. Something about the dead Jew spooked them.

"I'd be worried, too, if I suspected I'd killed a friend of my general," Valerius mumbled.

"What was that, General? Did you say something?" Linus asked.

"No, nothing," Valerius said as he dismounted. "Just let me see the body and be away from here."

Linus accompanied Valerius as he parted the soldiers standing around the body. "Soldier, you there, what did this man say?"

The soldier, wide-eyed with shock that the general of the Tenth was talking to him, stammered before he blurted out what had happened. "Sir, as this man lay dying, sir, he requested, sir, that he..."

"Soldier, if you leave out all the 'sirs,' you'll be finished much more quickly," Valerius grumbled.

"Yes, sir. I mean..."

"What happened, soldier?" Valerius barked, his patience running out and his temper rising as he thought about missing his ship because of a dead Jewish rebel.

"Sir, as this man was dying, he told us to give you back his sword. So we thought he might be an acquaintance of yours. We thought that impossible since he is nothing more than a Jewish rebel, but we thought we should tell you anyhow," the soldier said obviously relieved at never having to speak to the general again.

"Let me have a look," Valerius said. He knelt down and looked squarely into the face of the dead man. The Roman general was still not giving away even the smallest clue to his thinking.

But Valerius looked deep inside his mind and dwelled on the memory. The body of the rebel lay sprawled on the ground, his cuts still oozing blood.

So, Joseph, you have returned. You did not listen. What did I tell you about fighting a Roman legionary? Didn't I tell you what would happen?

When you left me on Masada, I never wanted to see you again. I wanted you to marry that slave you were with. But no, little man, you didn't listen. Valerius leaned forward and closed Joseph's eyelids.

"Sir," said Linus Eclectus, "what shall we do with the body?"

"What have you done with the rest of the rebels' bodies?"

"Well, Lord Commander, there is a deep pit out on the Mount of the Skulls, where we crucify criminals, and we just throw the bodies in the pit and cover them with dirt. I'll have the men take care of this one now and make sure your wagon is ready to leave."

"Bury this one in a proper grave. There is a Jewish burial ground out near the Mount of Olives. Your men said he was brave. He deserves a proper burial. Don't leave his body to the dogs."

With his final command given, Valerius made his way to the Roman patrol escorting him to Caesarea.

Chapter Forty-five

Present Day

The workmen wrestled with the huge wreaths adorning the necks of Patience and Fortitude, the lions in front of the massive beaux-arts building that fronted Fifth Avenue. The silent, stone animals wore holly wreaths every Christmas season. The huge, old-fashioned windows of the New York Public Library's main building at Forty-Second and Fifth looked out on a barren avenue devoid of the holiday shoppers and festive Christmas lights that dazzled New Yorkers and tourists for weeks. Christmas was over, and New York had settled down to the interminable months of gray that gripped the city during the winter.

Outside the majestic library, the first snows of January began to fall, driving twilight New York into an even deeper gloom. Taxis threw slushy puddles of water onto the sidewalks, narrowly missing pedestrians and sometimes, with luck, splashing them. The smell of roasting chestnuts and charring pretzels hawked by the latest wave of immigrants to New York scented the late afternoon air. Over the past several years, Afghans took over the pretzel and chestnut wagons. They were hard workers who fled the mess that the late, greatly-not-missed Osama bin Laden and the suicidal Taliban made of their country.

The Afghan pretzel vendors remained invisible to busy pedestrians. They were just another bunch of immigrants, like the millions of people who populated this great city from its founding in the seventeenth century. Each decade saw a new wave of immigrants arriving in New York. One could almost tell where the world's troubles were by the type of immigrant who landed in the five boroughs.

The nineteenth century potato famines in Ireland brought men and women whose children later became fire chiefs and police inspectors, mothers of priests and cardinals, feminists and activists. The pogroms in Central Europe brought in disenfranchised Jews who came to America seeking the great dream their ancestors dreamt for centuries. World War I emptied the Austro-Hungary Empire of citizens who wanted no part of a war fought for a toy emperor and his gussied-up ruling family.

The immigrants came by the hundreds of thousands—Germans, Poles, Bohemians, Hungarians, Slavs, Croats—and built their little neighborhoods, bringing with them their churches, their customs, and best of all, their food. All of these immigrants created a city whose fabric has known no equal in the history of man.

And it was still going on. Whether the immigrants were fleeing famine in Africa, wars in south Asia, or terrorist attacks in the Middle East, they came to America. They came to New York.

The pedestrians struggling with their own problems couldn't care less about the history of their hometown. New York was in a hurry, passing by the library without noticing that the lions had lost their wreaths and Christmas was over.

Five miles south of the library, a man walked to the memorial park erected on the site of the World Trade Center. He did this every morning. He said his prayers, reading from his breviary, and slowly returned to the little Catholic chapel on the Battery. And each morning, the cares of the world and a sinister cloud of evil followed him as he sought the refuge of the quaint old New York mansion that now housed a Catholic church and the Shrine of St. Elizabeth Ann Seton.

This morning, as always, he was alone. He walked the few blocks from the new World Trade Center construction site and rounded the street where his church stood. The building was smack-dab on the Battery overlooking the park and the upper harbor, but it officially was on State Street, a curving path that followed the rounded tip of Manhattan. The building that housed the church also followed the curve so the entrance was not the typical square steps-and-columns arrangement of the downtown churches.

This weekend morning he returned to the church, climbing the winding front staircase or "stoop" as the Dutch founders of New York would have called it. He opened the double doors and entered the building. As usual it was empty, and he was alone.

He prostrated himself in front of the simple white altar illuminated by the blue and white stained-glass window above it. He prayed with all his heart that his cursed discovery would never be found.

That Sunday afternoon in Rome was etched in his mind. Following a private mass in the Vatican chapel, Monsignor Edmund F. X. O'Brien, S. J. went to an early dinner with a cardinal archbishop, Giacomo di Sistio, said to be one of the most powerful churchmen in all of the church hierarchy.

"Tell me, Monsignor, what do you have?"

"Eminence, you know what I found. I reported my find to His Holiness. What more do you need to know?"

The cardinal signaled for another carafe of simple Frascati, looking at the American Jesuit while he did so. "We're in Rome, no? We drink the local wine. I have been coming to this bistro in Trastevere for years. We eat simple food here. We drink simple wine. This bistro serves us wine made in the Sabine Hills."

"Yes, your Eminence," though O'Brien wished for nothing more than a cold bottle of Peroni.

"Edmund, may I call you by your first name? The Holy Father has told me what you have found. You need to come into the bosom of the Church. You are no longer an outsider. Please listen to me."

♦ ♦ ♦

In the 1980s, the library system, like all of New York, suffered a deep decline. Employee furloughs, limited research facilities, and unfilled positions were the norm. Then in the 1990s, under the watch of Mayor Rudolph Giuliani, the city and its citizens' spirits soared, and the municipal coffers filled. By the time the ball dropped in Times Square ushering in the new millennium, directors of the New York library system could boast of having the most sophisticated computerized research network in the world.

The Fifth Avenue main rooms retained the classic style of the building. In its basement, below the footfalls of tourists and residents crossing Forty-Second Street, resided the library system's computer facilities. This is where the "new" librarians worked, far from the classic works and rich treasures some two stories above their heads.

Andrew Wagner was one of those "new" librarians. The fifty-year-old bachelor was captivated by the capabilities of the system's new computer network and transferred his academic affection for classical literature and ancient historical puzzles to the nineteen-inch frames of information that his computer delivered to his desktop.

When the director of the library, Martin Fallon, discovered Andrew's new passion, he asked him to categorize and computerize the library's vast collection of ancient language references. Fallon was a fellow graduate of the Oriental Institute in Chicago. He parlayed his graduate degree into research grants, teaching fellowships, more research grants, and finally, a position at the New York Public Library as its director of ancient languages.

He hired Andrew in the early 1990s. By then, Fallon was a division director. Andrew wasn't adept at political maneuvering, so he languished in the ancient languages department. Fallon meanwhile adroitly positioned himself into bigger and better jobs. Fallon had the incredible luck of always being available at the right time.

When the old director died suddenly, after ingesting thirty pills of every legally available narcotic, Fallon was there to help the shocked library board. He took the reins of a stunned and demoralized library system and quieted the troops. For his deft handling of a dire and embarrassing situation, the board handed Fallon the ultimate prize—the directorship.

Fallon's success stunned Andrew. He was almost Fallon's contemporary. Fallon was just five years older than he. Unfortunately, Andrew possessed none of Fallon's people skills nor any of his star power. Martin was a stand-out player on the St. John's basketball team. One of the library's board members owned a minority interest in a professional basketball team. The two of them got along famously.

Andrew and Martin rarely saw each other, except for exchanging a quick hello in the hallways. Yet, a few weeks ago, a private meeting between the two planted Andrew on a very strange career path that no one, absolutely no one, could have imagined.

It began with a voice mail message from Fallon's secretary requesting that he meet with the director at "his convenience." Andrew hustled up to Fallon's office that afternoon. He waited the obligatory ten minutes before Kathryn, Fallon's secretary, ushered him in.

"Andrew, how are you? We haven't spoken like this in a while. Are you getting on well with Mary?" Fallon shouted in his booming voice.

"Well, Marty, Mary and I haven't been an item for about three years. As for myself, yeah, I guess you can say I'm getting on well." Andrew knew that calling him "Marty" would rub Fallon the wrong way. Andrew had too many years at the library and was too low on the totem pole to fear the wrath of so high a personage as the director.

"Andrew, let's cut to the chase," Fallon said, visibly annoyed. He turned his back as he stared at the winter landscape of Bryant Park. Fallon spun around in his chair and gave Andrew his "earnest, concerned" look.

"Frankly, we need you here. I know you can do the job I'm asking you to. There's no one in this building who knows more about ancient Near East languages than you. Hell, you know more than me, and I graduated from the Institute before you!

"You've become quite adept at our new computer system. What I'm proposing is that you head a team that will propel this institution into the big leagues when it comes to ancient Near East languages. I'm creating a new department, and I want you to head it—the Division of the Near East. What do you think?"

What do I think? I'm waiting for the next shoe to drop, Andrew thought. Without waiting for his answer, Fallon moved expansively to the next subject.

"Of course, Andrew, I don't have board approval for this. That means I can throw you a title but no raise or staff, and you'll have to keep the same office. But I promise you, believe me, at the next board meeting I'll ram through approval for this in a heartbeat. I'll make it a three-point shot. Trust me."

Everything sounded fine to Andrew except that he didn't trust Fallon. Three-pointers didn't exist when Fallon played for St. John's, and Andrew felt that somehow he was getting railroaded into yet another dead-end job. Fallon was throwing him the bone of a new, unpaid promotion to keep Andrew from ever going anywhere within the library system.

"Sure, Marty, that sounds like a great idea. I was hoping to get my hands deeper into our Near East collection, and the computer system will get me closer than if I stayed in the reading room for a year of Sundays. Thanks. I accept."

He got up, knowing that the meeting was over, and started to walk toward the door. That's when Fallon called out. "Hey, Andrew. There's some good news here. We got a new researcher on loan from the Israel Antiquities Authority. She's got no place to situate, so I'm going to assign her to you. Don't look so glum. I hear she's a piece of ass."

What a perfect ending to a meeting with the director, Andrew thought, walking out of Fallon's office. *I get a new job with a new title, no pay raise, no staff, and the same crummy office space. But I have to look on the bright side. My new coworker is a "piece of ass."*

"Andrew," Fallon called down the hall as he walked away. "She's coming in next week at JFK. Why don't you show her our hospitality and pick her up. You can even put the car service on an expense form. I'll sign. I promise," Fallon called out.

"Will do, Martin." Andrew reverted to the director's full name when other library employees surrounded him. *No reason to piss off Marty totally in public. I do it enough in private.*

Andrew made his way to his office, replaying his meeting with Fallon. When Marty tapped Andrew for the new project, the library director couldn't have realized that he was throwing him a lifeline.

Ever since graduating from New York University, Andrew had been living a lie. He fancied himself the Indiana Jones-type archaeologist. He fantasized about going on digs, unearthing the next breakthrough in ancient history. He wanted to use his degree to do something really useful.

He daydreamed about the cute women in those impossibly short shorts who always volunteered for archaeological excursions. He thought about being somebody. In truth, he was little more than an over-educated file clerk for the New York Public Library.

But things were looking up for him. He had a new job, albeit at the same pay. And a mysterious, good-looking woman was soon to join him. Plus his job was gaining him some notoriety at the silly little parties his position at the New York Public Library required him to attend. Andrew had become a master at attending fund-raising cocktail parties.

In years past, Wall Street "Masters of the Universe" corralled all the women at these parties. Then it was the dot-com crowd. Now, it was nobody in particular, but that nobody crowd didn't include him. Andrew would stand in the corner of whatever reception he was attending, looking lost and forlorn. Occasionally, a woman would drift by and start a conversation. After explaining that he was a classicist with a knack for ancient languages, the woman usually drifted away, eyes glazed over, desperately looking for someone else.

When he got back to his desk, a beautifully inscribed envelope lay on his desk. Andrew picked it up, hefting the weight of the paper in his hand. He opened it. Attached to the invitation was a note from the director. His old buddy, Marty Fallon, said some of the library's most generous benefactors requested his presence.

Two minutes later, his phone rang. It was Fallon. He spent about three seconds on niceties then jumped right into the purpose of his call. "Why don't you knock off early, Andrew, and get that tuxedo dusted off. You'll need it for the reception tonight. And, by the way, your new assistant is supposed to land next week. Don't forget to pick her up," Fallon said jovially.

"Okay, Marty," Andrew said. He looked at the clock and decided to leave. He had to get ready for the party tonight. That was an order from the director.

With a wave of his hand to an administrative assistant outside his door, he walked to the elevator and out the employee's entrance. He made a beeline for the Lexington Avenue IRT, a few blocks east of the library.

Chapter Forty-Six

Andrew lived uptown on Eighty-Sixth Street. When he was growing up, they called it "Yorkville," then it was the "Upper East Side." Now, it's "Yorkville" again. He hadn't much time to get his tuxedo "dusted off." The reception was at Lincoln Center on the west side, and getting there from the east side was a pain in the ass. He had to go downtown to Grand Central, take the shuttle to Times Square, catch the uptown Seventh Avenue local to Sixty-Sixth Street, and walk four blocks. Sometimes, Andrew wished for a better-paying job so he could afford a taxi.

Andrew got out of the subway and walked east to his apartment. It was a floor-through walk-up all the way east on Eighty-Sixth. Old-time New Yorkers called it a railroad flat because the rooms followed one another in a straight line like rail cars. It wasn't very big, but it was a prestigious location. He took a shower and got ready for the party. His tuxedo was well-worn but in decent shape. Thankfully it was the winter, so his raincoat hid most of the tuxedo. Guys wearing tuxedos on the subway always got stares.

Andrew checked his tux one more time in the full-length mirror on his bedroom door then walked down the stairs. Jumping out onto

Eighty-Sixth Street, Andrew turned left and walked to the Lexington Avenue subway station. He looked at his watch. He had plenty of time to make the Lincoln Center party.

About forty-five minutes and three trains later, he emerged from the Sixty-Sixth Street subway station and walked the four blocks south to Lincoln Center. The broad plaza in the middle of Lincoln Center was one of Andrew's favorite places in all New York. He hunched his shoulders against the brisk wind blowing across the plaza and walked to the reception.

Little did he know that greater minds and more powerful people had other things in store for him. His useless degree in ancient languages would soon propel him onto a career path that he could only dream of. And all thanks to a former professor of his at NYU whose class he would attend religiously during his senior year. She had sent the invitation to the benefit to the library.

At sixty-two, Jill Benson was still a fantastically good-looking woman. Thirty years ago her male students thought so. Andrew's opinion hadn't changed. Professor Benson had retired from NYU after becoming a dean of the liberal arts school. Remaining single all her life despite her ongoing attraction to men, Dean Benson later joined the board of Lincoln Center at the behest of one of her many rich suitors.

No one cared that whenever he was away from board meetings, so was she. Or that they both returned with tans in the dead of a New York winter. But that was to be expected of her. Who else but Jill Benson, when she was a mere thirty-year-old professor, could persuade the greatest Roman classicist of all time to address her undergraduate class on his discovery of the key to the language of Etruria?

Granted, Etruria was not a hot topic in university circles. But to attract the foremost authority on even an obscure a topic as Etruria was a feather in the mortarboard for a struggling assistant professor on the arduous tenure track at a great urban university.

Andrew had attended the lecture she had arranged. The portly professor from Italy, Federico Pallotino, ignited a spark in Andrew. Here was the man who translated the fabled tablets of a tongue that was gone before Rome was a republic. *And he is speaking to me,* Andrew thought, sitting in the large gallery that served as a classroom.

The small, balding Italian brought his lecture to a close with Andrew still in a fog as to what his future would be. Professor Benson walked up to thank the Roman scholar and received a kiss and a rather warm hug from the man. Students in the audience and a smattering of jealous classics professors nodded to themselves knowingly as if they figured out exactly how that young woman got Dottore Pallotino to come lecture at NYU.

Not too much later, assistant professor Benson received a tenured appointment as a full professor in the NYU classics department. The catty university staff thought they knew all the reasons for Jill Benson's full professorship and later appointment as dean as well as they knew her tailor, her perfume preferences, and her choice in men. But what they failed to see was that behind her beauty was a first-class classicist and a prime-time academic politician.

Andrew would soon learn how prime-time a politician Jill Benson was.

Andrew entered the lobby of the New York State Theater. Upstairs, on the mezzanine, his first look at his old university professor evoked a classic moment. She was having cocktails and conversations with two very distinguished and foreign-looking gentlemen. Both the men seemed very, very interested.

The occasion for this evening's cocktail party was yet another fundraiser for the New York Public Library. This time, two obscure Asian artists, a pianist and flautist, were cajoled into donating their services to raise money for a good cause. For some unknown reason, Jill Benson specifically requested his presence. Still, Andrew couldn't help feeling he was just a low-level librarian sent to amuse the upper classes. This was the last evening Andrew would have to think of himself as a low-level library employee. He just didn't know it yet.

"Andrew, there you are." And the words came out of her mouth like he was the only person at the party. That was Jill Benson's magic. She made you feel like you were the only one in the world for her. *No matter that she had planned devious and cruel uses for you. She recognized you. She loved you. And you were the center of her universe,* Andrew thought to himself.

"Andrew, let me present you to two very important men who ask, as I do, for your help." She turned to the two men beside her and motioned for them to speak.

"Signore, I am Ettore Scala, the minister of antiquities for the civica of Rome, and this is Cardinal Archbishop Giacomo di Sistio. We need your help, and the lovely Professor Benson said you might avail us."

Signore Scala was the consummate diplomat, drawing Andrew closer into his circle.

Andrew was sucked in like an oyster at a Low-Country beach roast. *These people are asking for my help. Why? One's a top-ranking Italian government official and the other a Roman cardinal! What's he doing in a tux? Where are his ecclesiastical robes? What in the hell is going on?*

He looked at the door leading to the outdoor terrace as his only escape. *I have to get out of here. These guys are for real, and I'm not. Let me be anywhere, anyplace, but the direction this conversation is going. I'm a library clerk for God's sake, with a smattering of knowledge about ancient languages. What do these people want with me? Why is Professor Benson looking at me with her alluring smile? What in the hell am I getting into?*

Andrew telegraphed his worry all over his face. Jill Benson jumped right in. "Oh, Andrew, stop worrying. There's nothing these men are going to ask you that you can't do. I've suggested that you're the man we need. After all, weren't you the university's most promising ancient languages student before you decided to bury yourself in the library? And, if it weren't for you, the library's display of the Qumran Scrolls would have been a disaster. Here's your chance, boy, to help me, help yourself, and do something with your life."

Jill's use of the word "boy" cut to Andrew's heart. After all these years, he was still a "boy." So why turn to him for help? What did Jill know about his character, his yearning for something else that made her pluck him out of the obscurity of the library's stacks? And what was wrong with being a curator at the greatest library in the world's collection of ancient Near Eastern literature? What was she expecting of him? There had to be another motive, but Andrew couldn't fathom it.

She turned away from him and resumed talking to the two Italians. *Always the professional,* Andrew thought, *always working the crowd*. He noticed she was careful to call them the Qumran Scrolls, the term used by professional archaeologists, not their popular name, Dead Sea Scrolls. A sudden commotion in the lobby disrupted Andrew's thoughts.

White-jacketed waiters marched through the crowd, ringing chimes to alert the party crowd that serious musical business was about to begin. They looked like miniature bandleaders banging undersized glockenspiels, but like the rest of the New York elite, he entered the great hall.

The program was excellent. But what else to expect from Lincoln Center and the library's benefactors? The elegant crowd exited the hall, making their way to the escalators to the front doors into the wintry New York evening. Andrew ambled out, alone, nodding his head respectfully as he passed people he recognized who were "important" to the library. As he approached the escalator, he heard a voice crying out his name over the crowd. "Andrew! Andrew, would you wait for just a moment?"

He turned his head. There was Jill Benson, her two Italians in tow, coming toward him. *She's not going to leave me alone. I guess I'd better be ready for the onslaught.*

"Professor, er, Jill, I was just on my way home. Shall we connect tomorrow morning?" Andrew said.

"On your way home! You must join us for dinner; I insist. In fact, why don't you pick a nice out-of-the-way restaurant? These two men have had too much of New York society, and a simple Italian meal might be to their liking. Ettore has an embassy car waiting for us outside. Come, it should be fun," Benson said, linking arms with the Italians.

Andrew thought about her offer. She didn't give him much time. She started to walk toward the escalator and managed to push Andrew into the crowd.

"Gladly, Jill. Gentlemen, let me think for a minute as we walk to your car. Signore Scala, Eminence, where is the car?"

"Mr. Wagner," the Italian official answered, "I would be very disappointed if it were not right out in front. We old men can't walk very far in this chilly weather."

They walked together out the glass doors and through the Lincoln Center Plaza. True to his word, the Italian Embassy car—a plain black Ford Crown Victoria—idled in the special lane constructed just for Lincoln Center. Andrew waited while the three of them entered the back. He closed the door and sat in front. The taciturn driver, an extremely fit man in his late thirties, glanced at him through hooded eyes. The slight bulge under his right shoulder told Andrew that he was no plain driver, probably a senior ranking member of the Italian Carabinieri.

Andrew looked at the driver and said, "Let's go to Mulberry Street."

Chapter Forty-Seven

The Crown Vic drove south on Seventh Avenue. Jill Benson engaged the two men in an animated discussion in rapid-fire Italian. Andrew, sitting silently beside the equally quiet driver, didn't understand a word of it.

"When you get to Canal Street, take a left. You'll see Mulberry Street on your left, but a police barrier probably blocks it. That'll be a minor problem," Andrew told the driver.

All he said was "Si, Signore," and kept on driving. He turned the car onto Canal Street. It was late evening. The street was crowded. Stores overflowed with every knock-off in the Western World. "Gucci" handbags, "Rolex" watches, the ubiquitous "Polo" shirts lined the stalls. Not a single item was genuine. It didn't matter to the shoppers, as long as it looked like the real thing. The merchants made their dollar. The shoppers walked away happy. And somewhere, in the corporate towers of the retail giants, security officials fumed. The stores thinned out the farther east the car traveled. Soon, the towers of NYU took over the streets.

Andrew turned around and called Jill's attention to the landscape. "It looks like good old NYU is spreading like an oil spill," he said.

Benson looked at him and gave him a brief nod as if to say *don't interfere with my conversation*. He slunk back into his seat.

The driver brought the car to a stop at the corner of Canal and Mulberry. Dead ahead of him on the left, two New York City policemen manned a police barricade blocking the entrance to Mulberry Street. The driver made the left turn and pulled up to the barricade.

One of the cops, who looked like he graduated high school three weeks ago, held up a white-gloved hand. He approached the car, and the driver noiselessly slid his window down. He spoke softly to the policeman. The cop peered into the back and walked to his partner. The two of them had a short conversation, and they walked to the barricade to pull it aside. The cardinal waved his hand at the two cops as the car pulled through to Mulberry Street.

"We're looking for a restaurant named *SPQR*," Andrew told the driver. The driver nodded. He pulled up to the restaurant. Nobody moved. In a few minutes, the two cops walked into the restaurant. Soon, several men piled out and walked to their cars parked in front. They drove away. The driver pulled the Crown Vic into the open space.

Wow! Andrew thought, *somebody in this car's got real juice.* The driver got out of the car and walked to the sidewalk. He opened the back door and helped the Italian official out first, then Professor Benson, and finally, Cardinal di Sistio. Andrew got out unassisted. The driver walked into the restaurant. The four of them waited on the sidewalk until the driver returned and bent over to say something into Signore Scala's ear. He turned to Andrew.

"Signore Wagner, you have picked a most excellent place. Rocco tells me the restaurant is ready and waiting for us. Come. Let's go inside." He placed his arm in the middle of Jill's back. Andrew and the cardinal walked side by side through the etched glass entry doors.

The owner of the restaurant waited for them behind the maître d' stand. Behind him was a huge table covered with special antipasto dishes. The owner beamed at them and went directly to the cardinal.

"Eminenza," he said, kissing the cardinal's ring in the style of an old-time Catholic. "This way, please." When they got to the table, the driver, Andrew figured his name was Rocco, was already there. He stood in front of two opened bottles of a very expensive Chianti Classico. In his hand was an empty wine glass, stained slightly red.

Andrew turned to Professore Scala and said, "Don't tell me your driver's a wine expert, too."

"Oh yes, Rocco's Italian. He knows his wines. But he's an expert at tasting other things as well."

The four of them sat at the restaurant's signature table, a large round one nestled in the corner behind an etched-glass panel. They could see the entire dining room, but the other diners couldn't make them out. Andrew signaled for the waiter to bring menus. There was no need. Three waiters buzzed around their table, bearing plates of simple antipasto. The owner came over and addressed the table in soft Italian. The cardinal looked up at him and said, "*Per favore*, English please."

The owner pulled down on his tux jacket. "As you wish, Eminence. If there is anything I can do, just look my way. There's no need to call for anything. It's taken care of." He walked back to the maître d' station to greet his other patrons. They were left alone at the table, the food in front of them. Andrew looked up and asked, "Where's the driver?"

Scala answered, "I suspect he's in the kitchen supervising the staff. You know, Rocco looks at those food channels all day and fancies himself a chef." He beamed broadly at this little inside joke. Andrew just dug into his plate of roasted vegetables, white beans and pasta, and marinated mushrooms.

Rocco Inamorato was a member of the Carabinieri, the first "Armed Force of Italy" as declared in a March 2000 law passed by the Italian government. But he was more than that. As a member of the Carabinieri's Special Operations Group, Inamorato was an expert in combating terrorism and guarding Italy's highest officials.

Since the early 1800s when the Italian government first formed the Carabinieri, the select group of men to serve in its ranks had a special connection to the Vatican and to the pope. Inamorata was carrying on a two-hundred-year-old tradition watching out for the safety of top-ranking government officials and the Vatican's elite.

Jill Benson picked at her antipasto. Di Sistio and Scala ate with gusto, and the cardinal began to poach at Jill's plate. She said nothing, smiling at the three men.

After the waiters cleared the antipasto plates, Jill broke her unusual silence. "Andrew, what a wonderful place. How did you ever think of coming here? I haven't been to Little Italy in years!"

Andrew put down his fork and looked at her. "That's part of its problem. Except for the festival and the summer tourists, New Yorkers seemed to have forgotten about Little Italy. This place is wonderful, home to New York's original Italian community in the early 1900s. It was a lot bigger years ago. Even I remember it being bigger. But the old folks die, the young ones don't stay, and the Asian community spreads and takes over more and more of what used to be Little Italy."

The owner approached with an attractive, dark-haired woman. Before Andrew could put down his fork, Rocco was at the table, his hand inside his custom-made silk jacket. The owner looked at Rocco guardedly and spoke rapidly.

"Please, this is my wife, Concetta. She usually doesn't work on Tuesdays, but fate must have brought her in today. I have asked her to make sure that you are taken care of like you were sitting at our kitchen table." He backed away nervously, his eyes on Rocco. Giacomo quickly defused the tension.

"So, Signora, you've come 'specially for us?" he teased.

Concetta picked up on the tension and decided to play along with Giacomo in putting everyone to ease. "Yes, yes. Tuesday night is usually reserved for my women's club meetings at my church, but it was canceled tonight. I took the train in. I hate driving in the city. Every time I come into the city, I go home with a receipt from an auto body shop," she said, hoping that the little joke at her own expense would restore the table's jovial mood.

"You work with the Church? Where is it?" Giacomo asked, emphasizing the capital "C" in church.

"It's a local church, Our Holy Redeemer, out on Long Island. Unless you're from here, you won't know where it is. Maybe, gentlemen," Concetta beamed broadly at the three men, "you could join me next week. I think my female friends would welcome such elegant men in their presence. Even your watchdog," she said with a nod toward Rocco.

"Alas, I am back to Rome at the end of this week. Maybe next time," Giacomo said, clearly ending the conversation.

"Well, thank you, and come again. *Mangia!"* Concetta said, walking away from the table with perhaps too much of a wiggle.

The brief interlude was over. Rocco was back in the kitchen. Apparently, the diplomat's bodyguard met the owner's wife in the kitchen and vetted her; otherwise, he would have rushed to the table. Andrew shook his head at the little comedy that had just played out at the table. *Jeez, a church-going lady. She'd die if she knew she was flirting with a man who could become the next pope!*

"Andrew," Jill said, "this place is truly perfect. And the name of this restaurant—*SPQR*—you always were a pushover for Latin."

He smiled, pleased that his professor congratulated his choice of restaurants. There are several great restaurants in Little Italy. *SPQR* was a favorite. It was larger, a little bit better decorated, and the staff treated you like you were home. Plus, the name appealed to him. The initials stood for *Senatus Populusque Romanus*—the Senate and the Roman People. Those initials signified the pact between the ruling class—the Senate—and the common people. It was a favorite phrase in the old Roman Republic. Even today, you can see "*SPQR*" carved into ancient Roman buildings.

Andrew was about to continue when the same three waiters brought platters holding simply prepared fish. Rocco showed up holding a chilled bottle of Frascati, a country-style white wine from the hills just north of Rome.

Another waiter whisked away the red wine glasses and replaced them with the proper glass for enjoying white wine. Rocco silently poured the wine and walked away.

"Rocco sure knows his wines," Andrew said, somewhat moronically, as he twirled the pale golden liquid in his glass.

Scala looked up and said, "*Si.*"

The owner walked to the table, shooing away the waiters. "My honored guests, I have something special prepared for the pasta dish—fluffy dumplings in a red wine sauce, the kind you think you can get in Italy but no one serves anymore."

"How true, Signore," the cardinal agreed. "Even my favorite places in the Trastevere cater simply to tourists."

Andrew looked up at Cardinal di Sistio in surprise. Not only was the Trastevere across the Tiber from the Vatican, it was also the historic Jewish Quarter of Rome. What was a cardinal doing walking around a neighborhood that certainly had no love for the Catholic Church?

"Your Eminence," Andrew began, but the cardinal raised his hand and stopped him in mid-sentence.

"Young man, when you come to the Vatican and see me in all my trappings of my temporal power, then you may address me as 'Eminence.' Here, today, we are partners working together for the same outcome. Please, Andrew, call me Giacomo. However, do not—like your American clergy—call me 'Jocko.'" Jill Benson just beamed at Andrew as if to say that he had been accepted into some foolish boys' club.

All four of them passed on the fabulous pastries the waiters brought for dessert. They drained their espresso cups and rose to leave. Waiters rushed over with their coats. Andrew stood there forlornly, waiting for the damage. *This bill has got to be high, and no one's reaching for their wallet.*

The owner came over, inquiring whether everything was to their liking. Andrew looked at him and, holding his hand down by the seam of his pants, made the universal sign for the check. The owner looked at him and said nothing.

"Eminenza, I'm sorry, English, yes? Eminence, professors, thank you for coming to my restaurant. It was an honor and privilege to serve you." And he walked away.

Andrew stared at him. *This meal has gotta cost a grand. The old guys alone inhaled a couple hundred bucks of wine. How do they get away with it? Never paying for anything!* They walked through the front door, and Rocco was waiting for them by the car, its engine running and the heater warming the interior.

They heard a commotion at the end of Mulberry Street near Canal. Three burly men, dressed in black and looking like private security, were hustling a pretzel man off the sidewalk and pushing him and his wagon into the street. Rocco pushed the three of them into the back of the car, leaving Andrew to make his way into the front seat. He had barely sat down when Rocco locked all the doors and backed away from the curb with a squeal. He flew out of Mulberry Street, the cops holding traffic for him. He stopped briefly at Canal before turning east. Rocco stared at the pretzel man, he and his wagon dumped unceremoniously in the gutter. Andrew looked at the man, feeling sorry for the Middle Eastern immigrant who probably supported a large family by selling pretzels and chestnuts.

Rocco gunned the car eastward along Canal. The pretzel man rose to his knees and stared malevolently at the speeding car. He reached into his wagon for a cell phone.

Chapter Forty-Eight

Andrew rushed down the wide steps of the library's main building. He received a telephone call that morning from Ettore Scala inviting him for lunch at the Helmsley Palace. *If this were a repeat of last week's dinner, then I don't have to spend a dime,* he thought to himself. *It's going to be a killer day!*

It was a beautiful winter day in the city. The sun was bright, and the streets empty. Few came to New York in the dead of winter. This was the time when natives took over. He walked up Fifth Avenue and headed east to Madison Avenue. The Helmsley was nine blocks north, a brisk walk. He continued east on Fortieth Street, a nondescript block with worn-out buildings filled with textile wholesalers on the ground floor and cloth cutters on the upper floors. What was left of the New York garment district started here and headed south and west.

He passed through Fortieth and made his way to Madison Avenue. He loved the avenue. It was the one street in the city that maintained the gentility of an older New York. He loved the little shops. The book stores, the small bakeries, the odd designer here and there echoed a New York when people strolled the streets from merchant to merchant, buying their daily goods. Further uptown, the vulgar storefronts of international retailers poked their brassy door fronts onto the avenue. Madison Avenue was a relaxed, exclusive place to stroll.

His steps took him quickly into the fifties where old-time wealthy New York built their country homes. At the turn of the century, this was still a bucolic neighborhood. It was a good one-hour ride north from the exclusive confines of Madison Square.

Only when the subway went in did New York expand at a breakneck speed. And even then, there were pockets of farmland in the middle of the city. He remembered his grandmother telling him that the site of the United Nations used to be a slaughterhouse at the turn of the century—the twentieth. Butchers used to roll the carcasses of slaughtered sheep and cattle off the promontory that stuck out into the East River. Babi, he used to call his grandmother, would take the trolley to Forty-Second Street and the river to buy chickens from the slaughterhouse. Now the United Nations was there.

Nothing much has changed except there's no slaughterhouse. The people inside the majestic UN buildings just condone slaughter. They don't partake in it, except when they invited that madman Arafat to address them as if he were a civil human being.

Andrew looked down the avenue and saw the back of St. Patrick's Cathedral. When the cornerstone was laid for the building in 1858, its nearest neighbors were herds of cows. Today, it occupies some of the most expensive real estate in the world, especially now that the Japanese economy was in permanent recession.

At Fiftieth Street St. Patrick's loomed over the neighborhood. Tucked behind the cathedral was the parish house, and now, the Archbishop of New York's residence. Across the street stood the Helmsley Palace, the hotel built on top of the archbishop's old residence, the Villard Houses.

It tore Andrew's heart out when the Archdiocese of New York decided to sell the Villard Houses to the Helmsley real estate interests. But he had to agree, for all their vulgarity, the Helmsleys did a good job with the hotel. They maintained the magnificent plaza in front of the Villard Houses and incorporated the old building into the lobby. You couldn't expect much more from people who cheated on their New York sales tax. Both of them were dead, but they did a good job while alive.

Andrew entered the lobby and looked around. It was magnificent. He glanced at the paper in his hand and walked over to the bank of ornately decorated elevators. The door opened, and he punched the button for the fourteenth floor. He walked down the hall to room 1402. It had double doors. *Hmm,* Andrew thought, *Signore Scala rates a suite in the Helmsley? He must be more important than I thought. Why are we meeting here? Why not a conference room at the Italian Embassy?* He was about to knock when he saw the bell on the doorframe. A hotel room with a doorbell? Andrew was about to push the bell when the door silently opened.

"Welcome, Mr. Wagner." Andrew looked directly into the always-suspicious eyes of Rocco. The driver was also an efficient butler as the Italian ushered him into the suite. There, right at a table next to an open bar, sat his dining companions.

Signore Scala dispensed with niceties. He rose and gave Andrew a quick "hello" and walked him to the table. Jill Benson and the cardinal were in quiet conversation. Rocco stood by the wall, silent and ever-watchful.

Jill turned. "Andrew, how nice you could join us. Shall I ring for room service?"

Andrew didn't know what to say. He wondered why he was here. *Room service in this place must cost a fortune. What the hell was that guy doing standing there? He's a driver.*

Giacomo rose and grasped Andrew's hand in a warm, characteristically Italian embrace. "I am so glad you decided to work with us. Jill has high hopes for you. Signore Scala and I have been discussing your future. We have cleared it already with your Mr. Fallon. He's enthusiastic that we have selected you."

Andrew, still standing, drew back a bit. "Wait a minute. Just wait a minute. What are you talking about? Work with whom?" He rose from the table and started to walk away.

Rocco adroitly stepped in front of him. "Perhaps Mr. Wagner wishes something from the bar? Sit down. I'll bring it to the table." Andrew did as he was told.

"Now that that's settled, maybe we begin." Giacomo di Sistio settled back in his chair and motioned to Rocco for another bottle of water.

"First of all, I can assure you of the utmost confidentiality of everything that is said here. Rocco has swept the room for listening devices. The heavy, brocade curtains make it impossible to pick up any conversations using directional microphones on the outside.

"Why all this secrecy? What are we looking for? Again, let me assure you that should you choose to work with us, you shall have the backing of all the governments involved. I represent the Vatican, and to some extent, the free world. Scala represents Italy and the arts world. And, lovely Jill, your government."

At the mention of this, Andrew's eyes flickered from the cardinal to his former professor.

"What's the matter, Andrew? I'm not so much the radical professor you thought I was. Do you really think radical professors get named dean? I've been working with our dear old Uncle Sam for over twenty-five years. Agency heads come and go, but Jill's still around with her unimpeachable contacts in the underground.

"The underground!" she snorted. "Now you read about those sniveling bastards looking for pardons after being on the run for forty years. Forget about what they did and who they killed. They want a pardon!"

She pushed herself away from the table and walked over to the bar. Jill opened a bottle and poured herself three fingers of Scotch into a crystal old-fashioned glass. "Excuse me," she said as she walked to the suite's only bedroom.

It was when she was gone from the room that Andrew noticed the bottle she poured from was a bottle of Johnnie Walker Blue. *Holy Jesus,* Andrew thought. *That stuff costs fifty dollars a shot at the uptown Scotch bar, and Benson pours it like it was a boilermaker at the Blarney Stone.*

The table turned quiet after Benson's outburst. When she was gone, the cardinal placed his hand gently over Andrew's and said in a low voice, "Jill has a past with the 'underground.' Her first and only fiancé was on the wrong end of a shootout with a radical group in Oakland. He was an undercover federal agent. But few know that. Her contacts within the underground are invaluable, and she still provides us with an entrée into the world of the terrorists."

Andrew looked at his feet underneath the table. *I wish I could just click them and be back at the library. Something tells me this isn't Kansas.* The cardinal motioned to Rocco, who without asking, brought him a glass filled with Campari and ice. He looked at Andrew again. "Are you all right? Do you wish Rocco to bring you something or order from room service? Just tell him, and he'll get it."

"No thank you, your Eminence, I mean Giacomo. I have a feeling that this conversation isn't going to be about antiquities. So tell me, why am I here?"

The cardinal was about to answer when the telephone warbled softly. Rocco picked it up quickly. *"Pronto. Si. Si."* He placed the telephone down and walked toward the table. *"Eminenza, scusi,"* and he made a motion with his eyes. The cardinal excused himself and followed Rocco into another room.

Scala rubbed his hands and cleared his throat. "Andrew, we are alone here. Let me explain what I know. Professore Benson knows a little piece, as do I. Giacomo, however, knows it all. What we all know is that we need your help. Let me begin.

"About a year ago, a monsignor assigned to an antiquities project in Israel made an astonishing discovery. He relayed his information to the Holy Father. I take it His Holiness was equally astounded. He called Giacomo to his private chambers one evening and asked him to look into the affair. He told Giacomo to treat it as the highest papal matter, that is, only he, God, and the pope know what it is about.

"Tell me, Andrew, do you know anything about papal politics?"

"Truthfully, Ettore, only what I read in the papers when a new pope is about to be elected, plus the stuff that Andrew Greeley wrote about."

"Ah, yes, Fr. Greeley was a most interesting man, yes? But he was a Jesuit, and what can you expect from them! Let me share with you what is making the rounds of Vatican City and most of the political chambers in Italy.

"Our beloved pope died. The cardinals, in their wisdom and guided by the Holy Spirit, elevated another man with the same convictions to the chair of the Holy See. Now he has retired and we have another man in Peter's chair. But, still, no matter who occupies your White House or our Chair of Peter, we always cooperate fully with the United States to roust the elements of terrorism from whatever cesspool they hide in. But, I speak too much.

"Our cardinal, Giacomo di Sistio, was widely rumored to be the next pope. He was the most attractive of the *papabile*—you know, the cardinals whose names go on the ballots. So many times their names ended up in black smoke wafting from the Sistine Chapel's chimney.

"When the smoke turned white, all of Rome expected Giacomo to walk out on the terrace and give his blessing to the city and the world. But that was not to be. Nonetheless, our cardinal has very much to gain from making sure this thing works out in the end. He is still a *papabile.* And he has been entrusted with a secret that only one man in the Vatican knows. Listen to him.

"Giacomo is a worldly man, but he is also a very holy one. He loves Jesus very much. But he has no desire to be sitting on the throne of Peter welcoming Jesus to the Vatican when He comes the second time. You see?"

Andrew really didn't, but he nodded yes. "Your head moves up and down, but your eyes tell me something different. Let me put it plainly. What Giacomo knows, what you will know, if it isn't rectified, could very well mean the end of the world."

Chapter Forty-Nine

The Italian official's words sucked the oxygen out of the room, creating a silence so thick it masked the traffic on Madison Avenue. Andrew stared at his hands, crossed and uncrossed his legs, picked at his cuticles, anything not to focus on what Scala had said. One by one, as if summoned by a bell, Jill Benson and Giacomo di Sistio made their way back to the room. All four of them stared at the table, examining their hands.

The cardinal broke the uncomfortable silence. "So, you have heard Ettore. What do you think? Do you want to go ahead? If not, now is the time to push back from the table and walk through the door. We will never bother you again. If you wish to be part of us, I suggest we break for an early lunch. Rocco will arrange for room service."

"Tell me, how do you know this? The pope asked you to 'look into this affair.' What affair? What are you talking about?"

"My son, we will reveal more to you in time. But let me tell you this. The Holy Father received a private communication from one of his priests working in Jerusalem. It shook him to his inner being. I know. I was in his private chamber when he told me the message.

"We both agreed that the information was too explosive to keep to ourselves. Despite what many may think about the Vatican, we have little power to act on our own behalf. We need the cooperation of friendly governments.

"Through my offices, we contacted your government, ours, and a secret group of 'friends' working in Israeli security. Professor Benson has agreed—"

"Giacomo," Benson cut him off in mid-sentence, "I didn't agree to anything. I was drafted into this affair."

"This is true, Jill. But I must give this young man an explanation. No?"

No one said anything. Giacomo motioned Rocco away from his watchful stance against the wall and whispered something in his ear. The driver-butler left the room.

"Let us begin," intoned di Sistio. "Andrew, I know the most pressing question on your mind is 'Why me?' Your professor will explain. Jill, if you please."

She cleared her throat and straightened her white silk blouse. Her breasts strained against the shimmering fabric and Andrew caught both men looking intently at them. *God bless, Giacomo,* Andrew thought to himself. *He'll make a hell of a pope.*

"Your selection for this duty is no accident. In fact, we zeroed in on you when we learned the news. My, er, our government came to me for help. I am in no shape, despite the glances from Giacomo and Ettore, to play anything more than a consultative role. We need someone on the street to manage the task.

"When I was asked to help, I scoured my Rolodex. I mean no offense, but you weren't in it. You were, however, in an article that was laying on my desk. Remember when you took charge of the Dead Sea Scrolls exhibit? You received a number of accolades and got more than a few write-ups in the popular archaeological journals. So, I called Martin Fallon, and we met for lunch.

"Fallon is such a fool. All I mentioned was a secret governmental project, and he was all ears. For the past year, we have been monitoring your activity, especially your computer activity. You, Andrew, have taken up again with your studies of Near Eastern languages. That was very convenient for us."

Andrew's ears reddened at the mention of his computer activity. *What else do they know about me?*

"We also know," Benson continued, "that there is no permanent person in your life. You're free to move about. Furthermore, your new position that Fallon threw you is meaningless. It carries no authority, no perks, and no future. We are offering you a future."

At this point, the cardinal interrupted. "Professore Jill, if I may." She nodded her assent.

Giacomo di Sistio placed his elbows on the table and leaned forward. "I know you must be disturbed about how much we know about you. This is not, what do you Americans say, a 'set-up.' The library board has agreed that you be seconded to the Holy Office for Near Eastern Affairs. You will receive a salary equal to three times the amount the library pays you, and it will be tax-free. You will also receive what is possibly the most valuable document in the world—a Vatican City passport.

"I know you Americans treasure your blue book with the seal of the United States on it. I assure you, my English friends love their black passport, especially now that most Europeans carry the EU version. But an American passport can't get you into every country, and in some places, it will guarantee a bullet to your head. Trust me, you will come to treasure your Vatican passport. I have already made arrangements with friends in Washington for you to carry one. They have no problem."

Jill Benson jumped back into the conversation. "Andrew, Giacomo will fill you in on the particulars on your way back to Rome. He has arranged for the papal plane to take you and him back to the Vatican. But, let me tell you what I know.

"A Jesuit priest, a man we thought the Order had put out to pasture, has cracked the code of an obscure piece of copper tucked away with the Qumran Scrolls. For the past sixty-five years, it remained hidden from the scholars. The writing was in paleo-Hebraic, and none of the words matched what we know about the paleo-Hebraic language. This priest had nothing to do except concentrate on this piece of copper. He deciphered it. It definitely was not part of the Qumran library. How it got into the same caves as the other Qumran scrolls, we'll never know. But it is more important and more explosive than all 15,000 pieces of the Dead Sea Scrolls.

"We're not talking about the proof of Jesus or the validity of His mission as some scholars had hoped the scrolls would reveal. Don't get me wrong. That would be nice to know. But it wouldn't change two thousand years of history. Sure, a little turmoil among theologians. Front covers on the news. But, that's about it.

"What was discovered is much more important. It won't ignite a religious debate. It will ignite a holy war, the likes of which history has never seen. What our priest found was a deed, inscribed on a small, square piece of copper. It's a deed to the oil-bearing lands in the Middle East. And it gives the property in perpetuity to a Jewish family."

The import of what Jill Benson had just revealed began to sink into Andrew's thick head when a knock on the door followed by the sound of a plastic key slipping into the lock stopped all conversation. Rocco rushed into the room, pushing a room service wagon.

"Eminenza, gentlemen, Professore Benson, we must leave now, *subito*!" He ushered the four of them out the door past the room service wagon. As Rocco closed the door, Andrew saw a bloodied hand poke out from underneath the tablecloth covering the wagon.

Rocco pushed them out of the suite. They avoided the elevator on the fourteenth floor and walked down one flight. By the time they got to the twelfth floor landing, Giacomo was out of breath.

The putative future pope of the Roman Catholic Church looked at Andrew. "This is a young man's game. I must get back to Rome where I can hide behind my books and watch you young men do all the work."

Rocco rushed up to them. "*Eminenza,* come. I have cleared the elevators. Let's get to the basement and back to the embassy. You will be safe there. I have alerted my friends in the New York FBI office. They will meet us there and get you and Signore Scala to the plane safely. You too, Andrew."

Andrew just stood on the landing of the hotel's emergency stairs. *Me, too? What the hell am I doing here? How did I get caught up in this popular fiction thriller?* Andrew had no time to answer these questions in his mind. Rocco, with more force than he had ever shown, thrust Andrew through the service door on the twelfth floor out into the corridor of the hotel. The five of them made their way to an open elevator magically waiting for them.

Rocco was the last in. He looked either way about the corridor and checked the escape hatch on top of the elevator cab. All was clear. The doors closed. He inserted a New York Fire Department key into the elevator's control panel and sent the elevator car straight to the basement floor. Putting his arm around Giacomo and shielding the cardinal from sight, he walked through the service door into a covered truck bay and into the waiting Italian Embassy car. A hotel employee stood by the car's door, keys in hand. Rocco shoved Cardinal di Sistio unceremoniously into the back seat. Jill and Ettore also received strong pushes. A shout to Andrew got him into the front seat. The loading of the car took all of thirty seconds. Rocco grabbed the keys from the employee, threw him a double sawbuck, and stepped on the gas.

The Crown Vic, obviously souped-up to Italian government specifications, peeled out of the hotel's alleyway onto Fiftieth Street and made a left onto Lexington Avenue. Rocco maneuvered the car west until he got to Park Avenue. From there, it was a short ride to the embassy.

Rocco helped the two men out of the car. Jill, still spry at sixty-two, jumped out of the back seat. Andrew looked at his watch. The cheap digital timepiece read 3:16. Lunch lasted longer than he thought it would.

They took the embassy's small elevator to the second floor parlor, a private room for diplomatic use. An elegant silver coffee service was waiting for them. They continued their discussion until the winter night darkened the windows. It was time to go.

Both Italians were home. Jill lived a few blocks north on Park Avenue. But Andrew had to schlep all the way up to Eighty-Sixth. He looked around the room, waiting for someone to say good-night.

"I think it's time to retire for the evening," Cardinal di Sistio said. "Rocco, you too. Let Aldomo take Professore Benson and Mr. Wagner home." He glanced around the room. "We shall speak of this tomorrow."

A knock on the parlor door introduced yet another character into this bizarre play. A man similar to Rocco but without his refinement just stood at the doorway, indicating he was waiting for Jill and Andrew. Wearily, they took their leave and followed him to the elevator down to the embassy's private garage.

The Crown Vic was gone, replaced by a white Chrysler 300M. None of the embassy cars were fancy Cadillacs or Lincolns, but all of them had bloodlines that led right back to the drag strip. Andrew wondered what was under the Chrysler's hood as Aldomo drove smoothly up Park Avenue.

The car pulled up to Jill's apartment house. The doorman, bored by a slow night of no activity, rushed to the Chrysler and opened the back door. Jill got out with a quick squeeze of Andrew's hand and glided through her front door trailed by the doorman. She didn't even look back. Andrew rode in silence.

"Signore, your house. It is by the park, no?"

"Almost," he told the driver. "The house is between York and East End on the right. Turn down Eighty-Sixth and keep on going. I'll tell you when to stop."

The traffic was light. They got to his apartment house in a few minutes. Andrew thanked Aldomo and got out. He walked to his building, the last four-story building left on the street. The ground floor, where a full-service Gristede's used to be when he was growing up, was turned into a lobby and a garden apartment. Andrew slipped his key into the lobby door and walked up two flights to his apartment. He stumbled through his door and crashed into the bedroom, wondering what the hell he had gotten into. Gratefully, sleep came quickly.

Chapter Fifty

Walking up Eighty-Sixth Street to the Lexington Avenue subway the next morning, Andrew tried to sort through the events of the previous night. He knew he was asked to help in some kind of Italo-Vatican plot that the US government knew about. He knew that the driver was worried about someone chasing them. And he knew he was extremely tired.

He got out of the subway at Grand Central, less crowded now that half the Wall Streeters didn't work downtown anymore, and walked through the beautifully restored Grand Central Station. He made his way up to Forty-First to the employees' entrance of the library and saw a deep blue Lincoln waiting. The car was a Big Apple car—the library had an account with the service—and his name was printed in block letters on a sign the driver had stuck in the front window.

Holy shit! I forgot all about picking up that archaeologist at JFK. He yanked the car door open and told the driver he'd be right back.

"That's okay," the driver said, "I get paid thirty-five bucks an hour to wait."

Fallon went nuts when he saw a charge for waiting time on one of the car service bills, but Andrew wasn't worrying about Fallon. He had to get a packet of stuff he needed to read on the way to the airport. He ran into his office and grabbed the thick folder lying on his desk. He ignored the square, cream-colored envelope embossed with the papal seal. He mumbled a few words to his fellow employees and rushed to the car.

The Lincoln swerved west, starting the circuitous ride out of Manhattan to JFK. The driver slid the car down Second Avenue to the Queens Midtown Tunnel. "Sir," the driver asked, "you okay with the toll?"

Andrew nodded and answered, "Yeah, don't worry about it. I gotta meet an El Al plane at eleven. You think we'll make it?"

"No problem. Let's get the hell out of the city, and we'll be at JFK in no time."

The traffic gods were good to Andrew. There was neither construction nor any accidents on the Long Island Expressway. He dozed in the back, awakening only as the car glided to a mandatory security stop before entering JFK.

Worship of the traffic gods apparently didn't do any good inside JFK. The traffic was miserable. What made it worse was all the security. Every terminal had half a precinct of cops standing outside. The car crawled until it got to the El Al terminal. Then it stopped dead.

Andrew signed the receipt the driver handed him and got out of the Lincoln. He barely made it to the sidewalk outside the terminal when an El Al employee approached him. "You are meeting…?" the employee asked with no introductions, no niceties, no good mornings, just a brusque question.

Andrew rummaged through his briefcase and pulled out the folder marked "IAA" for Israel Antiquities Authority. He opened the folder and told the impatient employee the name of the passenger. "Jordan Barash; she's coming from Tel Aviv."

"That's impossible. The only El Al flight from Tel Aviv is LY0001, and it doesn't arrive until 17:45 hours. You either have the wrong flight, or you are six hours early. Come inside with me please."

They stepped through the first of four security screens. Satisfied that neither Andrew nor the El Al employee had any unidentifiable metal objects on them, the soldier let them through. Andrew and the employee continued to walk through the terminal when Andrew realized there was something wrong with this picture. "Hey! Wait a minute! Those are Israeli soldiers," Andrew said, with emphasis on *Israeli*.

"Quite," answered the El Al employee as they stopped for another security check, also manned by a soldier. They were now in the terminal proper. "This way."

They passed the ticket counters and made their way to the screening lines leading to the small handful of gates El Al maintained at JFK. Andrew kept his mouth shut. Something about foreign soldiers with guns patrolling on American soil made him uneasy and quite cooperative.

Before they went through the screen, the El Al employee asked Andrew to remove his shoes, belt, all metal jewelry, and empty his pockets. "When you get to the screening module, do not walk through. The guard will tell you when to proceed. Thank you for your interest in El Al," he said and walked away, leaving Andrew stranded at the security checkpoint.

He stepped into the module, waited until he was told to proceed, and started to dress on the other side of the checkpoint when a voice spoke behind him. "There's no need to dress in public, Mr. Wagner. Please come with me."

Andrew turned around and saw an officer. He looked like a lieutenant, but Andrew wasn't up on army insignia of foreign governments. Silently, he followed the officer. They stopped before a door marked "Private." The officer opened the door and waved Andrew in. The door closed.

The room was comfortably, but sparsely, furnished. This was obviously not a lounge for El Al's best customers. He looked to his left. There, behind a bar that would not be out of place in a Long Island basement, stood a squat, powerfully built young man.

"Drink, Mr. Wagner?"

It wasn't even eleven in the morning, but Andrew thought it would be politic to join the man. "Sure, I'll have a white—" stopping his request when he saw what was in the man's hand—something short, something brown, and something definitely not effete. "Gimme what you got," he said.

The man walked over with two water glasses filled with scotch. "Sit down, please. You're about five hours early because there is much more for you to know before Captain Barash arrives. Relax, this is probably the safest place in the city, short of our embassy. My name is William Hirschberg, and like you, I have an interest in ancient Near Eastern languages."

Andrew and William—he didn't look like a "Bill"—sat on the only couch in the room, sipping their drinks. *These Israelis aren't that bad after all,* he thought to himself as the scotch coursed down his throat. *I haven't had scotch for breakfast since my college days.*

The door leading to the terminal opened, and a voice boomed across the room. "Pour me one, too, William. I feel like drinking my breakfast."

Andrew looked up and saw an older version of William standing by the door. His left eye was hidden behind a black patch. His hair was too short to complete the pirate look, but Andrew had no doubt that the man was every bit as deadly as William Kidd. Meanwhile, Hirschberg jumped up at the sound of the voice, stiffened, and said, "Sir!"

"William, William, I am your father's brother, your uncle. Must you always treat me like one of those army scoundrels? Come, *boychik,* let's sit at the table." William's uncle looked at Andrew and waved him to the table. William walked over to the table with the three drinks.

"This is my Uncle Julian. He is a ranking member of the Israel Antiquities Authority and Miss Barash's direct boss."

"Andrew," William's uncle spoke in his booming voice, "my name is Julian Hirschberg. Let's talk."

Andrew said nothing, just thinking how weird the last seventeen hours had been. Julian's phone rang. He reached into his pocket. His meaty hand enveloped the tiny mobile phone. "Yes. He's here. Yes. Yes. She'll be here this afternoon. Yes. To the embassy. Good-bye."

He returned the phone to his pocket and took a swig of the scotch. "I dread the day these damn things have a television screen. Then we'll have no privacy at all. Enough of this merriment. Let's cut to the chase."

Andrew recoiled at the phrase "cut to the chase." This was the second time someone affiliated with this venture used that term. *What do they do, go to same secret spy school? And now, class, let us concentrate on saying, "cut to the chase."*

He also wondered, *How close is this man to current technology? After all, movies, television shows, even face-to-face conversations are commonplace with today's smartphones. Hasn't he ever heard of FaceTime on an iPhone?*

Julian's voice shook him out of his daydream.

"As I was saying, you know why we are getting together. One of your fellow citizens, a priest working in Jerusalem, has made an astounding discovery. Yes, we think Monsignor O'Brien has found a deed to the Arab oil. Not a bad thing, except the deed-holders are an unnamed Jewish family. Now, tracing that family's going to be difficult. There's a small matter of some two thousand years between the writing of the deed and its recent discovery.

"I think your priest is holding out on us. Three governments—ours, yours, and the Vatican—want you to cooperate with this priest and learn what he's keeping from us."

The cooperation among the Vatican, Israeli, and US governments was unusual but not uncommon. The Catholic Church had the best human intelligence network on earth. Hundreds of thousands of clergy kept their superiors apprised of what was happening locally. Word filtered upward until it reached the highest levels of the Vatican. In matters of great importance, the pope himself got involved. Such was the case with O'Brien's discovery.

Cardinal di Sistio had barely left the presence of the pope after their fateful late-night meeting when another prelate entered the papal chambers.

"Monsignore Enders," the pope said in his guttural German, "I have a delicate task you must do for me."

"Yes, Holiness," the younger man said, patiently waiting until his countryman and the man responsible for him entering the priesthood spoke again.

"With the utmost secrecy and discretion, you must reach out to our friends in Washington and Tel Aviv. Give them this message. 'We have entered the Pass to Megiddo.' They will understand. I am sending Cardinal di Sistio to the United States. He will make arrangements for them to meet with his surrogates. Go now and do this quickly."

"Yes, Holiness. May I tell them when the cardinal shall be arriving?"

"Not soon enough, my young friend."

The younger man left the pope in his study. Dressed, as always, in his white cassock and a white zucchetto topping the crown of his head, the pope settled in the black walnut chair he had brought with him to Rome from his beloved Germany.

Even before ascending to the chair of Peter, a younger Josef Ratzinger bore the weight of his church on his shoulders. As the ecclesiastical head of the Society for the Propagation of the Faith, he occupied the most sensitive office in the Vatican, save the one seat of power he now occupied. Hundreds of years ago, the organization he headed was known as the Holy Office. It was a period the church wished to forget—the Holy Inquisition. The position Ratzinger had held was formerly known in the sixteenth century as the Chief Inquisitor.

A less well-known fact about the pope was his role as the church's head of archaeological studies, especially those concerned with biblical themes. He was intimately aware of the Dead Sea Scrolls since he controlled the initial committee of scholars—all of them Catholic, except one. He fervently believed that even that committee and those that followed would never unlock all the secrets held in the two-thousand-year-old documents.

He was accused of suppressing the committee's scholarship, afraid it would reveal some unknown facts about the life of Christ. He locked his eyes on the simple wooden crucifix hanging above the kneeler he could no longer use and prayed aloud.

"Would it were so, dear Jesus, that we may have learned more about you. Nothing we would have learned could have changed two thousand years of history and longing for a heavenly life. But what you have placed on us now could not be worse."

The elderly Pope shocked the world with his resignation. Vatican-watchers blamed the inner workings of papal politics as wearing down the old man who was truly fit to be more of a scholar than the leader of the most populous Christian faith in the world. But for those very few who knew the world-ending problem he was wrestling with wondered if the knowledge of what he and the world faced weighed too heavily on his shoulders. His successor, a charismatic Argentinian of Italian parentage and a Jesuit, would now have to deal with it.

"I have to go to the bathroom," Andrew said, rising unsteadily to his feet. He walked to the back of the room and opened the bathroom door. He didn't even close the door when he lurched to the commode and threw up all the scotch. William and Julian heard him and left him alone. He kept on going until he got to the dry heaves stage. A few minutes later he had enough. He washed his face and walked-slid to the couch against the wall. "I'm taking a nap."

That's when the dreams began. He was stuck in a dry, dark cave. Figures in long white garments walked down a short flight of steps into a pool and emerged up on the other side, completely dry. One figure wore a short Roman sword. "Find him. Find him." Someone in the dream began shaking him. It wasn't a dream. Andrew opened his eyes and looked up at William.

"Andrew, Andrew, wake up. Let's go find her," William was shouting in his face.

"Find who? What am I doing in this cave? What…"

"Andrew, snap out of it. You've slept off the booze by now," William yelled at him. "It's almost 17:00 hours. Jordan's plane arrives in forty-five minutes. Wash up and let's walk to her gate." He looked around. The room was empty. *Where was Julian?*

Chapter Fifty-One

Reb Whitlow looked out the window. The natural fountain spritzed water a hundred feet high in the middle of the impossibly blue lake. *What was a beautiful lake like this doing here? What was a beautiful city like Geneva doing in this gray country?* Reb Whitlow's Switzerland was gray, not at all like the country of green meadows and belled milk cows in the travel posters. His employers were gray. "The Gray Men," he called them, and they were assembled around a polished conference table at a private bank in Geneva.

Geneva's private banks are a best-kept secret. One goes to Zurich for banking and financial matters. One goes to Geneva to imbibe drinks at cocktail receptions of the United Nations' offices and attend economic summits. There's not supposed to be any financial intricacy in Geneva. But no one told the Gray Men that. The Gray Men came here to plot the flow of the world's oil.

Reb Whitlow never paid attention to the conversation around the table. That wasn't his job. They would summon him to the table when they wanted him.

The locals said the stone bridge at the end of town was used by Hannibal to maneuver his elephants across the Alps. Reb had his share of elephants, courtesy of the silly little wars his former employer would foment wherever it was convenient for US foreign policy. Oh yeah, Whitlow had seen the elephant.

Reb hadn't started in this clandestine life. He was going to be a teacher. His résumé was perfect for a tweedy career at some prestigious university or, better yet, an obscure women's college with a lot of scholarship students who wouldn't dream of reporting a lecherous professor.

Reb knew all about scholarships and living at the low end of the college totem pole. You'd never know it from the paper he carried. It was perfect. Undergrad at Gonzaga in Washington; law school at Notre Dame; a PhD in international relations at Fordham; and post-doc at Georgetown.

The CIA came knocking for Reb when he was in his second year of post-doc work at Georgetown in Washington, DC. He wouldn't have gotten to Switzerland or to the high life offered by the salary the Gray Men paid if the CIA hadn't kicked him out. Oh, the boys in the Company loved him. They trained him, and they made him what he was. But the Company men who specialize in "wet work" know they don't have long-term careers in the CIA. A new assistant director gets named, develops a conscience, and purges the CIA's ranks of all the killers it had trained. Men like Whitlow were just shift employees, not career intelligence agents.

Reb had walked out of the CIA's headquarters in Langley with his separation papers in hand, a valid passport, and his 401(k) statement in his briefcase. He pushed the exit door of the CIA's headquarters, and there in front of him was a brand-new, dark green Jaguar.

"Mr. Whitlow, let me drive you to your car," the driver said. By the time Reb got to his BMW M3 sedan, he had a new job. He was now working for the Gray Men.

Whitlow pondered his change in careers. His first meeting with one of the Gray Men in the CIA parking lot was a while back. Still

Reb wondered how his new employers got his name. He specialized in a particular kind of work that the CIA never acknowledged. There were always rumors that, for men like him, there was a life after the CIA. And the life was lucrative, much more lucrative than government pay.

Were there these connections among "certain interest groups" that kept tabs on men like Reb Whitlow? He would never know. Nor would he ask. He just collected his paycheck.

"Mr. Whitlow, turn your attention here please," one of the men around the table said. "The fountain will still be in the lake when this meeting is over. Mr. Whitlow, the Jewess has landed in New York. Here are your tickets. I suggest you make her acquaintance. You know what to do. Get rid of her, that meddlesome priest, and bring us back the copper square."

Chapter Fifty-Two

The *souk* teemed with life. Daniel made his way through, roughly pushing the old women out of his way. *Why does my brother insist we meet in a place like this? Our great leader lured those accursed hotel devils into building their monuments in our fair capital. But no, Hassan has to meet in a common marketplace.*

Daniel continued to walk through the *souk*. He was an angry young man with no reason to be angry. Born to upper-middle-class Lebanese parents, Daniel Bensouk never faced the horrors of war other Lebanese children faced. True, he was too young to remember Beirut as the "Paris of the Middle East," but neither did he live through the troubles that flattened the country.

He spent his childhood with relatives in Atlanta whose construction business complemented his family's work in Lebanon. Daniel returned to Lebanon when all was quiet and the country was rebuilding. Even the fabled Corniche, a wide boulevard fronting the Mediterranean shore, was being redeveloped. No, there was no reason for his anger, except for his trip to Pakistan.

His family never would have guessed that Daniel Bensouk would become one of the world's most feared and secretive terrorists. He was never exposed to the madness that gripped the Middle East in the last quarter of the twentieth century. Evil had taken over Lebanon, and no one was safe, least of all the vulnerable children of wealthy parents. The Bensouks were wealthy Christian Arabs parlaying a small business started by Daniel's grandfather into a worldwide construction and real estate empire. Daniel's father chose to stand his ground in Lebanon, but he feared for his son.

When he was six, his father put him on a jet to live with his cousin in the United States. The little boy didn't know why he was leaving home, and he was promised he would come home soon. Daniel had a normal childhood in Atlanta, blending in well with other immigrants to the New South.

By all indications, Daniel Bensouk had turned into the perfect American. He played soccer at the local church, joined the Little League at Morgan Falls Park, and attended local public schools.

After high school, he attended the University of Georgia in Athens on a scholarship. Neither he nor his family needed the money, but his uncle encouraged him to accept the scholarship.

"Believe me, Daniel, if you get marked as a scholarship student, your days at university will be easy," Edouard Bensouk told his nephew as they drove the ninety minutes from Atlanta to Athens. His uncle's prediction came true.

Daniel floated through the University of Georgia in Athens, posing as a foreign exchange student when the pose was useful to get girls, and then as a middle-class American of Lebanese background when that pose was useful to get girls. His dark Lebanese good looks projected like a flame attracting the blonde, blue-eyed, Southern female moths.

He was a personable young man and tall for a man of Middle Eastern descent—over six feet. His family's wealth, in Lebanon and in America, insulated him from most hardships a foreign exchange student faced. He carried his wealth easily, never affecting the rich boy airs of some of the Arabian exchange students.

Daniel drove a late-model Toyota, a gift from his American uncle, and lived in off-campus housing. He studied business and graduated with a degree in insurance. He knew he would be involved in the construction and real estate business, but he wanted something to fall back on. Insurance was as good a background as any, he had thought.

Daniel lusted after the American lifestyle. After graduation, he traded in his Toyota for a BMW. He went to mass every Sunday with his cousins, and he worked for his Uncle Edouard as a property manager. The Bensouk family owned a string of apartment houses in south Atlanta, in a predominantly African American neighborhood. The people were middle-class, hard-working families who paid their rent every month and strived to get their children a better life.

Everybody knew he was the rent man, but nobody resented him. He always came with candy for the little ones, and he had been known to reach into his pocket to pay the utility bills of his elderly tenants. Life was good.

Daniel had one weakness. He was a ladies' man. It was a bad trait for a property manager. It got him into some scrapes that nearly cost him his life. Some of his tenants knew that a little lovin' went a long way in taking care of their rent for that month. But their boyfriends, and sometimes, their husbands, preferred they paid the rent in cash.

Daniel was leaving an apartment complex on Memorial Drive late one evening when a man in the apartment complex's parking lot stopped him. "Salaam, Brother."

He had no idea what he was talking about. All he knew was what his uncle told him: "If a black man stops you, pull out your piece, and don't take no shit."

Daniel reached into his jacket for the nine millimeter automatic he carried for protection. Georgia recently required a carry license to possess a concealed handgun. He applied for one as soon as the law changed. Daniel, nervous sweat and fear reeking from him, looked at the man.

"Peace, Brother. Why are you coming at me with a piece?"

Daniel peered into the darkness and saw a young black man dressed in Muslim garb. He knew that this area was a hotbed for a Muslim sect that followed the teachings of a reformed convict. A 1960s black radical used to rule the neighborhood, but he got himself caught in a shoot-out with DeKalb County police and now he was a guest of the state in the "Ironbar Hilton." His contacts told him there was a dangerous power struggle going on in the area.

He wanted no trouble. Despite what his Uncle Edouard had told him, Daniel preferred a peaceful solution. He showed the man his hands, palms turned up, and jingled his car keys in his pocket. "Hey, listen. I was just collecting the rent. I'm on my way back to my car. Here. Take twenty bucks and donate it to your favorite charity. Man, I don't want no trouble."

Daniel settled down. His fears drained from his face, and he walked calmly toward the man. He had enough firepower on him to take out the local police precinct. He just didn't want trouble. It was bad for business. It was bad for his uncle. And what's bad for his uncle was bad for him. Daniel was on an extended student visa. His uncle "knew" people in the Georgia congressional delegation, so his nephew got special treatment from the INS. But that special treatment would end in a heartbeat if he were involved in a shooting in south Atlanta.

"My brother," the man said, "I don't want your money. I know who you are, and you are good to us. But you are a brother Muslim, aren't you? I have come to invite you to our mosque. You must miss worshipping Allah up there in Sandy Springs."

Daniel lived with his uncle in an affluent northern suburb where the voters were overwhelmingly Republican. The little municipality had finally seceded from Fulton County, creating the state's seventh-largest city. That happened after an almost hopeless thirty-year effort by a group of hard-core secessionists got blessed by a newly elected Republican state legislature.

Most of the northern residents had no idea what was going on in the city. The majority of suburbanites didn't read the Atlanta paper. There were more red and blue plastic bags on suburban lawns—holding copies of *The Wall Street Journal* and *The New York Times*—than the clear plastic bags of *The Atlanta Journal-Constitution*. If it weren't for Daniel's monthly rent collecting duties, he would have no idea where Memorial Drive was.

"Ah, I see. You misunderstand. I am not a Muslim. Even though I am from the Middle East, I am Catholic. I appreciate your invitation. Here, let me offer you something for the mosque's programs," Daniel said, holding out two twenty-dollar bills.

"Thank you for your offering. In Allah's name I shall take it. But we wish to have your mind and spirit, not just your cash."

Daniel looked at the man again. "Who are you? Why are you coming to me in the middle of the night with this message?"

"My brother, I am but a messenger for Allah. Salaam," he said, silently fading back into the shadows.

Daniel walked away, troubled, and with much to think about. He clicked his key fob and killed the alarm. Sliding into the seat of his low-slung BMW, he drove the fifteen miles north back home and to an uncertain future.

Daniel was already sitting next morning at the breakfast table when his Uncle Edouard came down. He and his uncle spent most of their time separately visiting properties in the family's portfolio of real estate. Uncle Edouard managed not only his own properties, but also the entire holdings of the Bensouk family. Daniel started at the bottom—managing the south-side apartment rentals. Edouard and his two brothers looked after the Bensouk commercial properties, mainly one- and two-story office parks in the northern suburbs.

The Atlanta real estate community knew the Bensouks but not well. Nor did the family have a great reputation in the wide-open Atlanta property business. It wasn't the family's practice to develop property. Too risky, Edouard would say. Let others get their hands dirty in this damnable red clay, he would laugh. Once the building was up and running, Edouard would stalk the property, maybe for years. When the original developer fell onto hard times, which was the norm in the real estate business, Edouard would snap up the property for less than fifty percent of its value.

The original developer came out of the deal with a small profit, a big tax write-off, and cash to develop more office parks in an already overcrowded market.

The Bensouk brothers preyed on the developers' main weakness. They had little patience for managing. Edouard would say that he had never seen a developer happier than the day when the first shovel full of dirt was turned over on a new building site. The Bensouk brothers realized this early on and always stood ready to feed the building habits of their developer friends.

At the few real estate business socials during the year, the family was amiably treated. They contributed to all the popular charities backed by one real estate mogul or the other. They provided starter jobs for the relatives and children of their fellow property owners. And they never broke ranks with the real estate community during legislative battles.

All seemed to go well with the Bensouks and their Atlanta partners. The camaraderie was a front. Behind their backs, as they well knew, the Bensouks were reviled as moneylenders and vulture investors.

The brothers didn't mind. They retreated into the comfort of their large and well-off family. A gathering of just close relatives could number up to 150. Edouard's house in Sandy Springs was more of a catering facility than a home, he used to joke. Daniel was a part of all this. He lived in his uncle's house and was more like a son than a nephew.

The family expected him to lead its return to Lebanon as commercial developers in the Lebanese renaissance. His time in the United States, his uncles would tell him, was in preparation for the return of the Bensouk name to the top tiers of the Christian Arab business world.

At a post-Easter celebration, Daniel cornered his uncle for a serious discussion about the family. His "exile" in America did little to help him understand his roots.

"Edouard," Daniel said, dropping the familiar "uncle" as requested, "why are we Catholics in an Arab country?"

"By all rights, this is a story your father, my beloved brother, should tell you. But I am here, and he is not. Please, take your drink and let's go outside. No one will miss us.

"We are a fortunate family. We have been a family of record-keepers and scribes for as long as anyone can remember. We can reliably trace our ancestors to the original settlers of South Arabia and the first Christian missionaries. Some say that Peter himself preached to our people, while Paul roamed all over the Mediterranean converting the gentiles. Your father maintained the records, but most of all, he has in safekeeping for the family a medal that is said to have been touched by Jesus Himself. I doubt that is true, but it is very old, and only the first male in the family may hold it.

"When God calls your father back home, then you will hold the medal for the family. That medal has always represented our firm founding in the faith. It has not been easy. It is harder today than ever before.

"During the Muslim wars in the seventh century, our family resisted Muhammad and his followers. For this loyalty there has always been an altar dedicated to us in St. Peter's. It is graced with the presence of the Holy Eucharist, signified by a red votive light burning twenty-four hours a day. There is no sign, no plaque with our name on it, but it is there. Every pope for 1,400 years has held the well-being of our family *in pectore,* that is, in his heart, keeping our secret from the glare of the day.

"Someday, you will lead the family in its devotion. For now, let's return to the celebration inside and enjoy the food."

Chapter Fifty-Three

Daniel walked back with his uncle, his mind and heart heavy over the family history, and his determination even stronger to learn more about Islam.

Later that night, he lay in his bed, conflicted. Yes, his family came from a long line of ancient Christians, and he was raised as a Catholic. But something drew him to his family's past with Islam. He couldn't figure out what it was. There was something…something pulling him from long ago that called to him. He needed to heed that calling and discover for himself what it was. He would take the first step. He would determine if the stirrings in his soul were nothing more than a young man's inquisitiveness into a strange and forbidden religion or truly an ancient tug on his heart that came from he knew not where.

The next day, Daniel finished his property management duties early and drove to a mosque in suburban Atlanta. He walked into the vestibule, removed his shoes, and entered the building. He looked around. He was disappointed. Like many mosques in non-Arab countries, it drew Muslims from all over the world. The followers of Mohammed, like Christians, adhered to one faith, but their individual cultures affected how they practiced it. Daniel didn't know what he was looking for, but he knew he wouldn't find it in America.

He continued to search for the Islam he had constructed in his mind. Month after month he returned to the suburban mosque and nothing happened, nothing touched him. This was the turning point in his life, the time when he would form his twisted idea of Islam and sink ever deeper into the Muslim radicalism that was threatening the peaceful balance of civilization.

Daniel fell into a group of young men who, unlike him, were dissatisfied with their lives and the lives they led in America. Impoverished, uneducated, and, ultimately, dangerous, they embraced the radical Islam preached by the imam at the mosque.

He had nothing in common with them except for an unusual attraction to the "purity" of Islam preached by the imam. He couldn't define it. He didn't know the origin. Nor did he know that the strange pull on his soul that he felt would drag him into a totally unknown world.

After his father died, Daniel returned to Lebanon, forsook the Catholic faith, and converted to Islam. It didn't take long for a certain group within Islam to recognize the fires burning in the young man. They sent him to northern Pakistan to a special Islamic school, a madrassah that taught their way of life. It couldn't be further from the pure Islam that Daniel sought than if he sought instruction about Islam in a synagogue. The teachers in Pakistan specialized in hatred and a corruption of the Koran that created monsters out of little boys, killers out of young men, and out of special men like Daniel, zealots willing to die for them.

"So, tell me, Daniel," the mullah said over a pot of fresh mint tea, "what do you wish to do for us?"

Daniel looked at the mullah, unsure of what his answer should be. He had completed his schooling. He burned with the fire of rebellion. And he turned his back on his family and his religion. He sought to serve Islam, but unknowingly, all he had succeeded in doing was corrupting his soul to serve the mullahs of hate.

"You come from a connected and wealthy family. You were educated in America. You know the devil we fight against. You are intelligent, well-spoken, and good-looking. We have dozens of fighters willing to strap a bomb to their chests and run into a crowd. But you, my son, we have other plans for you. For you are destined to be the sword of Mohammed.

"You will leave here and return to Lebanon under a cover created by our friends in France. You will build a new life. And you will work our wondrous ways. Allah be with you."

The mullah left the small room never having touched his tea. Daniel sat still at the small table, wondering what his life would be like now that he was a fully committed soldier of Islam. He soon found out.

He lived alternately in Beirut and Paris. In the seven years since he "graduated" from the Pakistani school, he had become one of the most lethal terrorists in the Muslim network. He worked like a shark, always alone, sleeping little and never staying in one place. He rarely spoke with his family. His uncles, aunts, and cousins accepted his absence at family gatherings, believing his stories of worldwide travel on behalf of the French university. They also knew he kept a hand in the family business in Lebanon, running the construction trade as an absentee boss. They never suspected their nephew and cousin had become a contract killer for the Muslim underworld. True to the mullah's word, Daniel never strapped a bomb around his waist, killing a few dozen Jews. No, for him, life in the fight against the infidels would be selective, discreet, and lethal.

Only his brother, Hassan, knew who Daniel was. Like him, he converted and joined the terrorist forces of Islam. Because his handlers knew better, Hassan never rose above the role of courier, principally ferrying messages to and from his secretive brother.

Daniel was a wealthy man, having transferred his share of his father's empire to untraceable accounts in Geneva and moneychangers in France. He lived two lives. One was as a smooth-talking archaeology professor welcomed into the most prestigious universities in the world. The other skirted the seamy underbelly of humanity where idealism was thrown out the window and only personal gain, money, and the mullahs' twisted notion of right ruled.

Daniel glided through the academic world skillfully, playing his role as a Middle East archaeologist. Daniel the terrorist huddled in dank basements, steamy jungle hideouts in South America, and dry caves in the Middle East. Both Daniels were successful. Neither of their paths crossed except in the conflicted mind of Daniel himself.

"Señor, we have what you want, and you have what we want. So, we can make a business deal, no?" The disgusting little thug sat across from Daniel in a smoky Columbian café, trying to broker a drugs-for-guns deal. This was what Daniel's life had sunken to. He would ensure that drugs from the Middle East would find their way to South America. It amused him to know that the Colombians weren't satisfied with just being the largest cocaine cartel in the world. They wanted to rule heroin distribution in the United States, hoping to keep their Mexican rivals out of the picture. Poppies did not grow in Colombia. They grew in the Middle East under the firm control of the Muslim terrorist network.

In return, the Colombian drug cartels would ship stolen arms to the "freedom fighters" wherever Daniel told them. He hated this part of his job, wondering how he had allowed himself to sink so low.

His Middle Eastern contacts trusted him to broker the drug deals. He was a wealthy man and would not cheat them. They always suspected Daniel skimmed some profits from every deal, but he never took enough to alarm them. Daniel justified his profit-taking as a means of setting up his retirement fund. He had every intention of disappearing someday to a Caribbean island, never returning to the terrorist world he had entered.

He was a wanted man in the western capitals of the world. But no one knew for sure who he was or what he looked like. None of the terrorist and government leaders who gave him their contracts ever met him. Daniel worked through cut-outs, drop-offs, and wired money to untraceable accounts. He published no messages on the Internet. He gave no interviews on Al Jazeera and Fox News. He had no friends and divorced himself from his family. He would have been captured years ago had he been the usual thuggish operative living in the shadowy terrorist network.

His money, connections, and ability to disguise himself kept him free. To the normal world, he was a French archaeology professor, free to move around the world with his French passport and academic background. But he was also a very careful man and never took chances.

Hassan never took their father's advice to go to America where it was safer. He chose to stay in Lebanon. Over the years, his hatred developed and he embraced radical Islam. When Daniel returned and converted, nothing could have made Hassan happier. He knew just a little of what his brother did for the Islamic cause. He didn't know everything. No one, not even the mullahs who relied upon his services, knew everything about him.

Daniel sat on the bed in his Paris hotel room, water dripping from his hair wetting the screen of the mobile phone in his hand. The call went through effortlessly. It always gave Daniel a little thrill to know he was driving the American security experts crazy when he used these untraceable phones. But he was still careful. Unfortunately, the man on the other end of the line was rarely careful, and this gave Daniel fits.

"What do you want?" Daniel was never polite to his brother, and the longer they worked together, the surer he was that if he didn't kill Hassan first, his brother would get him killed.

"Daniel, my brother, I have an important job for you. So important that we must meet. But not in Paris. Meet me tomorrow at the *souk* in Beirut. Then we will talk. I have good news. You will finally be working in Israel."

Daniel ended the conversation without saying good-bye. Time and again he warned his brother not to use his name on the phone. But the idiot never learned. He didn't look forward to meeting Hassan. His younger brother always made him nervous and meeting in the bombed-out *souk* in Beirut made him doubly nervous. He didn't know the place well and would have preferred to meet at an American hotel. Meeting in the *souk* was Hassan's way of reminding him they were not tourists in the Arab world but freedom fighters for the Muslim cause.

He dried himself and jumped under the covers. Lying in bed with the Eiffel Tower's lights shining through the curtains, Daniel stared at the ceiling and pondered Hassan's words "working in Israel."

The homeland of the Jews was too dangerous for a valued professional like Daniel. He never worked in Israel. Only those too stupid to value their lives would pit themselves against that government's vaunted and much-feared security forces. And Daniel was not stupid.

He wondered what Israel would be like. The last time he was there was what, twenty years ago? And what about those girls he met, especially the blonde one with whom, he was sure, he had fallen in love?

It was odd that he never met her on the archaeological circuit. But then again, she probably never left Israel. With so much of value underground in that tortured little country, why leave? He never forgot her name. "Jordan," she had said, "like the almond."

Has she forgotten me? Probably. Beautiful women like her always have men in their lives. She wouldn't recognize me anyway. Thanks to the skilled surgeons in Geneva, I doubt even my own mother would recognize me.

Daniel's head sank deeper into the pillow. He grabbed the medal that hung around his neck. It was actually half a medal, so impossibly old that most of its features were rubbed off by generations of

Bensouk safekeepers. But the goldsmith's art was still visible. Daniel, like his ancestors, wondered why the family treasure was incomplete.

Chapter Fifty-Four

The El Al terminal still gave Andrew the creeps. He well understood the need for added security in these times, but the sight of armed soldiers from another country walking around in his local airport didn't fit the picture.

Andrew and William walked to the gate. Andrew stared at the screen that had the gate information. El Al flight LY0001 had landed. The Boeing 787-8 Dreamliner was somewhere out on the tarmac, inching its way toward the gate. Andrew stared out the window at the activity on the field. Planes from all over were waiting at gates, backing out of gates, waiting to get into a gate. It looked like a shopping mall parking lot, except the vehicles were a hell of a lot bigger.

The El Al jet pulled up to the gate. The plane was the newest out of the Seattle-based manufacturer. Only a handful of airlines had ordered them. Specially equipped for long-haul flights, the newer models came off the line with hardened cockpit doors that could resist a C-4 charge if anyone was stupid enough to use that explosive on a plane.

The El Al flights, he had heard, had a complement of air marshals that equaled ten percent of the passengers. Of course, the airlines never revealed their security measures, and the governments were equally tight-lipped. *It's sad,* Andrew thought, *that Israelis are safer at forty thousand feet than they are attending a bar mitzvah at home. Will this horror ever end? And what part am I to play in it?*

The gateway door opened, and the passengers streamed off. The initial group came from the first class section, so it was unlikely the mysterious Jordan Barash would be with them. No government flew junior employees in the front of the bus.

Andrew and William stood right in front of the exit. There was no way either of them would miss their passenger. A group of Hasidim trailed off the plane, dozens of children in tow. An American tour group, complete with sunburnt noses and plastic duffle bags, waddled down the passageway. A few single men passed by, some of them, Andrew was sure, carrying government-sanctioned guns.

Then a man Andrew recognized ducked through the passageway, animatedly putting the moves on an attractive woman to his left. He was some sort of network journalist, outfitted in his "straight from the battlefront dress" of a safari coat and custom-tailored khakis. The woman was more interested in the pattern of the carpet than in what he was saying. *Good for you, cutie pie, that guy must be a jerk.*

The two took several strides down the passageway. At the head of it, where William and Andrew were waiting, they parted amicably.

"Of course, I'll catch your special on the dig. I wouldn't miss it. I'll call you at the station, and we can go out and celebrate," she was saying. "I'd love to join you in your car back to Manhattan, but I have someone waiting for me. Business calls, you know," she said with a wave and a practiced brush-off.

She turned away from the network Romeo and looked squarely at William and Andrew. "I'm Jordan Barash," she said, holding out a well-tanned arm connected to a callused hand that definitely knew the wooden end of a pickaxe or a rifle butt.

"Miss Barash, it's good to meet you. I'm Andrew Wagner, and we'll be working together. This is William Hirschberg from your government."

Jordan looked at him. "I know who he is."

Hirschberg acted as if Andrew didn't exist. William took her hand. Andrew just stood there and stared. No archaeologist ever looked like her. She was the girl of his dreams dressed in those impossibly short shorts on a dig in Israel. Or, at least she would be, if she were on a dig and he were an archaeologist. She had just gotten off a transatlantic flight and looked better than Andrew did when he was freshly showered and shaved. And, did he think *girl*? No, Miss—he loved the sound of that word—Barash was a well-put-together woman. Andrew stood there, tongue-tied and feeling slightly ridiculous.

He recovered and the three of them walked down the terminal. Andrew kept stealing sidelong glances at Jordan, not saying anything, just content to listen to William's mindless chattering. At the exit from the terminal, Jordan stopped dead in her tracks.

"Mr. Wagner, there's no need for you to look at me, then look away so I won't catch you looking at me. We'll be working together, so you better get to know what I look like." Jordan Barash was an upfront woman.

He considered the invitation and acted on it. Jordan stood before him in her Ralph Lauren countrified look, blonde hair reaching to her shoulders, green eyes flashing at him in the wan terminal sunlight, and tanned skin poking out from the sleeves of her jacket.

"Miss Barash, I'm sorry for staring, but I had pictured you differently. I just thought that Sabras were, well, you know, different looking," Andrew said, realizing that he made no sense at all. "Sabra" was a term for women born in Israel after their parents emigrated there. He learned the word as a student at NYU.

"Mr. Wagner, no, let me call you Andrew, I am a Sabra, but not all of us come from a uniform background. My parents emigrated to Israel as teenagers on the first boat out of Eastern Europe. The rest of my family never got a chance. Their ashes lie in the camps."

Andrew stared at this beautiful woman with such a history of horror in her background. There was no need to place an adjective before or after the word "camps." He knew. The world knew. And the Israelis never forgot. And he knew there was no reason to mention it again.

"So that's where the blonde hair comes from," he said, trying to lighten the mood.

The ride back to the city was silent, the passengers lost in their own thoughts. Andrew alternated between trying to figure out how to get Jordan Barash naked and trying to figure out her role in this deal.

William sat back in a stupefied gaze, all liquored up from the scotch he drank. And Jordan Barash, the beautiful, the angelic Jordan Barash, sat back with her eyes closed.

Andrew's eyes kept drifting to the top of her jacket. Leaning back on the car seat had opened her jacket just enough to give him a good look at her cleavage. It wasn't much. Jordan wasn't, shall he say, an endowed woman, but what she had was attractive. Andrew caught a glint of gold at the top of her blouse. It looked like a medal.

He was very surprised. Unlike Catholics who wore a medal fashioned after every saint under the sun, the Jews he knew rarely wore anything, except maybe a Star of David. Religious icons had become very popular after the murdering terrorists destroyed the World Trade Center. Women and men took to wearing crosses, Miraculous Medals, Stars of David, and other religious representations. But Andrew hadn't seen too many medals around the necks of Jewish women. That he focused on her medal rather than her perky nipples poking through her bra was a sad commentary on his life. Andrew had seen his share of women's nipples but not too many medals on Jewish women. More surprisingly, not too many were half medals.

Chapter Fifty-Five

The phone rang a third time. McCoy jumped on it, almost yelling his name into the receiver. "Mr. McCoy, this is a friend of your government. I would like to invite you for a drink this evening. Let's make it inconspicuous. There's a bar you go to from time to time to relive your grammar school past. Your presence there would not be unusual. Nor would a meeting between you and one of your business friends raise any eyebrows. Shall we say at ten?"

The phone went dead. McCoy had received a lot of weird telephone calls in his career, most of them coming from the Washington headquarters. But none like this. How did the "friend" know he liked to hang out at the Wicked Wolf on First Avenue? It was a neighborhood place that was no longer his neighborhood, but McCoy went back there from time to time. Some of his no-life friends from his past would go there and relive the infinite worlds of maybe.

After a couple of drinks, the bunch of them played the game well. *Maybe if I did this or maybe if I did that.* In truth, they were all running out of maybes. All of them had reached the magic age of fifty, and time had run out.

James McCoy was in his last years with the Federal Bureau of Investigation. He had been a New York cop for a few years before getting his accounting degree and transferring to the FBI. A series of successful cases in outlying bureau offices caught the attention of higher-ups in Washington. Late in his career, McCoy received the prestigious assignment of running the FBI's New York office, the largest bureau in the FBI.

McCoy placed the handset back into the cradle. That evening McCoy was walking up First Avenue. The street was crowded with neighborhood people going about their business. McCoy's trained eye picked out the sole dope dealer on the block, a young guy, well-dressed and probably pushing to the club crowd. This was his old neighborhood, as safe as any in the city. It had its share of bad guys, but the residents could be pretty sure that they were kept far away from them.

He walked down the block and stopped in front of the Wicked Wolf. Unlike the old-time rummy bars with half-painted windows, the Wolf's windows were open for everyone to see in. The gin mills of McCoy's youth had their windows painted halfway up. He didn't know if it was to keep people from seeing in or the rumpots from seeing out and realizing that there was a world out there that wasn't at the bottom of a bottle.

McCoy walked through the double-doors and waved a hello to Frank. He was the bartender and brother of a grammar school classmate of his. Frank automatically reached behind the bar for McCoy's favorite gin. McCoy shook his head, indicating he was going to sit at a table.

There was just one table with a single man sitting at it. He obviously wasn't cruising for women. The guy was in his mid-sixties, maybe more, and looked like a rough character. His stare, his sense of alertness reminded McCoy of some of the older agents who had been in the terrorist battles of the early eighties. They had a stare that no one would ever forget. That's what this guy had.

He also had good taste in wine. *What did he do, bring it in himself?* McCoy knew the Wolf's wine list never ran to anything more than thirty bucks a bottle. The bottle of red the guy had in front of him started at a hundred bucks retail!

"Mr. McCoy, I presume. My name is Julian Hirschberg of the Israel Antiquities Authority. I am very pleased to meet you."

McCoy sat down and looked at him. *What the hell is this all about? What is he doing here?* Eileen, his favorite waitress, passed by, and McCoy grabbed her around the waist. He needed something, someone familiar. They'd been doing this for years, and she planted a big kiss on his head.

"What'll it be, Jimmy? You still drinking that English rotgut, or do you want an honest beer like your old man used to drink?"

McCoy looked at her. "You know what, Eileen, you convinced me to be a man. Gimme a draft and a shot of Beefeater's."

"McCoy, you're incorrigible. What's your darling wife gonna say? You sitting here, flirting with the waitresses, and not even having the decency to drink her national beverage?"

"Eileen, how many times do I have to tell you? Vodka is not the national beverage of the Russians. It's that soured mare's milk or whatever that shit is they call a drink. Just drag your cute little Polish ass back here with my drink and a couple of menus. Okay?"

McCoy turned to his tablemate. "Hey, Julian, you don't mind if I call you Julian, do you? This bar is the only place on the entire avenue where not one employee is Irish. How can it be a bar? I think it's because the owner is a Hungarian or something like that. Go ahead, see for yourself. See that hulking guy at the end of the bar by the cash register? That's the owner. He probably got beat up by the micks when he was kid. That's why he refuses to hire the Irish. That and the fact that a lot of the young guys coming over are hard men. You know what I mean?"

"Mr. McCoy, may I call you Jimmy? There's no need for you to impress me with your knowledge of world affairs. Yes, a lot of the young men coming out of Ireland are 'hard men' as you call them. They are also mostly thugs and thieves dealing in dope for guns. They keep the bastards who are killing my people every day alive. Like the owner of this bar, I have no use for the element that's coming out of Ireland today. And don't forget, it's not prejudice. Éamon de Valera, the first president of the Irish Republic, was Jewish.

"We are faced with a problem that falls squarely in your lap. You are the domestic police for the government, no? We have a domestic problem that you need to know about. Please, listen."

Eileen came back with McCoy's boilermaker and some menus. He and Julian fell silent. "I know when to leave. I'll keep the tables next to you empty, Jimmy, but you gotta make it worth my while." He waved his gold card at her, and Eileen smiled.

"Okay, Julian, let's talk. Better yet, you talk, I'll listen," McCoy said. He reached into his pocket for a cigarette.

Julian took out his lighter and lit McCoy's cigarette, thanking God that there was at least one American who still smoked.

McCoy grabbed his hand and looked at the battered Zippo in Julian's hand. It bore the badge of the Masada regiment, the top fighters in that tough nation. *This guy is no simple archaeologist,* McCoy thought.

Julian placed the lighter on the table, taking note of McCoy's recognition of his old regiment's badge. "Jimmy, as I said, we have a problem."

"I know. We all got problems. I have more problems than you can think of. I run the most important FBI bureau in the country. You think you can tell me about problems?"

"You have no idea of problems. Ah, here's the food. Let's eat." McCoy and Hirschberg dug into their steaks and chomped away silently. Neither wanted to break the silence and begin the real business.

Julian pushed away his plate. He was tempted to order another piece of beef—good steak was a rarity in the Middle East—but he didn't want to appear like a glutton. He signaled Frank for another bottle of wine, and the lanky bartender reached under the bar and withdrew another bottle from a case that Julian had delivered earlier in the afternoon.

Eileen brought the second bottle—already opened, the Wolf had no time for the usual sommelier bullshit—and cleared the plates. She refilled their glasses and walked away.

Both men reached for cigarettes, smiling at each other because they shared a secret vice.

"So, tell me, is what you're going to say official or unofficial? Do I have to report this meal and conversation to my bosses, or does it stay here with me?"

"What I tell you, your bosses won't even know. Your people in Washington might know, but you'll have to go to the White House to really find someone who knows. I am telling you this because you are the agent in charge of the New York office. And your boyhood friend, whose best man you were supposed to be, is up to his neck in deep, deep shit." McCoy looked at Hirschberg, wondering how much this guy really knew about him.

"We are not talking about a terrorist plot, as horrible as those consequences are. No, this is much more serious. We are talking, my FBI friend, about Armageddon."

The ash on Jimmy's cigarette grew long and drooped as he listened to the man seated across from him.

Chapter Fifty-Six

The embassy car made good time from JFK. It pulled up to the Marriott on Lexington Avenue and Fiftieth Street. The driver opened the car door. Jordan disappeared through the lobby doors. Andrew stayed in the car with William Hirschberg.

"She's something else, isn't she, old boy?" William nudged Andrew. "Whaddya say we stop for a nightcap?"

Andrew looked at William. *If I am ever going to stay in this game, I better get a wooden leg. I don't know where these guys put all the booze!* "No, William, I don't think so. Can the driver drop me off at my apartment? Tomorrow's a big day. Jordan's coming to my office at the library, and we're going to start the project. I'd better turn in. Thanks, though."

"Okay, if that's what you want. Tell the driver your address." The car stopped at Andrew's apartment house. The street was deserted. The block between York Avenue and East End Avenue was as close to country living as anyone in New York was going to get. Some of Andrew's buddies argued for the leafy serenity surrounding Gramercy Park, but Andrew stuck to his Yorkville roots and stayed uptown.

He got out of the car. The car sped away, and Andrew looked after it. He looked up and down the street, breathed in the cool air, and changed his mind. He turned on his heels and walked up Eighty-Sixth to First Avenue to a little deli that was open twenty-four hours a day.

Two Yemeni brothers owned the store. Knowing what he knew now, Andrew eyed the guys a little more closely. They hadn't a clue what was on his mind.

"Welcome here again," one of the brothers, Moussad, called out to him. Andrew liked the two guys. They ran a decent place, overpriced in everything except the essentials—beer, cigarettes, and milk. Andrew always bought his essentials there, especially since the deli was one of few that stocked Ballantine Ale.

He paid his bill, waved good-bye, and walked out onto the avenue. On the corner of Eighty-Sixth and First was a supermarket. The place closed at eleven, but it had an all-night redemption machine for cans and bottles. That meant a crowd of homeless men and women collected outside the store, pushing their wagons full of discarded bottles and cans. They fed their cans and bottles into the machine and collected a paper chit they would redeem the next day.

Andrew hated these people. He knew it wasn't politically correct, but he could care less. He worked at a shelter run by the archdiocese a few times and stayed up all night listening to the pitiful tales the men told. For every sad case of a good guy down on his luck, there were a dozen crack heads complicating their habits with another addiction. These guys would sit back, collect their welfare checks, and smoke them away. It was a shitty life, and there was no cure.

He wedged his way through the homeless as he left the deli. He knew some of them were dangerous, so he kept up his guard. As he rounded the corner, he nodded to the doorman manning the building that housed the supermarket. The doorman's main job at night was keeping the bums away from the tenants.

Imagine that, Andrew thought, *paying four grand a month for an apartment and having to wade through this human detritus every night.* He continued to walk down Eighty-Sixth toward the park. He never turned around. If he did, he would have seen one of the homeless men talking into a cell phone.

He crossed York Avenue and got closer to his apartment. At the end of Eighty-Sixth was East End Avenue, one of the few places in the city where the residents could be awakened in the morning by the birds. And real birds, not the flying rats New Yorkers called "pigeons" and birders called "rock doves."

Andrew opened his building's outer door, unlocked the inner door, and climbed the stairs to his apartment. He looked around the apartment, drank two Ballantines, and went to bed.

Andrew slept restlessly. He heard the birds before his alarm clock rang. He got up, showered and shaved, and dressed in a suit. Typical library dress was tweedy academic, but he had a meeting with Jordan Barash this morning. He told himself that he didn't want to impress her—she was too young for him, sort of—but he did spend extra time picking out the right tie.

He locked the three locks on his apartment door and bounded down the stairs. He looked good, and he felt good. This double-breasted navy suit hung in his closet for special occasions like these. Andrew opened the lobby door and walked out onto the street. In front of him, parked at the curb with the motor running, was the embassy car.

The driver got out and gave him a once-over. The slight bulge under his suit jacket reminded Andrew of the Italian Embassy's "driver," Rocco. *Jesus,* Andrew thought, *does every driver in this town pack a gun?*

The driver motioned for him to get in. Andrew was surprised. Then he caught himself at being surprised. *Nothing should surprise me anymore.* He opened the back door of the Lincoln Town Car and got in. There in the back seat was Jordan Barash, dressed in a very no-nonsense business suit.

"Good morning, Andrew. I thought I would save you the trouble of getting on the Number 4 subway."

The number and letter system the city adopted for its subways still threw Andrew. He grew up in a city where the trains had names, like the Lex, or the Seventh Avenue, or the Canarsie Line. He still had to think when someone asked him where the 9 train was or did the 7 stop here.

"Thank you, Miss Barash. It was very thoughtful of you."

"Please, drop the 'Miss.' We'll be working together as colleagues. I am looking forward to picking your brain. I have been told you are quite a Near Eastern scholar."

Andrew's cheeks reddened. He never had a conversation about his background with a woman who looked like Jordan Barash. He looked at her and felt like a simpleton. "Of course, once we get to my office, we can get down to work. I am quite enthusiastic about learning more about this piece of copper. I have only received dribs and drabs of information."

"Andrew, you know what we all know. We have an archaeological and political puzzle to unravel. So, let's cut to the chase."

Andrew nodded, thinking there was that phrase again: "cut to the chase." *Am I missing something by not being part of the club?*

The car moved slowly to midtown. Andrew knew that the fastest way to get into this part of the city was underground, but he welcomed the ride and being close to Jordan. The car eased its way down Fifth Avenue. As it neared the Public Library building, Andrew anticipated the turn onto Forty-First Street where the employees' entrance was. The car didn't stop. Andrew leaned forward to say something to the driver, but Jordan's hand pushed him back into the seat.

"We have decided to hold the meeting elsewhere. Trust us." The car continued down Fifth and turned onto Seventh Avenue at Twenty-Third Street, running down Seventh until it made its way into Chelsea. Andrew looked around. This was the real Chelsea, the neighborhood where he had been planning to start his life with his bride. He hadn't taken a good look at the neighborhood for thirty years. He wanted nothing to do with Chelsea, the place where his life should have begun.

His life fell apart uptown on the West Side at the end of a gun thirty years ago. His fiancée, his high-school sweetheart, was leaving her teaching job at a private school on West Fifty-Eighth Street when she got caught in the middle of a drug deal. Andrew met his once and never future mother-in-law at the city morgue on East Twenty-Third Street that afternoon. The blinds opened and there was his bride, her daughter, and his future lying on a gurney.

That was then. This is now. The car turned up Eighteenth Street and stopped in front of a renovated brownstone. The driver got out, looked around, and thumped the roof of the car with his hand. Jordan opened the door and got out. Andrew followed her. They walked to the stoop of the brownstone and mounted the stairs. They never had to ring the bell. The door opened silently. The first sight Andrew saw was the beaming face of Julian Hirschberg.

"Come in. Come in. Jordan, my love, you look beautiful. And Andrew, how good of you to come. Everyone is here. Come. Let us walk to the back where the parlor is. Everyone is here, everyone is here."

They followed him down the hall. Richly polished wooden floors gave off a lemony scent. Julian opened a set of double doors. They had walnut frames with etched glass panels. Andrew stopped to admire the doors before walking into the room. Entering the house was like taking a trip back to the New York of the 1880s. It was exquisite. *What a great place for a meeting!*

He and Jordan walked into the large room. At one end was a fireplace with a roaring fire spreading cheer into the room. The center held a large oval table, more like a dining table than a conference table. Comfortable dining chairs provided seating. There were the usual water glasses and water pitchers on the table. To the side, a large buffet held an ample supply of liquor.

Andrew looked around the table. Julian had done an admirable job of gathering all the players in one room. He was surprised to see Cardinal di Sistio who, Andrew thought, was going back to Rome this week. Actually, the rotund little cleric told Andrew he was going to be on the papal plane yesterday. But there he was. They were all there, plus another individual he hadn't seen in almost twenty-five years. "Jimmy, I don't, I don't..."

"Don't say anything. We can catch up later. This is more serious than your apologies or mine for not keeping in touch."

Jimmy's seriousness startled him. *I can't believe we haven't seen each other for over two decades, even though we had been best friends. For Crissake, McCoy was going to be my best man!* Andrew kept his mouth shut and continued to check out the room.

Standing against the walls were Rocco, the Italian Embassy driver, and the unnamed driver from the Israeli Embassy.

At the table sat Jill Benson, Ettore Scala, and Giacomo di Sistio. There were five places unfilled. Four of them were for Andrew, Jordan, Julian Hirschberg, and McCoy. They sat down. The fifth was empty. Rocco closed the double doors and stoked the fire. Someone knocked. Rocco opened them.

The gaunt figure of a Roman Catholic priest appeared in the doorway.

Chapter Fifty-Seven

Monsignor Edmund F. X. O'Brien, S. J. was the missing piece of the puzzle. He started this calamity with his discovery of the Copper Scroll fragment. After he alerted the Holy See, the Vatican secreted him away from Jerusalem and hid him in the open, assigning him to pastoral duties at a small church on the Battery in downtown New York. He was forbidden to correspond with any of his peers. His translation duties had ended. He was, in effect, on permanent leave from the Society of Jesus. The Vatican controlled his future and his every move.

"Monsignore, you know everyone here? No, I guess not. You haven't met these two. They will be your eyes and ears for the project. May I present Andrew Wagner and Jordan Barash. Andrew is a Near Eastern languages specialist with the New York Public Library. Jordan is with the Israel Antiquities Authority. Julian Hirschberg, whom you know, is here representing both the IAA and his government," Giacomo said.

At the mention of Julian's name, McCoy's eyes narrowed. He studied Hirschberg's open face and clear eyes. He knew Hirschberg for what he was. And he wasn't an archaeologist. The cardinal, noting the silent interplay between Hirschberg and McCoy, quickly assumed control of the meeting.

"What we need to do today, Monsignore, is close the circle you opened. Everything said in this room is confidential. Both governments here have acquiesced to the authority of the Holy See in this matter. What is at stake is too great to leave in the hands of one government. The people in this room have clearance at the highest levels. Mr. Hirschberg and Mr. McCoy are here to give us their unofficial cooperation. But jurisdiction rests with us. Monsignore, everyone, are we clear on that?"

Andrew looked into the faces around the table. Everyone was grim. Slight nods indicated the affirmative. The Vatican was in control. Giacomo di Sistio resumed speaking. "This house in Chelsea was made available to us by a particular friend. None of you will take any work papers or notes out of this house. You may use the bedrooms on the third and fourth floors should you wish. There is a full-time housekeeper. And Rocco will always be in attendance.

"Mr. McCoy, we have arranged a special leave for you from the FBI. This should not hurt, no? We know you are close to retiring. This project shall be your last. We have made arrangements with Washington to accelerate your retirement, and our friends in Miami have made available a property for you at a very advantageous price." McCoy just looked at the diminutive cardinal and nodded.

"Andrew and Jordan. You both have satisfying careers. We have done everything in our power to ensure that you will continue these careers at a higher level than you could have imagined. Starting today, both of you will be part of the Holy See's Office of Near Eastern Archaeology and Linguistics. I am the secretary of that office. You will have accommodations in Rome and, as I have said, Vatican passports.

"Jordan, I know you treasure your independence and your Israeli passport. But that document will do you no good in some places where you will have to travel. The seal of the Vatican City on a passport opens doors that you could never have gone through. Andrew, the same goes for you. You and Jordan will be working together as a team to unravel this knotty problem. Secrecy is paramount. You will report directly to us. Understood?"

Andrew and Jordan nodded their heads. A vocal response would just break the solemnity infusing the atmosphere in the room.

"Because this is a secular affair, we shall neither begin nor end the meetings with a prayer, however strange that may seem with two clergy in attendance. But, ladies and gentlemen, if you know how to pray, I suggest you do."

Cardinal di Sistio rose, indicating the meeting was over. Everyone else rose and wandered over to the buffet where Rocco was enthusiastically pouring drinks. He turned to Andrew and Jordan. "I suggest you two stay for a while. You might want to catch the monsignore before he leaves."

One by one, the participants left the dining room. Cardinal di Sistio was engaged in a rapt conversation with O'Brien. Andrew and Jordan just stood alone, awkwardly silent, nursing their drinks.

Cardinal di Sistio brought Monsignor O'Brien over to them. "I must be leaving now. My plane back to Rome is tomorrow morning, and the good cardinal archbishop of this magnificent archdiocese has been entreating me to eat dinner with him. I fear for the worst. We are dining in his residence, and you know the taste of the Irish.

"Please stay. Speak with Monsignore." He turned to O'Brien. "My dear Jesuit brother, why don't you take these two young people back to the garden? Rocco is quite proud of what he has accomplished in the dirt of New York City."

O'Brien announced he was going out to the deck for a quick cigarette. He looked to Andrew and Jordan. They sat alone at the table. The room was empty. They had the house to themselves except for Rocco who went upstairs. The Monsignor walked outside, a lighter in his hand. They would meet with him later. There were greater matters at hand, like working together, like maybe developing a relationship, like the possibility that they were in danger. Andrew spoke up first. "So, whaddya think?"

"That's very profound. Do you have any other brilliant comments?" Jordan said, obviously annoyed.

All at once it hit him. For the past week he had been followed by God knows who, in two car chases, in meetings with people whose agendas were unknown, and meeting people at airports he never knew. Then, this woman—this so-called archaeologist—had the nerve to taunt him!

"I've had enough of this bullshit. You and your copper crap and your secret little cabal can go to hell! For me, I am going back to work." Andrew grabbed his coat from the back of the chair where he hung it and stormed out of the dining room, slamming the double doors behind him. He had almost made it down the hall when he heard the dining room's doors open. Backlighted by the sun streaming in from the backyard garden, Jordan's image filled his vision like some kind of angel. She just stood there saying nothing. Andrew looked back once and started again to walk out the door.

Jordan cried out, "Andrew, wait. I'm sorry."

He stopped in his tracks and looked back. She was walking down the hall toward him, the heels of her low-slung business shoes clacking on the polished wood floor.

My God, Andrew thought. *She sure is beautiful. Now don't get your shorts in a knot over a perceived insult. Give her another chance.* Andrew turned from the door and walked toward his angel. Simultaneously, they apologized to each other. Andrew gave in first.

"Okay, that's enough. We both need a rest. The past two days have been murder. Is the car still outside? You can take it back to your hotel and drop me off at my apartment."

"Andrew, there's nothing I would relish more than a hot bath and watching junky American television wrapped in a terry cloth bathrobe. That's not going to happen. Neither of us is going anywhere pleasant."

Andrew regarded her silently. "I know. We've got to get to the bottom of what the monsignor found. He should be out in the garden. Let's go face the music."

Together, they moved through the narrow house and entered the kitchen. It was beautifully outfitted and looked like it could handle a crowd. Stainless steel appliances lined two walls, and an eternity of black-and-green granite countertops complemented the appliances. The kitchen had a back door leading out to the garden.

On the deck stood Monsignor O'Brien, alone, smoking, and looking over the neighbor's backyard. Jordan and Andrew walked into the garden.

Monsignor turned and said, "You know why this place is so safe? Take a look across the fence. See that house? John Sampesino, the head of the New York mob, owns it. I pity the poor junkie who jumps over that fence," he said with some irony and not a bit of Christian charity. He ground the cigarette out on the teak deck, causing Andrew to wince at the effrontery.

O'Brien walked to the back of the deck and looked down at Rocco's garden. It was only three feet wide but ran the length of the narrow property. Rocco planted a perfect Mediterranean plot—Roma tomatoes, eggplant, zucchini squash, a bunch of different herbs, and some flowers for the kitchen. The garden was doing well.

People shake their heads in amazement when they hear about gardening in New York. Andrew knew better. The soil, even in Manhattan, has a rich, dark, loamy texture. If the sun can get to a plot, shining through the high-rises that line nearly every street, then a garden has a good chance to grow.

Rocco's efforts did not go to waste. It was too early to tell what would grow, but the stalks of the perennial herbs bloomed profusely. He had the small eggplant and tomato plants covered in cloches, individual plastic tents that let in the light but kept out the cold. Rocco had established an elaborate watering system that would drip water slowly into the soil, avoiding the typical gardener's mistake of drowning the plants.

Monsignor lit another cigarette and turned to talk. "If I were you, I'd be careful in what I say. The old man probably has this garden wired." As a precaution, he turned on the garden hose.

Upstairs in his second floor bedroom, Rocco cursed loudly. The running water seriously affected the acoustical qualities of the listening system he had planted in the garden. Potatoes may have eyes, but Rocco's garden had ears.

The Jesuit priest settled on a teak bench in a sunny part of the garden. He motioned for Jordan and Andrew to pull up two chairs close to him. "Keep your voices down. That Vatican bastard also probably has a couple of parabolic mikes aimed at this garden."

Andrew scanned the rooftops nervously. All he saw were a bunch of satellite dishes to capture the world's entertainment. Cable reception in New York was lousy and expensive. For those who could afford it, a satellite dish was the way to go. And it was apparent that the Vatican could afford it.

"I'll presume you know little of me except what I have discovered. Let me fill you in on the details." O'Brien took the two of them through his work from his earliest days at the Dead Sea Scroll library to his ultimate discovery.

"The scroll scholars are very secretive, even after the supposed opening up of the windows in the mid-1990s. Part of that bogus 'opening up' was the loan of some scroll segments for a world tour. That's where you, Andrew, became familiar with the scrolls. You were, I take it, the curator of the scroll fragments when the library exhibited them."

Andrew nodded. O'Brien continued his monologue. "The scroll committee is largely controlled by the bible crowd; you know, those guys who look for the proof of the bible in the text of the scrolls. They look for answers to questions like 'Does this in the scrolls prove Jeremiah said that and did Jesus live there and so on?' Those guys are a pain in the ass. That same crowd dismisses the validity of the Copper Scroll, mainly because they can't understand it.

"For starters, it's written in a text which most Near Eastern language scholars have trouble deciphering. Also, the Copper Scroll is a bitch to read. It's not exactly in great shape. And finally, it is kept in safekeeping in a museum in Jordan. Most scholars don't want to travel across the river to examine the scroll.

"I was exiled to Jerusalem by the Society. My superiors wanted me out of the way. So when I was seconded to the scroll institute, I decided to concentrate on the most overlooked and least understood part of the Dead Sea Scrolls. That, naturally, was the Copper Scroll. This scroll is a valid part of the Dead Sea Scrolls, and yes, it is partly a treasure map. But no one knows what treasure the scrolls are talking about. Some scholars argue that the scroll points to the places where the priests hid the temple's treasure before the Romans sacked it.

"I can't argue that point, because contrary to what most people believe, I did not study the Copper Scroll."

At this admission, Andrew's face contorted. He thought about what his mother would say, that he should never make funny faces because if he died that instant, he would live eternally with that look on his face. "Just wait a minute. Are you telling us that you haven't discovered anything new in the Dead Sea Scrolls?"

"Yes," O'Brien added. "I did start investigating and trying to interpret the Copper Scroll. But I came upon a discovery late in my studies that diverted my attention from the scroll to the small copper square I found fused to the last leaf in the scroll. Trust me, you will know more about what I discovered as we get to know each other."

What the monsignor was saying directly impacted what Andrew had been led to believe. The only reason he signed on for this wild ride was the validity and existence of the Dead Sea Scrolls. Now

O'Brien was saying that the scrolls had nothing to do with his discovery? He was puzzled. He looked over to Jordan who just sat in the garden, her face passively fixed on the Roman Catholic prelate.

"Andrew, relax. Do you think each of the scrolls found in the Qumran caves has a little tag attached certifying it as part of the Dead Sea Scrolls?"

Andrew gave O'Brien a glaring look. He was in no mood for levity.

"I'm sorry, I apologize for that little jab. Let me start all over. We all know the scrolls are in about fifteen thousand pieces. They were all discovered over a period of time in the late 1940s and 1950s. We still don't know who wrote them and for what reason. You want to start an argument among biblical archaeologists? Tell 'em you know who wrote the Dead Sea Scrolls."

He stopped for a minute to reach into his pocket for another cigarette. O'Brien returned to his nervous habit after twenty years of abstinence. He missed the exotic fragrance of the Turkish cigarettes his colleagues at the Shrine smoked. Most of all, every time he took a puff on one of his Marlboros, he was reminded of the smell of the cigarettes his Jordanian friend, Mansour al-Jamedi, smoked.

Damn him! Damn Jamedi and his delivery of the Copper Scroll to the Shrine. If it weren't for him, we wouldn't be in this mess at all. O'Brien wandered away into the corner of the garden, leaving Jordan and Andrew by themselves. He lit his cigarette, watched the smoke curl up to the New York sky, lost in memories and ignoring the two people standing with him in the New York garden. Andrew took this pause to go over in his mind what he knew about the Dead Sea Scrolls.

Bedouin goat herders discovered the Dead Sea Scrolls in eleven caves along the northeast shore of the Dead Sea over a period of years from 1946 through 1957. The scholars assigned to study the scrolls have identified about 870 separate scrolls, but the scholars' work has remained largely out of the public eye. There are two types of scrolls:

one group is biblical, referring only to the Old Testament; the other, non-biblical, referring to the teachings of the sect or the group responsible for writing the scrolls. The common language of the scrolls is Hebrew, though some are written in Aramaic, the language thought to be spoken by Jesus. Authorship of the scrolls is widely debated. Some say the Zealots wrote the scrolls. Others say it was a new sect of Judaism. Almost everyone agrees that the scrolls have no connection to the emerging Christian sect of the first century CE.

One museum in Jerusalem, the Shrine of the Book, devotes itself to findings from Cave I and XI. Discoverers found the longest scroll, the Temple Scroll, in Cave XI. Generally, scholars agree on the timing of the scrolls, when they were written, what their purpose was, and how to preserve them. *When it comes to the Copper Scroll,* Andrew thought, *throw all the rules out the window.*

The Copper Scroll, so called because it is made out of copper, was found in Cave III. It's recorded in a form of Hebrew and paleo-Hebraic using unfamiliar words. The scroll is thought to be a list of sixty-four underground hiding places that purport to identify where gold, silver, jeweled items of worship, manuscripts, and other treasures whisked away from the Temple by the priests before the Romans sacked it are hidden throughout Israel. Scholars believe this scroll may be the key to the lost temple treasure. The anomaly about the Copper Scroll is its current location. It is in a museum in Jordan, which essentially takes it out of the mainstream of the scholars studying the Dead Sea Scrolls.

Andrew kept turning these facts over and over in his mind. What could the Jesuit have found that others missed for so many years?

Monsignor O'Brien finished his cigarette, coughed loudly, spat on the deck, and rejoined Andrew and Jordan. "I know we're outside, but I hope you don't mind that I scurried away to the corner of the garden to have my smoke. For some reason, I don't think you mind being alone. I may be just a worn-out, old priest, but there's, ah, something about you two."

Andrew and Jordan cast sidelong glances at each other. *What the hell is he talking about? Have we become an "item" already after just two days?*

He cleared his throat again. "As I was saying and let me underscore this, the Copper Scroll is an anomaly. It is not a religious text. It is not a text related to the sect at Qumran. Initially, that's what attracted me. But I haven't devoted my time to studying the Copper Scroll.

"When I was studying the Copper Scroll at the Shrine of the Book—you know, the Jordanian government delivered it into my hands in Jerusalem—I had exclusive access to it. And no other scholar supervised me. One evening I defied all scholarly conventions and picked it up in my hands. I felt a small crease on the back of one of the sections of the scroll. I looked at it more closely and discovered it was a totally separate piece, a small square of copper, actually.

"Somehow, over the millennia, it had become fused to the body proper of the scroll. I separated it from the scroll and began studying it. Trust me, it was a chore. It was written in a language related to but not really Hebrew, sort of a paleo-Hebraic language, like the language we believe was spoken in the time of Abraham."

"What's this about? Monsignor, I originally thought we were talking about the Copper Scroll. I thought were you were translating that text and found something in it. But it's not about the Copper Scroll. It's about an 'appendix' you found. What the hell is going on?"

"Patience, Andrew. It's a virtue you need to embrace more often. Yes, the square is copper. Yes, it was in the jar in Cave III of the Qumran caves where the Copper Scroll was found. But no, it's not part of the Dead Sea Scrolls. And better yet, they don't know it's missing."

With one voice, both Jordan and Andrew shrieked, "Missing?"

"Well," the Jesuit continued, "not missing. Something isn't missing if you know where it is. I have it with me down at the church, tucked away safely in the bosom of Jesus. But there's more no one knows. The scroll tells us how to identify the family who owns the oil."

Jordan and Andrew left the Chelsea townhouse soon after Monsignor finished revealing his secrets. In the car on the way uptown, Jordan agreed to meet Andrew for a late lunch the next day at the South Street Seaport.

During his college days at NYU, he would go to the seaport with his girlfriend and poke around. Andrew and his girlfriend, Sarah, would roam around the area, taking pictures of each other at the helm of the great ships' wheels, acting like goofy college kids. He couldn't say for sure, but he thought he fell in love with Sarah at the seaport. Two years later, they had planned to get married.

After her murder, it took Andrew nearly ten years to return to South Street. Since then, he had been a frequent visitor. In the winter, when it was deserted, he would reach out over the harbor and bring back the spirit of Sarah close to his chest. He liked the winter at the seaport. There was no one there to wonder why a grown man was looking into the water and sobbing.

This was late winter. There'd be just a sprinkling of tourists and a few die-hard lunchtime drinkers. The seaport was far from most Wall Street offices. And it was a long, cold walk down to the riverfront. Few office workers made the trek.

The tip of Manhattan was a great place to work in the summer. It really was ten degrees cooler than midtown. But you paid for it during the winter, when it was at least twenty degrees colder than midtown. Springtime brought the winds. They cleared the smog and smoke out of midtown Manhattan. The springtime winds downtown meant that gale force storms would batter the lonely pedestrians foolhardy enough to make it to the water.

He knew the seaport would be deserted, which suited him just fine. The only restaurant open would be that upstairs pizza place. But he really wasn't hungry. He wanted to get over to Monsignor's church, and see what he had hidden "in the bosom of Jesus."

Andrew was standing in front of the visitors' kiosk at the seaport entrance when a black Chrysler pulled up close to the seaport's dock. Jordan got out, accompanied by the driver and bodyguard.

"What's with the muscle?"

"Oh, it's just Julian. He gets these coded messages from Tel Aviv all the time. Last night, one came through that worried him. He told me, and indirectly you, that it was of no import, but just in case, he's got Schlomo assigned to me."

"Schlomo? You got a bodyguard named Schlomo!" Andrew teased.

"I wouldn't make fun of him if I were you. He's here to protect me. There's nothing Julian said about him being nice to you."

Andrew looked over to Schlomo and gave him a small wave. Hiding behind his dark Oakleys, Schlomo didn't acknowledge Andrew's presence.

"How do you feel about a pizza?"

"Let's just get a coffee and get over to the church," Jordan said.

He wanted to argue. He thought that lunch today would be the start of the two of them getting closer together. Obviously, that was not on her mind. They drank their coffees silently.

The Shrine of Elizabeth Ann Seton, the small church where Monsignor was posted, was a hike from the seaport. It was on the other side of Battery Park, which was at least ten blocks away. Andrew started for the Chrysler, but Jordan had other ideas.

"Andrew, let's walk."

That was fine with him. He was a native New Yorker. Walking in the city meant nothing. "Okay. I'll lead. You follow. And make sure you bring Schlomo over there," Andrew said, acknowledging the hulking bodyguard.

They crossed the wooden planks of the seaport deck and walked under the FDR Drive over to Fulton Street. Battery Park was due south on Water Street. Monsignor's little church fronted the park on State Street.

Andrew wondered why O'Brien ended up in such an out-of-the way place. It was the last Catholic church in the Archdiocese of New York, tucked underneath a massive financial skyscraper.

He would soon know, and the peaceful little church would be forever etched in his memory.

Chapter Fifty-Eight

Reb Whitlow watched the two of them take off for Battery Park and the small church on its borders. Munching on a hot dog, like any innocent tourist, he just stood there and watched. He bought another hot dog and threw ten bucks at the vendor. "Keep the change."

The vendor shouted the blessings of Allah on Whitlow and his family as the ex-CIA agent trailed after Jordan and Andrew. He knew they would not only lead him to the priest but to the hidden location of the copper square. When he was finished with the priest and the woman, he would retrieve the copper square and be on his way to JFK back to Geneva.

Once Whitlow was far enough away, the hot dog vendor reached for his cell phone and dialed an interconnect service that would put him in touch anonymously with a phone number in Lebanon. Halfway across the world, the phone rang. A man picked up and answered gruffly. He stood in the middle of a bombed-out hovel that stank of cordite, sweat, and the filthy cigarettes his men smoked. He neither smoked nor drank, as befitting a true devotee of Allah and the mullahs. He listened intently as the vendor in New York spoke. "I have found the priest."

The man disconnected the phone and threw it to the floor of the hideout in Lebanon. Crushing the disposable phone under his foot, he picked up another and pressed a programmed number.

"Our friends in Geneva are solving the problem. But prepare our back-up plan. Tell the chameleon we might need his services."

Chapter Fifty-Nine

Jordan and Andrew walked down Water Street to meet O'Brien. Andrew knew where it was. He kept his mouth shut because he wanted to see Jordan's reaction to the tiny Catholic church.

To begin with, it was unlike any church in the city. It was the private mansion of a wealthy seaport trader. Situated on a curving part of State Street, the mansion itself was built to match the curve of the street. The archdiocese had gutted the inside to create the nave for the sanctuary. The outside remained unchanged. The rectory where the priests lived was in the back of the house. The inside of the church was completely white, more like a Connecticut Congregational church than a Roman Catholic church in New York.

The church had few parishioners, but it filled its pews each morning with downtown workers starting their day with mass and communion. On holy days, the church did a land-office business. It was a quiet assignment, perfect for a retiring priest, or one the archdiocese wanted to hide.

Vatican intelligence knew that O'Brien's life was in danger. That's why the Holy See requested the Archdiocese of New York hide O'Brien in plain sight. Crowds of office workers passed the church every day, not realizing that up the stairs of the little building was a fully functioning parish church.

Months earlier, during a beautiful Roman autumn afternoon, Cardinal Giacomo di Sistio summoned Monsignor O'Brien to his office. Cardinal di Sistio was still the most powerful man in the Vatican, even after his patron's successor retired and the College of Cardinals elected another man instead of him.

A young Italian prelate ushered O'Brien into the antechamber of di Sistio's office. Housed in the Vatican proper, the office was the envy of museums worldwide. The work of Renaissance painters, household names to every student who ever took Art History 101 in college, adorned the walls. The Vatican got them cheap—five hundred years ago.

He still couldn't get over the magnificence of the Vatican buildings. Tourists got to see the ceiling of the Sistine Chapel in all of its restored, pristine glory. Inside the private rooms and galleries of the Vatican was a whole other wonder of the art world, rarely seen but deeply appreciated by all who came in contact with them. The thirty minutes he spent waiting to see His Eminence were well worth it.

The massive double doors to the cardinal's private office opened. Through them walked the rotund man who could have been pope. "Edmund, how good of you to take the time to see me," Cardinal di Sistio said in perfect American English.

Monsignor O'Brien, a fourth-vow Jesuit beholden to no one except his superior general and the pope himself, merely replied, "Eminence."

"Come, let us go inside." The cardinal motioned to sit at a seventeenth-century settee that was probably worth more than the gross national product of Botswana. He walked over to the sidepiece and produced two glasses and an excellent bottle of single-malt Jameson's. "Drink?"

O'Brien's personal budget had no room for liquor of such quality, so he readily agreed. He winced when his host dropped ice cubes into the two glasses. "Eminence, I prefer mine neat."

"Ah, yes, the appetite of the American Irish. Pardon me, I forget."

He was all set to argue with this mule-headed Italian who insisted on putting ice cubes made out of the filthy Roman water into this beautiful whiskey. But he held his tongue. *Why fight a losing battle? Di Sistio probably learned his drinking habits from the philistines in Washington who put ice into everything.*

The two men sat across from each other. O'Brien on the settee, di Sistio behind his Renaissance desk. They each played with their drinks, sipped them, and put the glasses down. It was as if neither of the men wanted to make the first statement. So, they both started to speak at the same time. The American smiled at the cardinal and deferred to the man's rank. "Excuse me, Eminence. You first."

"My dear Edmund, let me cut to the chase. You know what you have discovered. The knowledge that you possess could truly mean the end of the world. Our Arabian brothers of the book will never pass hegemony of their oil lands to a Jewish family. Yet their strange desert customs make it impossible for them to ignore the deed inscribed on copper. We are, as you Americans like to say, between a rock and a hard place. And we in the church are between an even harder rock and a harder place. For it was one of our sons who brought this predicament to light. Our retired Holy Father was well aware of this situation. He was painfully aware that he had to deal with this, let's say, because of where he came from. The feelings of our present pope are unknown but he must come to grip with this problem.

"We made a mistake once before, almost seventy years ago when we did not speak out forcefully enough for our Jewish brethren. Oh yes, we have been blamed, though I think the record will reveal that we did more than that American playwright accuses. We have been crucified for Pius's inaction as surely as Our Lord Jesus Christ was crucified for our sins. That's why we are determined not to make the same mistake again.

"What you have discovered involves not two countries or three, or the Jews or the Arabs. It involves the whole world. And who better to speak out for the whole world than the Vicar of Christ himself?

"Our retired Holy Father had been in direct contact with the leaders who matter. He prays for them daily. Ever since the end of World War II, our popes have been mindful of the great leaders who have ruled America. One in particular, God rest his soul. You know he and John Paul had the courage and grace to confront the evils of the communist system. Between them, they brought down the 'Evil Empire,' and freed the Slavic peoples who were so dear to our late Pontiff's heart.

"We have a new man on the seat, but nothing has changed. Before he went into seclusion at Castel Gandolfo, Benedict had been in contact with the leaders of Israel for whom he also prays daily as preservers of the One, True God. He had met with their leaders privately, here and elsewhere.

"They understood his wisdom and his leadership. And they believe the same of our present leader who has broadcast his cries and prayers for peace and cooperation throughout the world. That is why this intractable problem has become ours. The leaders of America, Israel, and their allies have agreed that we will adjudicate this. The Holy Father, even with what little he knows about this, and I have agreed that you will be our instrument of agreement.

"In two weeks' time, we will send you back to your native New York. Our brother Cardinal of New York has agreed to assign you to a small parish in downtown New York. Go with God, my Jesuit friend."

With that last blessing, Cardinal di Sistio rose from his desk, indicating that not only was the meeting over but also that he would not entertain any questions. A cardinal who spoke for the pope had given the monsignor his marching orders. As a priest of the Roman

Catholic Church, Edmund had but two choices: follow the orders or leave the church.

He left the cardinal's office and was escorted outside to St. Peter's Square. The immense plaza, where the faithful gathered to catch a glimpse of the pope, was sparsely populated. As he walked, he went over in his mind what the cardinal had said—and did not say—and who he was in the hierarchy of the church.

Giacomo di Sistio was said to have come from an ancient Roman family. So ancient, that he claimed to be able to trace his roots to the very beginnings of Christianity. Di Sistio was an archaeological buff. In the 1960s he acquired an old villa and its accompanying property that was on the outskirts of Rome proper. The land was said to have been held by his family until the 1700s, when it was lost in a fruitless battle against the House of Savoy.

Its last owners died in the confusion of World War II, and the property reverted to the state. Di Sistio was then the Bishop of Ravenna, ironically the last capital of the Roman Empire. He befriended an international textile merchant who bought the property for him. Di Sistio spent every weekend and vacation on the land, sprucing it up for his eventual return to Rome when he would excavate it for its historical value.

When he finally returned to Rome for his papal assignment, he contacted Eustore di Medici, a friend of his, and another member of the Roman aristocracy. He asked him if they could find archaeology students to help him excavate his villa in the Sabine Hills. Professore di Medici naturally thought of that good-looking American professor at NYU and contacted her.

Di Sistio was assigned to the Vatican, but he still held his post in Ravenna. Despite the distance, he was determined to be on site as much as possible.

That summer, NYU students, under the direction of Associate Professor Jill Benson, peeled back the soil under the villa to its lowest level. They discovered a foundation dating back to the first century CE. Professor Benson called di Sistio immediately. "Bishop, your Excellency, you must come to the dig. We have found something that you would be most interested in."

Di Sistio thanked Professor Benson and returned the telephone handset to its cradle. He made arrangements for a car. Two days later, he was in the Sabine Hills standing beside Professor Benson and her students.

"Your Excellency, see these pillars. We think they formed the doorway to the Roman villa that once occupied this site. It must have belonged to a minor official because it bears the *SPQR* legend. The owner of this house must have been very loyal to the Roman Republic even though he lived in imperial times. That's why, I think, *SPQR* is emblazoned on the pillars of his house.

"We have also found clay tablets in what we think was the cookhouse for the villa. The tablets are essentially grocery tallies, and they are addressed to one *V. Sixtus*. Maybe that's where your family name, di Sistio, comes from."

Bishop di Sistio walked around the excavation site, thinking silently. He called to Jill Benson, who stood around with her students, dressed in impossibly short shorts and a tank top. With no ceremony, she approached the ecclesiastical authority from Ravenna.

"Bishop, here are the tablets," she said, handing him three dusty squares of clay about the size of a book. "If you look closely at the bottom, you can see the inscription *VSIXTUS*. Bear in mind that Romans neither used spaces between letters nor did they use punctuation. So reading this tablet, the inscription says *V. Sixtus*. The nomen or family name is Sixtus. Perhaps this truly is the origin of your family name.

"Bishop, there's one more thing. Along with the tablets, we found a few items of Judaica." When Bishop di Sistio looked at her quizzically, she elaborated on her find.

"Judaica is the archaeologist's term for artifacts from the Jewish culture. When we find them, they usually indicate that at some point Jews lived at or visited a site, in this case, your villa. We can date them from the same time as the tablets, so Sixtus either had Jews living here, owned Jewish slaves, or brought the artifacts back with him from Judea on one of his many merchant trips. We just can't tell."

The bishop stepped away from the young American professor, holding the tablets. His hands trembled as he thought about their significance. *These are a connection with an ancestor so ancient only the earth knew his name. Now the earth has given up his identity to me.* He returned to the dig.

"Thank you, Professor. See that you send me the bill for your good works. I have enough money to extend your work through the end of the summer.

"Here," he said, giving her several thousand lira, "take your students to the town's wine shop and enjoy life. But make sure you take a bath," he called out joyfully.

The bishop returned to his car, clutching the tablets to his bosom. *So, V. Sixtus, is the "V" for "Valerius"? Can you see from your vantage point in heaven what your children have done? And thank you for clearing up the mystery about Jews in my lineage.*

He started up the car and returned to Ravenna. Along the way, he said prayers for his long-dead ancestors, both pagans and Jews.

Monsignor O'Brien was in his office at the Vatican one morning when his secretary gave him an envelope bearing the papal seal. In it was a note from Cardinal di Sistio, requesting that he leave for America immediately. Plans for an assignment had been made. He needed to stop by the secretary of state's office for travel documents. The pope had granted him a Vatican passport.

That was several months ago. Since then, he had been tending to his limited pastoral duties at the little church on the Battery. He had traded the warm climates of Jerusalem and Rome for the bitter winters in New York. He now sat in his rectory, pondering his future and the future of the two people whose fate brought them into his hands.

The wind blew viciously into their faces as Andrew and Jordan walked south to the church. Andrew swore downtown New York was the only geographical location on earth where the wind was always in your face. They got to Monsignor's church, wiping tears from their eyes caused by the biting wind.

They looked at each other before going inside. Somehow, they knew that once they stepped over the threshold to the church, their lives would change forever. They entered the vestibule, passing the rows of votive candles. Memories of his youth flooded Andrew's mind. They opened the doors to the sanctuary. The weak afternoon sun streamed through the blue and white stained glass window behind the church's marble altar. The whiteness of the interior dazzled them both.

They approached the altar. There, on the steps leading up to the altar, lay Monsignor O'Brien. He was dressed in the priestly undergarment known as the alb. He was praying and sobbing at the same time.

Chapter Sixty

Reb Whitlow threw popcorn to the seagulls perched on top of the monument to the US Merchant Marine at the south end of Battery Park. He kept his other hand firmly locked onto his leather briefcase. Inside was his custom-made H&K pistol loaded with special noise-suppressant rounds. They held a light load of powder but had enough force to pierce the human skull. In short, his pistol was a supremely effective killer's gun for those who liked to get close.

Whitlow landed at JFK that morning after an all-night plane ride from Geneva. He hated this assignment. True, Whitlow was an indiscriminate killer, but he still hated to kill women. He had no idea why Jordan Barash was part of the contract. He didn't ask questions. All he knew was that he was supposed to come to New York, get rid of the woman and the priest, and return to his home in Maine.

He ran an oyster farm as a cover for his real job. The farm had provided him marginal income in the past few years. Last year, he saw a noticeable uptick in revenue.

Caleb, the farm's manager, convinced Reb to invest in Belon seed oysters from France. The large flat mollusks were prized by chefs-of-the-moment at restaurants-of-the-moment in New York and San Francisco. Caleb had quadrupled the output from the oyster farm and now Reb was making a comfortable six-figure income after expenses. That's what he reported to the IRS. His Geneva income stayed in Switzerland in an account known only to him and the bank manager. The bank manager had seen Reb's hardware. He wouldn't be speaking to any of the tax authorities.

Reb made a big deal about searching the harbor with his binoculars. He looked like any other tourist eager to see and identify the ships anchored in the upper bay. He turned around and trained the powerful lenses on the little church across the street. He saw Jordan and Andrew enter. *Let me give them time with the kind priest, and then I'll go in.* He tossed more popcorn to the seagulls.

Chapter Sixty-One

Jordan and Andrew stood respectfully in the back of the church, waiting for Monsignor O'Brien to acknowledge their presence. The prostrate figure on the steps of the altar stirred and rose from the cold marble floor.

"Jordan, Andrew, we don't have much time. I feel that I am not going to live much longer. Let me tell you everything I know."

Andrew looked at the Jesuit, startled by his words of doom. "Monsignor, why would you say anything like that? You look no worse or no better than any other seventy-year-old man that I know." Andrew's attempt to cheer up the priest didn't work.

"Thank you for your levity. But my heart is heavy, and I believe the Lord is whispering to me. Don't worry. I am ready. But enough about me. I didn't bring you all the way here to chat about my health. Please come to the altar with me."

Both of them ascended the steps to the altar, flanking the priest like acolytes. He reached into his pocket and took out a key. He unlocked the tabernacle on the altar. Once the door was opened, he genuflected, as did Andrew out of habit. Jordan just stood there, unaware of the significance of the monsignor's actions.

O'Brien reached into the golden case and retrieved a small flannel bag, like a shoe bag, the kind you buy at a discount store. He laid the bag on the white linen of the altar. He opened the bag and took out a piece of copper about the size of a greeting card.

"This is what could cause the world so much trouble. This is the deed." He offered it to them as if it were a sacrament of the Catholic Church. "Go ahead, you can touch it. It's made of copper. It has survived these many years; it's difficult to damage it, though I wish I had the sense to destroy it a year ago."

Both Jordan and Andrew looked at the piece of copper with trained eyes. But neither of them could recognize the faint text inscribed into the metal. Here and there, there were words, but the piece of copper was a puzzle.

"Here, come to the altar. I shall translate it for you." Jordan and Andrew got closer to the altar. If Jordan were uncomfortable in this most Christian of churches, she did not show it. "Let me read it.

"Joseph of Jerusalem, favored of the king, I, Ahmal al-Fasheal, ruler of the desert, of all the lands from north to south and from east to west, from the lands of the black water to the blue waters of the pearl sea, give you and your family, your sons and their sons, their sons and their sons' sons, in perpetuity and forever, all the land as far as a camel can ride from east to west along the journey you took to return my daughter. You and yours shall rule forever over the land of black water from the dunes of the Empty Quarter to the pearl beds of the sea. This I have said. This I have written."

The priest was silent. He looked at Jordan and Andrew who also stood silently next to him, mesmerized by the words of the ancient king. O'Brien broke the silence. "His scribe sealed it with the personal mark of the king. I have traced the provenance of this deed. There was a Fasheal who ruled Arabia in the first century CE. The laws he handed to his people have been adopted for use today by the modern governments on the Arabian Peninsula. So you can say, in effect, that his word still rules. That is what makes this deed so important. There is no way any Arabian ruler can doubt its authenticity or its validity."

♦ ♦ ♦

The three of them were locked in a busy conversation over the meaning of the deed. They never heard Reb Whitlow enter the back of the church or open his briefcase. He crouched behind the last pew, out of sight and well hidden in the late afternoon shadows.

Whitlow saw his targets on the altar. With her mane of blonde hair, she was hard to miss. He removed his H&K special and chambered a bullet. All of a sudden, O'Brien suffered a hemorrhagic coughing attack. Jordan and Andrew grabbed him. He waved them away. Whitlow dove behind the pew.

"The deed isn't all there is," O'Brien said in a faint voice, obviously still winded from his coughing fit. "On the back there are crude Hebraic letters, obviously from a different hand. I have not told anyone about this message. It is the key to the ownership of this deed, and by extension, the oil-bearing lands of Arabia."

Monsignor O'Brien recited the words from memory. *"Be it known to all that the family of Joseph of Jerusalem bears a medallion given to him by King al-Fasheal, the father of Aleya, his only love, of the south lands. I have parted this medallion in two pieces and given the other part to her. May the two parts be united someday in love. When the two parts join, I will be joined with my love. And may our families enjoy forever the riches her father, the king, gave me."*

He had barely finished reading this when Jordan, fingering the medal around her neck, went pale and dropped to the floor of the church. Monsignor bent over to examine her. A pistol shot rang out and shattered the serenity of the little church. The hole in the front of O'Brien's head was tiny. The exit wound splattered his brains all over the altar.

Whitlow had missed. He wanted to kill the Jewess first, then the priest. Neither the priest nor the other fool would know what to do with a dead woman at their feet. It was different with her. She was a trained Israeli operative, and she would hunker down into defensive mode immediately, probably searing his image in her memory. He better get the hell out of the church in the brief confusion caused by the assassination.

He slipped out the vestibule into the wintry afternoon. He calmly looked at his watch and crossed the street aimlessly like any New York pedestrian.

The ex-CIA killer almost joined Monsignor O'Brien in the hereafter. Pumped full of adrenaline after the shooting, Whitlow wasn't paying attention to his surroundings. Midway through Water Street, which was a wide street for downtown, he looked to his side and saw a government sedan come barreling down the street. He barely had time to dive out of its way, landing in a puddle left over from that morning's street cleaning. Passers-by ran over to him and tried to help. He clutched his briefcase to his chest and shooed them away.

"No. I'm fine, thank you. Anybody know who that son-of-a-bitch was?" *Gotta keep up the pretense,* he thought. He got up and hailed a taxi. He had to get back to his hotel and report to his handlers in Geneva that he needed another attempt.

The government sedan screeched to a stop in front of the church, all four doors flying open. Just as McCoy and two FBI agents started to run up the steps, Jordan and Andrew came screaming out of the church doors, yelling for the police. McCoy flashed his badge to the gathering crowd of do-gooders to chase them away and had his agents cordon off the church.

"Wait here until the uniforms show up. Make sure they understand this is a federal investigation," he shouted to his men. McCoy didn't want the New York police screwing up his deal. Even though his superiors knew it, he was still acting way outside Bureau guidelines and on his own. If anything went wrong, bye-bye pension and bye-bye charter boat. Hopefully, he still had the Vatican in his back pocket.

Jordan and Andrew stood at the top of the steps surrounded by McCoy's agents. Andrew was shaken. Jordan was steely cold, a point McCoy did not miss.

McCoy ran up the steps and glanced at Jordan and Andrew. He turned to one of his men.

"Joe, you stay here. Ron, come inside with me."

The crowd outside swelled and turned when they collectively heard police sirens blasting down State Street. Three squad cars roared up the sidewalk and stopped parallel to the church. The NYPD sent weight to this one. The captain of the First Precinct showed up with a lieutenant in tow. A couple of blue shields—homicide detectives—followed them. Pulling up the rear in separate cars were Schlomo and Rocco.

McCoy was inside, missing all the commotion outside. He rolled the dead monsignor over. He looked up at his agent and said, "He wasn't the initial target. I can tell by the entry wound. The shooter would have tapped him twice in the chest, not take a chance on a head shot."

Captain D'Ambrosio charged into the church. He walked up to McCoy and pushed aside the other FBI agent. "Whaddya got on my turf? How the hell did you get here and know to call us?"

"Oh, Captain," McCoy said, "and how nice to see you, too. This is a federal case, but I do appreciate you boys directing traffic outside."

On a law enforcement organization chart, the bureau's special-agent-in-charge was equal to the police commissioner in any city. All agents, however, received strict instructions to treat all local police with due respect.

"Captain, we can discuss this uptown. Let's not do it here. But I have to tell you, this involves a terrorist plot, and you know we have first call on any terrorist activity. As far as I can tell, no one else was hurt or involved. And it was a professional hit. The shooter's long gone. You wanna help me clear the case, I'll give you all the credit you deserve. But you have to act independently of me, and I will not—cannot—share information with you. These are not my rules, Sam. You got a complaint, call Washington."

McCoy was on a first-name basis with every precinct commander in Manhattan, Brooklyn, and most of Queens. The bureau long ago wrote off the Bronx, and nobody cared about Staten Island. McCoy was a schmoozer, that's for sure, because his father taught him that you catch more flies with honey than with vinegar.

The ambulance pulled up, and McCoy let the uniforms direct the removal of the body. By that time, Schlomo and Rocco made their way through the yellow police tape. How they did it, McCoy didn't know, and didn't want to know. He looked at the two foreign bodyguards, both of whom he would bet worked for their respective intelligence agencies. McCoy said, "Schlomo, you win. She's alive. Rocco, you lose. He's dead."

The ambulance attendants put O'Brien's body into the back of the bus. With all the action gone, the crowd began to disperse. McCoy walked outside and lit a cigarette. He ran into Andrew, standing all alone. McCoy said nothing, embraced him, and whispered into his ear. "Tonight at the Wolf. Eleven o'clock. We need to talk."

The federal agents got back into their car, knowing full well they would drop the investigation. There was no trail to follow in a professional hit like this. As they drove uptown to the FBI office, McCoy wondered how his Russian contact knew something was going down. And how did the contact know where Jordan and Andrew were going to be?

Turning onto Water Street, they got stuck in a traffic jam. *Shit,* McCoy thought. *Why can't we run a blue light on top of our car?* He sat and fumed.

Schlomo took Jordan aside and talked to her privately. Jordan came over to Andrew and told him that they needed to get back to the Chelsea house. She said nothing about what Monsignor O'Brien had said about the medallion.

Schlomo and Rocco walked out of the church in front of them. Andrew and Jordan quickly jumped into Schlomo's car. Andrew was sure it was armored but didn't ask. Rocco followed them.

The cars pulled up to the Chelsea house. Schlomo got out. The passenger doors were still locked. Rocco angled his car behind them. He got out. The two of them swept the street with their eyes. Schlomo pressed a button on the key fob he carried. The passenger doors unlocked. He went over to the car and grabbed Jordan, shoving her inside the safety of the Chelsea house's front door. He let Andrew get out of the car by himself. All four of them walked into the house and followed the hallway back to the dining room.

Andrew peered through the glass doors. The etched glass distorted the faces, but he could tell who was sitting around the table—Julian Hirschberg, Jim McCoy, and surprise of surprises, Cardinal di Sistio. They walked in.

Julian played the ever-cheerful host. "You two must be dying for a drink after the day you've had. Can I get you anything?" Jordan and Andrew shook their heads.

McCoy piped up though. "Sure, Julian, how about a Johnnie Walker Blue."

Julian flashed his trademark beaming smile at the FBI agent. "Why go with the cheap stuff when you can have the best, eh, Jimmy?"

Andrew looked at the two of them. *So, it was Jimmy and Julian. How did they become such bosom buddies?* Andrew felt a little jealousy creeping into his chest. He and McCoy were grammar school friends, the closest two guys could be. It was no one's fault they fell apart. There was no good reason. It was just that after Sarah's death, Andrew's world fell out from under him. With it went all his friends. *Oh well, Jim and I will sort it out later this evening. Let's find out what's on people's minds.*

Rocco took his customary place against the back wall. Only this time, Schlomo joined him. *Oh great,* Andrew thought, *another budding friendship.*

Cardinal di Sistio cleared his throat, the Vatican diplomat's subtle way of letting everyone know he was ready to begin the meeting. "I promised not to introduce religion into these meetings, but no one can fault me for saying that the Holy Father sends his blessings and thinks of you daily. Who knows, my friends," he said looking directly at Julian and Jordan, "we may be wrong and you may be right, but who's counting on the other side?" This little bit of levity loosened the tension in the room. Everyone knew they were there for serious business.

"First off. Andrew and Jordan, I am sorry for the tragic incident you experienced. It has convinced us that you no longer have a safe refuge in America. Julian and I have been talking, and we think it best that both of you go to Israel. We must bring this to a head. And, Andrew, it's time we spoke truthfully.

"One of our brethren in the Middle East alerted us several months ago that the terrorist underground…and others, may I add…suspect that the church has uncovered a dangerous secret. They learned as much as we know about the deed. The instruments of Satan have been following us all, according to Rocco and the Carabinieri. That is why Rocco and the others have been assigned to us.

"I shudder to call people of the book—you know, we all claim common heritage to Abraham—instruments of Satan. But they act with evil intentions. And, as you have learned, they will not hesitate to kill and kill very efficiently. All of our governments are on the alert, but those very brave men can only do so much. We must be careful. How they know what we know can only be traced to what you Americans call a 'leak,' either in the Vatican or in Jerusalem."

At this statement, Julian rose to protest. Cardinal di Sistio persisted. "Julian, we have been working together for how many years? Ten? Twenty? Would I accuse you of treachery? Please, take your seat. Let us talk this over like reasonable men and women.

"I think we found this 'leak,' though I am not sure. It's us! The librarian, Osinsky, lived too well for a simple priest. Regrettably, I have not had the opportunity to question him. He has suffered a massive heart attack and now joins his mentor, our late great John Paul II, in the afterlife. We pray for his soul and his happy repose in the bosom of Jesus.

"Andrew, you must carry on the work of Monsignor O'Brien. We did not expect the good Jesuit to leave us in such a manner, but we were prepared to retire him deep inside the Vatican. His Holiness had agreed to this scenario. Unfortunately, and may his soul rest in peace, that is not necessary. So, Andrew, we need you now. We need your body and soul, heart and mind, will and intelligence. Agreed?"

Andrew just nodded, waiting for the other shoe to drop.

The cardinal continued. "We all need to be honest with each other. I shall start. It is no secret to anyone at this table that the news of this property deed must remain secret. We cannot use it as a bargaining chip with the terrorists. There is no leverage to be gained. Knowledge of the deed's contents is the death sentence for humanity. The Vatican, as we all have agreed, will manage this.

"Andrew, both Julian and Jordan are members of the Israeli intelligence community. Captain Barash is also an archaeologist, which gives her perfect cover to be in areas where Jews may not ordinarily go. Julian's post at the Israel Antiquities Authority is a total cover. Colonel Hirschberg is the second-ranking member of an intelligence division and a former commander in the country's elite regiment, the Masada.

"The only two people who are what they are represented to be are you, Andrew, and the late monsignor. Even your friend, Mr. McCoy, has been playing a role that far exceeds his authority. We had hoped to use Monsignor O'Brien to contact the other side and arrange a truce, if you will. That is now impossible. Andrew, will you act in his stead?"

Again, Andrew nodded, knowing that he no longer could get out.

Cardinal di Sistio acknowledged Andrew's nod and addressed McCoy directly. "Jimmy, will you please explain to us what you found at the crime scene?"

McCoy straightened up in his seat. He wasn't accustomed to briefing cardinals about crime scenes or murder victims. McCoy took his time before he answered, his gaze never leaving Andrew's eyes.

"The good monsignor was not the only target. You, Jordan, as you may have already guessed, were also the target. Why, we don't know. We know it is not the typical Middle Eastern terrorist community who shot at you. This was too professional a hit. The way the shooter melted in the crowds suggests to me that he is a renegade agent.

"I have my friends searching their files for suitable candidates. I know that's a waste of time. I just can't call him up and say, 'Mr. Shooter, would you mind coming to my office?' He went after you, Jordan, because there is another leak somewhere, and I'm betting one of the scroll scholars talked."

McCoy stopped for a moment and addressed the room, not looking for an answer from anyone. "Can I smoke in here?" Cardinal di Sistio motioned for Rocco to bring over an ashtray. McCoy looked up at the bodyguard. "Thanks." After lighting his cigarette, the FBI agent cleared his throat.

"Jordan, Andrew, what did Monsignor O'Brien reveal to you in the church? We will find out sooner or later. Where is the deed? I'm afraid that if we find out later, you'll both be long-dead."

Jordan and Andrew looked at each other. Andrew thought she never looked so vulnerable, so alone. His heart melted as it had never before. *I can't be falling in love with her. She's a tough-as-nails secret spy. There's no way we can get together.* But, he couldn't argue with his heart.

"I guess I should speak because it affects me," Jordan said, at first in a soft voice, then later picking up in volume and timbre. "There's more to the monsignor's discovery than the deed. By itself, the deed is explosive, but what good is a deed if the heirs cannot be traced?"

The men around the table murmured to themselves, the subtle volume of their surprise resonating off the paneled mahogany walls of the dining room. "O'Brien found another message etched on the back side of the square in a different hand and in Hebrew. It was written by my ancestor."

Jordan let her words sink in. Slowly, a crescendo of disbelief rose in the dining room like a symphony orchestra preparing itself for the first movement of the concertmaster's notes. They all looked at Jordan, waiting for her to finish.

"Monsignor O'Brien found the key to the identification of the heirs. It's a medallion," she said, reaching inside her blouse. "This one. And there is a matching half somewhere out there. We need to find it."

Chapter Sixty-Two

There's nothing darker than the ocean at night, especially from forty thousand feet. Andrew pressed his face against the small porthole in the door of the front cabin. Jordan had the window seat. She was asleep. Andrew didn't feel like pressing over her body to look out the window, so he ambled up to the front of the plane and bothered the flight attendants. "You don't mind if I just want to look out the window."

"Of course, sir," said a very attractive flight attendant. "May I get you something to drink?"

"No, thank you. I just want to play tourist, you know."

"Will this be your first time in Israel?"

"Yeah, I've always dreamed about going there. I studied the place all my life."

"You speak Hebrew?"

"Yeah, well sort of. Oh, forget it," Andrew said walking back to his seat. *No, I don't speak Hebrew. But I understand every goddamn language spoken by your enemies going back to the time before Abraham. And no, I don't want a drink. I have to keep my head clear. You see, I'm going to Israel to stop a plot that will blow up the world if I don't do something.*

Andrew found it refreshing to talk to himself. He could say things that would ordinarily put him in jail. He settled back into the seat and fidgeted. He stretched and looked through the window over Jordan's sleeping body. Way below, he saw lights twinkling on the ocean. He guessed they were oil tankers making their way to the gas pumps of America. *That's what I'm involved in. Making sure those tankers don't stop crossing the ocean.* He lay back in his seat, disgusted with himself and the world in general.

The plane's wheels hit the tarmac with a resounding thump. The noise and vibration shook Andrew out of an uneasy sleep. *These El Al boys don't pride themselves on smooth landings. Not like the Delta pilots who make noiseless landings seem like a customer right.* He had heard that El Al pilots get their planes on the ground as quickly as possible. Something about not being shot out of the air by a surface-to-air missile.

The plane taxied to the gate. Jordan awoke, looked at him, and smiled. "Welcome to Israel," she said, her white teeth contrasting beautifully against her tan skin and blonde hair.

God, she is achingly beautiful. Andrew felt like a sick puppy looking at her. Jordan had no reaction to him at all.

They were the first to line up at the plane's front door. First-class passengers always came off the plane first. *I could get used to this treatment,* he thought. *I like working for the pope. I wonder if the Vatican's got a retirement plan.*

Jordan and Andrew walked up the passageway to the terminal. Two young soldiers stood at the entrance. They saw Jordan and immediately snapped to attention. She looked at Andrew, embarrassed now that her real job was out in the open.

"Right this way, ma'am," said one fit soldier. The other grabbed Andrew's bag.

Jeez, do I look so old that I can't carry my own bag? The soldiers escorted the two of them to an army jeep. *No sedans in this country,* Andrew chuckled to himself.

"Captain, should we drop your guest off at his hotel or should we go to Government House?"

"Etan," Jordan said, reading his name off the patch above his left pocket, "let's take our guest to his hotel. I can report in later." She smiled sweetly at him then turned to Andrew, reserving a part of the smile for him.

The jeep pulled out of the Tel Aviv airport and hummed along the highway to the city. Andrew was beside himself. He was finally in Israel, the Middle East, and the place where all of his learning had been pointing him. And for a guide, he had the lovely Jordan Barash. Andrew looked at Jordan and smiled. She smiled back.

They jumped out of the jeep in front of the hotel. "Thank you, Lieutenant, you provide a very efficient taxi service." The young officer blushed at Jordan's words. Andrew looked at him. *What man wouldn't be captivated by a few words from Jordan Barash?*

A doorman rushed to grab his bags. *Jesus, it's déjà vu all over again. Does the whole country think I'm too old to carry my bags?*

At the front desk, the clerk welcomed them. "We have a king room overlooking the plaza. Will that be sufficient?"

Jordan blushed. "No, we aren't staying together. I am just escorting my colleague here."

"Yes, ma'am," the clerk said without missing a beat. "And the guest's name?"

Andrew jumped into the conversation. "My name is Wagner. Andrew Wagner."

"Yes, Mr. Wagner. Would that be…wait a minute." The clerk walked to the counter behind him and picked up a yellow slip of paper. "Mr. Wagner, would the lady accompanying you be Captain Barash?"

"Yes, how did you…"

"Never mind. Why do you want to know?"

"We have a message here for you, Captain. You are to call Government House at your earliest convenience. Please, use the phone over there."

She left him at the desk to take care of himself. She dialed the number and was patched in immediately on a secure line to Julian.

"Jordan, how are you? I am so glad you are back home." Even though he was the country's second-ranking intelligence officer, Jordan thought he was always ineffably polite. *I wonder if he says "sorry" when he drills a bullet into a target's forehead.*

"You left a message for me here in Tel Aviv?"

"You and Andrew need to come to Jerusalem. We have a request from the French government for you to assist one of their archaeologists. The man is supposedly a scrolls scholar. Jordan, I don't like this. It's out of my hands. This request came straight to me from Government House."

"You forget that I am an archaeologist and a damn good one at that. I get requests like this all the time. My picture has appeared in *Biblical Archaeology Review*. I'm not surprised that visiting colleagues request my attention."

"Our service is gender-blind. I am just telling you to be careful."

"I'll take your words under advisement. And, begging the colonel's pardon, that comment about being gender-blind, you're full of shit." She returned to the front desk. "I need a room for tonight."

Andrew looked at her, mulling over the possibilities with anticipatory delight. "What happened with your government obligation, Captain?" he asked.

Jordan looked at him sharply. His sarcasm wasn't lost on her. She was in no mood for any male bullshit. "We have to go to Jerusalem tomorrow, both of us. I'll see you tomorrow morning."

Andrew wasn't giving up that easily. "Can we declare a truce and have dinner? It's on the pope."

She cocked her head. "Sure, tonight in the hotel dining room. I don't feel like going out."

Andrew went to his room and crashed. The past weeks, combined with the all-night flight to Israel, wore him down. The telephone rudely interrupted his dreams. "Mr. Wagner," a crisp female voice intoned, "it is sixteen hundred hours."

"Thank you," he said bouncing the phone back on the hook. *Why is the rest of the world so goddamn militaristic? Why can't hotel operators outside the United States say, "It's four o'clock"?*

Still lying in bed, Andrew caught himself thinking of Sarah. *Is that why I am so attracted to Jordan? Because she's an older, more mature version of Sarah? Does her blonde hair and green eyes show me what Sarah would have looked like if she lived? Has that been my problem? Am I still in love with a ghost?* He collected his thoughts and jumped out of bed. *Sarah's dead, long dead. And Jordan's alive, and we're having dinner tonight. Shake out of it, Wagner.*

Andrew sat at a table for two nursing his drink and looking around nervously for any sign of Jordan. He didn't think she would slip in unnoticed. A commotion at the maître d' stand told him that she had arrived.

Andrew stood up. Jordan looked absolutely gorgeous. He hadn't known that she owned a single piece of feminine clothing. But there she was in a slinky black dress that hid nothing. Maybe tonight was his lucky night.

"Andrew, how are you feeling? Did you make it over the long flight?"

Andrew stared at her. The gold chain around her neck sparkled. Then his thoughts turned dark. At the base of the chain was that damned medallion. "Let's forget about everything tonight. We're here to enjoy dinner." He studied her face. Slowly, his hand reached across the table and grabbed hers.

Jordan looked at him and placed her hand over his. "Andrew, I am not who you think I am. You're not in love with me. You're in love with a memory. Until you realize that, nothing can happen. Let's enjoy dinner."

God bless women, Andrew thought. *They always know how to get to the heart of the matter. She's right. I've never gotten over the loss of my once and future bride.* He kept his thoughts to himself and gave Jordan a shocked look. *Is my anguish over my long-dead fiancée that visible?* They ate silently, then started to chat about the next day's travel plans.

"We drive to Jerusalem tomorrow to meet this French professor at the King David Hotel. That's the best hotel in Jerusalem. You're booked there as well. I'm returning to my apartment. I don't know who this guy is. Julian's suspicious. But then again, Julian is suspicious of everybody that he doesn't know personally.

"I don't know how this deed thing is going to shake out. I suspect our governments will bury it, and it will be erased from official memory. I think it is better that way. No one, the least of all me, should have to bear this burden."

Andrew's distraction kept him off topic. "Jordan, okay, you nailed it. Yes, I am still in love with a long-dead woman. It's just…just that you look like my Sarah if she had lived. I'm sorry. No more pining over what could have been between us."

"Go ahead, not being friends never stopped you," she said teasingly.

"How do you know that the medallion around your neck is the one Monsignor O'Brien was talking about? Let's face it. The medal he talked about should be about two thousand years old. Even my grandmother cleaned out her attic once in a while."

"I don't want to answer your question with a question but at least let me get this one in. Why don't you think it is the same medal? Some families, you know, can trace their ancestry back several hundred years. Who's to say that my family hasn't kept the story about this medal alive for longer than that?"

"Come on, Jordan. Tracing back ancestry a couple of thousand years? That's for royalty."

"Royalty, schmoyalty! What the hell is royalty? Just a bunch of people whose ancestors were bigger thugs than yours. Are you trying to tell me only 'royalty' can keep family records? That's the trouble with you Americans. You're from nowhere. None of you people stay in the same place."

Jordan's green eyes flashed. Andrew had obviously touched on her sore point.

"My family had been in the same European village for hundreds of years until those Nazi bastards came through. And yes, we have records."

Andrew looked chastened. "Okay, okay, I apologize. But think about another thing. If your family's been wearing that medal for two thousand years, why isn't it worn smooth?"

"You're an archaeologist wannabe, right?"

"That was a low blow."

"You're right. I'm sorry. But really, haven't you seen gold work several thousands of years old that looked like the goldsmith fashioned it last week?"

"Again, I agree. But the stuff you're talking about has been buried in some godforsaken desert or underground tomb for all that time. I wouldn't exactly call your cleavage a dry and forbidding place," Andrew said, purposefully looking down the front of her dress.

"Here's where I have to come clean. No one in my family ever wore it. It passed down from mother to daughter in a cedar box. Every hundred years or so a new box was built, and the medallion was carefully placed inside. I just started to wear it. When I learned about this assignment from Julian, it was as if the medal were talking to me, begging me to wear it as a talisman. I don't know. I can't explain it."

Jordan's voice trailed off to a quiet whisper. She looked down at her plate and played with the remainder of her food. She put down her utensils and fixed her beautiful green eyes firmly on Andrew's face. "Let's go to Jerusalem. Julian has arranged for you to study at the Shrine of the Book. That is a very high compliment. People just don't get off the plane and walk into that research institute. You can stay there during the day, and I'll take care of the French archaeologist by myself. I think he'll fascinate you. Like you, he's a Near Eastern scholar, a philologist, but I am told by my contacts he's from a very old Lebanese family.

"We'll meet for dinner in two days, all of us. Don't worry about me, I'll be fine. It'll be fun to be a simple archaeologist again. This army routine wears thin after a while."

"Jordan, what's the name of this French archaeologist? I may recognize him from the literature if he's done any good work."

"Wait a minute. Let me take a look." Jordan whipped out her smartphone.

I wonder if she remembers when all you could do with one of those was write on it with a cumbersome stylus, Andrew joked to himself.

Poking the tiny buttons, Jordan came up with the answer to Andrew's question. "Here it is. His name is Dr. Bensouk, Daniel Bensouk, with the University of Paris."

Jordan caught her breath. She never really looked up his name. *Daniel. Could it be that Daniel? No, that's a common first name in Lebanon, and he never told me his last name. And, if it were, would I recognize him?* She turned away from Andrew, knowing full well she would recognize the Daniel who captured her heart.

Chapter Sixty-Three

Mr. Whitlow, we think it is time for you to take an extended vacation. Your adventure in New York has drawn too much publicity, and while you are the consummate professional and have left no tracks, who knows what the FBI will uncover?"

Reb Whitlow sat on one side of the table in the understated conference room used by the Gray Men. Not one of his employers showed any concern over the aborted hit on Jordan Barash. Reb himself wasn't worried. He had served these men and their interests well over the past six years and made a fortune to boot. *Maybe it was time to go to ground.* He sat there, half-listening to the gray-suited man across from him, fixing his gaze on the water spewing out of Lake Lucerne.

One of the Gray Men turned to him, snapping his fingers to get Reb's attention. "Mr. Whitlow, please. You must cooperate with us. Please pay attention!"

The man never raised his voice, but Reb Whitlow got the message. His eyes bored directly into the eyes of the four men in the room.

"We have arranged for a transfer of some of your assets to an untraceable account in Zurich. Here is your ticket. When you get to Zurich, look for 39 Banhofstrasse. The office you want is above a confectionary, uh, how do you say it in America, a candy store. You will see Herr Strunz. You may either return to your farm in Maine, or our preference, take up residence in a schloss that we have arranged for you in Chile. You ski, no? The Chilean winter is almost upon us, and you will find the powder excellent. Satisfied? Then all is taken care of."

Reb never had a chance to answer. Nor did he care. He knew he had no choice when it came to plans made by the Gray Men.

"You take care of yourself, Mr. Whitlow, and come back to us rested and ready for your next assignment. Take this envelope. Thank you."

Whitlow knew he was dismissed. He left without saying so much as a thank-you or good-bye. These were not sentimental men. He hefted the envelope, then opened it. It contained a ticket to Zurich and ten thousand Swiss francs. *Thank God this country doesn't participate in the euro system,* he thought. He'd have a hell of a time spending euros in Chile.

Whitlow left the building and went directly to Geneva's quaint airport. Despite being an important international destination, the city's airport had the feel of an old-time bus station in the American Midwest.

The forty-five minute flight was smooth, passing over the beautiful Swiss countryside. At the Zurich airport, he caught the train to the center city and checked into his hotel. He thought about calling for a woman, but it was too late. Undoubtedly, Herr Strunz would arrange that. The Gray Men always did.

Reb left the hotel and strolled to Zurich's world-famous Banhofstrasse. He spied the confectionary and noticed the doorway next to the storefront. He pushed the door open and walked up the short flight of stairs. The door at the end of the hallway identified the office as a travel agency. Reb walked in without knocking.

A slender, balding man turned around. "Mr. Whitlow, yes? Come with me." He led Reb into an inner office past his secretary, a platinum-dyed blonde with black eyebrows.

"Here, Mr. Whitlow, is what you need. I have arranged for a transfer of a substantial amount of your assets to our local branch in Santiago, Chile. Here is a one-way first-class ticket. Enjoy yourself. Call me if there's anything you wish."

Reb started to walk out of the man's office, but stopped as the "travel agent" called after him. "Mr. Whitlow, my secretary Karin wishes to take you to dinner this evening. Would that be suitable?"

Reb looked at the woman behind the desk. She slipped her tongue between her lips to show Reb the golden ball that pierced the front of her tongue. "Sure, fine. I am at the..."

"We know where you are, Mr. Whitlow."

That evening, Reb was fussing with himself after getting out of the shower. There was a knock on the door. He opened it. Karin stood there in leathers, her hair spiked, and her lips smeared with deep red lipstick.

God, Reb thought to himself, *we may have invented punk rock, but these European women have elevated it to a fine art.*

"Mr. Whitlow, I thought you might enjoy a club I have discovered in Old Town. Shall we?"

This part of Zurich wasn't the quaint tourist attraction that its name implied. True, it was the oldest part of the city. But it was also the area where the Zurich police had contained the city's prostitution and drug traffic. The police left it alone as long as its inhabitants didn't spill over into the more respectable parts of the city.

Reb took Karin's arm and locked his hotel door behind him. He left with a song in his heart and a condom in his wallet.

The winter sun was characteristically bright in the morning when Fritz Angermueller walked his beat along the Limmat River. Angermueller was a rookie policeman assigned to the beginner's beat in the Zurich police department. He patrolled the border between Old Town and respectable Zurich.

He trained his eyes on the joggers running along the Limmat and watched for the occasional junkie who may have crawled out of his hiding place to sit by the river. One of his rookie duties was to make sure the riverbank was kept clean of all trash. He would radio headquarters, and they would dispatch a cleaning crew to it pick up. Angermueller was responsible for the human trash.

He looked over the wall and spied a bundle of rags lying in the bushes. *Probably a bunch of junkies fought over those clothes that the Ladies' Guild donates to clothing bins. Those dumbasses couldn't make up their minds what to do with the clothes, so they just left them there.* Fritz leaped over the wall, propelled by muscles finely tuned by months in the academy gymnasium.

His suspicion grew the closer he got to the rags. The jumbled-up rags had too much definition to be just an assortment of clothes strewn on the grass. He stood over the pile. His face flushed with excitement as he hovered over his discovery. The rookie policeman had stumbled on the rare homicide in Zurich. Alone on the riverbank, he pumped his fist into the air. He knew this discovery could get him out of rookie status more quickly than he ever thought. He bent over the body. With care not to disturb the crime scene, he turned the body face up with his baton as he was taught in the police academy. Reb Whitlow's dead eyes stared, unblinking, into the morning sun.

Chapter Sixty-four

Daniel checked into the King David Hotel in Jerusalem the morning after Andrew and Jordan had arrived using one of his many passports. This was issued in Lyons by the French government. It identified his occupation as university professor. He was able to travel freely throughout the Middle East and throughout the world for that matter. No one knew his real identity. The Jews called him the "Desert Chameleon." Only Hassan, his brother, knew who he was and what he did. Even his family thought he was a prosperous construction executive and university professor.

The call came from Switzerland two nights ago. It was routed through several exchanges. The men in Geneva thought they were calling Syria. He picked up the telephone in his construction office in Beirut.

He accepted the assignment, reluctantly. Killing a woman, even if she were a Jew and an army officer, was distasteful. But it would be easy. Posing as an archaeologist, he would convince her that he wished to see Masada out in the Judean desert. Even though it was an important place in Jewish history and a tourist attraction, few people took the effort to climb up the mountain.

The tourists were too lazy, and the Jews no longer cared. Better they concentrate on the *Via Dolorosa* and the other bogus sites in Jerusalem that catered to the Christian crowd looking for Jesus.

Once they were on top of the mount, he would shoot her with a .22 pistol and roll her body over the side of the mountain. He would be back in Beirut, complaining to the Israel Antiquities Authority that the woman never met him. Her body wouldn't be found for months, if ever. The desert predators would take care of her.

Daniel flew to Tel Aviv and went straight to Jerusalem to the King David Hotel. He accepted his room key from the desk clerk and went up to his room. He pulled a slip of paper out of his pocket and dialed a number. "Yes, perfect. I shall be here." In one hour, a beautiful blonde European woman—he always demanded this type—would be in his bed.

The next morning, Andrew unknowingly passed Daniel sitting at the hotel coffee bar. He was walking toward the hotel exit to meet Jordan. Andrew knew she and the French university professor were scheduled to ride out to Masada and visit the top of the mount. The Frenchman had offered, in return, a personal tour of Petra in Jordan, as if she hadn't been there already.

Jordan promised to first drop Andrew off at the research institute, and then she would run back and pick up her French guest at the King David.

Andrew stepped outside the hotel and saw Jordan sitting in an army jeep. Jordan kissed Andrew lightly on the cheek. "Hop in. I'm your personal chauffeur today."

Andrew looked at her, realizing he got his longed-for wish. There she was, outfitted for an archaeological hike up Masada dressed in those impossibly short shorts he always fantasized about.

"Why are you smiling?"

"Never mind. Just keep on driving."

Jordan pulled the jeep up in front of the research institute. "I told them the Vatican had authorized you to go through Monsignor's research papers. You shouldn't have a problem. I'll see you tomorrow for lunch or dinner with the French guy. It's funny. I think I might know him, but you know those Lebanese. About three hundred thousand of them share the same name. I'll find out soon. I'm staying out at Masada tonight. It's too much of a hassle to drive there and back in one day.

She gunned the jeep and sped off back to the King David to meet the mysterious French archaeologist. Andrew walked into the Shrine of the Book and was greeted by a serious-looking receptionist. "Yes, this way, Mr. Wagner."

Jordan drove back to the King David. She left the jeep in front of the hotel and had a smile on her face as she strode through the lobby toward the front desk. She was going to ask the clerk to ring for the Frenchman. She got halfway across the floor when a very attractive man rose from his chair and approached her.

"Dr. Barash?" Daniel said, holding out his hand.

"Yes, but I'm not a 'doctor' yet," Jordan answered, studying the man in front of her. She was not particularly fond of Middle Eastern men, especially Arabs. He was dressed in the typical business casual affected by all men once they landed in Israel. Then, she saw the gold chain hanging around his neck. *Ugh! What a greaseball!* "How did you know who I was?"

"Dr. Barash, even in France, we receive copies of *Biblical Archaeology Review*. When your picture appears, we take notice. You have to admit that your face stands out when compared to the chiseled rock statues that usually grace the covers of that esteemed magazine."

He said it with such grace and charm that Jordan was immediately disarmed. *Maybe this won't be such a bad assignment after all.* She turned away from him to check her mobile and caught him looking at her. Jordan was used to flirtatious stares from men, but why did her heart flutter so when this man looked at her?

"Excuse me, Dr. Bensouk. I have to check my messages."

"Of course, my beautiful lady."

Jordan walked away toward a small phone alcove and flipped open her mobile. Sweat formed on her upper lip, and she felt light-headed. *"Beautiful lady." He called me "beautiful lady." It can't be him! He looks so different. It was so long ago. I must be making this up. But he has those faint scars behind his ears and underneath his chin. Was he in an accident? Why has he changed so? But the eyes. The eyes don't lie. They never change. And neither does my heart.* Jordan shut her mobile and walked back to him.

"Dr. Bensouk, the roads to Masada are good and well guarded, yet I'm afraid I must tell all my visitors about the presence of the guards. I find that many Europeans think Israel is like America's Wild West."

Daniel looked at her, regarding her all the more for her presence of mind. *She recognizes me, but she really doesn't know who I am.* "It never crossed my mind, Dr. Barash. Paris has had its share of terrorist incidents. You must not forget that we have a large Middle Eastern population in my city. Also, Dr. Barash, I may teach in Paris, but I am a Lebanese."

His continental cordiality was a refreshing change from the gruff attitude of Israeli men. She kept looking at him, wondering if he really were the same man who walked behind her up Masada so long ago. The trip to the shore, the wine shop. Her mind told her this couldn't be the same man, but her heart kept telling her differently. How would she know?

"Dr. Bensouk, it's quite a drive to Masada. That's why I have planned a two-day trip. There's an inn at the base of Masada. Actually, it's more like a hostel. A kibbutz just outside of Jericho runs it. It's comfortable. Better yet, it enables us to avoid the long drive back in the dark. The Israel Antiquities Authority has arranged and paid for the rooms. We'll stay there tonight and return by mid-afternoon tomorrow.

"When we return to Jerusalem, I've arranged for us to spend more time with Andrew Wagner. He is an expert in ancient Near Eastern languages. The three of us will either have a late lunch or dinner at a café in the old city. It will be a pleasant social occasion."

"Of that I'm sure. Your colleague and I shall be like two leaves with you, the flower, between us."

Jordan blushed. *I'm really too old for this nonsense. I guess what they say about French men is true. But he's not French. He's Lebanese,* she reminded herself.

"Dr. Bensouk, you are really very charming, and I know I shall enjoy my time with you. But you can't go trekking up Masada dressed like that. You did bring field clothes, didn't you?"

"Wait here. I shall return completely outfitted and packed in just a few minutes. I must admit, even I look dashing in a pith helmet!"

Jordan laughed and shooed him away. She sat down and tried to rid herself of the warm feeling that coursed through her body, especially through some parts that she hadn't used in a long time. Flushed with embarrassment, she hid her face in a guide to Masada and waited for the charming Dr. Bensouk to come down in his "dashing" pith helmet.

Back in his room, Daniel packed his bags carefully. It was a simple archaeologist's field pack. But no archaeologist carried a special .22 caliber pistol with Talon bullets in its clip. He dropped the pistol casually into his bag and walked out the door. He looked around. There was no trace that he had ever been there. After this assignment, he was on his way to the Caribbean where he would stay for a long, long time.

He walked to the elevator. The light on the panel told him he had reached the lobby. He bounded out of the hotel's express elevator, looking for Jordan, an Atlanta Braves baseball cap perched on his head.

"That's your pith helmet?" Jordan called out cheerfully.

"We are not in the middle of Africa, are we, Dr. Barash? Or, if I may, Jordan."

Jordan looked into his deep brown eyes. Warm feelings flooded her body. "Of course, Daniel."

Throughout the trip to Masada, Daniel remained silent. *This assignment is no good. Not only is she a woman, she is a beautiful woman. And this is the woman I wanted to marry so long ago at that beautiful seaside resort.* He was sure of that. *I don't care if she holds the key, whatever that is. I don't care that she is a captain in the army. But if I don't do the job, someone else will. And they'll come after me.*

"Deep thoughts, Daniel?" Jordan asked.

"No, it's just that I have trouble with my notes. They are written in French. We are speaking in English. And soon we will be at a site where the common language is Latin, and the signs are in Hebrew. Surely you can understand my quandary."

"No one has ever put it so well," Jordan said, throwing back her head coquettishly. *What the hell is wrong with me? I'm acting like a teenager on her first date!*

They drove to Masada in silence, both of them wrestling with memories they had buried so long ago. Daniel just looked at her and smiled, painfully aware that soon he would kill her. *I can't kill her,* Daniel thought to himself. *Somehow, some way we must escape. We can leave our past behind and be together.* He closed his eyes and prayed…to Jesus and Allah.

Jordan looked at him, knowing fully this was the young man she shared that summer with. But he had changed. *He's had plastic surgery. Why? He's not that old.* His cheeks were different. His nose was different, more refined, like a nose created by a very skilled reconstructive surgeon. His hairline had moved back. *This man has had extensive surgery to change his looks. Is he running from something or someone?* While her mind pondered this puzzle next to her, she knew in her heart, in the very depths of her soul, that this was her Daniel. There was a deeper connection. She didn't know what it was.

Jordan slowed the jeep as it approached another checkpoint. She got out of the car and walked to the soldier. "We are two archaeologists and are on our way to Masada. Our government has extended its courtesy to my guest, a French university professor. Let us pass."

The soldier looked at her with dead eyes. "Your papers, please."

Jordan looked back at Daniel and shrugged. He smiled back at her and kept a low profile. He didn't need those Jew soldiers examining his belongings.

Jordan took the soldier aside and took out her army identification papers. He looked at them and snapped to attention to salute her. Jordan held his arm to his side. "No, you fool, just let us pass."

"Yes, ma'am."

"What was that all about?"

"I must apologize. The government is on high alert for one reason or another. It's nothing. We are always on high alert. Let's go."

"There is a good reason for you to be on 'high alert.' Remember, I am an international university professor traveling to the most dangerous parts of the world in pursuit of my studies. Dealing with terrorists, in one form or another, is part of my job."

Jordan stepped on the gas and drove toward Masada. They were close enough to see its looming presence over the desert landscape. She pulled up to the inn at the base of the mountain. Getting out of the jeep, she couldn't pass up flaunting her knowledge of the site. "Daniel, we are now at the site of the original Roman base camp. This is the very same area where Titus directed the building of the ramp that led to the downfall of the Jewish heroes on the mount."

Daniel looked around. He was truly amazed. The outline of the camp was very clear, and the ramp leading up the side of the mountain still existed after almost two thousand years. *Just think,* he thought to himself, *how many thousands of lives were used and discarded to build that ramp. And for what? To rid the place of a thousand Jews? Why has this accursed land always been the locus of battles?*

"Daniel, are you listening to me? We'll explore the top of Masada tomorrow. For today, we'll just walk around the base camp. That okay with you?"

"Absolutely. May I request your company at dinner?"

Jordan warmed up again. *There's only one place for dinner here, and we're the only ones at the inn. Why does he make it sound like a romantic evening for two?* "I would be honored. Put on your 'pith helmet' and let's go exploring."

Chapter Sixty-five

They took off together, Jordan animatedly explaining every fact about Masada. It was hot. It was the Judean desert. After two hours walking around the mountain, they returned to the inn, tired, dusty, and sweaty. As Jordan turned down the hallway to her room, Daniel called after her.

"Dinner tonight."

Jordan just waved and kept on walking. She got back to her room and looked through her bag, cursing her stupidity in packing only "archaeologist chic." In other words, she packed nothing but jeans, khakis, and field jackets. Even her nightgown was nothing more than an oversized tee shirt. *Nightgown! What am I thinking?* She took a shower in the tepid water provided by the inn and got dressed.

Jordan felt naked without her medal. She had left it in Jerusalem, not chancing losing it at Masada. She left the top three buttons of her blouse strategically open. Satisfied with herself, she walked the short way to the dining room.

Daniel was all alone, of course. But he had the staff dim the lights and place two candles on the table. Never mind that the candles were the squat kosher kind found in many Jewish households; they were still candles, and they radiated a special charm. Daniel rose to greet her and gave her a wary peck on the cheek. "If there were ever an archaeologists' calendar, your picture would grace every month."

She blushed. He blushed.

The moment was broken by the coarse entry of the only waiter in the house. He drew near them, carrying a plastic washbasin. The basin was full of ice, and inside, Jordan could barely see, was something green.

He placed the washbasin ceremoniously on the table. Jordan looked at it. "Daniel, champagne! French champagne!"

"But of course. I am, after all, from the University of Paris."

The meal that followed was worse than the blandest hospital food. It didn't matter. By the time the waiter plopped the gray matter on the table, masquerading as meat, she was pleasantly feeling the effects of the champagne. Once or twice, their knees touched under the table, but they both withdrew them as if they were shocked by an electrical charge.

They finished the champagne but left their food mostly uneaten. Daniel waved off the horrible coffee, suggesting they return to their rooms to prepare for the day ahead.

They walked down the hall together. Daniel got to his room first and turned to Jordan to say good-night. She never gave him the chance. A quick but firm kiss on his lips silenced all talk. She turned and walked to her room.

Daniel opened his door and walked into the room. It was a miserable hovel. The mattress was thin and the bed cramped. It was after nine. The water had been turned off. Gratefully, the hotel staff had left him a basin of water to wash.

He undressed and got into bed, his medallion secure around his neck. The champagne affected him, too. When he was near her, his medallion grew warmer, pressing into his flesh as if to telegraph a message. *Stop! This is nonsense,* he thought to himself, as he drew the covers up to his chin. He slept, but it was not an easy sleep. He knew he couldn't do it. Now he had to figure out what to do.

Midway through the night, his door opened. Daniel reached down into his duffel bag, his hand on the .22. He peered into the darkness. "Jordan? Is something the matter?"

"Yes. No. You." She slipped her tee shirt over her shoulders and nestled next to Daniel in the cramped bed. "Daniel."

"Yes?"

"You're my Daniel."

"I am. And you're my Jordan."

"Daniel, make love to me."

Nothing changes in the desert. The Judean sun rose hot and fast, just as it did two thousand years ago, just as it will two thousand years from now. The windows in the Masada Inn were strategically positioned so that the sun streamed in on the room's inhabitants at first light. Each room with its single window faced east.

Jordan was the first to get up. She rose from the bed and looked at the sleeping form of Daniel. His arm was thrown across his chest, his thick eyelashes resting on his cheeks. His gold chain reflected the sun's early rays.

The chain! That was something Jordan totally ignored last night. The greaseball chain was the last thing on her mind. She sat on the bed and playfully tugged at Daniel's chest hairs.

"Ouch! What are you doing, she-devil?" Daniel called out in mock hurt.

"Nothing that I didn't do last night. Or have you forgotten already?"

Daniel looked up at the woman hovering over him. This was no European prostitute. This was the woman he would bring with him to the Caribbean. *I have plenty of money. I don't need this assignment. How do I prepare her for the full story? She is a Jew. She is an army officer. How would she feel knowing that she slept with the Desert Chameleon?*

Jordan bent over to nuzzle Daniel's chest. Her arm caught on the sheet, and it dropped away from his body. His chest was bare. His medallion was in full view, glinting in the morning sun streaming through the window. She stared at the medallion around his neck. Her world went black. She couldn't speak. Her body shook.

Jordan sat up on the bed, her hand to her chest, grasping for the medallion that wasn't there.

"Jordan, what is it? What's the matter?"

She didn't know what to say. *How could this happen? Only two people in the entire world have this half-medallion. What are the chances those two people would meet on the dusty plains of Masada? What drew us here?* She just stared at Daniel's chest. "Daniel, you were the one so many years ago. You were the one who said let's plan our future by looking into the past. You were also the one who made me go gushy every time I was near you. For some reason, here at Masada, we are together. I don't know what it is. But I know it means something.

"Daniel, stay here. I have to get back to Jerusalem now. I'll be back by mid-afternoon. I'll arrange for a guide to take you to the top of Masada while I'm gone." Jordan threw her clothes on and ran toward the door. She turned and said, "Wait for me, my love."

She jumped into the jeep and drove way too fast for the rough desert roads. She grabbed her army credentials out of her bag and pinned them to the sun visor. *I'll be damned if I'll stop at those army checkpoints. They better get a close look at my ID as I go whizzing by.* She had to get her medallion and see if it completed Daniel's.

Fortunately for her, there was no traffic on the road from Masada. When she approached the only checkpoint, the same junior lieutenant was on duty. He immediately recognized the beautiful blonde captain and waved her through.

"Bennie, what did you do that for? We are supposed to stop and inspect all cars that pass here. Do you want to get us on report?" asked the other junior lieutenant assigned to the hellish guard duty.

"Relax, Dov, that was the captain from yesterday. Remember, you couldn't keep your eyes off her butt as she walked back to the jeep? She doesn't have her passenger with her, and she's driving like a bat out of hell. Lovers' quarrel, you think?"

Back at the inn, Daniel sat on the porch sipping coffee. He was trying to figure a way out of his old life and into his new future. He got out of his chair and threw the remnants of his cup onto the desert floor. *God, this is miserable stuff! Why do they make coffee like the Americans? They pass warm water through a paper bag filled with ground camel dung and call it coffee.* He longed for the soothing taste of the thick, sweet coffee he enjoyed in Beirut. *Never mind, I'll soon have all the fresh coffee that I could ever want.* He had made up his mind. Now, he had to put the plan into action.

He walked outside to the south side of the building, away from the massive mount of Masada. He withdrew the cell phone from his pocket and made the first of several untraceable calls. The phone rang in Geneva. A buff young man in a severe gray suit picked it up. "Yes?"

"It will happen tonight."

The young man placed the phone back into its secure cradle. *The Gray Men in Geneva will be pleased.*

Daniel thumbed the off button, then the on button. This practice made sure the phone's memory was clear. He made another call. Again, the signal bounced through several transponders, making it untraceable.

It was eleven p.m. in Cali. A telephone rang in a massive house in the city's wealthy quarter. Outside the house, men with machine pistols and guard dogs patrolled the well-lighted grounds. A slightly inebriated Arturo picked up his special phone. *"Si?"*

"Arturo, this is Josef. I desire a Caribbean vacation. Is my house ready?"

"*Si.* You know where it is."

Daniel broke off the conversation.

Arturo called two men to his side. "That loco Arab is coming for a visit. Make sure he gets safely to his villa on the coast. Then kill him. Be careful, I hear he is a dangerous man. And yes, find another connection for us in the Middle East. It should be easy in that part of the world. There will always be some other terrorist willing to trade drugs for guns." Arturo went back to the constant party in his *hacienda,* thinking nothing of his latest business transaction.

Daniel folded his phone and put it back into his pocket. *I shall take that hike to Masada. The desert air will clear my mind.* He walked back into the inn for another cup of that undrinkable coffee.

Jordan raced out of Jerusalem, stopping only to fill the jeep's tank using her privileged army card. Her medallion felt warm against her chest. She knew what she had to do. She had to tell Daniel the whole story, get him to come back to Jerusalem, and then what? She couldn't go to Julian. She didn't trust him. The Vatican would never harbor a Jew and an Arab. No, she would go to the United States. Safely ensconced there, she and Daniel could lay a claim to the oil wealth. They could start a foundation and channel the oil money through it.

She was no fool. They wouldn't get the oil money, of course. But she had a plan to get some of it. *America is full of law firms that specialized in corporate blackmail.* She had the deed. They had the medallions. Andrew could verify Monsignor's translation. In sum, they had enough evidence for a very good law firm to put together a legal challenge to the world's oil wealth.

Of course, this would all be done in complete secrecy, unless the oil barons opted not to go along with her plan. *That would never happen,* she reasoned. The oil barons would gladly pay them billions of dollars just to settle and go away.

In America, she and Daniel would control the charitable foundation they would create and make sure the money the barons paid them would go back to the people from whom the oil was stolen in the first place. Slowly, they hoped to change the conditions that fostered terrorism.

Even though those fools run around setting off bombs and screaming "Allah!" their masters are safe at home screaming "Money!" and "Political power!" She and Daniel could give the little people of the world both—money and from it, political power. This could be the legacy of the secret of the Copper Scroll!

She reached into her bag and fingered the flannel bag that she had taken from the church altar in the confusion after Monsignor O'Brien's murder. No one knew that the crafty priest had spirited the deed away from the Shrine of the Book. And no one knew she had the deed. There would be no contesting their claim—hers and Daniel's. Together, they had the matching parts of the medallion, and she had the deed.

Chapter Sixty-Six

Jordan kept on driving down the empty desert road, pushing the jeep's little engine as hard as she could. She barreled through the checkpoint. Bennie and Dov just looked and shook their heads. "Maybe she changed her mind," Bennie said.

The jeep slid to a stop in the dry dirt in front of the inn. Jordan grabbed her bag, touched the medallion around her neck, and ran into the inn.

"Where is he?" She grabbed the desk clerk and shoved her army credentials into his face. "Where is the university professor?"

In the middle of her fury, Daniel walked through the front door, slapping the desert dust off his pants. It was early evening.

Jordan spun around and ran to him. "Daniel, Daniel." She collapsed in his arms, all the adrenaline of the last few hours draining out of her. When she collected her thoughts, she said gently, "There is much I have to tell you about our future."

The sun was setting, bathing the desert rocks and the mount of Masada in an orange-golden glow. After they picked at their dinner, they walked out together, luxuriating in the cool air of the early desert evening. Daniel looked at her, his arm encircling her waist. "There is much I have to tell you. You may not want to hear it, but I want you to know that from this point, it is only you that I think about…that I care about.

"Jordan," Daniel said, while looking toward Masada, "can we get to the top now? I feel a special pull for that place. I can't explain it. It's as if something of me is up there. And it's much stronger now that I have you by my side."

Jordan thought about what he said, strangely having the same weird attraction to Masada. It wasn't like she hadn't been there before. She was an archaeologist. And her unit trained there, and that's where she was commissioned. She debated whether to tell Daniel how they were going to get to the top or to just grab him and put him in the jeep and drive off. I better tell him, she decided, he's going to find out soon enough.

"There's a special military road that gets to the top. We used it all the time in training."

Daniel looked at her, feigning ignorance. "We? Training? I don't understand, Jordan."

"Get in the jeep."

They got to the top a lot quicker than the Roman army. Daniel afforded himself the luxury of being a wide-eyed tourist for just a minute. The ruins were beautifully preserved and excavated. Even in the dying light of the day, he could see the still-vibrant colors of the murals decorating the walls of King Herod's palace.

"Let's walk to the other side of the mount, away from this ramp. That way, if the Roman army comes charging up the ramp again, we can get away," he said with a smile and a little laugh.

They walked, hand in hand, across the top of Masada to a spot shared by two lovers two thousand years ago. "Jordan, there is so much I have to tell you. When I am finished, if you want to throw me over the top, I'll understand. I deserve it. But, let me try."

"Shh, shh, my love. Let me go first. Whatever you have to say cannot be as startling as what I have." He said nothing, just drinking in the beauty of her face.

"Daniel, I am not what you think. Oh, yes, I am a fairly accomplished archaeologist. That is true. But I am also a captain in my government's intelligence service. I have spent my life battling the murdering terrorists that afflict my poor country. This past month I have become involved in a tale straight out of Hollywood."

"Jordan, I know."

"Just listen. About a year ago, a Jesuit priest finished deciphering a piece of copper inscribed with paleo-Hebraic writing. The copper piece was fused to the back of the Copper Scroll.

"O'Brien's find, a small, metal square, is a remarkable document whose existence, if it became known, could upset the balance of power—not only in the Middle East but throughout the world. It is a frightening discovery, an ancient time bomb waiting to explode! Daniel, it was a two-thousand-year-old deed to the most lucrative oil-bearing lands in the Middle East.

"But, there's more. The deed gave these lands to a young, Jewish merchant and to his family in perpetuity. The king who granted this deed has descendants living today. That means the terms of the covenant are enforceable.

"On the back of the scroll was a key—*the* key—to the deed. It identifies the owners of the deed by this." She reached inside her blouse and took out her medal. "And this," she said, reaching inside his shirt and taking out his medal.

"Daniel, I don't know how this happened. How in the whole world we met? How we came to be in this place, you and I, carrying a two-thousand-year-old legacy around our necks? But it is. It is fate."

Daniel looked at her. He knew he could never tell her who he was. He also knew he had to get her away from Israel, out of sight, as soon as possible. Now he knew why his masters wanted her dead. Maybe him, too.

"Jordan, I am not who you think I am. True, like you, my professional life is real. But I am not just a simple university professor. My family is wealthy—very wealthy. They were wealthy many years ago, and with the blossoming of Lebanon, they have climbed back on top.

"After what you have told me, I know our lives are in danger. I deal with it all the time, owing to my family's prominence in these unsettled lands. I own a villa in the Caribbean and pay heavily for protection there. Let's leave tomorrow. We can fly to America and board a plane for the Caribbean."

"Daniel, yes, I do want to go with you and spend the rest of my life with you but listen to what I want to do. We can make contact with a New York law firm from your villa in the Caribbean. It is outfitted with the necessary communications equipment, yes?"

"Jordan, you could run a Fortune 500 corporation from my patio overlooking the ocean."

"Good. We need to somehow make our ownership known and press a claim against the oil interests. I am not naïve. No one will honor the deed but imagine the effect that it will have on the 'interests.' They would gladly pay us to go away."

Jordan kept on talking, at times running out of breath, for she had so much to say. "We could funnel the proceeds of the oil cartels' payment through your family construction company and establish a foundation in the Netherlands Antilles. We could silence the terrorists' bombs forever with cash. Think about it, Daniel. What a future! And we could be the start of it."

He reached over and held her in his arms. "My love, there is nothing more I would like than to end the reign of terror. I have seen it firsthand and wish no more of it. But, after what you have told me, I believe neither of us is safe in this part of this world. Let's go back to Jerusalem and make plans to leave. It's not too soon to return. I have seen enough of Masada, already."

Jordan and Daniel left behind the magic of Masada. They got into the jeep and rode back to the King David Hotel, each lost in thoughts about the future.

Arriving at the hotel, Jordan gave the jeep's keys to a disdainful valet. He was more used to parking Mercedes and the occasional Rolls. Never, *never*, did a dusty army jeep pull up for parking in his lot. Walking to the front desk, they looked at each other and came to a decision. "I think we better get our separate keys," Jordan said.

"What, you've become modest?" Daniel teased.

"No, I'm a target. I was a target in New York. And I'm probably one here."

"My love, I can't tell you why I feel it, but I can almost guarantee you're safe with me. Who stalks a university professor?"

"I don't think so. Separate rooms."

They got their keys. On the way to the lobby elevators, Jordan stopped at the concierge's desk. "My guest and I want to have dinner at that café near the Street of the Potters. Would you know if it is still open? We need reservations for two, maybe three, tomorrow at 14:00 hours."

"One minute, madam," the concierge murmured, looking into his incomparable sourcebook, his personal compilation of everything and everyplace in Jerusalem and beyond.

"Yes, madam, it will be open tomorrow. Shall I book you for lunch? Dinner isn't served until 19:00 hours."

"That will be fine," Jordan said, joining Daniel at the bank of elevators.

As the elevator door closed behind them, a cleaning man from a contract service studied them. He made sure who they were before making the call. He walked to his wagon in the back of the lobby by the service entrance. He reached for a phone secreted away in his cleaning bucket. A phone rang in the West Bank. "I know where they'll be."

Daniel kissed Jordan in the elevator and left for his room. Hers was on a higher floor. He argued with her about them keeping separate rooms—he was firmly convinced there was no danger—but she prevailed.

Jordan got out of the elevator, looking forward to tomorrow.

She undressed, shaking the dust of the desert out of her clothes and out of her hair. She just wanted to drop into bed but felt dirty. And she was too keyed up.

After a nice, warm bath using the luxurious bath oils the King David Hotel provided, Jordan dried herself and slipped naked into her bed. She drifted off into a light sleep, still troubled by what she knew.

Half-awake and half-asleep, Jordan heard the locks on her door give way to an expert hand. First the door lock, then the double lock, and then the chain. She wished she had her pistol. Her best defense was the telephone. As she reached for the phone, the man approached the bed.

"Do you really want to call room service?" Daniel smiled.

Later, lying in each other's arms, Jordan looked at him. "What are you thinking?"

"I am thinking that this is the first day of the rest of our lives."

Chapter Sixty-Seven

The hot water ran in streams down his chest. Somewhere out there, he heard a voice. "What? What did you say?" Of course, the running water drowned out all sound. *Why do women insist on talking when you're in the shower, then expect you to hear it? Never mind,* he thought to himself and shouted out, "Okay, dear."

Listen to me, I sound like we're married already. He opened the massive shower door in Jordan's suite—*how did she get this room?* he wondered—and walked into the bedroom to get dressed. He started to ask her what she was saying when there was a knock at the door. Jordan froze. He smiled. "My love, relax, we are in a hotel. People are always knocking."

He opened the door with a calm assurance. The bell clerk handed him a thick envelope. He thanked the clerk and closed the door.

"Who was that, Daniel? Last night's girlfriend who got lost?"

"Never mind her. I have found another girlfriend." He smiled and grabbed her around the waist, waving the envelope in front of her.

"What's in that envelope, our getaway cash?"

"Almost. This package contains our tickets. The concierge took care of the travel arrangements overnight."

He opened the package. "That's strange. We fly to London, and from Heathrow there is a direct flight to the Caribbean."

"What's so strange about it? If you lived in England, wouldn't you want a direct flight to the Caribbean? Does the weather ever get nice in London? Let me look at the tickets."

She flipped through the computer printout of the itinerary. "Daniel, you better tip the concierge big-time. He saved you a bundle of money. It seems to be about half as expensive to fly to London, then to the Caribbean, instead of going through the States."

"I'll make it worth his while. We probably won't be seeing him again, ever," Daniel said.

"If we're leaving late this afternoon, there's still time for lunch, right?"

"Jordan, it'll be a tight squeeze. Can't we forget about lunch? Think tropical, think sweet drinks with little umbrellas in them, think you and me on the beautiful Caribbean beach. Forget about falafel and that hideous red Israeli wine."

"Listen, you renegade. You lay off our cooking, and I won't make fun of the 195 cousins that always show up at every Arab affair. Let's start this relationship right." She grabbed him by the chin and kissed him lightly on the lips. He grabbed her tighter and kissed her more forcefully, pushing her down on the bed.

"Wait a minute. Remember lunch? Tight schedule? I promised to meet Andrew. And now I need to say good-bye. Let's get dressed and get going. Go ahead, get back to your room and get packed."

Jordan collected her stuff, making sure the flannel bag was in her suitcase. She met Daniel in the lobby. He was standing by the concierge's desk waiting for her. The concierge was beaming. *Daniel has taken care of him,* Jordan thought.

She grabbed his arm, and together, they walked out the front door. Her army jeep was waiting at the curb. The valet was grinning as well. *Okay, Daniel's really spreading the wealth!* They got into the jeep and started toward the café.

A block away, the engine in a beat-up Audi turned over. Hassan, Daniel's brother, looked with intense hatred in his eyes at the jeep that just passed him.

"Why are you so adamant about this lunch? Is it just because we're meeting Andrew?"

"Andrew is the reason we're together. We owe it to him to get together one last time and say good-bye. He's going to be a huge help to us in the future. And we have to make sure he knows that. So, the lunch isn't just about us. It's about our future and what we're all going to do to get rid of the evil *djinn* that stalk this land."

"*Djinn,* my love? Since when have Jewish girls become afraid of *djinn*?"

"Shut up." And Jordan kissed him with a passion that reached across two thousand years. "Daniel, Andrew is sort of special to me. Don't worry. There was never anything between us. But, if it weren't for him..."

"Don't worry. I shall sit there eating the stale falafel and drinking the horrible wine, acting like I'm having the time of my life."

"Daniel, I promise, I swear, I shall never bring this subject up again. But, falafel is not the sum total of Israeli cooking." Jordan turned and punched him playfully on the arm. She wasn't looking at the road. She heard Daniel yell.

"Jordan! Watch it! You almost hit that piece-of-shit Audi that just passed us. Let's try to make it to the Caribbean in one piece, please."

"I didn't even come close. Besides, what the hell is that guy doing driving like a madman down this street? Arab drivers!"

Jordan knew Jerusalem well. She followed the twists and turns in the street, never once consulting a map like most Jerusalem drivers. She slowed the car and kept her hands on the wheel.

"There it is. Just up the street," she said, pointing her chin in the direction of the café. She kept her two hands firmly on the wheel and made sure Daniel saw that. Daniel directed her to a no-parking zone in front of the café. He got out and flipped a couple of bills at two teenagers standing outside the café. He warned them in Arabic to look after the jeep. They looked back at him as if to say, "Who would steal this?"

They moved toward a table near the back. "Let's go back here behind the drinks case."

"Why do you want to sit back here? Behind the server's station where they store the drinks?"

"Darling, despite my job as a university professor, I still have a background in construction. Drinks cases are made of stainless steel, and they're stronger than any of these walls that surround us. This is Israel. We always need to sit in the safest places.

"Let's forget about construction. Let's talk about the past that has become our future. This is the café we spent time in years ago, no? Drink a glass of wine with me and read the walls. But make sure it's not that horrible red wine. For a land that has been making wine for over two thousand years, you have never gotten the hang of producing a decent red. Now the French..."

"Enough of the French." Jordan ordered a carafe of wine. "Don't worry, Daniel. It's white wine."

A few blocks away from where Daniel and Jordan sat, Andrew threw a hurried glance at his watch and wiped the sweat from his face. He was late. He picked up his pace and practically ran down the street. The lousy map he held was unreadable. He stopped and asked a policeman for directions. The cop pointed down the block.

"It's about a hundred meters," the cop said, obviously bored from a lifetime of giving American tourists directions.

As he hustled down the block, Andrew got caught in a knot of senior citizens, Americans from the look of them. One of them, an old guy, was telling the crowd of equally old ladies about the time he served on an aircraft carrier in the war. "And, you know," Andrew overheard him saying as he struggled through the crowd, "the strangest duty we had was escorting those refugee ships here to Israel. It wasn't called Israel; it was called Palestine then. Here we were, just coming off the greatest victory in the Pacific, and we got orders to go up past Diego Garcia, through the straits, and into the Mediterranean. We picked up the refugee convoy off the coast of Italy and sailed next to them like a mother duck and her babies."

Andrew struggled to get past the seniors. The guy kept on talking. "It was sad, nothing like you ever saw. I was proud to do it, but I wanted to get back to the States to my Mae," he said, looking at a woman standing next to him with love and affection that could only come from decades of devotion to each other.

Andrew still tried to get around the crowd, but he stopped and listened. The World War II vet captivated him. His white hair was still cut in the brush back style, and he had that confident look on his face that told the world he went to war and won. *What did Tom Brokaw call them?* Andrew thought, wracking his brain for the title of Brokaw's book. The Greatest Generation, *that's right, all those American men and women went to war or kept the home fires going so we could be where we are today. I wonder what Israel's "Greatest Generation" bequeathed to their children and grandchildren?*

"Hey, young fellow, where're you running to?" shouted the old sailor.

"Ah, Willie, let him run. He's probably got a sweetie waiting for him," his wife said.

Andrew blew her a kiss as the crowd of senior citizen tourists parted to let him through. Once in the clear, he began to run again. The café was still the equivalent of a football field away. *I better get a move on if I'm going to make lunch.*

Daniel drained his wineglass and reached for the carafe. "You know, this isn't so bad. My apologies to you for my previous remarks."

Jordan shot him a glance and, looking worried, said, "I wonder where Andrew is. We have to leave soon."

All of a sudden there was a scuffle at the front of the café. "Sir, sir, you cannot barge in here like that. Sir, you need reservations. Sir!"

The man wasn't listening. His gaze was fixed on the table at the back. Daniel looked up. *Hassan! What is Hassan doing here?!*

Jordan looked at the crazed-looking Arab, and then at Daniel. She realized that Daniel recognized him. *What's going on?*

Hassan stood in the middle of the café, opened his jacket, and reached for the detonator strapped around his waist. "For you, my brother. Allah be praised!"

Chapter Sixty-Eight

The men sat around the conference table. The water jet spurted from the surface of Lake Lucerne, providing an impressive sight for any who cared to look out of the floor-to-ceiling windows.

The telephone on the credenza rang. One of the attendants in the conference room picked it up, listened, and brought the phone to the table. The man sitting at the head of table took the call. "Yes. Thank you."

He addressed the rest of the seated men. "It is done. The woman had the piece of copper in her bag. Our people in the hotel have verified that. The woman, that treacherous Arab, their medals, and the deed, all are gone. The bomb vaporized them."

"What about the others?" asked a man at the other end.

"Others? There are no others. They are all with us. If you mean the librarian, the evidence is gone. Who would believe the fool's story?"

Chapter Sixty-Nine

Hassan's crude bomb rocked the ancient walls of the Old City café. The explosion killed chattering tourists and lunching locals instantly. The concussion from the bomb blew out the front of the café, injuring countless passersby and knocked a school bus on its side.

Within minutes, government authorities responded. Bomb experts from the fire department, the army, and the police cordoned off the scene. Only Orthodox rabbis were allowed to enter and begin their gruesome duty of securing the pieces of human flesh strewn about the wrecked café.

Not a single bomb expert commenced a search for survivors. As one official later said in a comment that was broadcast around the world on the cable news channels, "A blast like that leaves no survivors."

The front of the café and the street outside was a mob scene of firemen, police, soldiers, and curious onlookers. Some were praying and some just watching in stunned silence. The grief had yet to hit.

No one watched the back of the café. No one saw the two people scramble out of the rubble and climb through the wide back window of Gamaliel's warehouse. And no one noticed that the woman clutched a flannel bag in her bleeding hand.

About the Author

John J. Jedlicka is a journalist with over two decades in the newspaper, magazine, and Internet news business. He holds a degree in classics and has a lifelong hobby studying and translating Latin. The New York City native is married and lives in Atlanta with his wife, Eileen.